With special thanks to the following:
Editing: RG and Emily Moore
Proofreading: Leslie Ogle
Cover design: The author in conjunction with TM Media
Interior Design: Kim Martin with Jera Web Creations, LLC

Library of Congress Control Number: 2008922401

ISBN: Hardcover   978-0-9801709-2-4

The author is formerly published under the name Rene Reid Yarnell. Books published under this name include Your First Year in Network Marketing (Random House); The New Entrepreneurs (Quantum Leap); 'Til Death Do Us Part… (Quantum Leap); Your First Steps in Network Marketing (Quantum Leap).

Relationships/romance/ politics/9/11/terrorism/prisoner abuse/current history/death and dying/care giving/loss and recovery/Catholicism. A Quantum Leap Publication.

Printed in the United States of America

Book distribution: AtlasBooks
Phone: 1-800-537-6727
Email: info@atlasbooks.com

Author's Website:
www.ReneReid.com

PEACE AMIDST CONFLICT

RENE REID

In memory of
My mother, Helen Bright Harrington,
My stepfather, Lin Harrington,
My dearest friend, Father Frank Murphy,
My doctor friend, Dr. Jerry Howle
For all that you taught me
by your example throughout your lifetime
but most especially in your final stages of life

Dedicated to
the one who saw the pilgrim soul in me
With love and gratitude for the joyful times we shared
and for the growth we fostered in each other
for as long as we were blessed to be in each other's lives

The pursuit of peace, whether between nations, communities, or couples, must never be abandoned no matter how unattainable it may seem.

Author's Note

Just imagine "what if," a writer friend said to me one day. Such is the power of fiction. And so I began envisioning a world with judicious, humane leaders as the heads of state; a world moving toward peaceful solutions to what seem irreparable differences between nations; a world where even lovers can rise above their own self-created impasses to take the needed steps toward living together in harmony.

This is a story of love and politics set against the stark, historical background of 9/11. The political events leading up to and following the terrorist attack are shockingly true. For Jenny Roberts, this is a spiritual journey and, for Kyle Anderson and his brother, Josh, it is a political quest converging in self discovery, love and loss, understanding and healing. Set amidst the most significant crisis of our time, these fictitious characters are given the opportunity to carry out what could be in a more perfect world.

Warmly,
Rene Reid

ONE

In Flight

As the plane dipped toward Denpasar Airport, Kyle Anderson looked down at the white sands and crashing waves of the Bali coastline. Jenny Roberts, his partner of two years, dozed in the seat next to him. He could hardly believe she had come all this way just to be with him. After all the turmoil they had come through, he was even more appreciative of their having this time away together.

Kyle had never loved anyone as much as he loved Jenny. *She can be so stubborn,* he thought, especially whenever he brought up the subject of marriage. She was happy with their relationship just as it was, but Kyle wanted more. He ran his fingers through his blond hair, now filtered with gray, and thought of all the things he loved about her: the way she curled up next to him when he read to her; the way she listened with her full being; the way their bodies molded together when they slept; and he loved the delicate, natural scent of her skin. No one had ever made him feel the way she did. A snippet of lyrics from *South Pacific* filtered through his head: *Most people live on a lonely island, lost in the middle of a foggy sea. Most people long for another island, one where they know they would like to be.* And Kyle wanted to be with Jenny.

He leaned over and brushed her golden brown bangs out of her eyes. "Time to wake up, sweet pea. We're about to land." Jenny stirred and smiled up at him.

When they stepped off the plane, a team of marshals was on hand to whisk their group quickly through customs. Among the many public figures they had flown in with were judges, law enforcement officials, and politicians, and local security was there to make certain that no trouble occurred. The majority of the dignitaries were coming from Asia and all over the South Pacific, eagerly anticipating a weeklong workshop highlighting the American judicial system and its newest methods of law enforcement.

"Thank God countries are less inclined today to see their challenges as isolated and unique," Kyle said as they rode to their hotel. "Technology is making the world more united than ever before. After this workshop, state departments in many countries will be able to share much more information."

"Improving communication is a boon for everyone," Jenny said. "You and I could give one heck of a workshop about that, huh?" She gave his ribs a gentle poke.

"Yeah, we've definitely had enough practice," he teased with a glimmer in his eye. He continued to chat enthusiastically about his hopes that the impending workshop would give officials from Pacific island nations a rare opportunity to learn how America handled security. The sessions were designed to cover the newest methods for intelligence services, police, prosecutors, and judges, with topics including customs and border protection, immigration and customs enforcement, the elimination of safe havens, and improving communication between intelligence services throughout the world. As California's attorney general, Kyle was passionate about his specialty, state laws.

"You're so intense when you talk about your work," Jenny said as their car pulled up to the hotel. "Yet you're so light-hearted when you're relaxing with me."

"I run the gamut of extremes—that's for sure."

"You know, it's a good thing I didn't meet your twin first. But if I had, I wouldn't have been treated to the last two years of learning how to adapt to the pendulum of your moods."

"But you got the handsome one," Kyle said. "Poor Josh, he's such a plain guy." Jenny laughed knowing that, after nearly three years, it was still difficult to tell the identical twins apart.

Checking into the Kuta Beach Resort, the entourage was welcomed with delicious fruit drinks while a Balinese band played bamboo instruments. During the welcome session, they learned that Bali was one of 27 provincial regions of the Republic of Indonesia. About 80 percent of the Balinese were Hindu and the rest were a blend of Muslim and other religious traditions. Kyle and Jenny were looking forward to getting to know the culture and enjoying a peaceful escape in paradise.

Eager to get away from the group and be alone with each other, they headed up to their room. Relaxing on the balcony, Jenny rested her head against Kyle's chest as they gazed at the view from their room overlooking the white sands and dazzling blue of the Indian Ocean.

"Kyle, your eyes are almost the same color of the ocean out there—and they're sparkling just as brightly."

He kissed her softly. "I can't decide what to do first," he said, holding her closer, "go down to the beach, take you to bed, or wander into town. It's a dreadful dilemma."

"I vote for number two," she said, winking.

Afterwards, they got ready for a romp in the pool. As Jenny pulled her cover-up over her bathing suit, she checked herself in the mirror.

Approaching her from behind, Kyle rested his chin on the top of her head, and put his arms around her. "Not bad for a woman in her fifties," he said. Then, taking her hand, he led her out the door.

Wanting to stay in communication with home, Kyle stopped at the front desk to arrange fax transmittals to their room while Jenny headed to the pool. When Kyle arrived, he gave her a quick kiss and headed straight for the towering waterslide. Grabbing a slide mat, he hiked up three stories to the top. They were both in high spirits, particularly after surviving such a personally challenging year. Jenny jumped into the water and waited at the bottom of the slide. As she watched him slide down, Kyle was hooting loudly, swishing from side to side. As he splashed into the pool, Jenny caught him in her arms and they sank under the water. They came up together, laughing uncontrollably.

"I could feel butterflies in my stomach when I rounded that last curve," he said.

"Me too," Jenny said. After both of them taking many turns on the slide, Jenny pondered. "Why can't we have a waterslide at home? You just can't come down it without feeling good."

"All we have to do is keep this in our minds whenever we need a boost," he said, "but it is a pity that my bathtub is too small for one of these." Kyle was feeling better than he had in months about everything in his life: teaching the workshop, carrying out his duties as attorney general and, most of all, having Jenny by his side.

As a professional speaker, Jenny was familiar with being a workshop leader. But on this trip she was travelling only as Kyle's companion. She would have traveled to the ends of the earth for him to show him how much she loved him, and she welcomed the chance to be with him simply as his partner, to lend him emotional support. There were many obstacles to her taking the trip, but she longed to spend some time with Kyle, just the two of them, on the magical island of Bali—a place Jenny had dreamt about ever since she first saw *South Pacific* performed. For her, the trip was a break from grieving the recent deaths of both her mother and stepfather. Also, her close friend, Father Mike O'Malley, was barely hanging onto life. Reluctantly leaving her dying friend in the care of his nieces and nephews, she chose to be with Kyle. For Kyle, the trip was a much-needed vacation after a difficult two years of dealing with a high-pressure political job coupled with a grueling divorce.

After their antics in the pool, they came back to the room to shower and change for dinner. Kyle had planned an evening of dining and dancing at the neighboring Sari nightclub, a popular place for Westerners visiting the area. They had a lovely, romantic dinner, but did little dancing. Exhausted from their day of travel and fun, they ambled back down the beach toward their hotel. With their arms around each other's waists, they silently watched the ocean and listened to the breaking of the waves.

They returned to their room just before 10 o'clock. Kyle turned on the television while Jenny went to the bathroom to get ready for bed. Kyle quickly found the CNN channel.

"What the hell??"

Still brushing her teeth, Jenny emerged from the bathroom. "What is it, Kyle?" As she saw the scene unfolding on the screen, Jenny put her arms around Kyle. They both stared in disbelief at what appeared to be a science fiction movie. A plane was crashing into the North Tower of the World Trade Center.

The news channel replayed the scene from a different angle, or so they both thought at first. But they were witnessing a second plane crashing into the South Tower. *One might be an accident*, Jenny thought. *But two?*

They stood mesmerized, listening as announcers shared what little was known. Gradually, it was concluded to be a terrorist attack. Jenny felt far away from loved ones and, momentarily, she wished she were home, but she was grateful she was with Kyle. The same scenes continued to play over and over, and confused announcers speculated on what had happened.

"Oh, shit!" Kyle suddenly exclaimed, turning to Jenny. "Josh had a meeting at Morgan Stanley yesterday morning."

Jenny looked confused. "So . . . ?"

". . . in the Morgan Stanley office . . . in the World Trade Center! Oh, shit. Oh, God, please, no."

While Kyle had pursued his law degree at the University of California, Los Angeles, Josh had gone to Boston to study international peace relations at Brandeis University. Shortly after graduating, Josh went to work for Amnesty International in New York, where he remained until he received what he termed "the chance of a lifetime to make a difference." Offered a job in the Office of the Secretary of State when Colin Powell was appointed to the office by President Bush earlier in the year, Josh had joined their team.

Kyle was already dialing his brother's cell phone, but his call was sent directly to Josh's voicemail. Next he called the hotel where Josh was staying in New York. He dialed and continued to nervously hit redial, but the lines were busy and he couldn't get through. "Oh, please God," he cried. "No, no, no...."

Two

Early Bird

September 11, 2001

Josh Anderson never believed in being any later than five minutes early. Leaving his hotel room, he decided to walk the mile or so to the World Trade Center. It was a crisp fall morning and the air felt good as he breathed it in.

After rounding the corner from Church Street and turning onto Vessey, Josh entered the South Tower and then headed downstairs to the coffee shop. The waitress recognized him from recent visits and started making his decaf, non-fat latté before he even sat down.

"Here's your 'weak skinny,' Mr. Anderson," she said.

"You're pretty skinny yourself, Joanne, but you sure don't seem weak," he retorted. She winked at him as she moved to the next table.

He sipped his coffee while thumbing through the *New York Times*. He missed the *Times* since he and Emmy had moved to the District of Columbia. The *Washington Post* had its own special political character but the *Times*—there just wasn't another paper quite like it, at least not in Josh's opinion. He felt good being in Manhattan, absolutely the city of cities for him.

About 8:30 AM Josh headed up to Larry Bancock's office on the 56th floor. Larry was the community relations manager for Morgan Stanley and was meeting with Josh to determine the extent to which his company would help fund the world hunger program about which Josh had convinced them to contribute when he was with Amnesty International. Even as a staff member of the State Department, Josh had continued his efforts for peace by addressing people's most basic needs. Peace would be a natural outcome if the "haves" shared their resources with the "have nots," Josh always preached. The morning meeting was an extension of his convictions.

Sitting at Larry's desk, Josh checked his email. Soon, one of the secretary's came in to let him know that Larry was on his way up. Josh decided to go to the elevator to meet him. The elevators, located in the core of the tall tower, were the geometric center that gave the structure its needed support. While standing at the elevator bank waiting for Larry, Josh heard an odd sound, a kind of clanging as if something was falling through the elevator shaft. Then, through the crack in the doors, he saw a poof of dust.

Just then, a man rounded the corner, frantically yelling, "Number one just blew!"

Josh ran to the north side of the building's perimeter and saw the top part of the twin tower ablaze. Other Morgan Stanley employees were grouping around him, and everyone was incredulous. Rumors began flying about a private plane errantly crashing into Tower One. Then the loudspeaker system assured everyone in Tower Two that they were safe. "Stay where you are," a man's voice intoned. "There's a problem in the North Tower." More people came rushing out of their offices and raced to the north windows, mesmerized as they looked out at their twin building ablaze. The voice on the loudspeaker returned: "If you choose to leave, do so by the stairs."

Instinctively, Josh wanted to get out. He spotted Larry in the crowd and told him, "Let's get out of here. Now!"

Suddenly, there was mass pandemonium. Larry and Josh made their ways back to the elevator and took it down to the sky lobby on the 40th floor. Rick Rescorla, the head of security for Morgan Stanley, was already there with a bullhorn directing everyone toward the stairs. As they passed by Rick, Larry told him how glad he was that Rick had prepared the employees for an emergency evacuation. Going down the stairwell was fairly orderly at first, though the stairwell was packed tightly with people. There was a kind of communal spirit. Everyone assumed there had been a light aircraft accident—maybe the pilot had a heart attack. Those moving more slowly stayed on the inside, by the railing. After 15 or 20 minutes, the escapees reached the 10th floor, just in time for what felt like an earthquake. The building began jiggling like a bowl of Jell-O. Josh thought maybe a huge chunk of the North Tower had fallen onto the South Tower. For the first time, he felt a real sense of panic. Smoke began to fill the stairwell. Josh encouraged those around him to use handkerchiefs or their jackets to cover their faces when suddenly the lights went off, and everything went black.

Three

Duty Calls

SEPTEMBER 11, 2001

After innumerable tries, Kyle could still not reach Josh. Attempting to set aside his own personal trauma, he slipped back into his official role as attorney general, and he phoned the governor of California, Jed Bradley. Anxious to discuss the implications of what the attack might mean for California, Bradley eagerly took Kyle's call. "I'm so sorry about your brother," Bradley said after Kyle had filled him in. "If there's anything I can do..."

"I just have to keep trying, Jed. Josh is a survivor if ever I knew one," Kyle said, not quite believing his own confident voice.

The governor wasn't sure how much Kyle knew, so he quickly summarized the state of affairs as he knew them. "The attacks involved the hijacking of four commercial airliners, Kyle. Two aircrafts were flown into the World Trade Center in New York City and a third into the Pentagon in Arlington, Virginia. A fourth aircraft, apparently heading for the nation's Capitol, crashed somewhere in a field in Pennsylvania."

"The destination of all the planes was California, three to Los Angeles and one to San Francisco," Jed continued. "In light of this, we need to take precautionary steps to protect our state. I'm in the process of evacuating the airports in L.A. and San Francisco."

"Absolutely," Kyle agreed, thinking, *How could Washington not have known this was coming?* Kyle encouraged the governor to dispatch some of California's search-and-rescue squads to New York. During the call, word came in to the governor that civilian air travel had been suspended across the United States. After hanging up and briefing Jenny on what had been said, Kyle told her, "We're stranded on this island, sweet pea."

Jenny just shrugged, unable to shake off the bleakness of what was happening.

Unable to return to the States, and with little sleep, Kyle made calls throughout the night, doing his best to conduct business from Bali. By morning, he received a fax from Jed that helped him piece together the events of the September 11 attack:

> 8:46 AM—American Airlines Flight 11, having departed Boston 47 minutes earlier, crashed into the North Tower of the World Trade Center, setting the building on fire.

> 9:03 AM—United Airlines Flight 175, having departed Boston 32 minutes earlier, crashed into the South Tower of the World Trade Center and exploded, setting the building on fire.

> 9:37 AM—American Airlines Flight 77, having departed Washington's Dulles International Airport one hour and 17 minutes earlier, crashed into the Pentagon, sending up a huge plume of smoke.

> 9:40 AM—The FAA halted all flights at U.S. airports, the first time in U.S. history that air traffic nationwide has been shut down.

> 10:03 AM—United Airlines Flight 93, having departed Newark, N.J. one hour and 21 minutes earlier, crashed in a field in Pennsylvania, southeast of Pittsburgh.

> 10:05 AM—The South Tower of the World Trade Center collapsed, plummeting into the streets below.

> 10:10 AM—A large section of the Pentagon collapsed.

> 10:28 AM—The World Trade Center's North Tower collapsed from the top down, releasing a tremendous cloud of debris and smoke.

Already on his fifth cup of black coffee by 9:30 AM, Kyle studied the sequence of events. It was still the evening of September 11 in the

United States. Kyle watched President Bush onscreen as he addressed the nation: "Thousands of lives were suddenly ended by evil," the president said. Appearing exhausted and distressed at the end of one of the longest and most unforgettable days in American history, Bush asked for prayers for the victims and for their families and friends.

"These acts shattered steel," Bush stated, "but they cannot dent the steel of American resolve."

After barely sleeping all night, Kyle and Jenny were exhausted. They awoke to a phone call from the workshop leader expressing his deepest sympathy and informing Kyle that the workshop was cancelled. After trying again to reach Josh, Kyle went downstairs where the hotel was abuzz with the news. There was so much support there in the midst of this American tragedy. Kyle kept trying to reach Josh throughout the day, but he still couldn't get through to him. Kyle feared the worst, but he held onto hope.

Four

Going Down

Oh my God, this is a terrorist attack, Josh thought, but he kept that thought to himself. He didn't want to instill panic in the dark stairwell. He knew enough about structural integrity to recognize that the vibration he was feeling couldn't last much longer without the building being shaken apart.

After a few seconds, the emergency lights flickered. Josh passed a woman frozen in place on the stairs, her knuckles nearly white from grasping the handrail. Then he turned around and began coaxing her to let go and follow him. She finally started walking again on her own power, and Josh moved at her pace so that she wouldn't freeze up again. At that point, some people began to rush down the stairs, knocking into others. By then, Josh was stepping over high-heeled shoes, purses, and even briefcases left lying on the steps.

As Josh continued to descend, his imagination wandered. What would he do if something terrible happened? He pictured himself finding some kind of slide in the rubble, and shooting down the rest of the way. But he didn't imagine himself dying. He tried to stay focused on the woman he was helping and getting her to safety.

The most surreal part of his experience came when he finally reached the lobby. It looked like an atomic bomb had gone off. There were ashes everywhere and one woman standing there was sobbing and gasping for breath, her arms wrapped tightly around one of the lobby columns. Josh followed the directives of the policemen who were there ushering everyone to the basement exit.

Josh yelled to a fireman coming through the plaza entrance: "The stairwell is filled with smoke. People need oxygen!" He was still ushering the woman from the stairwell and, moving her quickly through the crowds, they caught up to Larry in the basement of the building. As Josh rushed past the underground delis and coffee shops, he saw full cups of coffee, bowls of cereal, and half-finished plates of bacon and eggs, all just sitting on the tables. In contrast to an hour earlier when he'd been enjoying his coffee and news, there were no people in any of the shops. The scene reminded him of Pompeii. People had left the basement in such a panic that they hadn't even take their coffees with them. Once they were out of the basement exit and on the sidewalk, Josh crossed the street and sat down on the curb. Clearing his lungs of the smoke's effects, Josh happened to glance to his left to see what looked like a huge pool of some reddish substance. He kept staring at it, trying to figure out what it was. The red covered about 10 or 15 feet in diameter. Then he looked up and saw what he thought at first was debris falling from the building. But then he realized it wasn't wreckage or remnants from the building. It was people . . . jumping. Some jumped holding hands. That's when it dawned on him that the reddish pool was human blood.

Josh tried to call Emmy, his partner of eight years, but cell phones weren't working. People were lined up in long queues at phone booths. Josh made his way toward City Hall and then headed west until he was about 15 blocks from the towers. People everywhere were crying with bewilderment. Suddenly, he heard a loud crack and looked back to see the top of the South Tower begin to fall. That was when Josh decided to run.

Five

Reliving the Day

The room phone rang and Kyle grabbed it. In no time, Jenny heard him exclaim, "Josh, thank God you're alive!" Kyle motioned to her to pick up the extension.

By the time she brought the receiver to her ear, Josh was telling Kyle about how he had gotten out. But there were so many others."

"I'm so relieved to hear your voice," Kyle told his twin, choking back tears.

"You know, bro, it never occurred to me that I was going to die. I guess I'm just too damned arrogant to think it could happen to me."

"Jenny's on the line now, too."

"Hey, Jen, how's my favorite California girl?" Josh asked, trying to sound natural.

"Oh, Josh, I'm so glad you're . . ."

"Yeah, me, too," Josh interrupted, sighing.

"Can you tell us what happened?" Kyle asked. "I mean, don't unless . . ."

"Bro, I think it would make me feel better to get it off my chest again. Emmy's listened to it a few times already, after she nearly squeezed me to death when I finally got home."

Kyle and Jenny were rapt with attention as Josh began recounting his day.

"...and in spite of an announcement telling us to stay where we were, something told me to get the hell out of there. See, Tower Two, where the Morgan Stanley office is, had the most problems, even though it was the second one hit. Some of the people in the office had lived through the earlier bombing back in '93. One of the things that saved many of us was that the Port Authority had upgraded the stairwells since the first attack. They were well-marked and well-lit. So people could escape more efficiently this time. If it weren't for that . . . and Morgan Stanley's security guy, Rick Rescorla, a whole lot more people would have died. Rick's practice drills really paid off. He was a saint in my book."

"Was?" Kyle asked softly.

"Yeah. He didn't make it." Josh paused. All three were silently choking back tears. After a moment, Josh continued.

"You probably know that there was only an hour between the building getting hit and its collapse."

"You probably wouldn't have been there if it weren't for those Republicans you work for," Kyle said, only half kidding. Republican bashing had always been one of the brothers' favorite things to do in private. In their public personas, Kyle and Josh managed to maintain more diplomacy.

"I guess I also have them to thank for all the soul searching I've been doing since," Josh replied. "But you're right. I've had a long history with Morgan Stanley. They were strong contributors to Amnesty International while I was working there and now, with my new job, the State Department hopes they will continue to support our third-world projects. We need all the resources we can muster. Anyway, the meeting was set for 9:00 AM., but I arrived an hour early. God, it was such a clear, beautiful autumn day. You've been there, bro. You know how much security there is to go through since the last bombing in 1993."

"You bet I know. Did you take the elevator up to the sky lobby?" Kyle inquired.

"Yeah, and then I transferred to the other elevator banks. I was a little early, so I went to Larry's desk to check my email while waiting for him to arrive."

"I don't get it," Kyle said. "If the terrorists wanted as many as possible dead, why didn't they hit the buildings later?"

"I think they miscalculated. The number of deaths could have been higher. On the Morgan Stanley floors, less than half of the employees had arrived at work."

"What floor were you on?"

"Fifty-sixth," Josh answered. "Where the terrorists got lucky was the way the buildings collapsed. I don't think even *they* expected that would happen."

"I heard that may have been the only time of day they could get that many planes leaving the East Coast for the West Coast with full tanks of fuel. Having enough fuel to create the largest possible explosion was obviously part of the strategy," Kyle added. "So what happened next?"

Josh continued to fill Kyle and Jenny in on the details of his escape.

"Those who waited and got on the upper elevators 10 minutes later died," Josh explained, "because, by then, our building had been hit."

"How long was it before the tower fell after you got out of it?"

"Minutes."

"How did you finally get out?" Jenny asked.

"A bus. But it was weird. After I stopped running, I was near a bus stop. There was a line of people who couldn't get on the bus that was sitting there. A man turned to me and said, 'The driver won't let us on. We don't have exact change.'"

"What?" Kyle and Jenny simultaneously exclaimed.

"Can you believe it? So I pushed my way to the front of the line and hollered at the driver, 'Are you nuts?' Then I turned to the crowd, threw up my hands, and shouted, 'Everybody on!' and we all loaded onto the bus. The driver, obviously in his own state of shock, drove us all the way to Central Park South, and then ordered us off. As I stepped off the bus and looked back, I couldn't see the North Tower anymore. I asked the cop at the entrance to the park, 'What happened to Tower One?' In the quietest tone, he answered, 'It's gone …'"

Josh choked up at that point, and Kyle suggested they talk again later. All three were emotionally spent. After ending the call, Kyle immediately called NYC Mayor Rudy Giuliani on his private line. Kyle got through and expressed his sadness for the city's losses, and his support for Giuliani in the days to come. The mayor confessed his fear that the WTC attacks might only be the beginning.

Six

Hindus vs. Muslims

SEPTEMBER 13 - 16, 2001

Throughout the next 48 hours, Kyle and Jenny discovered that the U.S. government had officially named Osama bin Laden as the prime suspect in the 9/11 attacks. At first bin Laden denied this accusation, suggesting the hijackings were the fault of Jews or of the CIA. But in subsequent statements and interviews, he expressed admiration for whoever was responsible. In several public statements, bin Laden took credit for "inspiring" what he called the "blessed attacks" of September 11.

"How can the man be so callous?" Jenny exclaimed to Kyle. "How could anyone kill so many people and be proud of it?"

"I'm as sickened as you but not surprised," he replied. "Bin Laden's hatred for America first developed when his homeland of Saudi Arabia allowed the U.S. military to prosecute the war against Iraq from Saudi soil. Washington had multiple warnings that he was planning something. I've even had them coming across my desk. But what I learned today from Jed is simply beyond belief. He told me that while U.S. air traffic has been shut down, more than 140 passengers, most of them Saudis and many immediate relatives of Osama bin Laden, were flown out of the country."

"That makes no sense."

"Well, that depends on whose sense you're talking about. Many will say that the White House avoided a major international crisis by getting Saudis out of the country. They'll claim those relatives aren't responsible for bin Laden's actions. The exodus was orchestrated by the Saudi Arabian ambassador, Prince Bandar. He's so close to the Bush family that they call him Bandar Bush."

"And your take?"

"President Bush and his father are joined at the hip with the bin Laden family in various oil dealings. That's why they were allowed to leave!" Kyle was angry. "You watch. We're going to end up at war, but Osama bin Laden will come out unscathed. You just watch . . . this is not about bin Laden; this is about oil and greed, plain and simple."

"But Kyle, if he's responsible for this tragedy, obviously we'll get him. How hard can it be for an entire nation to catch one man?"

Later that afternoon, Jenny called home to check on her son. He had his own condo but often stayed at her house when she was away to help with her speaking business. Chad assured her that all was well, and she made a second call to Father O'Malley.

"How are you, Mike?" Jenny asked, still feeling uneasy for having left him to join Kyle on the Bali trip.

"I'm in good hands, love. My niece keeps cooking for me with the hope that I will eat all her glorious food and become magically healed." Jenny knew that Mike had come a long way in accepting his impending death. Mike asked about Jenny's trip, trusting that she was enjoying her much-deserved time away.

"Well, we're stuck here until they lift the blackout on air travel. By any chance, were you watching the news when the towers went down?" Mike hailed from the Bronx, and Jenny couldn't imagine how he must feel about the tragedy.

"No, I was sleeping. But I woke soon after and moved into the living room to watch as the news replayed the horrible scenes over and over again. I talked to my youngest brother, Jimmy. He is still on the force in New York and is heavily involved in the rescue work. God help us, Jenny, what is our world coming to?"

"I have no idea, Mike, but it's a mess. Kyle is doing everything he can from here to safeguard California from any potential fallout."

"How's he doing?" Mike asked, knowing how much Kyle had struggled through the past two years.

"He's so caught up in this tragedy that he hasn't had time to think about anything else. And his twin was there, Mike! But Josh got out okay, thank God. But both he and Kyle are terribly upset with the government bureaucracy in Washington that allowed the attacks to slip through its intelligence."

"Government intelligence? That's an oxymoron if I ever heard one!" Like Kyle, Mike was a Democrat, and they shared both a common passion for social justice and a common loathing for Washington officials who bungled the responsibilities entrusted to them. "I think Kyle and I could come up with a more suitable name to give the counter terrorist agencies who are supposed to prevent this kind of thing from happening."

Kyle was engaged in conversation with someone on the other line but signaled across the room to say hi to Mike.

"You and Kyle would have a heyday sorting through all of this together," Jenny teased Mike. "Kyle sends his love and prayers."

"Get home safely, "Mike said, "and take all the time you need. God doesn't seem to be calling me home yet. I really am in good hands."

Surrounded mostly by Hindus and a small number of Muslims in Bali, Kyle and Jenny were torn between the apprehension of being in enemy territory and the eagerness to seize the opportunity to learn more about Islamic beliefs and Muslims' attitudes toward Americans.

Like most Americans, neither Kyle nor Jenny knew much about the differences between Hinduism and Islam. But they decided to mingle among the people in Bali and, in doing so, they learned that there were oceans of differences between the two belief systems.

Heading into a small café after a stroll on the beach, Jenny and Kyle looked around for a table, but there were none empty. A heavyset, gray-haired man nearby smiled and gestured to them to join him at his table. As they seated themselves, the man introduced himself as Amal and, shortly into the conversation, he revealed that he was a Hindu.

"In actual fact," Amal explained, stroking his full beard, "Hindus and Muslims lead lives mostly in isolation from one another, except for personal friendships. Even living in close proximity for a thousand years has not welded Hindus and Muslims into one people. In many parts of the world, they are still at war, and probably always will be."

As their order of *punjabi kadhi* arrived, highly recommended by Amal, he continued to answer their questions. "Believe me, Muslim fundamentalism finds no virtue in any non-Muslim culture. People like bin Laden only believe in destroying every other culture and superimposing Muslim culture. Many religions can be fanatical, but it is only Muslims . . . and Christians," he added sheepishly, "who seem to thrive on fundamentalism."

"Just to be clear," said Jenny, "you mean the belief that religious or political doctrine should be implemented literally." Jenny understood that well due to her own Catholic upbringing.

"Exactly," Amal replied. "Muslims stick to the traditional orthodox belief that there is no God except Allah, and Muhammad is Allah's prophet. No Muslim is allowed to question that belief."

"And for Hindus?" Jenny inquired.

"There is nothing like that in Hinduism. For us, everything can be questioned, and all kinds of religious innovations and digressions are accepted. We respect that questioning, but Islamic law has less respect for non-Muslims. Historically, the policy of Muslim rulers was to keep their minority in a privileged position and see to it that there was no integration with the 'inferior' Hindus."

They parted from Amal after lunch, thanking him for his religious clarifications. As Kyle and Jenny wandered through the marketplaces that afternoon, they found it easier to strike up conversations based on Amal's enlightening discourse, and the people with whom they spoke expressed their sorrow over the tragedy back in the States.

For a while, they sat on a park bench with a young mother, watching while her children played. "The purpose of Hinduism is to give God consciousness," she told them. "You see, if this is done first, the understanding that all spirit souls are equally loved by the creator will follow automatically. I believe that we are all calling on the same God. For me as a Hindu, it is not good to feel that my religion is true, and the other religions are false."

"Do you hold the Koran as sacred?" Jenny asked.

"Much of it I do find inspiring," she replied, but I do not take it as literally as a Muslim would. For example, according to the Koran, the purpose of Islam is to convert or kill any non-Muslim."

"Is the interpretation of that the main difference between Hindus and Muslims?" Kyle asked.

"The Hindu says, 'Everything is God,' while the Muslim says, 'Everything is God's.' But for thousands of years, we lived in harmony with each other, respecting our differences. It has only been since the 20th century that our religions have been driven apart."

Soon after, Jenny and Kyle headed back to their hotel. On their way back to the room, they stopped for coffee in the hotel restaurant. There they met an older Muslim man named Harith. He told them he had been in Bali for the past several months on business. He recommended they order the Mirembe Kawomera dark roast. "It's full-bodied and may even grow hair on your chest," he said, eyeing Jenny and obviously enjoying his own humor. "More importantly, the sales support a cooperative of Jewish, Christian, and Muslim coffee farmers working together to build peace in Uganda. That's why I'm here. I'm looking for Hindu farmers who may want to join our cooperative."

After Kyle and Jenny had learned more about the co-op and its purpose, the topic naturally shifted to Osama bin Laden. "What you must know," Harith explained, "is that although Osama bin Laden and the members of al Qaeda and I are all Muslims, we are light years apart. Bin Laden cannot simply be called a Muslim, or even a fundamentalist Muslim. He is an extreme, radical, fundamentalist Muslim terrorist."

Harith removed his rounded, brimless wool cap. "Bin Laden is among those who believe that the world is divided into two: the house of Islam and the house of war. Such people view the Islam as being permanently at war with non-Muslims. This is the meaning of *extreme*."

"And radical means something else?" Kyle asked.

"Oh, yes," Harith explained. "A radical is one who believes that he has a divine right from God to impose his will on others. Add that to being an extremist, and you have something really serious to contend with. Whereas almost all Muslims believe that there must be no compulsion in choosing Islam, bin Laden believes that the West must accept Islam, by force, if necessary. This makes him a fundamentalist, calling for a holy war against the United States."

"So, where do you fit into all of this?" Jenny asked.

Harith chuckled. "I'm an old man. My philosophy has mellowed over time. I am quite content to believe what I believe and teach my children the same. I do not worry about western thinking." He paused to take a sip of coffee. "And, finally, bin Laden has called on all Muslims to kill any Americans and Jews that they can. This makes him a terrorist. Such a man is not troubled by collateral damage, for example, of even those Muslims who were killed in his terrorist attack in New York City."

"How can that be?" Jenny asked incredulously.

"His reasoning is that some of those killed were good Muslims. Because they died during a holy war, they will be given special treatment in paradise. Those who were non-observant Muslims will simply be hastened to hell, where they belong."

Throughout their conversation, Harith repeatedly conveyed his sympathy with the United States. Without any prompting, he assured them that few Muslims thought as Osama bin Laden did. As Americans, they were no more in danger among Muslins here in Bali than they would be anyplace else.

Jenny and Kyle exchanged looks of relief.

"Your country's greatest concern should be with jihadism—the attempt to use religion for political purposes," Harith cautioned. "The ones you should be most fearful of are not pious Muslims in the Middle East but the alienated and uprooted young Muslims who see jihad as the answer to their personal search for identity. They can crop up everywhere in the world, and you have no way of anticipating their moves or of linking them to one another. I guarantee you that will be the biggest challenge for the Western world."

"You know, Jenny," Kyle said after they returned to their room, "this thing has been brewing for a long time. Intelligence officials had several warnings that terrorists might attack the United States on its home soil—even using airplanes as weapons—well before September 11th. I received some of those reports through my office, and I was shocked that the CIA's New York office took no action on the information. Or, at least, that's how it looked to me. And I saw in old reports from a joint inquiry of the House and Senate intelligence committees going back to 1998 that U.S. intelligence had information on a group of unidentified Arabs planning to make another attack on the World Trade Center, this time flying explosives-laden airplanes into the Twin Towers."

"How could our government ignore all those warnings?" Jenny asked. "I find that hard to believe."

"One report stated that the FAA found the plot highly unlikely given the state of Afghanistan's aviation program, and it was confident that a flight originating outside the United States would be detected before it reached its target inside the country."

"You mean it never occurred to the government that the terrorists would use our own airplanes?"

"Apparently not. As early as 1994, the government received information that international terrorists had seriously considered the use of airplanes as a means of carrying out terrorist attacks. And even as recently as July of this year, I received a briefing prepared for senior government officials that warned of a significant terrorist attack against U.S. and/or Israeli interests in the coming weeks. It stated that the attack would be spectacular, designed to inflict mass casualties, and that it would occur with little or no warning."

"Kyle, I feel so disillusioned. You know I voted for Bush because I thought he could best lead our country, but when other people find out how much he knew before September 11th, well, I have to wonder if they're going to feel like I do right now."

"I think you can count on that, sweet pea. Josh mentioned he had an opportunity to sit in on a meeting with Attorney General John Ashcroft. He said Ashcroft explained that the reason we were blindsided was largely because of what he calls 'the wall' that exists between law enforcement and intelligence agents. It's absurd but, by law, they weren't allowed to share information. But that isn't enough to excuse them in my mind. There were still other hindrances. There was a memo sent out on September 4 of this year from Richard Clarke, the administration's counterterrorism advisor."

"Just one week before the attacks?"

"Yep. Josh told me that Clarke knows more about Osama bin Laden and al Qaeda than anyone in the entire country. Clarke was trying to call an urgent meeting about this very issue last January but he was shunned by the top senior officials. No one took him seriously. Finally, eight months later, they got around to having the meeting Clarke had requested to discuss his national security policy directive. The principals at the meeting signed off on the objectives, which were to eliminate the al Qaeda network, and use all elements of national power to do so, and to eliminate sanctuaries for al Qaeda and related terrorist networks. And if diplomatic efforts to do so failed, they would then consider additional measures. Clarke was so frustrated that they waited eight months to meet with him that he shot off a memo blasting the DOD and the CIA. He urged policy makers to imagine a day when hundreds of Americans lay dead after a terrorist attack and then ask themselves what else they could have done."

"And that's exactly what happened," said Jenny. "With so much detailed information available, I just can't understand why the attacks weren't prevented."

"Well, in defense of the CIA, the intelligence reports generally didn't contain specific information as to where, when, and how a terrorist attack might occur. Also, there was a voluminous amount of threat information to sift through. What I'm telling you," Kyle said, pinching his index finger and thumb together, "represents only a *tiny* percentage of everything that came through to the intelligence community during this period, most of which pointed to the possibility of attacks against U.S. interests overseas. Even so, my sense is that the intelligence agencies were so protective of their information that they were slow to share with each other."

Jenny's mind was reeling with all Kyle had told her. She just couldn't fathom how such sophisticated intelligence organizations could have been so ill prepared. "But even with the information they did have, Kyle, wasn't it a matter of sifting through what was credible information and what wasn't?"

"Yes," Kyle said, "but here's the real travesty." Kyle could feel himself becoming angrier and angrier as he thought about it. "Throughout this whole mound of reports, there was a consistent and critically important theme repeated again and again—Osama bin Laden's intent to launch terrorist attacks inside the United States."

The September 11th crisis had definitely put a damper on Kyle's spirits, but one good thing was coming out of it. He was aware of how much he and Jenny were being drawn even closer together by sharing this time in their country's history.

That night, Kyle and Jenny talked about world affairs before they fell asleep. Although he now knew Josh was safe, he still slept fitfully. He was awakened early the next morning by a phone call. Groping for the receiver, he picked it up on the fourth ring.

"Hey, bro," came Josh's familiar greeting. "Got a question for you. What does the CIA stand for since 9/11?"

"I have no idea," Kyle mumbled, wiping the sleep from his eyes.

"The Center for Incompetent Action. Hah! And what does NSA stand for?"

Kyle groaned.

"The agency that Never Saw Anything," Josh said, chortling. "And what do you call the outfit Fooled By its own Ineptness?"

"Okay, the FBI. Now stop. I can't take any more. It's too early in the morning for this."

"Shit, I forgot about the time difference. I'm just getting off work. Anyway, I wanted to let you know that a new department has just been established in the Pentagon, and everyone is scrambling to be included."

"Not another pun, please."

"Rumor has it that George Tenet is going to give up his post as director of the CIA and become head of the newly created CYA." Even as he made a joke about it, Josh knew Tenet would take the brunt of blame for the intelligence failure. "Seriously though, Tenet did everything but stand on his head and fart *The Star Spangled Banner* to get the administration's attention about the recent terrorist threat."

Kyle laughed and sat up in bed as Jenny began to stir.

"Yep," Josh continued. "Everyone wants to be under the protection of the Cover Your Ass department right now. You ain't never seen so much scrambling to protect backsides and point fingers as is going on right now in Washington.

"Do tell."

"It's bizarre," Josh described. "About two o'clock this morning, Richard Clarke was heading back to the White House after taking a short break from meetings to shower and clean up. Returning, he fully expected to be examining what our counter attacks should be on al Qaeda, what our vulnerabilities are, and what we can do about them in the short term."

"Of course," Kyle agreed. "That makes perfect sense."

"Well, he told my boss that he walked into a series of discussions about—are you ready? —*Iraq*. Powell couldn't believe it, but he did know that toppling Saddam Hussein has been the agenda of this administration from the get-go."

Kyle was stunned. None of the warnings of terrorist attacks that had flooded the government or passed through his office had ever mentioned Iraq.

Josh explained to his brother that everyone in Washington was playing catch-up, with recent memos flying between the Offices of the Secretary of Defense and the Secretary of State. Josh had copies of the unclassified memos, and he read aloud from them to his brother. One stated that the FAA had sent four information circulars to the airline industry between June 22 and July 31, warning them of the possibility of attacks using airplanes, essentially urging U.S. pilots and air traffic controllers to maintain a high degree of alertness.

"During this same time on June 28," Josh continued, "Condoleezza Rice is quoted as having said, 'It is highly likely that a significant al Qaeda attack is in the near future, within several weeks.'"

"Josh, this is information every attorney general should have had—especially those of us in critical states. Can you send some of these to me now?"

"Bro, don't feel bad that you're not among the first to know things as significant as these reports. Rumor also has it that the White House informed—get ready again— Prince Bandar about the plan to attack Iraq, even *before* Colin Powell was clued in. Kyle was finding it difficult to believe what his twin was telling him.

"Yeah, just two days after 9/11, word is spreading that Bandar and the president sat on the Truman balcony smoking cigars and shootin' the shit like good ol' boys. And it is well known now that fifteen out of nineteen of the terrorists were Saudi, that Osama bin Laden was Saudi, and that al Qaeda's membership and funding were largely Saudi. But not one sign that President Bush did *anything* to curb the Saudi's involvement in terror, not to mention curbing his relationship with the Saudis. Instead, the Saudi evacuation began with full White House approval. Anyway, got to run. Talk to you later."

Shaking his head in disbelief, Kyle hung up the phone. Because of the top-level secrecy of information coming into him, he had always been fairly closed about his work but, under the circumstances, he felt free to relate to Jenny his conversation with Josh. Fully awake now and propped up on one elbow, Jenny listened intently as Kyle filled her in.

"Kyle, after everything that has happened these past couple of days, I don't know what to think anymore. You once predicted I'd say this, so here goes: I can't believe I voted for Bush. Should I prepare myself for a hundred lashes?"

"As much as I dislike Republican administrations," Kyle told her, "and Bush's in particular, no president could have seen this coming with the information he was fed by the intelligence community. But as for those hundred lashes…" Kyle batted his eyes at her as his head disappeared under the covers.

As they continued to keep up almost hourly throughout the day on the progress in the States, Kyle recalled to Jenny something that Robert Kennedy had once said about terrorism: "What is objectionable, what is dangerous, about extremists is not that they are extreme, but that they are intolerant. The evil is not what they say about their cause, but what they say about their opponents."

"I'm having a really hard time taking all of this in, but one of the questions that we have to ask ourselves is, *why?*" Jenny said. "Why would a group of people hate us so much that they would sacrifice their lives for the cause?"

"That is *the* question," Kyle replied without pause. "This attack is driven by their hate for America's foreign policy. But one thing also seems clear. Their hatred for us is, in part, driven by their religious principles."

"That complicates things."

"Most definitely. When people act in the name of their God, by whatever name they call him, they can be both righteous and uncompromising. But what I fear most is that our response to this attack will be just as religiously righteous. There will be little attempt to ascertain what this is really about. Both sides will see the other as evil, and both will press forward in the name of God. Scary, isn't it?"

Jenny was a lifelong Catholic and Kyle a recent convert. Religion played an important role in their lives and relationship, but Jenny thought that the terrorists approach was totally unreasonable.

"One of the things I love about you is your mind," Jenny said.

"Oh, it's my mind, is it? And what about my body?" he teased.

Standing on tiptoe, Jenny put her arms around his neck and pulled her body close to his. Caressing her tenderly, Kyle, a full nine inches taller than Jenny, leaned over to kiss her. Her body, her soul, her entire being desired him.

"I love you, Kyle Anderson," she said.

"I love you, Jenny Roberts."

He led her to the bed, and each slowly removed the other's clothes. With nothing held back, effortlessly they molded their lips, their bodies, and their souls into a single expression of their deepest love for each other. Afterward, exhausted, they fell asleep in each other's arms.

When they woke up the next morning, the airports still had not reopened. Kyle and Jenny continued to stay tuned to CNN. President Bush had declared that the United States was in a state of war. The latest report surmised that 19 radical, extremist, fundamentalist Islamic terrorists hijacked four jetliners and piloted them toward the White House, the Capitol, and the two World Trade Towers. The first plane apparently was unable to find the White House and made a kamikaze run at part of the Pentagon. The passengers allegedly took control of the plane headed toward the Capitol and crashed it into the ground southeast of Pittsburgh. The other two planes hit the towers. At first, about 7,000 lives were believed to have been lost but, upon further checking, many duplicate names were found on the lists. Gradually, the number was understood to be closer to 3,000 deaths.

Seeing Senator Bob Graham speaking on CNN, Kyle turned up the volume. "Do you remember this senator?" Kyle asked Jenny. "He's chairman of the Senate Intelligence Committee."

Jenny listened with Kyle as the senator explained that the goal of the hearings wasn't "to point a finger or pin blame on anyone, but to correct problems that might have prevented our government from detecting and disrupting al Qaeda's plot. Collectively there was enough information that law enforcement should have done a better job of seeing what was coming and, with any luck, stopping it."

Kyle checked his email. Amid all of the depressing messages, there was an uplifting one from a friend in Manhattan. It was an excerpt from a poem written by an eighth-grade Brooklyn student named Amanda.

A shattered city is all that is left behind.
These acts of hatred have left us blind.
Too blind to see what the world would be,
With peace and love and all people free.

"Out of the mouths of babes," Kyle said after reading the poem to Jenny. "It's such a shame. So much hatred lies ahead, and America will know no other way to handle this than massive retaliation."

A shiver ran through Jenny as she thought about his words. She and Kyle had gone through their own conflict and had come through it. They had learned how to set boundaries and demand respect, but settling their differences did not require "an eye for an eye." Being together through this atrocity drew Jenny even closer to Kyle.

When they sighted other Americans in Bali, Kyle and Jenny acknowledged them with a spirit of oneness. Natives of the island treated them with quiet compassion. There was an overwhelming sense that something shattering had happened, and the experience was shared in a single breath of solidarity by the entire world.

After countless hours on hold on the phone, Jenny was finally able to book their return home. Seated on the aircraft, Jenny noticed some Americans eyeing Muslims and Hindus with suspicion. Had she and Kyle not had the good fortune to spend time among people of both religions, they too may have felt suspicious. But there was a seriousness about Kyle that Jenny couldn't help but notice. As she watched him, she thought about all they had come through in their two years together. Kyle had faced his divorce and depression, and Jenny her parents' deaths, and they both had dealt with their crises head-on. After many struggles, they had made a commitment to a steadfast relationship with each other. Now Kyle was returning home to face a tragedy of national and international consequences, one that would inevitably create enormous inner turmoil for him as California's attorney general.

"Those look like serious thoughts running through your head," Jenny said softly.

"How can you tell?" Kyle whispered as he leaned closer.

"It shows on your face. I can see it right here." With her finger, she traced the lines between his brows and above the arch of his nose.

After a short pause, he said softly, "America will soon be at war. And I don't want to see that happen."

"Who does?" Jenny asked.

"Plenty of good Christian Americans are chafing at the bit at this very moment to gun down some terrorists," Kyle said with a sigh, not to mention some of our key leaders in Washington. And why not? A man has just led a crusade against us and won the first battle. The only reasonable political response is to attack 'the evil one' back."

"You don't agree?"

"As JFK said, 'If we cannot now end our differences, at least we can help make the world safe for diversity.'"

Jenny leaned over and kissed Kyle on the cheek. He turned his head, and his lips met hers. For a moment, as the airplane soared up through the clouds, she was lost completely in him.

"Seriously," Kyle said, coming out of their romantic reverie, "as a Catholic Christian and a lifelong Democrat, I have to accept that I am odd-man-out in the Republican-dominated political world I live in. I can see going into Afghanistan and plucking bin Laden out. And we need to shut down the al Qaeda network. But that isn't how our Republican Congress and our Republican president and his neoconservative staff are likely to handle the matter. They aren't likely to honor the rules of a just war."

"What are the rules?" Jenny asked. She realized that this was a subject she and Kyle had never broached.

"In the Church's view, the rules dictate that all other means should be tried before engaging in warfare. This is one of the big attractions Catholicism held for my brother. Only after every peaceful effort has been exhausted, only after all other means have proven ineffective or impractical, should war be considered. And then our commitment should be to avoid inflicting harm on non-combatants—on anyone not directly involved in the war. Politically and spiritually, I agree with this. It scares me to think of what lies ahead for all of us."

Kyle's apprehension engulfed Jenny as well. With these attacks, the world would never again be the same. Kyle had a job to do. And Jenny had a friend to care for. It was time for them both to go home, back to their respective responsibilities.

Part I

Five Years Earlier

Seven

Jenny's Divorce

Jenny didn't need anyone's help. She was determined to get through her divorce from Matt by herself. But if she did choose to let someone in, it most definitely would not be a priest. She had been married to an ex-priest who had broken her heart over and over. But now, for reasons unexplainable to herself, here she was about to discuss it at length with Father Mike O'Malley.

Her thoughts wandered back to her first meeting with Mike. They had been introduced at a Monday night football gathering the previous year at the home of the O'Connors, friends of Jenny's known for their hospitality and great parties. At the party, Jenny shared with Mike that before her marriage to Matt she had been wed to a former Catholic priest. Mike shared with Jenny that he had left his ministry with the intention of getting married, but he ultimately chose to return to the priesthood. Consequently, they both felt an instant connection to one another, and their friendship grew.

When she and Matt separated a few months later, Mike was a constant source of support. Jenny remained reluctant to seek Mike's counsel about her impending divorce, but Mike persisted that she confide in him. She received emails of gentle persuasion from him but she kept her feelings to herself. Finally, Jenny agreed to get together with him for a day trip to Lake Tahoe.

As she and Mike drove the road to the lake, Jenny reveled in the freshness of the mountain air. The glistening sun on the majesty of the mountains made her feel warm and protected.

During the drive, Jenny reviewed her life with Matt Roberts, her husband of the past seven years. When she met Matt, they were both in their forties and she was at the height of her career as a radio talk show host. She loved chatting with the interesting guests and sparring with the callers on topics of local and national politics, and she was at the height of personal confidence. However, with all that had transpired with Matt, her self-image was now at its lowest, and her head was still reeling from the fact that she, a lifelong Catholic, could be going through divorce.

Of course we faced challenges, she thought, but overall, their lifestyle had been above average. When she married, Jenny voluntarily gave up her radio career to free herself to work more closely with Matt. They traveled throughout Europe, Japan, Australia, New Zealand, and across America delivering motivational talks and training heads of companies in communication skills. Chad, Jenny's son from her first marriage to Don Neuman, had adapted well to the marriage. It had been hard on Chad when his father died and just as hard on Jenny being a widow at such a young age. But her marriage to Matt helped heal them both.

Matt and Jenny made a great professional team. They were husband and wife, business partners, and speaking associates. As part of the American Speakers Bureau, a company that provided organizations with appropriate speakers, they were never without engagements. They had the freedom to travel where they wanted, work with whom they wanted, and stay as long as they wanted. Their income was beyond Jenny's wildest dreams, and their life was essentially without stress. Matt was just under five-foot-ten, small-framed, and three years younger than Jenny. Matt's dynamism as a speaker was what first caught Jenny's attention. Impressed after attending one of his talks, she invited him to be a guest on her talk show. He presented himself as confident, persuasive, and a born leader. There was instant chemistry between them, and they were married within the year.

After six years, Matt was driven to be at the helm of his own ship instead of merely one of the crew on someone else's vessel. After considerable discussion, Matt and Jenny entered into a partnership with several others to establish their own company. But, early into the project, the partners ran out of money. That's when Jenny discovered that Matt was more of an idealist than a businessman. Far from greedy, Matt would share anything he had with anyone, and that was one of the qualities Jenny had loved most about him. But when Matt volunteered that he and Jenny would single-handedly keep the company afloat financially while the others stayed on as equal partners, Matt and Jenny differed in their outlook on business. She was aghast that he would even consider trying to continue under those circumstances.

"You can't run a business like this," she said, trying to reason with him. "You can't give people who have little or no investment in the project the same return and equal voting rights as those actually putting up the money. And besides, you and I don't have enough to keep this going. Please, Matt, let's give it up before we lose everything."

Of course, to the partners, Matt was the hero and Jenny the wicked witch. Matt lost all respect for her judgment and she for his. Quietly, he moved out of the house, leaving only a brief note on the bathroom counter: "You were the first to abandon me. Now it's my turn."

Jenny wasn't surprised, but she had convinced herself that somehow they would work it out. The newness of their business, she thought, would hold them together. Instead, it tore them apart.

During Matt and Jenny's separation, some of the speakers they had brought on board alerted Jenny to the fact that Matt was having an emotional involvement—as opposed to an actual affair—with Dianne Flemming, the only other female partner in their newly established company. Jenny fully grasped the intellectual reality: Dianne was the admiring female partner, and Jenny the fault-finding wife. But still Jenny was heartbroken. She learned of the relationship only after she had been voted out of her own company by Dianne and the other partners. Only Matt, her not-quite ex-husband, had abstained from voting.

All of these thoughts were tumbling over in Jenny's mind as Mike and she headed east on U.S. Route 50. Suddenly, she spoke.

"Mike, why is it that most men only leave a relationship when they have someone else in the wings? Can't they stand on their own feet for ten minutes?"

"Most men aren't strong enough to go it alone," he replied. "When it comes to relationships, women are much stronger than men."

Jenny loved Mike's Irish wit coupled with his New York accent. *"Women are much stronga than men."* With his kind, rounded face, she likened him to a guardian angel sent to watch over her.

"You know, Mike, statistics may not bear it out, but that's been my experience. In nearly every breakup, the woman stays by herself for a time, usually a long time. More often than not, the man already has one foot in a new relationship before he is out of the old one. And only with that relationship in place does he seem to have the courage to move on."

"Are you surprised by this with Matt?"

"Oh, God, yes, but I shouldn't be . . . for two reasons. The night before we got married, Matt asked me for a commitment: that I would never put myself in a vulnerable position with another man. That meant that I would not be off in a corner at a party flirting with someone of the opposite sex, nor would I even agree to have lunch alone with a man. I lived by this rule throughout our marriage. But in hindsight, I think Matt may have been projecting his own vulnerability in this area. In the end, it was his closeness to Dianne that added to his decision to divorce me."

"It sounds like the tables were turned, Jenny. It was he and not you who . . ."

"Exactly," Jenny said. "But the other reason I shouldn't have been surprised is that this is the same way it happened with me. He had been living with a woman when he reached out to me. I thought the relationship between them was completely over. I guess it was for him; but from a brief conversation I had with her, it definitely wasn't over. It is his pattern. Matt has not spent a great deal of his life living alone. He has almost always had a woman. I don't know if he could go it alone for very long."

"You must feel some anger toward them both," Mike stated.

"I'm more stunned than angry. Dianne always told me that I was the reason she got into the partnership. Then, one day, for reasons that were hard for me to understand, we had a minor falling out. I think about all those times I kept trying to put things back on track between us. But now I understand that, at least subconsciously, she had to find reason to be angry with me. How else could she . . ."

"Betray you?"

"Yes. My heart feels betrayed. Under the circumstances, it took some gall for her to vote me out of the company *and* take my husband. But my head understands what happened. Matt is a man who needs to be adored by his woman. With no financial investment in the company, Dianne could afford to hope against hope, while I had to face reality. From Matt's perspective, she became the appreciative woman and I, the disparaging wife."

"But your relationship before that seemed so good."

"It was! Before that, Matt and I led a charmed life. Matt would often say that our time together traveling around the world 'was a wee bit of heaven.' I'm sorry to see it end. But what makes this divorce extra painful is that it isn't just my marriage that's ending. It feels like my whole world is collapsing around me. Matt will go on doing what he has always done with his new lady friend. But, for me, my entire life is shutting down. I am moving out of our home. I'm losing my speaking partner, my business partner, my husband, and our family life. My son has run for cover and moved into his own place. I feel stripped of everything, Mike. And I'm scared."

"Maybe it would help if you focused on appreciating how fortunate you were to have had such a good life for so long."

Mike was right. Jenny knew the best thing she could do was concentrate on the positive years with Matt. And there were many. She looked across at Father Mike and admired this modern-day knight. He was dressed casually, saving his priestly garb for when he said Mass or attended formal functions. He struck Jenny as the grown-up version of the slightly pudgy Gerber baby, with his salt and pepper hair forming a curl in front. Mike had grown up in the Bronx with six brothers and sisters and attended Our Lady of Sorrows parish school, where Regis Philbin was a schoolmate. As in many Irish Catholic families, two of his brothers joined the New York City police force. Mike claimed his Irish wit came from his father and his sense of organization came from his mother. Nearly six feet tall Mike had a full, round Irish face with probing eyes that remained focused on the person with whom he was talking; Mike had a knack for getting others to talk about whatever burning issues were on their minds.

Father Mike was also passionate about the religion of politics and the politics of religion. Among his many responsibilities, he was director of the diocesan planning office, a job he created to help pastors and parish councils work through differences. If they couldn't reach agreement, he would serve as a mediator between them. This work often took him from the city of Sacramento out to Elk Grove and Folsom. He also served as director of the Newman Center at California State University, Sacramento. Named in honor of John Henry Cardinal Newman, this was one of thousands of Catholic ministry centers affiliated with universities throughout the world. Mike was equally wonderful with college students and loved his connection to Cal State. Mike had a unique gift for making people feel at ease.

Jenny wasn't sure why she had finally given in to spending this day with Mike. She was adamant about not having any more priests in her life. As deeply as she had loved her first husband, Don, who was a former priest, the pain of learning that he had died from a brain aneurysm while in Thailand had been devastating. He had gone there in search of himself, as he often did when he traveled. More than a decade had passed since then, but the memories of him were ever-present. She was finally able to admit, at least to herself, that their life together had left deep scars—even deeper than the pain of losing him through death. He had a need to wander and search for life's meaning. She attributed his struggle with his priesthood for his inability to settle into a life with her. She was grateful for the child they had together and focused on providing stability for Chad and for herself. She felt sure she could get through the pain of yet another loss without the spiritual guidance of a priest. She hadn't even sought the counsel of her own parish priest, Father Tom Jeffrey, whom everyone called Father Jeff. Yet here she was with Mike. Father Persuasive would be a better name for him, she thought, chuckling to herself. And despite all of her inner protests, she was enjoying the day so far.

She had no difficulty understanding Mike's thought processes, particularly as she reflected back on Don, and other priests she had casually known over the years. Most of them loved the priesthood and endured the celibacy requirement as an obligatory part of their commitment. Many would have loved to have been married and to experience what Matt and she had, even for a little while.

"Mike, do you think we'll ever see married priests in our lifetime?"

"You can count on it! It *has* to happen, hopefully not long after we have a new pope, or we'll all have to become Episcopalians."

They arrived at a popular local restaurant, Garwood's, and chose a table on the deck overlooking Lake Tahoe. It was a beautiful afternoon and, once seated, Jenny raised her face upward to feel the sun on her cheeks. She needed all the solar healing power she could take in. She and Mike talked quietly while they watched the sailboats on the water and waited for their food to be served. Father Mike said a prayer once their meal had been placed in front of them.

"It's good to see you eating," Mike commented. "You haven't been doing enough of that. How much weight have you lost?"

"About twenty pounds. Adkins has nothing on the divorce diet. This one is far more effective." This was the closest Jenny had come to humor in weeks.

"If you don't mind my saying so, you need to put just a little back on. You're really thin, Jenny." Mike gazed at her five-foot-three frame. It looked fragile and overpowered by her brown eyes, which oozed sadness.

"I know. I will get my appetite back. There just have been so many changes in my life. And this latest bit of information about Matt's affair with my business partner . . . "

"Are you surprised?"

"Yes. After all of Matt's emphasis on fidelity and never putting ourselves in a vulnerable situation, I am flabbergasted that he would make that connection with Dianne. I *am* angry, more toward him than her. It's just a bit harder when it's between your husband and your friend."

"You tend to overly trust people, Jenny, perhaps without their earning it."

"I guess I do. Whatever I feel, I think I understand why it happened, and that helps ease the pain."

"Understanding is the key to moving passed conflict. Without awareness of what provoked the other side, there can be no forgiveness, no reconciliation, no healing, and no peace."

"That's profound," Jenny mused, reaching for her glass of iced tea.

"It is," Mike said. "I learned that from some very knowledgeable people during my life. You seem to have a pretty good grasp of what has happened between you and Matt and, eventually, you will resolve it with him."

"What? Get back together with him?"

"I wouldn't predict that. I just mean that you are laying the groundwork to move on from the relationship without carrying a lot of bitterness." Mike paused as he took a sip of water. "I gather that you both are beloved in your industry. God help the person who is perceived as the home wrecker."

"The truth is, she didn't break us up. She just happened to be there when it all fell apart. And she was apparently able to support Matt when I couldn't. For his own sake, I wish Matt could be by himself for a little while. You know, go it alone and develop his own inner strength without needing someone else to reinforce it."

"But you said you knew how we men are," Mike teased.

"Yeah, and I'm starting to get clearer on what I want in my next relationship. Not that I'm ready for that yet, but I will be."

"So you'll marry again?" Mike asked.

"I don't know, but right now I don't think so. Not out of a sense of failure. My marriage to Matt was anything but that. But it is ending. I have to come to terms with that."

"I like the way you distinguish between failure and endings. You have such a healthy attitude. Most people would feel bitter."

"No, I really don't feel bitter, but I've lost a lot of self-confidence. And, for that matter, beyond procreation, I find myself questioning the purpose of marriage. It just seems like the expectations that go with marriage set it up to fail. It doesn't seem to be a viable system for those of us who have already raised our children and have been through marriages once or twice."

"So what now?" Mike asked.

"That is the question of all questions. If not marriage, then what?" Jenny sipped her iced tea and reflected before she answered. "In my own case, I want someone I can love and who will love me. I want intimacy. And I want to grow personally and spiritually and help my partner do the same. But I don't see myself bound by legalities or financial interdependence. That's the part that seems to make so many people feel they've *failed* at marriage. The expectations are unrealistic. I want someone who already has a life and will respect that I have one too. So instead of marriage, I guess I am looking for a kind of committed, spiritual relationship."

"Spiritual relationship . . . hmm. I gather by that that you don't mean *religious* as such."

"No. I mean someone who has values and lives by them; someone who recognizes God in his life and wants to grow closer to him; someone who would support me in that as well."

"I'd like to talk to you more about that idea sometime, after you've had time to work through your present situation. I'm here for you in whatever way I can be." Mike reached over and squeezed Jenny's hand.

"I know, Mike, and I really thank you for that."

The sun was blazing onto the deck and Mike suggested they go for a walk along the shore. They left the restaurant and drove a ways down the road to a lovely spot to stroll along the water's edge.

After a full day at Tahoe, Mike drove Jenny to her home in the Land Park section of Sacramento. She had bought the house with Don in the early eighties. It was an older home situated on almost an acre of land. Set back from the street and across from the park, it was in need of fixing up again, but it was hers, and she was glad she had held onto it during her marriage to Matt.

Mike said goodnight and promised to check on her the next day; then he headed to his apartment, a midtown two-bedroom on a quaint street lined with towering elms. The eclectic nature of that area, with its little restaurants, coffee shops, and outdoor cafes, made it comfortable for him to meet with people from all walks of life. Midtown ran from Sixteenth Street to Alhambra Boulevard and included an artful blend of architecture—refurbished mansions, Victorian flats, contemporary townhouses, and small apartments like his own. He loved to walk to the various bookstores, art galleries, boutiques, and theaters.

From that day on, Jenny saw or spoke to Mike almost everyday. At his encouragement, she began keeping a journal as an outlet to express her sadness and a way to discover herself and the life she wanted to create. She struggled through the months that followed, still feeling excruciating loss. She intentionally isolated herself from everyone except Mike. Having him in her life was comforting and their friendship continued to grow.

Eight

Home for the Funeral

As identical twins, Josh and Kyle Anderson experienced the world differently from the "untwinned" world. The boys, adopted at birth by a Mormon couple unable to bear children, had a strict but loving childhood. Two years later, the couple adopted a baby girl named Cassie to round out the family. Growing up in Santa Monica, the kids loved the beaches, the surfing, and the fun-in-the-sun lifestyle of Southern California.

Josh and Kyle were popular and good-looking, and they were often elected to class offices. Josh was the daring one, while Kyle was more staid. At dances and athletic events, each always had a girl on his arm. Once at the junior prom, Josh preferred his brother's date, and Kyle was more interested in the girl Josh brought. Dressed alike, hair combed in the same short, preppy style, they had only to exchange cars to pull off the switch. The unsuspecting girls never knew. Kyle was more of an intellectual, and he went out for debate while Josh chose basketball and track. Had the subject of debating or sports come up, it might have been one of the few ways the girls could tell them apart.

By 1970, both boys were eager to be out on their own—each for a different reason. Josh wanted to get away from the strict discipline of his parents. Kyle welcomed the chance to get away from living in the shadow of his twin. Although Kyle appeared to be the more dominant of the two, Josh's athletic prowess drew more attention. There were times Kyle felt jealous of Josh but held it inside. It was an emotion he wasn't proud of and did all he could to cover it up. But now he could be free to branch out and let his own separate identity emerge.

Kyle loved California and took up residence at the University of California, Los Angeles where he earned his undergraduate degree and then went on to pursue his law degree. He never had any doubt that law was his chosen field. While pursuing his Juris Doctorate, Kyle was hospitalized for a minor blood clot. In the hospital, he met Jo, the nurse who took care of him. Theirs was a natural convergence of nurse and patient, Jo a caregiver, and Kyle a man who needed to be nurtured. Two years later, the couple married. Five years into their marriage, they had a son, Kevin. In 1984, Kyle ran successfully for Los Angeles district attorney. Kyle distinguished himself as a compassionate but no-nonsense public official. Despite his youthfulness, he commanded respect. While Kyle served in that office, his wife gave birth to their second son, Marty. In 1990, Kyle accepted an appointment to the State Senate. Two years later, he ran for election to keep the seat and won by a high margin of voters. He was the state's rising political star.

Josh, the more rebellious of the two, chose to move far away from home and spread his wings. He chose Brandeis University, just outside of Boston, for one reason: K.C. Jones was the head basketball coach. After his idol moved on to coach at Harvard, Josh briefly considered following him there but knew he didn't have the grades to make it. For the first couple of years of college, Josh jumped from major to major, finally selecting international peace relations because he was drawn to one of the professors in that department. Josh respected the professor for his passion and could see himself in that career. Right out of college, Josh went to work for Amnesty International. He never married and would tell his concerned parents that he was married to his job. He had many girlfriends until, in 1993, he met Emmy.

That same year, the Anderson children received word from their mother that their father was gravely ill. For the first time in years, Josh joined his brother and sister as they all converged on the family house to say goodbye to the man who had chosen to raise them. Kyle was especially close to their father, while Josh and Cassie were closer to their mother. Seeing his father on his deathbed left Kyle feeling alone and vulnerable. It was the first time he had to face death, and he wasn't handling it well.

Josh grabbed a Bud Light from the refrigerator and offered one to Kyle. Declining, his brother chose a Diet Coke, and Josh led the way out to the back porch. For a few moments, they let the silence linger.

"So, how does it feel to be home?" Kyle finally asked his twin.

"In spite of Dad's illness, it feels good to be here. Mom looks good. But Cassie looks like hell. Too much weight and too many kids maybe."

Kyle didn't respond. After another pause, he spoke in a low voice. "Josh, I'm not ready for Dad to die."

"Who is?" Josh responded.

"But losing him is really hard," Kyle said. "I feel like my world is falling apart, and I find myself wondering about our real dad."

"You mean the sperm donor? Dad's our dad."

"Whatever," Kyle retorted as his thoughts wandered. "Mother still drives me a little crazy, but Dad was always reassuring. He was my rock. I don't know why I'm not able to be the kind of dad he was."

"The fact that our parents ditched us might add to the problem."

"Wouldn't you like to know why they gave us up?" Kyle asked. "Maybe there were some good reasons."

"I used to wonder, but not anymore. Maybe that's part of the reason I never wanted kids. I've got Emmy now. She keeps me balanced and makes up for whatever might be screwed up with me. Before I met her, I was just running around."

"I'm really happy for you two," Kyle said. "I have my career, but I'm not all that good at family life. It was better when the boys were little, but now that they're growing up, I don't know how to handle them. And Jo and I are just two ships passing in the night. We hardly talk to each other anymore. So I throw myself into my work."

"Does Jo know how you feel?" Josh asked.

"She must, but we don't talk about it. Jo's life centers on the boys. The fact that she's there for them is good, because I'm not. In a way, I think I'd be happier living by myself."

"You living alone would last about ten minutes," Josh teased him. "You're definitely the kind of guy who needs a woman in his life."

"Speak for yourself."

Life had pulled the twins apart, but their father's illness and funeral brought them back together. Afterward, Kyle and Josh stayed in close communication.

Four years later, in 1997, the twins returned to the old homestead for another sad occasion. What began as diabetes ended with everything imaginable breaking down in Cassie's body—her kidneys, her liver and, finally, her heart. Their mother was devastated over Cassie's death. Emmy came with Josh for the funeral, but Kyle came alone. Like the death of their father, the death of their sister weighed heavily on him.

"I hadn't kept in very close touch with her these last several years," Kyle said to his brother. "When did you talk to Sis last?"

"I spoke with her a few times during her illness. But I stopped when she was too sick to take my calls. I relayed information through her husband and kids after that."

"I called her once, but I didn't take her illness all that seriously. It never dawned on me that she was going to die," Kyle said. "I feel terrible that I wasn't a better brother." He paused. "I don't know what I would do if anything ever happened to you, Josh."

"I'm too damn stubborn to die," Josh replied. "Besides, I haven't lived long enough to have left my mark yet."

Emmy walked up and joined the conversation. With her arm around Josh's shoulder, she told Kyle, "Josh wants to get involved in politics eventually and turn the world upside down with his ideas on creating world peace."

"Emmy, he's been getting ready for it all of his life. He was the only guy in high school who tried to make peace on the football field. 'Why can't those guys just share that frickin' ball instead of fighting over who gets it,' he used to say."

Josh rolled his eyes.

"Funny you should mention politics, though," Kyle said. "My dreams aren't quite so grandiose, but I'm thinking about running for attorney general of California."

"Hey, that's great, bro!"

"And how does Jo feel about it?" Emmy asked.

"She doesn't seem to care either way," Kyle replied.

"Are things any better with you two and the boys?" Josh inquired.

"No, not really," Kyle said. "We just seem to tolerate each other. I don't feel terribly loved by anyone in my household. No one listens to me. They all do their thing, so I do mine."

"With all of that going on, are you sure about your decision to run for attorney general?"

"No, but I think I can win, and that gives me a sense of fulfillment. Who knows? Maybe I can even do some good in that role."

Whenever Josh was troubled about something, he turned it into a joke. "Well, when you get the job, just don't become one of those 'Asshole Gurus,' like so many AGs."

"I'll do my best," Kyle said as he faked a punch at his brother.

Josh's joking sometimes got under Kyle's skin. Kyle found himself still thinking about it the next morning and wondered whether his own self-centeredness and controlling manner had played a part in his marriage going downhill. He had always needed attention in school and, because he excelled at everything intellectual, he had gotten plenty of accolades—maybe not as many as his brother who was the star basketball player. But, as the top member of the debate team, he did earn a scholarship to college. He was used to succeeding at just about anything he pursued—anything except his marriage. After 20 years with Jo, he felt ignored, unimportant, and unloved. He wasn't blaming her. He respected her as a person and as a mother. But they were no longer nurturing each other as husband and wife. Being good at his job was what brought Kyle satisfaction.

Josh had responsibilities at work that required him to return home immediately after Cassie's burial. Kyle drove his brother and Emmy to the airport the next morning and allowed himself an extra day with his mother. He was overwrought with concern about her well-being and felt closer to her after they had gone through two family deaths together.

"How are you, Mother?" Kyle asked. "I'm worried about leaving you alone."

"I'll be all right," Glennys said, looking significantly older now than she had a few years earlier at her husband's funeral. A tall woman, she was thin and drawn. The skin around her throat hung more loosely and shook as she spoke. "I feel sad. I am eighty-eight now and am feeling very lonely. I'm lucky to have my health and my independence. I can still drive and take care of my home. For these things, I am most grateful to the Lord. But death is a very difficult part of life, isn't it?"

"It is for me. I took Dad's death really hard. And now Cassie's. There are some religions that find joyfulness in death. But I don't get it. It seems so horrible to me."

"There isn't a day that goes by that I don't think about your father. And Cassie and I talked almost everyday. She was always bringing the children over to see me. I am going to miss her terribly." She rarely showed her emotions, but now her lower lip was quivering.

Kyle had stayed in close touch with Josh since their dad's death, but now he felt guilty about his neglect of his mother and his sister . . . and his wife and boys. Kyle sat on the couch beside his mother and held her hand. "You and Dad were good parents to us growing up. I wish I had half of whatever it is you two seemed to come naturally equipped with."

"I gather things aren't going well for you with Jo," his mother said. "I pray for you everyday. I so want you to work things out. Divorce wouldn't be good for any of you. And the boys are still so young."

"I know, Mother." Kyle thought about how to discuss such a profound subject with her. It had been years since he had bared his soul to his mother. "Did you and Dad ever come close to divorcing?"

"Not really. It's the Mormon way, you know. We are family-oriented. Mormons' lives from the very start are about raising our children. We just know that and accept it. Maybe it would help you to go back and read the Book of Mormon . . . or to attend church once in a while."

Kyle wondered if it was possible to have a meaningful discussion on this subject with such a devout woman. She was so steeped in the Latter Day Saints way of thinking. Obviously, she knew that Josh had become a Catholic and he himself had been exploring other Christian religions. Josh had converted because of the Church's social justice issues from birth to the death penalty and war to peace. For the moment, Kyle sidestepped any talk of religion and continued sharing feelings about his marriage.

"Jo and I have gravitated so far apart. I don't know if we can ever come back again. Her life is the boys, and mine is my work. At times, I feel a kind of jealousy over the way she loves them more than me. That's not good. I know it. But I do feel it."

"No, that's not healthy. They are your children. They are your first responsibility," Kyle's mother said firmly.

"More than Jo? I thought my wife should be my first responsibility and my children after her. But it's not that way . . . for either of us. She puts them first and I put my work first. I love what I do and dread going home. I sit off in a corner, smoke my pipe, and read. The boys were so sweet when they were babies, but I don't know how to relate to them now. And they don't even pretend to want to spend time with me. They have their friends, and that is their world."

"Marriage is so sacred, Son. You can't just give up. Have you looked into yourself at all? You know how controlling you could be with your brother. Could it be you are that way in your marriage?"

"No more than Dad was with you and us kids. I loved Dad so much. And I thought the way he was in our family was the way it was supposed to be. A father rules. Everyone else marches to his orders."

Glennys laughed. Now it wasn't *that* bad," she said. "But he was definitely the head of our family."

"You see, Mother, I'm not. And I want to be respected the way Dad was. But nobody pays any attention. Times have changed. Jo is not like you were as a wife and mother. And maybe that's the kind of woman I need." Kyle smiled as he looked at his mother and began humming the tune to "I want a girl, just like the girl who married dear old Dad."

"Jo's good with the boys."

"I couldn't agree more. She *is* a good mother and I am grateful that one of us is a good parent. But I need a good wife—someone who adores me, finds my jokes funny, and thinks I'm a hero in my work."

"You are a hero in your work. Look how popular you are with the people. You make me so proud."

"Really? You've never told me that. Actually, neither has Jo."

"Don't be silly," Glennys said brushing his arm. "I've always been proud of you. And you know it."

Kyle paused. "No, I didn't know it. Even as a kid, you always attended Josh's basketball games. But you rarely came to my debates. Dad was busy but he got there to see me once in a while."

"Are you saying you were jealous of your brother?"

"It's hard to admit that at forty-eight years old, but yes!"

Glennys reached over to the coffee table and began flipping through the Book of Mormon that lay in its place of honor. She seemed uncertain of herself. Laying the book back down, she said in a firm tone, "Now you best not go looking for reasons in your growing-up years to explain away your marital problems. Your father and I did the best we knew how to raise you as good Mormon children. We were a close family and everyone in this town knew it."

Kyle realized he was treading on dangerous waters. He didn't mean for their discussion to go there. "Sorry, Mother. I didn't mean to . . ."

"I'm sorry, too, Son. I didn't mean to raise my voice at you. I guess I'm not quite myself now." Glennys wasn't the type to wear her emotions on her sleeve. She didn't cry easily.

Kyle's heart ached as he saw his mother's bottom lip quivering. *Damn me,* he thought. *What kind of person am I that I would make my mother cry . . . and on the day after she lost her only daughter.* He reached over and pulled his mother close to him. Holding her was a rare moment of shared physical affection for Kyle with his mother. They sat quietly, each carrying their own anguish and each trying not to burden the other with any more encumbrances than they already had.

It was Glennys who broke the silence: "I wish I could do something for you, my dear Kyle," his mother said as she reached up and put her arms around him. "Your sadness seems as heavy as my own. Maybe more so."

Nine

After The Divorce

On New Year's Eve, 1997, Jenny's divorce was finalized. Knowing how she was feeling, Mike invited her to lunch on New Year's Day. He chose his favorite hangout in Old Town Sacramento.

"How are you?" he asked Jenny once they were seated.

"Sad. Maybe glad that it's over. I need some kind of finality so I can get on with my life."

"Keep your focus on the future. It's only when you stop and think about your losses that you'll start to feel bad."

"You're right," Jenny said. "But I'm feeling emptiness, sadness . . . the fact that what used to be isn't there anymore. Sometimes I think those feelings will never go away, but I know from experience that they will . . . eventually."

"Well, take it at your own pace. Don't dwell on the sadness, but deal with it as it happens so that you'll complete the grieving process. And know that some of the feelings will always be with you." Then Mike reached into his jacket pocket and removed an envelope. "I brought this from the monastery while I was there saying Mass this morning."

In his spare time, Mike served as chaplain for the Carmelite sisters, whom he came to refer to as "my girls." The Carmelite monastery sat high on a hill overlooking the Sacramento Valley. The sisters had established their home there nearly 50 years earlier and, once they were no longer cloistered, had become an integral part of the local community.

As Jenny's eyes scanned the card within, tears began running down her cheeks. It was so fitting: a quote from theologian Dietrich Bonhoeffer, whom she had read years ago during her theological studies. She cleared her throat and read the card aloud: "'Nothing can make up for the absence of someone we love, and it would be wrong to try to find a substitute. We must simply hold out and see it through. That sounds very hard at first, but at the same time it is a great consolation. For the gap, as long as it remains unfilled, preserves the bond between us. It is nonsense to say that God fills the gap. God does not fill it, but on the contrary, keeps it empty and so helps us to keep alive our forever communion with each other even at the cost of pain.'" Jenny's eyes met Mike's as she finished reading.

"Bonhoeffer wrote that from his prison cell in Berlin," Mike explained, "to his friends Eberhard and Renate Bethge on Christmas Eve, 1943, when Eberhard was feeling the pain of separation from his family waiting to be drafted into the German army, to a war that was already lost."

Placing the card back into its envelope, Jenny said softly, "I will frame this and put it someplace special in my house. You always seem to have the perfect words for me."

By the following June, Jenny was ready to venture out of her self-imposed isolation and embark on her first speaking engagement since her divorce. Jenny was fortunate in that she and Matt had built a solid business with numerous audio tapes and CD's that continued selling even when she wasn't on the road, so getting back on the speaking circuit was more to provide her with a sense of purpose than an income. It took all the courage she could muster to face the St. Louis audience alone, without Matt by her side. Her palms were sweaty and her old confidence was gone, but in its place something new was taking hold of her. She was beginning to realize that, after the pain of the divorce, her message was more human. She was more in touch with her audience than when she had been on the top of the success ladder. In her stardom days with Matt, she was more of an instructor, but now she felt freer to acknowledge her struggles and share how she worked through them.

While Jenny was in St. Louis, she reluctantly phoned Matt's mother, Alice, whom she had yet to talk to about the divorce. It was a difficult call to make since she and Alice had been close. Jenny felt remiss in not having been in touch before. Matt's sister answered the phone and informed Jenny that her mother was in the hospital in intensive care but had expressed a strong desire to see Jenny. Jenny drove to the hospital immediately. When she walked into the room, Alice was sitting up, almost as if she were waiting for Jenny's arrival. Like old times, they had a wonderful three-hour conversation about life in general and Jenny's life with Matt in particular. Jenny was able to tell Alice that, despite everything, Matt had been a good husband to her. Jenny felt it was important that his mother know that. Alice told Jenny that she instinctively knew Jenny had done everything possible to hold their marriage together.

"I'm a little tired now," Alice said as she reached out to Jenny, indicating her readiness to get back into bed. "I need to sleep now, but when I wake up, we'll have some more girl talk."

Alice never regained total consciousness. In retrospect, Jenny thanked God again and again for leading her to make that visit.

Back home, Jenny felt like she was beginning a new life. Mike stopped by a few days later and, guiding him to her back deck, Jenny caught him up on her visit with Matt's mother.

"You seem different," Mike said. "It shows in your body language and in your eyes."

"I've *neva* felt more at peace than I do right now," Jenny said, mimicking Mike's Bronx accent. "Something important happened there. I do feel that I gained some closure for that part of my life. Maybe now, I'm ready to open myself to the next chapter."

"Remember that conversation we had months ago when we drove to Lake Tahoe and had lunch?"

"Yeah, we talked about what kind of a relationship I wanted next, something more akin to a spiritual partnership."

"That was an enthralling concept," Mike said. "Do you still feel that way?"

"I know I don't want to be married in the traditional sense again. God knows I've tried that. Like so many, I was raised with the belief and the dream of a one-man, one-woman relationship wherein each would fulfill the other in all aspects of their lives and the couple would be together until death. At the risk of sounding irreligious, I believe in that for young couples still looking forward to creating a family but, at this stage of my life, that is no longer my fantasy."

"If not that, then what?" he asked.

Yes, exactly. If not that, then what? Jenny thought as she sipped some of the foam from her latté. "Mike, I've thought so much about that. I always saw myself married only once and certainly forever to one man. I thought that man was Don. I loved him so much. But that wasn't meant to be."

"Well, it takes two people to make that happen. From what you told me about Don, I know he was troubled. Even if Don had lived, he wasn't in an emotionally healthy place."

"No, we weren't *ever* in the same place at the same time. He could never commit or settle down into a stable life with Chad and me. Our life was a revolving door. He was always running to something or from something. I was never sure which."

"But you are stronger now and maybe a bit wiser," Mike said.

"I hope so. I've stopped asking myself what's wrong with me, and I no longer equate the ending of my marriage with failure. I've been fortunate enough to have two marriages that brought much good into my life. They *ended* but I never saw either as having *failed*. Had Don lived, who knows? We might have wound up divorced. So, as I move on from my marriage to Matt, I find myself replacing the old questions with new ones."

"Like what?"

"What am I supposed to do with my life now? Where am I being led next, and who will be with me on this next phase of the journey? I've lived most of my life as if the outcome was all that mattered—you know, a happily-ever-after fairytale ending. But what I'm coming to understand is that life is the journey, and I want to live more fully in the now."

Mike reached out and touched her hand. "Undoubtedly, what you're asking describes some pain, but those questions also help you to avoid the need to blame anyone for the so-called 'failure' and to appreciate the good of what you experienced with Matt. I see you growing, Jenny, and getting in touch with your true self, in your life and your career."

"I hope I am. I'm no longer interested in breaking a record or climbing a higher mountain. I just want to be better than I was before. And I want to draw people into my life who are striving for this too. Those friendships that are based on helping each other through our search are the ones that I see becoming primary for me now." Jenny smiled at him and added, "People like you, for instance."

Mike took a sip of his tea and looked out to admire Jenny's garden before he spoke again. Jenny followed his gaze and observed the buckeye and the elderberry trees growing in her yard and the bushes of pale pink California wild rose. Along the side of the house, she had planted the state flower, neon orange California poppies. She learned that poppies could be fooled into blooming all summer with just a little water. The outer perimeter of her yard was lined with sycamores and tall oak trees. In many ways, Jenny felt her yard was a reflection of the blossoming going on within her.

Mike seemed to pick up on her thoughts. "As you grow, it sounds like your vision is becoming a more communal one. I can see that fitting for me as well."

"How so?" Jenny asked.

"Well, you know that I left the priesthood for about ten years. After all my years as an administrator for the Catholic school system in Washington, I taught school administration at the university level during my time out. I thought I would meet someone and get married. Ironically, the woman I fell in love with unknowingly helped me see how much I missed being a priest—preaching the Gospel, ministering to people. My significant friendships were more communally oriented. Eventually I contacted my bishop in Washington; he accepted me back and assigned me to Sacramento."

"So let me be sure I understand. You gave up the choice of having sexual intimacy with one woman in order to have intimate relationships that are non-sexual on a wider scale."

Mike nodded, pleased that Jenny grasped the concept. "I used to believe that we each had only one soul mate over our lifetimes. But part of my return to the priesthood was my coming to understand that those truly blessed with intimacy need not feel limited to one person or even one form in a lifetime."

"I think intimacy is one of the deepest possible connections in a relationship. Two people come together to help each other touch the innermost core of their being. Mike, this is fascinating. You returned to celibate vows in order to relate on an intimate level with other people in your life. You traded sexual intimacy with one person for emotional intimacy with many. I've never heard anyone describe it that way before. But I get it."

"Believe me, Jenny, I'm the least judgmental guy you'll ever meet when it comes to priests falling in love with women. I know many priests who are secretly married and some who have families and are still active priests. This is quite common, especially in third-world countries. I left the priesthood partially in search of that special woman. But I found I couldn't live without the priesthood."

"You're a good priest, Mike. And, it's true: People are more inclined to open up to you because you are a priest."

"I know. I think it is completely unnecessary that, as priests, we have to make a choice. But it is what it is. I love the priesthood. I am a priest at this moment in the Church when marriage is forbidden. And, given these facts, I have chosen priesthood over marriage. But it wouldn't be my preference. I sincerely hope, with the reign of the next pope, this situation will change like it has in. many rites in the Church."

While Jenny got up to pour Mike more tea, he asked, "Did I ever tell you about the young monk who was given his first assignment at the monastery? The abbot asked him to copy the sacred writings, using his talent to transform them into beautiful script.

"'Father Abbot,' the monk asked, 'if I am going to dedicate my entire life to this project, would it not be wise to give me an original from which to work rather than a copy?'

"'How right you are, my son,' the abbot said. 'I will go back to the sacred archives and bring you the earliest version of our sacred teachings. It will be good for me to look them over myself.'

"Time passed, and the abbot did not return. Concerned, the young monk found his way back to the sacred archives, where few monks were allowed to enter and where only original works were kept. There he found the abbot banging his head against the library wall.

"'Abbot, what is it? What is it?' repeated the young monk.

"The abbot lifted his head forlornly and said to the young monk. 'The word isn't celibate, it's *celebrate!*'"

Jenny laughed uncontrollably, and Mike joined in. Raising her glass, she announced, "Here's to more focus on celebrating!"

The more she came to know Mike, the more she saw him truly living this philosophy. He collected people. He was not just everyone's friend, he was their confidant, their confessor, their closest buddy, *their* priest. But Jenny was still soul-searching about relationships in her own life. Looking at Mike and speaking intently, Jenny asked, "Do you think it's possible to have two or more soul mates at the same time?"

"There is nothing more precious in life than a spiritual bond between soul mates," Mike said. "I'm not sure if I know where one crosses the line from experiencing intimacy with a friend to being soul mates. It seems like the apex of an intimate relationship. I read once that intimacy is the mystery of truly encountering another person."

"I think that's true. And, obviously, one need not be sexual in order to be intimate. They are two clearly distinct characteristics of a relationship."

"Yes, but if you reach the place where you feel you have two intimate soul mates in your life, and then one of them becomes sexual, that one should become the primary bond. Balancing the two then becomes more complex. For both relationships to survive takes profound maturity for all the involved parties."

Jenny let that sink in. It was more than she could get her mind around for the moment. If a spiritual partner should ever come into her life, someone with whom she could be both intimate and sexual, she couldn't imagine it taking away from her close friendship with Mike. "Whatever else happens, you and I will always be friends, Mike. I can't think of anything I couldn't talk to you about."

"I feel the same, Jenny. You are very, very special in my life."

The sun was setting, and the evening air began to feel chilly. But the warmth Jenny felt in her heart made up for the coolness of the breeze. Mike and Jenny were destined to be always close friends. His priesthood defined the rules, and they knew the boundaries.

Ten

Pleased To Meet You

1998

I can feel the fragile edges of my life, such as they are, being rewoven into a durable fabric of vibrant colors. Each twine seems resilient and, when interlaced, creates a dynamic pattern, shaping a new and exciting motif, Jenny wrote in her journal.

She had just returned from Australia where she had joined her old team of associates to deliver a motivational workshop to a group of women in Melbourne. She was grateful that Matt had not accompanied them. Any illusion about returning to her old life had faded. She felt born anew, and secure in herself without leaning on someone else for professional competence.

Back at last on the speaking circuit, Jenny was already anticipating her second international engagement. While it had been intimidating for her to fly to Australia alone (and to drive on the opposite side of the road), she was put at ease by the new and old acquaintances she met along the way. The trip covered a five-city tour from Sydney to Perth. Jenny knew she had more growing to do but was fully aware that, after having gone through so much personal desolation, she was able to touch the lives of people in her audiences in a deeper and more meaningful way. Following the tour, she spent a week with friends on Hamilton Island near the Great Barrier Reef. When the trip ended, she was happy to return to the familiarity of her home, her routine, and her close friends.

Newspapers had piled up while Jenny was gone. One headline, dated August 7, immediately caught her attention: "Al Qaeda Attacks Two U.S. Embassies in Africa." Too busy to keep up with the news while abroad, Jenny scanned the article, learning that a bomb planted in what appeared to be a gasoline tanker exploded near the entrance of the American embassy in Dar es Salaam, Tanzania. It destroyed the ingress to the embassy complex, set cars ablaze, and knocked over trees. American officials reported that five members of the Tanzanian staff had been killed and 72 embassy workers wounded, 15 seriously. Within minutes, a truck bomb 400 miles away ripped out doors and windows and destroyed much of the interior of the embassy in the heart of the Kenyan capital, Nairobi, while embassy workers were having their mid-morning coffee break. At least 74 people died there, and more than 1,600 were injured. The rear half of the embassy was torn away and another building entirely gutted. Jenny grimaced as she read that dismembered body parts were found lying everywhere, and broken bodies hung from the exposed upper floors of the embassy.

President Clinton condemned the bombers as inhuman and stated, "We will use every means at our disposal to bring them to justice, no matter what or how long it takes."

"Why?" Jenny said aloud to her empty house. "Who are these people, and what are they trying to prove?"

As she continued flipping through the stack of papers, an August 20 headline read, "U.S. Retaliates for Embassy Bombings." Skimming the article, Jenny learned that, although no one had claimed responsibility for the bombings, U.S. intelligence agencies were sure it was the work of Osama bin Laden, a terrorist who had recently been identified as the greatest threat to the United States. President Clinton ordered a cruise missile attack on a bin Laden camp at Zhawar Kili in eastern Afghanistan, hoping Osama bin Laden might be there. Twenty-one people were killed and scores wounded, but neither bin Laden nor any of the top members of al Qaeda were among them. Another attack was made on a purported chemical factory in Khartoum, Sudan, which CIA intelligence showed was owned by bin Laden and was producing chemical weapons. The intelligence proved wrong. *Amazing*, Jenny thought. She didn't know which strike troubled her more—the first action of the terrorists or the futile U.S. reaction. *So many lives needlessly destroyed*, Jenny thought.

Still mulling over the world situation, Jenny spotted a postcard from Mike from her stack of mail. He was in Ireland, leading a pilgrimage, which several mutual friends from Sacramento attended. Among those on the trip was Gene Vechio, one of the state senators in California's legislature. He, an Italian Catholic and conservative Republican, and Father Mike, an Irish Catholic and avowed Democrat, were becoming fast friends despite their differences. Especially since Gene's wife had recently passed away.

Jenny read the card, laughing when she got to the last line: "To balance the many castles and abbeys, we have added regular trips to the 'shrine' depicted on the front." Jenny turned the card over to find a picture of O'Malley's Bar.

A week later, when Mike returned, Jenny drove with him to the wine country to visit a retired priest friend who lived in Sonoma, not far from Napa Valley. It was fall, and the world outside their car windows was a display of orange, red, and yellow leaves blending to resemble a Monet painting.

On their drives together, Mike often brought along a theological article to review and discuss as they traveled. But this time, Mike showed Jenny a personal journal explaining that it was a diary written by someone he had recently met, a man who was thinking of becoming a Catholic. Sister Marsha from the Carmelite Monastery had introduced the man, Kyle Anderson, to Mike, and they'd had a few chats about spiritual matters. Jenny knew of Anderson. He had been Sacramento's district attorney in 1988 when she had her radio talk show. She recalled interviewing him when the county supervisors had appointed him to fill a vacancy in the California Senate. He won reelection after that and then he ran for and won the post of California attorney general. Jenny had seen him at a few political gatherings, but they'd only exchanged social chat. She thought he was good looking and, more importantly, he seemed to be doing his job well but she'd known he was married and had never given him any further thought.

As Mike drove, Jenny read portions of Kyle's journal aloud, a captivating account of a week that he had spent at Mount St. Carmel

Abbey in Santa Fe, New Mexico. He wrote that his twin brother, Josh, a convert to Catholicism, had gone there many times and, at Josh's encouragement, Kyle spent a week there seeking solace. From his journaling, it was apparent that Kyle, as a non-Catholic, was in awe of the silence, the regimen, and the kindness and wisdom of the monks.

Kyle wrote that he had bonded with one brother in particular, an elderly, heavy-set man with a jovial, rounded face and, in the tradition of many monks, he sported a tonsure. Kyle noted that Josh liked this saintly man, Brother Anthony, but for not-so-saintly reasons. Like Josh, Anthony had played basketball in school. Kyle liked Brother Anthony for his cheeriness and wisdom, and he wrote frequently about him in his journal. As she read, Jenny found that much of Brother Anthony's shared wisdom applied to her own circumstances.

"You cannot maneuver your way through the difficulties that confront you," Kyle quoted Anthony. "To try to take charge of the circumstances is to play God, to think that we actually know better than our Supreme Power. It fills us with pride instead of humility, and that is why it never works. Let God direct us. Do not try to tell God what to do."

Jenny paused and turned to Mike. "How simple life would be if I could just live by that one principle."

"You do pretty well, love."

"What about you?"

"There is no doubt in my mind that God led me back to the priesthood after my ten-year leave . . . and then to Sacramento," Mike said. "Unlike earlier phases of my life, that part was especially God-driven. I know I am where he wants me to be and doing the work he wants me to do."

Jenny smiled and went back to reading the journal. "You'll like this part, Mike," she said. "Kyle explains Anthony's perspective on his choice of a monastic life.

"Anthony says that the monastery is a place of confinement representing a microcosm of the world. The task for the monks living here is to face reality straight on. He says that all of us are in a monastery of sorts, but most of us have little awareness of it, and it is not often that we truly confront reality. The family is a kind of imprisonment, a monastery, even much like a political office. He says we should be grateful for the places that confine us because it is only there that we can learn the significance of liberation through love."

Kyle explained in his journal that Jeremy was the liaison with visitors. Except for the brother who ran the gift shop, Jeremy was the one designated to interact with the outside world. When Jenny finished reading, she thought how nice it would be to talk to Kyle about his experience. It took her back to her own early days of religious studies.

Mike confided in Jenny that Kyle was facing divorce. "He's afraid, given his office, that it's going to be very public."

"Aha, that explains his time at the monastery and his need for solitude and reflection," Jenny said.

"Yes, to his credit. I'm not a proponent of divorce, but he apparently gave it a great deal of thought before taking this step." Mike paused, and then his voice took on a serious tone. "Jenny, would you consider letting Kyle read your journal? I think some of what you've written could be helpful to him."

Jenny had been faithful about writing after her divorce and had shared the journal with Mike over the months.

"It's so personal . . . but if you think it would help . . ."

"Only if you're comfortable with it, love," Mike said.

They rode in silence while Jenny contemplated Mike's request. Finally, she spoke up. "I guess it would be okay, Mike. I'll make you out a copy." Until she began keeping the journal, Jenny had never been able to really express her feelings about Don's death. She was younger and in too much pain to be able to analyze it. But she had written about the rise and fall of her marriage to Matt and described in detail the process of her recovery. The day after their trip, she delivered a copy of her journal to Mike.

A week later, on a Friday afternoon, Jenny was surprised to find a message on her answering machine from Kyle Anderson. Mike had apparently wasted no time in getting it to him. Kyle's message expressed his thanks to Jenny for sharing her journal with him, and he expressed gratitude to Father Mike for having been the intermediary to get it to him. Due to her schedule, it wasn't until the following Monday that she had a chance to return his call. She was surprised how easily she got through to him in his office.

"You express yourself beautifully," Kyle told her. "Your thoughts are having a strong impact on me. I'd like to come out of my divorce as positive as you have."

"I enjoyed your journal as well, Kyle. What an experience for you to have. It must have helped you think through your decision."

"No question about that," he said. "I don't think I could have pursued the divorce if I hadn't met Brother Anthony. I'm not sure he would want to hear that, but it's true."

"I understand more than you know," Jenny said.

The following night, Mike and Jenny attended an Irish celebration together at the home of the Irish Consulate. As they entered the party, Jenny spotted Kyle. After formal introductions, the three of them chatted until the host and hostess pulled Father Mike away to meet another guest.

Left alone with Kyle, Jenny asked him about his work. He mentioned the edition of the *Women's Rights Handbook* that his office had just completed. He described the updates, explaining that the book contained the most current information on new laws and services that benefit women.

"I think I'm most proud of the work we did on hiring practices— issues related to pregnancy and sexual harassment," Kyle told her, and proceeded to outline the process. They were soon chatting about all sorts of things, and both felt sparks flying. On the ride home with Mike, Jenny couldn't stop talking about Kyle. She felt as giddy as a schoolgirl.

Three days later, Jenny attended a political rally with Mike and, again, Kyle was present. His eyes lit up when he saw her, and he stuck close to Jenny during the event. Because they had both shared their innermost thoughts via their journals, they quickly formed a unique bond. Jenny thought it was interesting to reconnect with someone about whom she knew more from the inside than the outside. Whereas most couples were initially attracted to each other based on outward appearances, Kyle and Jenny were attracted primarily because of their journal-sharing. Kyle's trim, six-foot frame commonly attracted women, and he was a handsome man with a youthful Norwegian demeanor that belied his fifty years. Jenny's slim, petite frame and her large, inquisitive brown eyes always held Kyle spellbound.

The two began nurturing their friendship by meeting frequently for afternoon walks and conversations at the Cal State Quad, a good place to steal away unnoticed. Kyle reminded Jenny of Don in many ways. Not only his appearance, but his personality, intelligence, sensitivity, love of books and poetry, even his spiritual interests. Although Kyle came across as staid, she surmised that there was a radical underneath, dying to come out. Like Don, Kyle was a staunch Democrat, and he talked about politics constantly. He enjoyed kidding Jenny about her "rich Republican friends." In between their visits, Jenny found herself frequently thinking of Kyle. There were so many wonderful things about him. She was drawn to him but also recognized that he was in the early stages of divorce. Jenny talked this over with Mike.

"Take it slowly," he said. "Don't back away just because the time isn't right, but don't dive in headfirst, either."

So, ever so slowly, Kyle and Jenny began building a friendship.

Eleven

Growing Closer

Over the first few months of getting to know Kyle Anderson, Jenny learned that he was much more than a politician. He showered her with books he loved. He treasured the classics. He was one of the few non-Catholics who had read *The Confessions of St. Augustine.* He enjoyed playing the violin, and was always learning a new piece of music. Their time together ran the gamut of shared interests.

One summer evening after dinner and a long walk by the river, they stopped by a local hangout and found it empty. As they sipped wine and chatted, Kyle's feelings for Jenny were overpowering. When a romantic ballad came over the sound system, he stood and pulled her up to dance. After a few moments of slow swaying, locked in each other's arms, Kyle leaned down and kissed her, long and slow. Then he moved his lips to her cheek, and then to her neck. Jenny shuddered with delight. *Slow dancing has nothing on slow kissing,* Jenny thought.

"Let's get out of here," he whispered as he nuzzled her ear. Arriving at Jenny's house, they resumed their kissing: hungry, passionate, lingering kisses that made them both want more. Instinctively, Jenny knew the time was right. She stood and held out a hand to Kyle. He took it, and she led him into her bedroom. They slowly undressed each other, and he guided her onto the bed. They caressed each other's bodies, touching where they had not dared to touch before. Lost in the moment, they hungrily expressed their love.

The next morning, Kyle awoke to the smell of fresh coffee. He sat up in bed just as Jenny brought in a tray of filled mugs and croissants with honey butter.

"Morning, Mr. Anderson. Did you sleep well?"

"Famously," Kyle replied with a grin. "Best sleep I've had in a while."

Jenny sat the large tray on the bed, and slid gingerly back under the covers. He turned and kissed her on her bare shoulder.

"I was wondering about something," Jenny said. "You know those embassy bombings that happened last year?"

"Sure. The work of Osama bin Laden, a rich terrorist pissed off about the U.S. support of Israel."

"America has been pretty unwavering in its commitment to stand by Israel," Jenny said. "But I don't fully understand our position there. I do think it has seriously hurt our efforts to build better relations with the rest of the Middle East."

Kyle nodded in agreement and realized again how much he loved Jenny's inquisitive mind. "About six months before those bombings, bin Laden gave advance warning. A copy of it came across my desk at the end of last year from George Tenet, the head of the CIA. Essentially, bin Laden declared war on the United States in an effort to liberate Muslims from America's grip. It was a demand for our armies to move out of the lands of Islam. Apparently the bombings were his way of showing that he meant it. I think he's capable of even worse things if we don't comply."

"But why *do* we give so much support to Israel?"

"You don't ask easy questions, you know. And the answer depends on whom you ask. Politically, the Jewish coalition has a powerful lobbying presence in Washington. But I think it also has to do with religion as much as politics. Look how Jews have long been treated by other nations. That is why Israel was created and surely much of the reason the United States is committed to supporting it. From your own religious studies, I'm sure you understand that the emergence of a modern state of Israel is seen as proof of God's covenant with Abraham. The Old Testament itself lays the groundwork for believers to anticipate the return of the Jews to Israel and expansion of Israel's borders to take in all the land between the Nile and the Euphrates."

"Religion is a strong factor for both Americans and Muslims," Jenny mused. "And they both believe they are right and that God is on their side. Jews, with strong support from Christians steeped in the Old Testament, hold the belief that the Jewish Temple must be rebuilt on its original site, which would require that the Dome of the Rock, one of the holiest places in Islam, be demolished. So, Israel must be the epicenter of God's intervention in history. But how does that differ from Muslims wanting to protect their sacred mosques?"

"You have a better grasp of this than I do," Kyle replied, sipping his coffee. "It is a complex situation. Look at the Holocaust. War is often steeped in religious history."

"Well, I was bothered by the way Clinton retaliated for the embassy bombings," said Jenny.

"If we could ask him, I doubt Clinton would say he did the right thing either. He was under a lot of pressure to act. Presidents, whether Democrats or Republicans," he winked at her, "have to rely on their intelligence agencies and, in this case, they weren't so intelligent. We didn't even have an embassy in Afghanistan at that time and, without that, the CIA had no viable spy operation and could hardly give accurate information to the White House."

"You mean to tell me that we lost unnecessary lives and spent millions of dollars based on false information?" Jenny asked.

"It happens all the time, sweet pea. The CIA information came from a mix of defectors and opposition groups, neither of which are traditionally very reliable. The CIA knew they screwed up. The only one who came out of that whole interchange a winner was Osama bin Laden. I think our raid helped elevate his reputation among Muslims. Our attack was so incompetent that we turned him into a folk hero, and I'm afraid we haven't heard the last of him."

For a few months after moving out of the house with his family, Kyle had lived in the University Inn connected to Cal State. In July, he took Jenny to see a house he was thinking of purchasing. It was a small 1920s bungalow with a back deck, just a stone's throw from the river, located in River Park, East Sacramento. She instantly fell in love with its charm, the fireplace in the living room, and the openness of the kitchen and living areas. Turning to Kyle, she gave it a "two thumbs up" signal.

Kyle bought the house, and Jenny helped him move in. Not far from the Cal State campus, the neighborhood was a quaint pedestrian community with sidewalks and old-fashioned lamps. It was conducive to strolling along the American River or bicycling to nearby parks. Jenny loved to walk with Kyle under the graceful olive trees in East Portal Park.

Kyle had no reservations about public displays of affection. As they shopped for furnishings for his house, he kissed her in Macy's. He kissed her in Pier One. He kissed her on the street corner. Kyle didn't seem to care who saw them. He had an unencumbered feeling of new love, like something he had once felt in high school, but better. He laughed at everything and made Jenny laugh. Life was simple and carefree. Almost.

One evening after work, Kyle stopped by Jenny's unannounced. He heard intimate laughter coming from Jenny's patio, and he felt a surge of jealously. Rounding the corner of the house, he saw Jenny, her back toward him, and she was rubbing the shoulders of another man. A sudden rage hit Kyle from nowhere and, for a moment, he didn't know whether to stay or leave. He chose the former and marched stiffly up the patio stairs. Seeing him, Jenny broke out in a grin, and Kyle saw that the man she was massaging was Father Mike. But the realization only made him more angry.

"Well, don't you two look cozy," Kyle said heatedly as he opened the screen door and entered the patio.

Jenny felt confused. Kyle sounded as if he was jealous, but jealous of whom? Mike?? Mike, however, felt Kyle's mano a mano mood. He was puzzled that Kyle felt somehow challenged by his presence, but he also had an impending engagement, so he quickly rose from his chair to say his goodbyes.

"Good to see you Kyle, but I'm off. Dinner engagement across town," Turning to Jenny, he gave her a quick hug. Then he then smiled at Kyle. "Sit yourself down; you're in for a treat."

Kyle just glared at the pair as Mike turned and left. Jenny knew something was wrong.

"Come on, Kyle, have a seat and let me rid you of some tension."

Kyle just stared at her but didn't move. Jenny was becoming alarmed. "Kyle, what's wrong?"

"What the hell were you doing touching Mike like that?"

"Excuse me??"

"Touching him, rubbing on him. And for that matter, he's around all the fucking time."

Huh? Jenny thought. She realized that it *was* jealously he was feeling. But she knew she hadn't been doing anything inappropriate. Mike often stopped by. Why should that change just because she was seeing Kyle?

"What's going on between you and Mike? I know you like priests, Jenny; you married one. So fess up."

Jenny was floored. Not only was Kyle's behavior totally out of character, she felt genuinely frightened. It was as if Kyle's doppelgänger had appeared from some parallel dimension.

"Kyle, I don't understand. Mike has been my friend for years. God, he even introduced us! I can't believe you would even *suggest* that anything was going on between us aside from friendship. And for you to imply that about my marriage to Don, well, that's totally inappropriate."

As if snapping out of a trance, Kyle felt suddenly ashamed. "I just...I was just ...oh, Jenny, I'm sorry. I don't know what came over me but I saw you rubbing his shoulders, and I...well, I overreacted."

"You can say that again."

"Can you forgive me?"

"Of course," Jenny said, moving to embrace him. Hugging him, she felt him trembling. "Silly man, don't you know how much I care for you? Isn't it evident by the way I touch you, look at you?"

"Yes," Kyle whispered. "But when I saw you touching another man that way, I felt so betrayed."

"It wasn't just another man, Kyle, it was Mike. My friend, not my lover. You, my dear, are my lover." Jenny leaned back and gazed into Kyle's eyes. "If it makes you feel better, I won't give Mike any more shoulder rubs."

Kyle leaned down and kissed her, and she melted into his arms.

Thanksgiving brought Jenny's family and friends together. She cooked her usual turkey stuffed with cornbread, sausage, and walnut dressing. Her mother, Ellen, made her special lemon meringue pie—the family called it angel pie—and her cranberry-apple dish crusted with crumbled brown sugar and nuts. Her husband, Earl, had a strong sweet tooth and insisted she make both because they were his favorites. Kyle brought a bottle of Courvoisier as an after-dinner treat, and Mike showed up with succulent-looking petits fours. Jenny noticed Kyle stiffen a bit when Mike made his entrance, but he appeared relaxed by dinnertime.

Mike had said nothing to Jenny about the patio incident; Jenny had told him that Kyle had just had a rough day at work, and that had been the reason for his mood. Mike felt that Jenny hadn't told him everything, but he hadn't pressured her for further details. Still, Mike felt the tension from Kyle.

Jenny's son, Chad, was also in attendance, and he and Kyle quickly paired off for a game of chess. Jenny was so happy that Chad and Kyle were bonding so well.

When everyone was seated for the feast, Jenny looked around the table and felt at peace. *I've come a long way since my divorce,* Jenny thought, hardly believing that it had been almost two years since it was final. She felt truly blessed.

Later that night, Jenny was already in bed when Kyle called to say goodnight and wish her a peaceful sleep. "I had a wonderful time with your family, Jenny, even though Chad did beat me twice at chess."

Jenny was happy that Kyle and Chad were getting along so well.

"I wish you were here with me right now," Kyle continued, "but at least it's nice to hear your voice. Has anyone ever told you what a soothing voice you have?"

"Mmm, I think I've heard something like before," she said softly.

"Well, mmm, it just makes me feel good to hear it. Listen, I have something I want to read to you. Be warned, though, it's mushy."

"I like having mushy things read to me," Jenny said.

"Okay, now I didn't write it, but I could have." Kyle read her a

Hafiz poem, and then paused before the final verse. "This reminds me of us," he told her, and then continued.

> The subject tonight is love
> And for tomorrow night as well.
> As a matter of fact,
> I know of no better topic for us to discuss
> Until we all die!

From that moment on, one line from the poem became their oft repeated mantra. "The subject tonight is us." "The subject tonight is dinner." "The subject tonight is when I will see you next." "The subject tonight is love."

During the weeks leading up to Christmas, Jenny began to notice that Kyle had frequent mood swings. No doubt the pressures of his job accounted for his sometimes drifting into his own thoughts, or his eyes projecting an aura of sadness. Then, one evening when he arrived at her house, he burst into the foyer exuding the excitement of a five-year-old child dashing to presents on Christmas morning.

"Guess who's coming next week?" Kyle prodded Jenny.

"Uh, Santa Claus and his reindeer?"

"Josh!!" Kyle explained that his brother had some work to do for Amnesty International in California, and he was bringing Emmy with him. After hearing so much about the couple, Jenny was thrilled that she would finally get to meet them.

Arriving in time for the annual state Christmas party, the four of them dined and danced the evening away. At one point, Jenny excused herself to "powder her nose." When she returned, Kyle asked her to dance, but she soon found she was dancing with Josh. It took her more than a minute before she realized the twins had made a switch.

When Jenny arrived back at the table, Emmy was laughing and told her, "It used to happen to me all the time. They've been pulling this one on girlfriends since high school."

In the spirit of the season, Kyle and Jenny were learning to share their usual traditions with each other. They attended more holiday parties and continued to grow closer to one another, although it seemed to Jenny that he was more relaxed when with his friends than when with hers. Kyle was comfortable with Jenny's family but not so much with her many friends. He even teased about having to drive her and Emmy to Mandy O'Connor's ladies' luncheon, calling the group "a bunch of rich Republican women." He made other offhand comments about how much time she spent socializing. She gathered from his occasional verbal slights that he was experiencing a kind of jealousy of her friends, and she thought back to their brief tiff on the patio. However, Kyle continued to be loving and attentive toward her. He prided himself in putting her first above anything or anyone else.

"This past year with you has been like a dream," Kyle told her on Christmas Eve. "I didn't know anyone like you existed. But sometimes I feel like our relationship isn't balanced. I feel like you're more important to me than I am to you."

"Kyle . . . I . . ."

"You don't have to say anything. It's okay."

"Yes, I do," Jenny said. "I've noticed your discomfort regarding my friends, so let me explain something. When Matt and I separated, it was more than just the ending of a marriage. It ended my whole life as I'd known it. I felt lost and alone and like I had been dumped at the bottom of a ravine. I really wasn't sure how to pick myself up and go on. But I climbed out and created a new life for myself. I started giving workshops again. I feel a more solid spiritual foundation under me now, and I'm happy about where my life is." Jenny paused and looked at him warmly. "And now that you're in my life, I've found a happiness that I never knew was possible. I just don't want to move too quickly, Kyle. You need time to figure out what kind of life you want for yourself, and I don't want to rush you. Besides, I still need time to sort things out for myself too. I don't think it's as simple as boy meets girl, boy and girl fall in love, boy and girl get married and live happily ever after."

"Why not?" he asked. "I read that story, and I rather liked the ending. But seriously, I guess I understand."

"I'm glad you do, Kyle. In my past relationships, I feel like I've molded myself too much to my partners. I haven't always given myself room to hold on to the parts of my life that help preserve my own identity. I don't mean to be inflexible with you, but I don't want to make that mistake again."

"Then kiss me, sweet pea, and all will be understood."

Shortly after Christmas when Jenny and Mike got together, she related her Christmas Eve discussion with Kyle. "I think it's all worked out," she told Mike.

"After all the conversations we've had, it is clear to me what you are looking for," Mike confirmed. "Someone who wants to grow and will support you in your growth. And you both have to be willing to talk about the difficult parts of your lives, the subjects that you may be scared to bring up out of concern for rocking the boat."

"I remember when we talked about this," Jenny said. "You predicted it wouldn't be easy for me to keep a close circle of friends and invite a romantic involvement into the circle, too. Here I am finally coming out of the pain of my divorce, and Kyle is still at the beginning of his. One minute he's up, and the next he's down," Jenny explained to Mike. "I'm handling that as best I can."

"You were up and down yourself right after your divorce. Actually, maybe more down than up. Keep using your experience to show Kyle compassion. That's what he needs more than anything right now—to be understood and to be loved . . . in spite of himself."

Kyle invited Jenny to spend New Year's Eve on a yacht, cruising the San Francisco bay. Everything about the evening was enchanting, including the ambiance. The interior of the cabin was decorated with shimmering ceiling ornaments. The tables were elegantly set with an array of balloons as centerpieces. The men wore tuxes and paper top hats of varying colors, and the women were in evening gowns and sparkling tiaras. They were served a lavish four-course Italian dinner catered by Allioto's restaurant: tomatoes and fresh mozzarella served with warm Italian bread, bowtie pasta with basil pesto sauce, ossobuco succulently falling off the bone and set on a bed of fresh spinach, and crème brulèe topped with vanilla ice cream and Grand Marnier. Kyle chatted with several of his political acquaintances at the festivities, and he and Jenny burned up the dance floor. As they counted down the seconds until they would leave the second millennium behind and welcome in the third one, confetti sprinkled the guests with good cheer. A brilliant array of colorful fireworks filled the sky around the ship. As the band played *Auld Lang Syne,* Kyle and Jenny raised their champagne flutes and Kyle offered a toast. "Here's to us and to our future together."

"A wonderful resolution," Jenny replied. As the clock struck midnight, they sealed their New Year's resolution with a kiss.

Twelve

Love or Obsession?

JANUARY - JUNE 2000

The impact of his divorce continued to take its toll on Kyle, and his mood swings became more frequent. Shortly after the first of the year, with Josh and Jenny's encouragement, Kyle began seeing a psychiatrist, Dr. Harvey Monroe. Kyle described Dr. Monroe to Jenny as a psychiatrist who was anything but stuffy. "He even built his own airplane," Kyle excitedly told her.

During sessions with Dr. Monroe, Kyle held nothing back. He told the psychiatrist about his concerns for his boys, his struggles with his ex-wife, and his fear of his private life spilling over into his public life. He spoke of his father's and sister's deaths, and his adoption. But most of all, Kyle talked about his increasing love for Jenny. After the first few weeks, Dr. Monroe had heard nearly everything possible about her. Kyle talked about her so often that even he found himself repeating things, especially about how she "just has too many friends."

"Doc, I love her like I've never loved anyone before. But her friendship with Mike is too important to her, and she used to be married to an ex-priest and . . ."

"Do you fear that she's in love with Mike?"

"Well, I don't think so. I mean, she loves him, yes, but not that way. But it's just not normal. How could he introduce us and then vie with me for her time?" Kyle asked. "And he's a *priest,* for God's sake! He's not supposed to have women in his life!"

During the next session, Kyle was upset about Jenny spending time with her "rich, Republican friends"—the most despicable of them being the O'Connors. Then he immediately softened and began talking about her as if he was a middle school student with a crush. On subsequent visits, Kyle complained that Jenny was not available enough to him, that she made more money than he did, and that she didn't like marriage but wanted him permanently in her life. He wondered if Jenny would ever give up her home to live with him in River House. There was always something stirred up within him.

Dr. Monroe began to have suspicions, and he sent Kyle for testing.

On Valentine's Day, Kyle invited Jenny to a stage show: *I Love You. You're Perfect. Now Change.* Given how close the subject matter was to both of them, they thoroughly enjoyed the performance, laughing hysterically at the situation. Afterward, over a light dinner of breaded calamari and salad, they exchanged cards.

"Mm, mush, mush," Kyle grinned as he opened the card from Jenny. She had chosen a romantic message. In his card to her, he expressed his gratitude for her support through his recent therapy.

Jenny had some experience dealing with depression with her first husband, and she felt she understood the syndrome. Like Don, Kyle would have a break in the darkness when he would come alive. Then he would sink again. And the more he lapsed into his depression, the more the "helper" personality in Jenny would surface.

In March, at Kyle's request, Jenny accompanied him to see Dr. Monroe. The doctor's eyes sparkled and he smiled as he greeted them. His dark brown beard tickled Jenny's face as he gave her a warm hug that signaled he knew more about her than she may have wanted him to know.

The doctor directed them to the couch, and seated himself in a chair across from them. "It's good to finally meet you," he said addressing Jenny.

Yes, he definitely knows a lot about me, Jenny thought. "I've heard a lot about you too, Dr. Monroe," she responded.

"Please, call me Harvey. And thank you for coming. It was important to Kyle to have you come in."

Kyle looked gratefully at Jenny and squeezed her hand.

"Let me begin by asking if you have any questions for me," Harvey said to Jenny.

"Yes, your constant changing of Kyle's meds. Every week he seems to be on a different dosage," Jenny said.

Harvey had tried many variations of Kyle's medications and raised and lowered his doses until he felt he had finally found a level that seemed to stabilize him. "This was one of the reasons I was eager to have you come in. You see, Jenny, treating depression alone is one thing. But, over the weeks, I have learned that Kyle is not just depressed. He's bipolar, a manic-depressive. Finding the balance for someone who is bipolar—experiencing mood swings from one end of the spectrum to the other—is far more challenging."

Jenny's heart felt as if it had stopped. Silence permeated the room. Absorbing what Harvey had just said, Jenny slowly turned to Kyle. "Did you know this?"

"Well," he replied, looking a little anxiously at Harvey, "I knew we were exploring possibilities. We weren't certain until recently."

Recalling the mood swings she had seen in Kyle, Jenny said, "That explains a lot. So what do we do? I mean, how can I help?"

"By continuing to love Kyle and giving him your support. Given your relationship with Kyle, you will be in a position to help assess his progress. I have added lithium to his medications, and it seems to be keeping him better balanced."

They spent the rest of the session discussing Kyle's ongoing battle with accepting Jenny as she was versus trying to change her. Both Kyle and Jenny described the irony and reality of the stage show they had recently attended. The closer a theme strikes home, Harvey told them, the funnier it can be, but the more seriously it should be taken.

Jenny left the meeting with greater understanding and concern. She had been through mood swings once before with Don. Was she up for dealing with it a second time? She was lost in her thoughts during the ride home. *Is it possible for a bipolar personality to ever be truly stabilized? Or would there always be ups and downs in his moods? I'll always be afraid that he will leave me on one of his downturns.* Jenny thought back to the numerous times in her life that she had dealt with feeling abandoned. Kyle's issues could wind up playing havoc with her peace of mind.

"No matter how well-developed we think we are, we all have issues to work through," Harvey had said during their meeting. "Who knows? Maybe the secret to a healthy relationship is nothing more than finding another person who has a compatible set of dysfunctions."

Jenny recognized that she had her own issues to manage. Hopefully, success for their relationship was simply a matter of synchronizing their respective struggles.

For the moment, they were an almost perfect combination of personality types. Kyle was devoted to Jenny and grateful for her support. In turn, with his dependence on her, Jenny had less fear that he might leave her. Plus, he needed her, and she needed to be needed. As long as the seesaw was balanced in this way, their relationship worked well. For once, Jenny felt that both her head and her heart were in the same place—guiding her to take things slowly.

"There are so many life possibilities you haven't even thought about yet," she told Kyle as they rode. "You may decide you want to become a full-time violinist or a professor of English literature."

"Or a circus performer," he teased.

Jenny thought for a moment and then asked, "Do you want some time alone?"

She knew that spending time alone was particularly difficult for Kyle. It was one of the many issues that dominated his discussions with Harvey.

"No, definitely not," he told Jenny. "Heck, I wasn't even in the womb alone. I've never enjoyed being alone." Harvey had told him that there was nothing wrong with wanting to be with someone and that some people needed more companionship than others. But he had suggested that Kyle spend time by himself now and then, that it would be good for him and his relationship with Jenny. Kyle thought about that conversation as he drove.

"What do you think about when you're at home and Jenny isn't with you?" Harvey had asked him.

"Where she is? Who is she with? Is she having a better time with them than she is with me?"

"I guess you don't need me to tell you that isn't healthy," Harvey had replied.

"I can't seem to help it. That's where my thoughts go."

"It sounds to me like your challenge isn't about being physically alone; it's about being alone with your thoughts. Why do you think you give in to such negative thinking?"

Kyle had let the question hang in the air. Outside the window that day, the sky was overcast, looking much like he felt when he had to be by himself. After a moment, he'd felt a lump in his throat.

"Kyle," Harvey said gently, "Let me ask you something. Do you believe you're a lovable person? Do you believe a woman could love you . . . for no particular reason except she just does?"

Kyle hadn't been able to speak. He simply shook his head from side to side and tears flowed down his cheeks.

Harvey had handed him a tissue and let him cry for a few minutes. "Why not, Kyle?

Brushing the tears aside, Kyle had whispered, "I don't know. Maybe so that I can perform for her or be funny or . . .

". . . or control even her feelings about you. When she's not with you, you have no control. Does that scare you? Having absolutely no control over how someone feels about you?"

"I like being in control," he'd told Harvey. "How else do you think I could run this state? I have to be a take-charge person to do my job."

"Well, I think we've stumbled onto something very important here. When you're in control, you like yourself. When you are in a place where you're not in control, you doubt yourself. You doubt everything, including that you are worthy of being loved. Or that you are attractive enough in and of yourself to another person. You're in a great place doing your job or winning an election. That, my man, is power and you love it. But being home alone and not being in a place to 'win' Jenny's affection leaves you vulnerable and scared. So you try to win her with your overpowering domination. But that simply won't work for long. So here's your assignment for the week. Just be. Just allow things to happen. Stop trying so hard to make them happen. Can you do that?"

At the time, Kyle had nodded but, even now, he still wasn't sure.

With his medications reasonably balanced, Kyle was gradually able to go on with life more normally. Only his closest staff members knew that he was in therapy. Outside that small circle, he was able to conduct himself as though nothing were amiss.

Jenny was still the recipient of Kyle's mood swings, though. One evening when she was at home, the phone rang every five minutes, as many as seven or eight times in a row. Jenny and Kyle had already talked earlier while he was at work and agreed that they would spend the evening apart in their respective homes, giving both some personal time. The caller ID indicated that the calls were coming from Kyle's home number. Respecting her own needs, and as difficult as it was not to pick up the phone, Jenny resolved not to answer. She still did not fully grasp that he was experiencing a manic phase; she just knew it wasn't healthy behavior.

The next morning, Jenny read about one of Kyle's professional goals in the *Sacramento Bee*. Kyle had formed a task force on gasoline pricing. The task force, made up of representatives from the oil industry, gasoline station owners, consumers, and environmentalists, was searching for ways to control California's gas prices. Kyle was proud of the fact that he had built a good reputation. He was a popular attorney general, admittedly with a bit of arrogance, but generally he was seen as a supporter of the people who had avoided being in the pockets of big business. Like any politician, he understood that he had to walk a tightrope between supporting those whose campaign money put him in office and supporting the people who elected him. Jenny sipped her coffee as she read.

> "The price spikes that sent pump prices soaring last year and again this year to above two dollars a gallon in some parts of the state erode the competitiveness of California businesses and reduce the real income of Californians," Attorney General Anderson said. "The high gasoline prices we are seeing today have been a long time in the making. It would be unrealistic to suggest there is a quick fix or simple solution. What we need are major strides

> in making "California's gasoline market
> competitive, finding ways to increase
> supplies, and becoming more aggressive
> about fuel conservation."

Putting the paper down, Jenny felt proud of Kyle. She loved his passion for serving the public and doing what he thought was best. But on a personal level, she was still worried about him.

At work, Kyle Anderson was fully on top of many pressing issues. The CIA and FBI kept him informed on matters of consequence to California. Memos from the CIA had increased significantly since he first took office.

Sitting at his desk in his wood-paneled office in late March, Kyle received a memo marked "confidential" from his CIA contact. It updated Kyle about potential terrorists arriving in southern California. Setting his coffee cup down, Kyle leaned over his desk and began to read:

> RISK ALERT: Two men residing in California are being watched closely by our agency. Their names are Khalid Almihdhar and Nawaf Alhazmi. They are known al Qaeda members and have been under surveillance since December of last year while attending a meeting in Kuala Lumpar, Malaysia, that involved eleven other young operatives, all associated with al Qaeda.
>
> Once they arrived in Kuala Lumpur, the Malaysian security services placed them under constant observation on behalf of the CIA. From the airport, the two men traveled 20 miles south to the weekend getaway for Yazid Sufaat, an al Qaeda member who earned a degree in biological sciences from California State University, Sacramento and specialized in the research of the acute infectious disease known as anthrax.

This is getting awfully close to home, Kyle thought. Two suspected terrorists living in his state and their associate was a specialist in chemical warfare and had attended college in Kyle's neighborhood. He read on:

We had no further information until March 4 when our
Bangkok station learned that Alhazmi had departed for Los
Angeles on January 15. He eventually moved into an apartment
in San Diego. Although there was no record of Almihdhar's
departure, we have just learned that he was traveling on the
same flight with Alhazmi.

These goons have been here for two months, and I am just learning about this?
Kyle shook his head in disbelief. He immediately picked up the phone
and called Blake, his chief of staff. "I want you to call our FBI contact
and check the TIPOFF watch list for the names of two guys." Kyle filled
Blake in on the essential details and spelled the names twice to be sure
Blake wrote them correctly.

Within the hour, Blake was in Kyle's office with a report. "No such
names are on the watch list, and the FBI claims to know nothing about
a meeting in Malaysia. Our FBI guy was a little miffed that we thought
we had information his office didn't have—especially about Almihdhar
having a U.S. visa. His advice was to watch the guys but, since they
don't have them on the watch list or in their files, there probably isn't
much to it."

Later that month, while Kyle was in Washington attending the
national attorneys general conference, Jenny was asked to speak to a
group in New York, one of her favorite cities to visit. On their first
Saturday afternoon home after returning from their respective trips,
they lay beside each other on the floor in front of Kyle's fireplace.
Time apart had served to pull them closer together. Kyle took out a
book of Yeats poems and put Beethoven's Pathetique Sonata in the
CD player. Then he read to Jenny.

> When you are old and gray and full of sleep,
> And nodding by the fire, take down this book,
> And slowly read, and dream of the soft look
> Your eyes had once, and of their shadows deep;
>
> How many loved your moments of glad grace,
> And loved your beauty with love false or true,
> But one man loved the pilgrim soul in you,
> And loved the sorrows of your changing face;

And bending down beside the glowing bars,
Murmur, a little sadly, how Love fled
And paced upon the mountains overhead
And hid his face amid a crowd of stars.

Kyle put his arms around Jenny and whispered, "I've finally figured out what it is I love so much about you. It's your pilgrim soul. I always see it behind your eyes, searching for something that will give you greater insight into yourself, and you're helping me do that, too. I've never known anyone quite like you, Jenny."

Jenny was growing to feel the same way about Kyle, but she still held back. The ink on his divorce papers was barely dry, and he was now dealing with the bipolar diagnosis. Jenny vowed to move slowly.

Kyle invited her to Calistoga for the weekend to celebrate her birthday at a small, out-of-the-way historic spot—Mount View Hotel and Spa. Amid shared mud baths, massages, and dinners in the garden, their time was filled with laughter and loving moments. On Sunday, they drove along St. Helena Highway and, when they saw a sign for a brand name that was familiar to both of them, Louis Martini Winery, they turned onto the property. The vineyard was one of the oldest in Sonoma County, and the rugged Mayacamas mountains were ideal for growing premium wine grapes. Many of the vines were 30 to 50 years old. They bought a bottle of Monte Rosso Cabernet and spread a picnic blanket on the grass. In the glorious setting, Kyle shared a poem that he had written over the past month:

Love captures your eye before it captures you.
It is a fleeting glimpse, a flicker in the sunlight.
You alone will notice as it sparkles in the heavens
At the peripheral edge of sight.

You can see its passage,
The mirror of its reflection
Everywhere . . . it's there.
Open your heart to see
How love moves so timidly,
Reaping sweet fruit of the vine
As bitter grapes yield delicate wine.

Jenny had moved closer, watching his face and listening to his voice as he concluded the final verse. She could feel Kyle's love pour out as he read the poem in this very vineyard setting. And the words were exquisitely descriptive of how his love for her had emerged inside of him. He was right. She could literally see love moving "timidly," bringing the vineyard surrounding them to life at that very moment. She leaned in and they kissed longingly and lovingly. It was a moment when the world was suspended in time—or so she wished—if only she could hold it in abeyance indefinitely.

Spiritual discussions with Jenny coupled with Josh's ongoing encouragement led Kyle to continue thinking seriously about converting to Catholicism. When he'd made his decision, Kyle phoned Brother Anthony to discuss the details.

"I'm ready to be baptized," he told Anthony. "I wanted you to be one of the first to know."

"I'm proud of you," Anthony told him. "You've been in my prayers since your first visit here. Not necessarily that you would become a Catholic. Just that you would find your way."

"You helped lead the way," Kyle said feeling reassured. Anthony said he would speak with Father Mike to set the plans in motion, and the date for Kyle to be baptized was set, as is traditional, for the Easter Vigil service on Holy Saturday.

When the time arrived, it was a magical evening for Kyle. After months of preparation, like his fellow catechumen, he was focused on this moment more than anything he could remember in his life. Josh and Emmy flew out for the event. Outside the church, a bonfire lit the darkness and warmed the coolness of the night. The Pascal Candle, named after the PASCH, the passion, death and resurrection of Christ, was blessed and lit, symbolizing Christ as the light of the world. Father Mike picked up the candle and led the congregation into the dimly lit church as he led the chant, "Christ our Light," and all responded in chant, "Thanks be to God." The altar boys and girls lit their candles from the Easter candle Father Mike held; then each person lit his or her candle from the altar boys' and girls'. Soon, the dark church was lit by candlelight. As the Gospel reading announced the resurrection of Christ, the lights came on, the bells rang, and songs of alleluia filled the church. The altar was overflowing with flowers of every color.

Jenny felt a radiance emanating from Kyle as he passed her going toward the baptismal font. She was filled with an indescribable joy watching Mike anoint Kyle with Holy water: The two dearest men in her life—Kyle and Mike—inexorably bound to one another through the celebration of this sacrament.

Jenny and Kyle spent Easter Sunday with Jenny's family. Kyle called his mother but avoided mentioning his conversion. Being a devout Mormon, she wouldn't have been thrilled. First one son a Catholic, and now the other. Instead Kyle talked about everything except the most important event in his life.

Mike was happy for Kyle and praised him for his determination and follow-through.

"Kyle is doing the best I've ever seen him," Mike told Jenny as he helped her with Easter dinner preparations.

"I'm sensing another noticeable, heartening change in our relationship since his final decision to become a Catholic," Jenny said, "and it's a very comforting change."

What I'm seeing," Mike offered as he helped her take the leg of lamb out of the oven, "is that his rebirth through baptism seems almost symbolic of the surge in your relationship. He was born again into a new life, learning to love with the love of Christ, experiencing belief in himself, perhaps more than ever before."

"The whole process was a reawakening for me too," Jenny said. "I found a kind of freshness in my life-long faith that was enhanced by his wide-eyed enthrallment in everything he was learning about the Catholic Church."

There was no question that Kyle was eager to move their bond to the next level. Often, as they sat out on his deck, he would slip into his own thoughts. When Jenny drew him out, she learned that he was troubled by the lack of definition or direction in their relationship. They had long discussions about the nature of marriage. Jenny explained that she felt permanently bound to Kyle, but Kyle argued for a permanent, legal bond. So it was more than a small surprise when

Kyle sent Jenny a note that, for the first time, mirrored her hope for the kind of life she longed to have with him.

> My dear Jenny,
>   You know that I want you to marry me, but I also know that I don't have to have that as proof that you love me.
>   So, no marriage: Just a simple allegiance defined concretely in the large and small acts of love we show to each other every day will be enough for me. Let us only promise our lives to each other, to honor each other's freedom, so that, in the process, we lose ourselves in kindness and care for each other.
>   At one time in my life, I would have thought it too simple a commitment, one that sounds like nothing at all. But it is, in truth, the most beautiful, profound, and joyous blessing one person can bestow on another.
>   Please accept this simple commitment as my gift to you. I love you with all my heart, and I know that you love me the same. K

Yes! Yes! Jenny thought as she read the note. *This is exactly what I want!* She immediately phoned Kyle to express her delight.

Over the next several weeks, Kyle invited a handful of their Catholic friends to his house, including Mike, for spiritual discussions. Now that Kyle was officially Catholic, he wanted to initiate provocative discussion about what their faith meant to each of them. Ensuing discussions covered a myriad of topics: Hafiz's poem, *The Subject Tonight is Love,* and the writings of such authors as Thomas Moore, Gary Zukav, and Scott Peck. It was a lively group.

One evening after the group had dispersed, Kyle and Jenny sat on his deck, snuggling under the stars and discussing the many definitions of love.

"I think I've figured out what love really is," Kyle told her. "It's choosing to totally extend oneself to another, like we're doing. Risking personal security in order to nurture another human being."

"It's transcending," Jenny said, "and I think we're moving in the right direction." She paused and looked lovingly at him. "Kyle, I've never wanted anything to succeed so much in my whole life as I want our relationship to succeed. I love you more than I know how to say."

"I love you, too, sweet pea. As long as I can keep my need to control or possess you at bay, our love *can* be transcending."

Unfortunately, less than a week later, Kyle was struggling with their arrangement. His mood swings placed an overbearing cloud over their life. He decided that he needed something more solid—primarily, for Jenny to be with him every night when he came home from work. Her outside activities and other friendships continued to frustrate him and, from his perspective, only served to take her away from him. During a phone call, it came to a head.

"I just don't think you understand me," he told her. "My day is filled with so much responsibility and stress and decision-making. I just want to know that when I come home, we can spend time together. I'm having a hard time trusting you on the nights you're not with me. When you're out doing your thing, and I don't know what it is exactly—Monday night football at the O'Connors or dinner with Mike—I picture a lot of flirtation going on, and it tears me up inside."

"Have you discussed this with Dr. Monroe?"

"A bit. And I don't think all that socializing is really who you are."

"Certainly I see myself as more of an introvert than an extrovert," Jenny said. "But I do love time with my friends. And I don't think it's healthy for me to give them up so that I can spend all my time with you. You're welcome to join me, but lately you don't seem to want to."

"That's because being with *only* you is what makes me the happiest. I don't need a lot of other people in my life."

"But our relationship isn't going to work if you won't accept me for who I am, Kyle. You can't just make me a puppet on a string with you as the puppeteer."

"Why not?" Kyle smiled. "That sounds pretty good to me."

"I hope you're joking."

But he wasn't. He was consumed with thoughts of how Jenny spent her time away from him.

Jenny loved her time with Kyle. But was there something wrong with her, she wondered, that she also wanted time with her friends? *Maybe I'm afraid to put all my eggs into one basket,* she thought. Husbands had come and gone in her life. But friends had always been there through her crises. How could Kyle ask her to give up her friendships?

"Look, why don't you come over and spend the night with me tonight?" Kyle said.

"Sweetie, I'd really love to, but I have to be up, dressed, and out of the house early in the morning to meet with the convention planners for my talk Saturday."

Silence followed. Then Kyle exploded. "Damn it, Jenny. There's always something or someone standing between us. I have a job to do, too, you know, but you don't see me putting that between us."

"Kyle, just because I have things I have to do doesn't mean I don't love you," she said.

"Yeah, well, your actions speak louder than your words, don't they?" The phone went dead.

Jenny called Kyle back. She wasted no time on pleasantries when he answered.

"Damn it, Kyle, we have a good thing going between us," she said after he answered. "Don't screw it up. You are making me crazy. Literally! I can't handle your judging me and criticizing me all the time. I'm not one of your staff members. I am not your child. And I refuse to be your mother or your guardian. I want to be your partner and I want us to love and respect each other for who we are. So just stop it. Do you hear me? I have a life outside of you and you can't force me to give that up. I'm really angry and I'm not going to take this anymore."

Jenny's outburst left him speechless for a moment. When he regained his thoughts, he was even angrier. "You don't want a boyfriend, Jenny. You want an occasional companion—on *your* terms. You want me around now and then. That's not enough for me. I want more in our relationship and I'm sick and tired of begging for your time and attention."

"You don't have to beg. That's not what partners do with each other. Grow up, Kyle, and call me when you get through puberty." Jenny slammed the receiver down.

Furious, Kyle called her back but only got her answering machine. He stomped around his living room and yelled obscenities at the walls. No matter how much he paced, he couldn't stop shaking. "Are you happy, Harvey? I'm out here by myself, just like you said I should be," he yelled aloud. "But I don't like it!"

The next morning, Kyle called Dr. Monroe and poured out his frustration.

"Why do I do that? Why do I try to make Jenny do what I want? Why do I get so frightened when getting together doesn't seem as important to her as it is to me?"

"'Frightened' is a well-chosen word," Harvey said compassionately. "When was the last time you just let things happen in any part of your life without trying to exert control? I mean, can you name a time when you felt you didn't have control over a situation?"

"Sure. Jenny has surprise me and showed up a couple of times at my office."

"Well, how did it make you feel?"

"Loved. Appreciated. Happy."

"Good. Until our next appointment, I want you to search your memory for other examples, situations when you weren't in control or felt like you didn't have to exert control. Go back as far as you can remember. Write down these moments and how they made you feel."

"That could take hours, days, weeks . . .," Kyle protested.

"For your sake, I hope it does, but I think it will take far less time than you think," Harvey said. "You have a lot of letting go to do."

"The thought of letting go scares me," Kyle admitted. "If I ran my professional life that way . . ."

"Well, we're talking about your personal life, not your job. What makes you so good at your job appears to make you an abysmal partner in your personal life. You excel at getting others to do what you believe is right for the State of California, and I suspect they usually come away thinking it's their idea, but that same tactic doesn't work in a relationship. Not a genuine one. And Jenny is too smart for you to pull the wool over her eyes. I suspect when you go back in time, you'll see that it won't be easy to recall times when you allowed things to unfold on their own. But if you really love her, and yourself, you can overcome a lifetime of this habit and learn an entirely new style of loving another person and allowing that person to love you back. You won't have to do somersaults or cartwheels to get her attention. She will just love you because you are loveable. By the way, you haven't been skipping your meds, have you?"

"Maybe a few times," Kyle confessed, "when things get hectic."

"Well, that explains some of your recent behavior," Harvey said. "Kyle, you must take your medication regularly, no excuses. The drugs are just as important as your therapy with me.

Kyle promised to take his medication religiously, and he hung up feeling both frightened and hopeful.

Good intentions weren't enough to turn the situation around over night. Kyle called and apologized to Jenny, but the same argument cropped up over and over becoming more heated each time. Finally, by mid-May, Jenny wrote Kyle a letter declaring that they needed to take some time apart. She assured him that it was temporary and suggested they go their separate ways for awhile; then they could meet to review and discuss their relationship. In closing, she reflected on her hope that they would work things out.

> Kyle, I hope you will use this time to reflect on what I've said, to grow spiritually, and to do some soul-searching. I will do the same. I love so many things about you and how we spend our time together. But I must stand up for myself and take some action that you will pay attention to in order to get you to stop your obsession with control and to treat me with more consistent kindness. I will call you on the fifteenth of June.

Two days later, Kyle sent a response that he agreed they both needed a break from the tumult of their relationship.

> Jenny, I sincerely apologize for my harsh words and for any hurt I have caused you. Believe me, it was not my intention.
>
> Although our Christian calling is to "bear with one another," there is only so much a person can handle. The outburst of your upsetting letter confirmed your exhaustion with my behavior. And my apprehension about our relationship came out in my irate responses to you of late. I guess the bubble burst for both of us and we need some time to heal.
>
> In the solitude of reflection, I hope we each will come to appreciate more the richness of our time together.
>
> You saved my life and helped me reach a new and better place—something for which I will always be grateful. And I can claim to have shown you some delightful, silly days and one solid poem.
>
> My love and prayers for you always, Kyle

From Jenny's perspective, there were no rules or restrictions about this time out. They could each use it however they wanted. She knew that it was entirely possible that Kyle would begin dating and perhaps find someone who was more in sync with what he wanted. While part of her feared that might happen, the other part reasoned that, if there was something real between them, they would both feel the sadness and emptiness left by the other. That was part of their discovery.

Jenny had no interest in dating. She wanted to be with Kyle. But she wanted a healthy relationship with him. In her journal, she admitted to herself that she wanted him on her terms, and she knew that he wanted her on his. Therein lay the problem. Could they let go of their own wants enough to desire what was best for them as a couple? And in that process, could they find a middle ground that would work for both of them?

Jenny felt the pain of their separation but knew that she had been the one to initiate it. She distracted herself by rereading some of her favorite books. In the pages of Thomas Moore's *SoulMates* she found a section that reflected exactly how she felt about the challenge she and Kyle were facing.

> Ordinarily we assume that a relationship should be smooth and complete, and when trouble arrives, we think the relationship itself is open to doubt. But matters of soul lie beyond simple judgments of good and bad, or smooth and rough . . . Religion recognizes pain and failure as important in the soul's deepening and sophistication. We can apply this insight to relationships as well: pain and difficulty can sometimes serve as the pathway to a new level of involvement. They do not necessarily mean that there is something inherently wrong with the relationship; on the contrary, relationship troubles may be a challenging initiation into greater intimacy.

Jenny prayed that Thomas Moore was right. Struggles had always made or broken relationships for her. She wanted Kyle in her life and, through this separation process, she hoped to discover on what level their love was meant to be. She admitted to herself that this time apart was not just about him. It was also about her. She had been both widowed and divorced, going through immense pain twice

before, and she wasn't sure she was ready to risk that again. She loved
her life now. But she enjoyed her freedom. She had good friends in
her life. If she continued a relationship with Kyle, somehow, on some
level, her life would be altered. Was she willing to allow change . . . to
risk the pain . . . to trust him? Could she trust him to love her enough
to stay with her? Could Kyle, with his bipolar ups and downs, be
stable in her life? No man ever had—neither her father nor her
husbands. Why would Kyle be any different? For Jenny, nothing in
the world hurt more than being abandoned.

While Jenny was clear-headed enough to analyze the problem, Kyle
was feeling deep anguish. He loved Jenny. He cherished her and
treasured every moment with her. All he wanted was a simple life with
her where they spent their time together. He wanted her so much that
he inadvertently found himself trying to overpower her . . . to take
charge of her the way he was skilled at taking charge in his work. What
was that old adage about not trying to capture the butterfly? Better to
let it go and, if it chooses, it may come back to land on your shoulder.
But what if it didn't? What if it flew away and never came back? The
fear of that happening took him deeper into depression. He couldn't
bear the thought of living without her. No matter how hard he tried,
he couldn't stop wanting to capture the butterfly.

The following week, Kyle sent Jenny a letter, opening his message
with a Wordsworth poem.

> I wandered lonely as a cloud
> That floats on high o'er vales and hills,
> When all at once I saw a crowd,
> A host of golden daffodils;
> Beside the lake, beneath the trees,
> Fluttering and dancing in the breeze.
>
> For oft, when on my couch I lie
> In vacant or in pensive mood,
> They flash upon that inward eye
> Which is the bliss of solitude;
> And then my heart with pleasure fills,
> And dances with the daffodils.

I believe that a loving relationship is a living thing, a marriage of true minds and hearts, which grows and deepens through the sunlight and shadows, the joys and sorrows of life. Love does not keep score of wrongs but rejoices when right prevails. Love is patient and kind. Love sees all things and believes all things. Love, the greatest love, never gives up on the other. So I'm not giving up on our relationship.

I want to earn your trust with my love. And my gift to you, for as long as you want it, is to respect our time-out, but know that I love you with all my heart, in absentia, and I will dream of dancing with you in the daffodils. K

The letter warmed Jenny's heart, and she discussed it with Mike. "It's funny, but I can see that I have a well-grooved pattern in my close relationships with men," she told him. "I fall in love with a man who is extremely powerful and dynamic on the outside but who is needy and dependent on the inside. I become the helper, the person working to hold the relationship together and to help him pull himself together. This was the case with Don and Matt, and now Kyle. How do I always end up choosing the same kinds of partners?"

"You are a helper type," Mike said. "That's not a bad thing, but it does put you in a vulnerable place where you are likely to keep getting hurt. However, Kyle has some things of his own to work on."

"You mean like jealousy. I know he's jealous of my time with you," Jenny said. "But what man wouldn't be threatened by another man who genuinely loves me, even if he is a priest? Kyle was married for twenty years. His life experience has been a close relationship between one man and one woman—a relationship that made up the core of his life. During that same time, I've been single more than I've been married and have built a circle of friends to make up the whole of my life. If I'm honest with myself, I trust the endurance of my friendships more than I trust the longevity of a life with one man. So, I guess what it comes down to is . . . I'm afraid."

"Well, it's good for you to be moving slowly. Give it time."

"I do need more time. Actually, *Kyle* needs more time. And I want to use this period to reflect on my shortcomings and learn how to be myself in a relationship and to say upfront what I really mean. This time is invaluable if I use it well." Jenny's voice softened. "But I do miss him. In spite of the problems, I can't imagine what it would be like *not* to have him in my life."

Mike assured Jenny that she was doing the right thing.

Kyle buried himself in his work. Except for a couple of brief conversations with Mike and Josh, he kept to himself. After spending long hours at the office, he went home and read. Occasionally, he practiced the violin. He fell asleep and woke up each morning to start his routine over again. He prayed that Jenny would come to the realization that they belonged together. There were few times in Kyle's life that he had concluded that doing nothing was the right action plan, and he knew this was one of those times. He also recognized that this was the kind of behavioral change Harvey was asking him to practice. And it was one of the most difficult things he'd ever done.

It wasn't easy for Mike, but he served as a kind of go-between for Kyle and Jenny. He assured Kyle that this was temporary and encouraged Jenny that she had made the right call. Mike knew that Jenny felt comfortable talking with him about the relationship because she knew there was no one who had her best interests more at heart than he. Jenny felt reassured in knowing that Mike loved her enough to want the problems between Kyle and her to smooth themselves out.

It wasn't that Mike was above feelings of jealousy. He was human and, deep down, he sometimes wished he'd never introduced Jenny to Kyle. At times, he even wished that Kyle would go away and take with him the giant waves of emotional turbulence he created in Jenny's life. But he knew that wouldn't be best for Jenny. She needed something that Mike could not give her—a sexually intimate relationship. She deserved to have someone special in her life. Mike knew that Kyle Anderson and Jenny Roberts were two gifted individuals. They had the potential to make each other happy. What Mike couldn't know was whether one or both of them were willing to expend the effort that being together would take. He hoped they would not get back together until they were both ready to assume the many responsibilities that love entails.

During his years out of the priesthood, Mike had faced his own soul-searching, not unlike what Jenny and Kyle were going through.

He had met a woman who became important to him. Mike loved her, but he could not fully let go of his priesthood. He missed preaching the Gospel and serving a multitude of people. She and Mike had explored every alternative, including her staying in his life even as he returned to his ministry. He desperately wanted her, but he questioned what kind of life it would be for her to live as the secret lover of a priest. She pleaded with him to let her be a part of his life after he returned to the priesthood, and to have a woman he loved and to serve God as a priest—that would have been the best of all worlds for him. But he could not pretend that it was the best life for her. Placing her well-being above his own desires, he walked away, leaving her behind when he accepted his new appointment in Sacramento, California.

With the wisdom of experience and hindsight, Mike counseled Kyle to listen with ears open to what Jenny needed, to love her enough to put her needs first.

And to Jenny he suggested that perhaps she and Kyle hadn't been together long enough to grasp the life struggles through which Kyle had come. "Dig deep, love," he told her. "Find out who he really is and stay open to discovering if the two of you are best suited to accompany each other on your life journeys."

"Whenever we talk about this, I notice you always bring it back to *understanding*," Jenny replied.

"Understanding can unlock many seemingly locked doors, love. But it demands letting go of the need to control the outcome. It takes a great deal of courage to search for real truth."

"Sometimes I think I'm listening only for the parts that I want to hear," she admitted.

"We all do that from time to time. But the deeper the desire to really understand, the more unafraid we must be. It's like moving through the dark to pursue the unknown." Shifting his voice, Mike said more softly, "I think Kyle is going through some transitions of his own. I received a letter from him today. Would you like to read it?"

Eager to know about what Kyle was going through, she read the letter, absorbing every word.

May 20, 2000

Dear Mike,

I am so sorry our love for Jenny sometimes pushes us apart instead of drawing us together. It should not be so. You were right when you told me that she is the most insightful person you know. And I hope her love and friendship will be big enough and strong enough to allow me back into her life. After all, that is the fundamental nature of love. At this tumultuous time of my life, you have been like an angel to me. You have kept me from drifting into despair. You have helped me to grow in arid soil. You have treated me as if I am the person I would like to be. I am so grateful!

Thank you again for helping bring me into the Catholic Church. Because of you, I now experience the relentless, unconditional love of Christ as expressed in the Gospels and elaborated throughout the ages.

Let us be willing to risk pain. Let us go forward with our friendship. Be my teacher, and I will be your student. Sister Marsha knew that we were right for each other. After all, not even Jenny will listen to opera with me! As Brother Anthony said to me, "I love you whether you like it or not."

Kyle

Kyle's feelings toward Mike had been like a seesaw—low on Mike one day and high on him the next. Jenny was thrilled to see him express such gratitude. She looked up from the letter smiling at Mike.

"You are so dear to me, Jenny," Mike told her, "But I did consider stepping out of your life so I wouldn't cause any problems for you with Kyle. Maybe now it's going to be okay."

"I would be devastated if you did, Mike. It is wrong for me to have to let go of my friends in order to have a relationship with Kyle. But I also know you'd have been reluctant to introduce us if you'd anticipated Kyle wanting to shove you aside."

"I want what's best for you and Kyle. I really do." Mike reflected back to his past situation. He had faced a crossroads of his own and made a difficult choice. From the deepest recesses of his heart, he prayed that Jenny and Kyle would make selfless choices, which he knew was the real meaning of loving another person.

During their month apart, Kyle was always on the edge of Jenny's thoughts, jumping into her mind when she least expected. Fortunately, for her, she could keep up on Kyle's career by reading the newspaper. She'd recently read that he was working with the California Gambling Control Commission, and she absorbed every word about him with the fascination of a proud consort, or maybe more like an adoring groupie.

One morning as Jenny scanned the paper looking for his name, a headline jumped out at her: "Attorney General Agrees to Meeting With Military Picketers." The article announced that protestors were meeting in Sacramento to prepare for their annual demonstration outside of the military base located in Fort Bennington in the Southern California desert. Kyle planned to meet with a group of priests and nuns and other pacifists prior to their planned march on the Republican National Convention to be held in Los Angeles at the end of August. The group, SOA Watch, claimed that Fort Bennington was a training ground for terrorists. The U.S. Army base, known as the School of Americas, was called the School of Assassins by the watch group. In their view, it had simply been transferred to California from its former location in Latin America and was still heavily involved in training soldiers in terrorist activity and inhumane methods of warfare.

The article reported that SOA Watch had the names and photos of a number of graduates of the school, and the watch members feared that soon there would be a serious attack on the United States by some of the people trained at the School of Americas facility. They claimed no government agency would listen or respond to them. But they were grateful that California's attorney general had agreed to meet with them and hear them out.

Jenny called Mike to ask if he was familiar with SOA Watch. He said he had personally met Father Roy Bourgois, its founder, while he was working back east. He felt certain that what Father Roy proclaimed was true. With a lilt in his voice, Mike suggested that the two of them might consider joining the march outside the Republican convention.

"That'd let your attorney general friend know that you value social justice issues over your 'rich Republican friends,' now wouldn't it?"

Jenny agreed in principle and, after she hung up, she checked the Internet for more information, learning that SOA Watch was a nonviolent grassroots movement founded in 1990 and dedicated to using protest and resistance as well as lobbying and media work to change oppressive U.S. foreign policy. School of Americas graduates are responsible for some of the worst human rights abuses in Latin America. In 1996, the Pentagon was forced to release training manuals used at the school that advocated torture, extortion, and execution. The School of America's nearly 60,000 graduates included notorious dictators like Manuel Noriega. Jenny recalled the 1980 assassination in El Salvador of Archbishop Oscar Romero, seven Jesuit priests, and three American nuns, and read that three-quarters of the Salvadoran officers implicated in the murders were trained at SOA. The more she read, the more furious she became.

Jenny then clicked on a legislative link on the SOA Watch website. There she read that the protest group was calling for a congressional vote. The group had been unsuccessful in getting Congress to consider an amendment that would cut funding for the military base. However, one Democrat representative promised that there would be a vote on this issue the following year.

Jenny longed to discuss this with Kyle. He had so much knowledge, and she respected his insights. She wondered how much of Kyle's newly evolved Catholicism was influencing his thinking. So far, he had managed to solve problems and stay low-key on controversial issues. But this one could be explosive. By meeting with the group, he was thrusting himself into the middle of a contentious issue. Jenny admired his courage but also worried that it would lead to his political downfall. Jenny had an eerie sense about this issue.

Reading about Kyle and keeping him in her daily prayers helped Jenny feel close to him, but she yearned to see him again. It had taken real discipline for her to hold the line. She was tempted to pick up the phone and call him. *No, let it go*, she thought. *It's still too soon.* She had to respect the space between them until there was no upheaval left inside of her and, in its place, serenity had taken over. By June 15th, she felt cleansed and ready for communication.

Just before leaving to go to Texas for her high school reunion, Jenny cautiously reopened communication with Kyle. She wanted her reunion with Kyle to be right, too, and he was receptive to her call, suggesting they meet for a hike on the rim trail along Lake Tahoe. Summer was in full swing, and the day was perfect. After an hour, they found a beautiful spot off the beaten track. Leaning against a tree, Kyle sat down behind Jenny and put his arms around her as they both gazed at the green reflection of Emerald Bay.

"I've missed you," Jenny said, nestling her head into the familiar place on Kyle's chest.

"I've missed you, too, more than I can tell you. It's been hell to live without you."

"Do you think we belong together, or are we just kidding ourselves? Maybe we're too different. We love each other but . . ."

She could feel his arms tighten around her. "Let's not try to figure it all out today. Let's just take one day at a time." For a long while they sat close together, silently looking out at the lake.

Jenny eventually broke the silence. "I was fascinated reading about your meeting with SOA Watch. How did it go—I mean, apart from what I read in the news reports. How did it really go?"

"I talked separately with both sides. You know, mediation is one of my favorite parts of the job."

"That's because you're good at it." Jenny smiled up at him.

"The governor and most Republicans in Washington are supportive of keeping School of Americas open for business at the military base. They look upon SOA Watch as a bunch of pacifists who don't understand our need to keep our American businesses on a solid footing in foreign countries," Kyle said. "The school, they say, is helping third-world countries preserve democracy."

"And what does the watch group say?" Jenny asked.

"I was really taken with Father Roy Bourgois," Kyle said. "He's really dedicated to his cause."

"And Mike told me that he's a good guy," Jenny said.

Nodding agreement, Kyle continued. "He said the democracy position *sounds* good but asked me, 'How do you teach democracy through the barrel of a gun?' Father Roy showed me a handbook that was part of the training program and pointed out why he and his group call it the School of Assassins. He had marked up the manual, indicating the places where the school was less about defense—the traditional purpose of a military base—and more about teaching how to attack, torture, and kill. The tone of the manual seems indifferent to the 'collateral dammage' of innocent people's lives being taken.

"That sounds sub-human. Both my father and my stepfather fought in World War II. When they spoke about it, they made me feel that war is supposed to be about defending our country, not about instilling soldiers with a mentality that denigrates human life."

"That basically sums up Father Roy's position," Kyle said. "He was adamant that the school has to be shut down. His commitment is so strong that he's already served prison time because of his beliefs."

"You're stepping into some dangerous ground politically. Are you prepared for that?" Jenny asked.

"I don't know but, since my conversion, I feel more of a responsibility to use my office for humanitarian issues. If I get into trouble, then so be it. At least I will go down for a worthy cause."

"It sounds like a lot of good came from our time-out." Jenny squeezed his hand and gently stroked his fingers.

"Yeah, I got a hell of a lot of work done." He smiled. "And just so you know, I didn't even feel the desire to go out and find another woman. I lived with solitude and did a lot of thinking about my behavior. For reasons I'm not sure I understand, my relationship with you is more volatile than with anyone I've ever been with."

"For me, too." Jenny turned and looked at him. "It's usually you who begins the 'warfare,' but then I've been right there, ready to jump in and accelerate the problem. You can make me crazy, Kyle. I have never been as angry with anyone as I was with you. And I've never lost my temper so badly."

"It must say something about the depth of our feelings," he said as he nibbled her ear and pulled her closer.

"And our vulnerabilities," Jenny added as she gave him an affirming, sexy smile and nodded in agreement. They sat quietly holding hands and watching the sun set on the lake. A young couple sailed by on a small catamaran, laughing and making loud noises.

"I want to have fun like that again with you. I've missed you so much." Kyle leaned over and Jenny turned toward him so that their lips met. They held the kiss while hungrily groping each other. He pulled her on top of him, and they molded their bodies to each other. They managed to stop short of making love right there on the trail.

"I want you so much. Let's go home," Kyle said.

"Do you think you can let up on me some and just love me and be steady?" Jenny asked, looking into his eyes.

"Well, I do have this overwhelming desire to possess you. I just hope 'being steady' doesn't mean putting up with all of your idiosyncrasies," Kyle half-teased.

"I did get a little better at being alone during our time apart. But you know what I need from you?"

"Besides love, what?" Jenny asked.

"Patience with me. I have a lot of growing to do. I was married for so long. I'm not used to being by myself, and I'm not very good at it."

"You know the answer isn't for me to fill all the emptiness inside of you, Kyle. It would be good for you to learn to appreciate solitude."

"I know," Kyle said. "I've talked about this with Harvey. He's working with me on some things that go back to my father's death and my urge to know more about my natural father. He thinks that my intimacy skills might have been hindered at an early age and that I identified too much with my twin."

"What an interesting insight! I do promise to be understanding. I love you, and I want our relationship to work. I have changes to make, too, and I've already started. But I'd rather show them to you than talk about them or make bogus promises."

"We know what my shortcomings are," Kyle said, raising his eyebrows as he spoke. "They can jump out and bite you. But I want to know about your reflections. What are you trying to change?"

"A couple of things. I realize in part that having a broad base of friends is a protection against my fear of being abandoned by a man. That way, if the man leaves me, I'll still have a circle of I can rely on."

"If you're really thinking about those things, it gives me hope, sweet pea. I want so much more with you, but I think I want too much closeness and you want too little—at least from me."

"Another interesting insight!" Jenny exclaimed. "Somewhere between our two extremes, hopefully, we can find a balance."

"So what else?"

"I realize how afraid I am of saying anything that might displease you . . . or anyone, for that matter. But I especially don't like displeasing *you*. I don't want controversy. I hate fighting. So I avoid saying the difficult things that might cause you to be angry with me. And that's not healthy. I want to be more committed to telling you the truth . . ." Jenny paused, searching for the right words ". . . about myself or my feelings or about you . . . without fear of repercussions."

"I want that too," Kyle said. "But I've given you reason to be afraid of my temper. I can understand why you don't want to set me off. "

Jenny was grateful for his acknowledgement of his part in this.

"So, Jenny, where are we going for dinner tonight?"

"Oh, I wish I could but I have to pack. I'm leaving for Texas tomorrow. I'm going for my high school reunion and to spend some time helping settle my dad's estate."

"What?"

"You know my dad died several years ago, and his wife passed away just before we met. Well, I had a call from the executor of the estate and he needs me to figure outwhat to do with their house. I hadn't planned on attending the reunion, but I might as well since I'll be there anyway."

"Well, I'll miss you," Kyle said, a little disappointment in his voice. "You be careful and, when you get back, we'll officially celebrate the end of our separation."

"Good idea," she said, turning to kiss him. "I'll miss you too."

"Just remember," Kyle whispered as he hugged her tighter, "'How many loved your moments of glad grace, and loved your beauty with love false or true. But one man loved the pilgrim soul in you and loved the sorrows of your changing face.' I'll be waiting for you."

Thirteen

Jenny's World Shaken

JULY - OCTOBER 2000

There is something refreshing about going back in time and gaining perspective with friends we've known all our lives, Jenny thought, as she drove onto the familiar grounds and around the circular drive of her old high school building in Dallas. How often she had walked in the woods there. As she eyed the brick gymnasium, she remembered the hours she had devoted to practicing volleyball and basketball. She couldn't wait to find Kerry McCormick. She and Jenny were best friends in high school and had stayed in frequent touch by phone. In their conversations over the last few months, Kerry had told Jenny about her marital struggles, and Jenny had shared her feelings about Kyle—what she loved about him, what challenged her and, of course, their recent timeout and getting back together.

Kerry had earned her masters' degree in psychology. Jenny was eager to listen to Kerry because she could speak not only from professional experience but from personal as well. Once they located each other, the old friends found a bench shaded by trees and sat down. It took no time at all for them to get immediately into the heart of things that mattered.

"So you're still married," Jenny prompted.

"Hanging on by a thread. I'm not sure we're going to make it," Kerry admitted. As she spoke, she lowered her head, and her shoulder-length blond hair fell into her face.

Jenny saw how much her friend was hurting. "Why are relationships so hard today?" Jenny asked. "When you hear about the olden days, people just seemed to make it. Period. No serious fights. No mid-life crises. They just stayed together."

"They had fewer choices."

"And we have too many," Jenny said.

"And you, girlfriend, have fabulous choices. I always hold you up as the woman I want to be in my next life."

"Kerry, if you only knew . . ."

"I do know. Remember who you're talking to. Even with all the anguish and endings you've gone through, I still want to be *you* in my next life. You have more choices than me. I have financial considerations that limit mine. Besides everything else, we've spent all our money. You don't have that to contend with, and it gives you more freedom to make healthy choices."

Kerry and Jenny described their situations to each other, just like old times. How often they had talked about the boys in their lives throughout their school years. But that was then, and this was now. Kerry wasn't sure what she was going to do. "I need more time to decide what really matters—security or freedom."

"From what you say, you don't seem to have much of either now."

"Touché! But I've been in my relationship for twenty years. You're just beginning yours. Ultimately your choice comes down to one thing: how much you're willing to give up in order to be in a relationship with someone who has issues."

"Don't we all have issues?" Jenny asked. "I know I've got my share of them."

"But in some relationships, you're able to maintain a lot of personal freedom and still honor the relationship and keep it primary," Kerry said. "But that isn't likely when you're involved with a narcissistic personality type. Believe me, I know. And this isn't likely to change."

"Do you think that's what's going on with Kyle . . . in addition to his mood swings?"

"Trust me when I say that I recognize the symptoms. The bipolar part of him can be more or less regulated with medication. But someone with narcissistic tendencies, that's another story."

"I thought narcissism was just a fancy way of describing someone who's self-centered," Jenny said.

"Oh, no. It's much more complicated than that. People with narcissistic personality disorder take in things differently than the rest of us. When you and I experience hurt, it might make us feel bad for a while, but it doesn't wreck our whole world. It's like we have a built-in protection around our hearts that keeps the pain from overwhelming us. But people with this tendency—they don't have that. A hurtful situation comes along, and they can only experience it internally. Whereas you and I can shake it off or feel the pain from a broader perspective, they are more likely to be oblivious to how it affects you and can only react to the way it affects them."

"It's almost as if others are 'doing' this to them," Jenny added as she began to get a sense of the problem.

"Yes, in Kyle's case, I suspect that it'd not be easy for him to empathize with a painful situation that happens to you. Generally, someone with this symptom can function just fine in his professional life but, in his personal life, it's hard for him to put himself in the other person's place. If you two have a problem, it will be rare for him to have any awareness that you're feeling pain too. And you can't just write it off as self-centeredness. It really is a personality disorder. He isn't always in control of how he reacts to situations. For those of us who haven't experienced it, we can't begin to know what it's like."

"Oh, boy! What am I in for?" Jenny asked. "I'm in love with him, Kerry, and I'm getting more and more involved. Is there any hope? Can a person have a relationship with someone like this?"

"Oh, yes, but it's a *lot* of work."

Jenny had a strong sense that Kerry was speaking from professional *and* personal experience. But she wasn't directly saying so.

"In Kyle's case, he may be experiencing narcissistic tendencies without having the full-blown disorder," Kerry said. "With dramatic changes in his behavior coupled with intense effort, he could work through it. But he'd have to find a way to get out of himself and become more focused on others. For your sake, it'd be easier for you to move on. But if you love him . . ."

"I do. I really do. But I wish love didn't have to be so complex."

"Believe me, Jenny, I understand the tug-of-war inside of you. And, if you really love him, you'll probably make it work. You'll just say to yourself, 'Damn the torpedoes. Full speed ahead!'" The two friends hugged tightly, knowing they were both facing serious crossroads in their lives.

While in Texas, Jenny had agreed to meet the co-beneficiaries of her stepmother's estate. Jenny had never lived with her father and stepmother nor even gone to their home when she was a child. But, as an adult, she visited them from time to time, beginning when Chad was seven, just old enough to enjoy summers at their home in the hill country on Lake LBJ.

During the endless drive from Dallas over the flatlands of Texas, Jenny thought back to early 1993, the last time she had seen her father. It was when she was with Matt on a speaking tour in Austin. She recalled how tumultuous the world was that year: a series of bombing raids were going on over southern Iraq, and a car bomb was planted by terrorists in the underground parking garage below Tower One of the World Trade Center, killing a few people and injuring over a thousand workers and firefighters. But the mayhem in the world, Jenny remembered, was in radical contrast to her personal life that year. After she and Matt had finished their workshop in Austin, he drove with her to meet her father, who was hospitalized about an hour away in Burnet, Texas. He was dying of cancer. In the military when Jenny was born, her mother had divorced her father when Jenny was a baby. Her dad and his second wife, Dixie, had been married ever since.

"Jenny, I'm so glad to see you," her dad had whispered from his hospital bed. He could barely speak.

Jenny leaned over and gave him a hug. Then, stepping back, she put her arm around Matt's waist. "Dad, I want you to meet my husband. This is Matt."

As a former hospice volunteer, Matt had spent a great deal of time at sick beds. He was at ease with the circumstances. Matt reached out to her dad and spoke quietly as he leaned over him. "I'm going to take good care of your daughter, Mr. Shaw. There is nothing I wouldn't do for her."

"Call me Bill. I can't tell you how much it means to me to know that she is with someone who loves her and will care for her, someone who won't leave her. I may not have been able to be a part of her childhood, but I've worried about her nonetheless, especially these last few years."

"There is no reason to worry now," Matt reassured him. "She's with me. And I won't ever leave her." As her father lay dying, Jenny felt love pervading the room—her father's commingled with her husband's. The feeling was warm and protective, like nothing she had felt before or since.

Jenny's entire childhood had been entrusted to women—her grandmother, her mother, the nuns, her guardians. Always to women. That day at the hospital bed was the first time in her life that she felt safeguarded and cherished by not one but *two* men. In the end, though, Matt didn't keep the promise. He said he would never leave her. But she would relish that moment as long as she lived.

Shortly after their visit, Jenny's father passed away. At his funeral, she was struck by how admired he was. Tears streamed down her face as others eulogized his life for all the good he'd done. But the truth was, she wasn't crying for her father. She was crying for herself. Jenny thought about how little contact she and her father had over most of her life. Her heart cried out, *Why them, Dad? Why not me?*

Now, years later, her dad's wife, Dixie, had passed away as well. Dixie's nephew, Johnny, let Jenny into the house. It felt strange for Jenny to be wandering around their empty home. Even though she had not been close to her father, his and Dixie's deaths still affected her. Perhaps they represented the end of an era. Or maybe it was more basic—without him, Jenny realized that she would not be in the world at all.

Johnny guided her to things she might want by which to remember her dad. She took one of his medals that he must have won as a paratrooper in World War II. She scanned through photo albums and carefully selected a picture of him in his military uniform—the way he looked when she was born. Jenny could see herself in him. She had her father's eyes and olive complexion and her mother's smile and petite body. She took his framed graduation certificate from Southern

Methodist University and the letters she had written him while she was studying theology. She was surprised to see how many photos of his only child he had accumulated over the years—an indication that Jenny must have mattered more than she knew. Jenny gathered pictures up and, at the last minute, Johnny handed her a small jewelry box with her dad's gold ring. As Jenny finished sifting through all the things Johnny had gathered together for her, she recalled how her mother had joked that she wanted to lay a claim against the estate for back child support. Jenny suggested there might be a statute of limitations. After all, it had been thirty-some years since her father's legal obligations had ended.

Jenny returned home from handling her father's estate to find her world turned upside down. Her mother, Ellen Emerson, had always been independent. Jenny knew something had to be seriously wrong when Ellen asked Jenny to drive her to the doctor. Ellen had started to feel ill while she and Earl were walking to the clubhouse in their condominium complex for a Fourth of July party. Ellen had been diagnosed with leukemia 11 years earlier. But she had beaten the odds, so much so that it was easy to forget she had ever had the disease. Jenny knew that, whatever this was, it had to be significant. Otherwise her mother would have driven herself. Even Jenny's step-dad was alarmed, so he accompanied them.

"Your lungs are really bad, Ellen. I'm afraid you may have a touch of pneumonia," Dr. DeWitt said. "I want to admit you to the hospital."

Ellen started to cry. Instinctively, she felt that her malady was more critical than the doctor was letting on.

"There's no need to cry," he told her. "I just want you there for observation."

Jenny checked her mom into Mercy General that afternoon. Then she went to her mother's house, gathered Ellen's nightgown and toiletries, and brought them back to her mother's room. Ellen was already settled in her bed. Jenny took instruction from her mother on what she needed to do for Earl, whose eyesight continued to worsen due to diabetes. She stayed until her mother fell asleep. Distressed over her mother's hospitalization, she turned to Kyle for reassurance.

The next day, gazing out of her bedroom window at her garden, Jenny was lost in her own world. Kyle approached her from behind and gently held her. As she turned in his arms, he sensed that she needed him in a way she had not before. He leaned over and kissed her warmly and longingly.

"I want so much to protect you from whatever you think might be happening," he said.

Jenny turned, her eyes meeting his. She saw no mania, no hysteria, just calmness. She had seen this gentle side of Kyle before, but the added compassion was new. He had lost one parent with whom he was very close. In this moment, he could empathize with her fear. She felt an overwhelming sense of his love as they embraced. Without words, she led him to the bed.

"I love you, Kyle, now and forever. I'm afraid of what is happening in my life, but I'm less afraid with you by my side."

With renewed energy, Jenny took on the added responsibilities. She made regular visits to the hospital, spending quality time with Ellen. It gave mother and daughter a chance to talk about things that they might not otherwise have discussed. Each day, Jenny took Earl out to lunch and then to visit his wife in the hospital.

Ellen wasn't getting any better. It wasn't obvious exactly what was wrong with her lungs, but the doctor's best guess was that it was emphysema. Ellen's years of smoking had caught up to her, even though she had quit the habit nearly 20 years earlier. When Ellen begged to be discharged, the doctor granted her wish on the condition that Jenny hire a home healthcare service to stop in regularly to take her vitals and help look after her.

Early one morning, Jenny's mother called. "Jenny, Earl has fallen and he's bleeding." Ellen's voice was almost inaudible.

"I'll be right there," Jenny said as she threw the covers back and leapt out of bed.

It normally took seven minutes to get to her mom's house, but she made it in five. She found Earl sitting on the edge of the tub in his bathrobe, holding the right side of his head with a bloodied washrag. She cleaned him up as well as she could and discovered that the cut was coming from the top of his earlobe. He must have hit a vein. It was a little gash, but blood was gushing everywhere.

"How did you do this?" Jenny asked, making conversation while she continued to hold his head to try to stop the bleeding.

"I fell out of bed," he said. "I must have hit my head on the corner of the bedside table as I went down."

After about 10 minutes, the bleeding still had not let up. Jenny called the healthcare service taking care of her mom and asked what she should do. The nurse on duty advised her to call 911.

"The paramedics are trained to take care of that sort of thing," he said. "But if he needs to be taken to the doctor, drive him yourself. It's free if they just make a house call, but if they have to take him somewhere, that's when it gets expensive."

Jenny made the call and, within minutes, the paramedics arrived. Four uniformed men and women walked through the door and up the stairs. Within no time, they had Earl's head wrapped in gauze. He looked like a soldier wounded in battle. They offered to drive Earl to ER but, on the advice of the service, Jenny drove him herself.

Three hours and four stitches later, they returned home. As Jenny pulled into the driveway, she saw that the nurse from home healthcare had arrived. She got Earl situated downstairs and went up to her mother's room. When she entered, she saw the nurse with panicked look on her face.

"Call 911 now. Your mother's vitals are dropping quickly."

"How bad?" Jenny asked anxiously.

"Seventy over thirty."

Jenny did and an ambulance arrived soon after. Jenny realized she had lived her whole life without calling 911 but now, in less than four hours, she had called it twice.

Downstairs, Earl was confused and frightened. Jenny promised him she'd be back in touch with him soon to let him know how Ellen was. Jenny climbed into the ambulance with her mom. Her cell phone rang just minutes later.

At the hospital, Ellen was quickly admitted and soon diagnosed with C-diff, Clostridium difficile, an infectious colon disorder. She was assigned to the same ward in which she'd previously stayed, and the nurses who'd so lovingly cared for her before assured her they'd take good care of her. Ellen smiled weakly.

"It's nice to see y'all," she murmured in her soft southern accent, "but, to be honest, I'd rather be home."

This time, Ellen was even more unhappy about being hospitalized than previously. C-diff caused horrible diarrhea, was very contagious, and it could linger indefinitely.

Jenny spent a good part of each day visiting with her mom. Kyle often stopped by after work and visited with Ellen as well. He and Ellen enjoyed long, wonderful talks. One evening as the daylight faded and twilight settled into the room, Kyle sat on the side of Ellen's bed and asked her about Jenny's childhood.

"What was Jenny like as a little girl?"

"Pretty much the way she is now," Ellen said. "Sweet. Happy. And she could never sit still. She was always involved with something at school, always on the phone lining something up."

"Yeah, always on the phone—that describes her pretty well. Every time she gets in her car and turns on the motor, she dials her phone. I think she believes that car won't run without the cell phone in use."

They both laughed.

"Jenny is so special," Ellen said. "She's the greatest happiness of my life. I've always been so proud of her. She always made me happy, except . . ."

"Except what?"

"Except when she went into that, that . . ." Ellen couldn't bring herself to cuss, but she wanted to "... that *blasted* convent school to study theology. They wanted to lure her into the convent and, according to the rules then, if she took that step, I would never be able to do ordinary things with her again. We couldn't go shopping. She couldn't come home for a few days. When I went to visit her, we couldn't even eat together. I just wanted to die. Every time I thought about her throwing her life away like that, it was as if she had died."

"Most parents would love for their daughter to pursue a life working in the Church," Kyle said. "I don't understand."

"That blasted Church has been the devil personified in my life. Overbearing, just like my own mother. See, I was young when I met

Jenny's father, only seventeen. I wanted out from under my mother's control so badly that I ran off to Oklahoma and married Bill. He was a paratrooper, and it was the middle of World War II. What I didn't anticipate, though, was what I would do when he went back to his assignment after his furlough. Once I had Jenny, I wound up back at my mother's for part of that time."

"If she was so controlling, she must have been furious with you."

"Oh, she was," Ellen said. "She and that blasted priest, Father Stanton, forced us to get married in the Church. Then, later, when I left Bill and wanted a divorce, I had to deal with the Church laws to undo it. Father Stanton promised that he would get me an annulment. Mine was a classic case of being too young *and* non-consenting to getting married in the Church. He said it shouldn't be a problem. But it was. Seventeen years later, my so-called annulment still hadn't come through. So, with Jenny away at that school, I got tired of waiting and married Earl in front of a judge. But my mother and the Church had a strong hold on my conscience. Aside from all that, I had to make a living for two of us and Bill wasn't coming through with any child support."

During another visit, Ellen told Kyle about her own childhood.

"My father left us when I was five. Mother had three of us at the time. I was the oldest, and the fourth, my baby sister, was on the way. Somehow, Mother managed to raise us all fairly well throughout the Great Depression."

Kyle wondered if his own mother would have fared so well under the circumstances. "Did your father know your mother was pregnant when he left?"

"Oh, yes. I'm sure that was the final straw that made him run. He returned when I was twelve, begging Mother to take him back. For a moment, she almost weakened. But in the end, she refused. She had bitterness toward all men after that, and she never remarried."

"Was it hard for you to leave your marriage?"

"Oh, yes," Ellen said. "I remember someone telling me I'd better be sure, so I thought about it for several months before I left."

"Jenny has a vague memory of the two of you walking out of the trailer you lived in on the Southern Methodist University campus. She told me you were carrying a suitcase, a brown one with yellow stripes, and she was carrying her own little suitcase."

"It was actually my makeup case she was carrying. Her clothes were in the big suitcase. I doubt if she could really remember that. She may just remember my telling her about it."

"I'll bet it was hard to do," Kyle pondered.

"It was a real turning point. I had to work hard to hold us together. A wonderful family, the Ayers, had babysat Jenny while her dad was in school and I worked. After leaving Bill I had to depend on them much more. I left Jenny with them more than I would have liked to because of my work."

"Jenny has talked about them. She described living with the Ayers while you traveled."

"Oh, that was a happy time for me—maybe one of the first after my divorce. I worked for a company directing road shows in small towns around the country. Local people volunteered to be in the shows, and their family and friends would pay to see the shows. I loved working with the townspeople. The only unhappy part was being away from Jenny."

"Jenny said the Ayers would drive her to spend weekends with you. The part I remember her most talking about was her sadness going back and forth between you and the Ayers," Kyle said.

"I know it was hard on Jenny. I did the best I could. Jenny had an unusual childhood because of it. Unusual but happy," Ellen said. "We never had our own house until she was thirteen, and I was only thirty-two. We found a place near her high school, the same Catholic academy I had attended."

"Well, you and Jenny have made up for lost time. You may have been apart a lot back then, but you and she are so close now. If anything ever happened to you, she would be devastated."

"Well, don't you worry. I am going to get better. Besides, Earl needs me now just as much as Jenny does."

Kyle stopped in to see Ellen several more times over the course of her hospital stay, and they both looked forward to their visits.

After two weeks, Ellen was released from the hospital. The C-diff was still present, and she returned home almost worse than when she went in. Her blood pressure was fluctuating at around 110 or 115 over 50, not where it should be, but much better than when she had been rushed to the hospital. Jenny arranged Ellen's bedroom with conveniences such as a portable toilet, a small refrigerator, a television with remote—all by her bedside within five square feet of each other. Jenny's son, Chad, helped out as much as he could, sometimes running Earl around on errands or helping him pay bills. Jenny felt blessed to have such a fine son.

One afternoon, shortly after returning home from the hospital, Ellen and Jenny chatted while Chad took Earl to the grocery.

"So, how's the backyard coming along?" Ellen asked.

Between visits to her mother's house, Jenny had busied herself by doing some extensive landscaping. She had always wanted a pond and was now creating several with small waterfalls and tapered creeks connecting them. From her sickbed, Ellen shared in Jenny's excitement regarding her lawn's makeover.

"The pond in the backyard is finished, Mom, and I'm now working on one right outside of the master bedroom. When I wake up in the morning, I want to be looking at the water and hearing it flow. It's such a relaxing sound. I've been working with an architect to get the bedroom just the way I want it. The fun part will be landscaping around it. Maybe you'll be able to go with me to the nursery," Jenny added, not quite believing that her mother was up to the task.

"I'm going to be getting well soon, Jenny," Ellen assured her. "I may not be well enough to get out, but I have found some lovely ideas for you." Ellen retrieved some landscaping magazines from her bedside table. "Just look at this!" She eagerly showed Jenny some pictures she had found.

"Oh, Mom, these are great," Jenny told her, thrilled that her mom was focusing outward from her illness.

"I may not be able to get out yet," Ellen said, "but I can still help!" They spent the rest of Jenny's visit looking at the magazines.

When Ellen's birthday rolled around, she was still too sick to leave the house. Jenny had hoped that her mom would be well enough to come to her house and celebrate in the refurbished garden, but in lieu of that, Jenny took some photos and had them enlarged, decorating Ellen's room with the colorful images. Jenny also wrote Ellen a heartfelt letter, expressing her deep love for her mother. She poured out her feelings of gratitude for all that Ellen had done for her over the years. Jenny wanted to reassure her mom—and herself—that she *would* get better.

August 17, 2000

Happy Birthday, Mom!

These past few weeks have been special to me. After all the years that you have taken care of me, it feels good to finally be able to give back to you, and I know you will get better soon. You are getting stronger. I can see it. But, like Dr. DeWitt said, it will just take time.

When I think back to my earliest childhood, I remember feeling pulled apart somewhat. I wanted to be with you more, and that just couldn't always be. But I never blamed you for it, never. I'm sorry for bringing you so much sadness when I left home to do my convent studies. I never meant to hurt you. Working in the Church was something I had always dreamed of doing, since I was seven years old. My training there laid a beautiful foundation for my life. I have a spiritual basis that underlies much of what I do, and I feel comfortable with that.

Since that time, and particularly since Chad was born, we have had a great deal of time to share with each other. I loved our time together in the Bay Area, and now Sacramento. I think about the time you had with Chad when he was so little, when you were teaching him to paint. I remember when he had chicken pox and the four of us were all living in your condo in Burlingame. You came to Sacramento just as I was beginning my radio career. And I loved the time when you and Chad and I—three generations—all worked in my office together. That was one of the beautiful memories I have of my time with Matt. And I'm grateful for all the years since then that you have helped me in the office. We more than made up for lost time!

You have lived with me through both my marriages. They have definitely been the most joyful and the most painful parts of my life, and I would never have gotten through those experiences without your love and support. Thank you so much for standing by me through these times and helping in my struggle to regain my life at each of these intervals.

> You are the best mom that anyone could ever have! If there
> is anything I can do for you now, I am here. I would go to the
> ends of the earth for you. I love you so much.
>
> Your grateful daughter, Jenny

Tears were pouring down Jenny's face as she finished the letter. She couldn't imagine life without her mother, yet she knew that might ultimately come to pass.

With Chad's help and that of the home healthcare service, Ellen was well cared for. Chad often came over after work and on weekends to help and to keep Earl company. Ellen had always done things for Earl, but now it was up to Chad and Jenny.

Jenny did a good job managing Ellen's care, but Ellen was getting harder to please as her health continued to worsen. As a patient, Ellen was sweet and appreciative and rarely drew the subject to herself or her illness. If she was asked how she was feeling, she always assured everyone that she was going to get better. But when friends came to see her, Ellen was much more adept at focusing the conversation on how things were going in *their* lives.

This was especially true with Kyle. Due to their many bedside conversations, both during her hospital stays and in her home, Ellen had grown very fond of him. She sensed he truly loved Jenny, and that alone opened the way to her heart. Ellen beamed as she saw Kyle at the door with Jenny behind him.

"How is your world going?" Ellen asked him one afternoon.

"Honestly? Things are pretty intense right now," he stated somberly.

"Can you talk about it?" Ellen asked. She respected that there were certain confidential topics he was not at liberty to discuss.

"Have you been reading the paper or watching the news the last few days?" Kyle asked.

"I've had the news channel on and 'the breaking story,'" she said, mimicking a newscaster's voice, "is the explosion on the USS Cole."

"Yeah, that's what has me concerned," Kyle said.

"It wasn't just an accident?" Ellen asked. She'd heard that, just before the huge blast, two men were seen standing on the deck of a small vessel alongside the USS Cole. The news report said that a hole, about 40 by 40 feet, was blown into its hull, killing 17 sailors and wounding 39 more.

"No, it was definitely an attack," Kyle said. "It has all the earmarks of a carefully planned, well-financed operation, and the bomb materials were expertly prepared. Muslim suicide bombers blew up an explosives-laden boat next to the USS Cole while the destroyer was in the Aden, Yemen, harbor. They're sure the blast was premeditated."

Ellen's brow furrowed. "Why would anyone intentionally commit suicide to carry out an attack?"

"I don't understand that, either," Kyle said. "Suicide bombers are driven by a deep belief that America is evil and the darkest enemy of Islam. They believe that their actions are blessed by Allah and they'll experience eternal peace after death."

Ellen flinched at the word *death*. "For all of us, I hope death does bring eternal peace. But I can't imagine *choosing* to die," she said.

"What hasn't been on the news," Kyle confided, "is that we have reason to believe that a man by the name of Jamal Ahmed Badawi is likely the mastermind behind the attack. He's a key member of the al Qaeda network, and it appears that the operation was financed by Osama bin Laden, the same man who orchestrated the attacks on the American embassies in Africa a couple of years ago. He's a dangerous man and determined to bring down the United States." *Even now, he has operatives living in California,* Kyle thought. "I have a feeling this is all connected. This bombing may be a precursor to something bigger."

Using the remote, Ellen turned up the volume on the television as she noticed the topic on the news again. President Clinton was standing aboard the USS Cole, speaking at a ceremony attended by many of the nation's leaders and the families of the dead and wounded.

Clinton described the unidentified attackers as people who allowed their religious, political, racial, or ethnic views to distort their view of the world. "For them, it is their way or no way," Clinton said. But such people "can never heal or build harmony or bring people together."

Can anyone bring people together on this issue? Kyle wondered. *How has history kept the Middle East and the West so far apart? So much killing in the name of God.*

"They all had their own stories and their own dreams," said President Clinton. He read each of the 17 sailors' names. Speaking directly to parents, brothers, sisters, and other loved ones, Clinton closed his remarks: "We are all mindful of the limits of our poor words to lift your spirits or warm your hearts."

"I like Clinton's style," Kyle commented. "He's not afraid to show his emotions, which proves he's human."

Ellen, a lifelong Republican, nodded in agreement as they continued to watch. The president said the crew of the Cole found common ground and a shared commitment to their country amid their diversity. The screen flashed back to the CNN newscaster, who continued to report that Osama bin Laden, the elusive Islamic militant who had publicly pledged to drive the U.S. military out of the Middle East, was the focus of the USS Cole bombing investigation. Bin Laden, a millionaire, Saudi-born dissident, was wanted by the FBI in the 1998 terrorist bombings of the U.S. embassies in Kenya and Tanzania, which killed 224 people. He was believed to be living in Afghanistan.

"This looks like a declaration of war," Ellen said.

"I know," Kyle agreed. "Some of the terrorists connected with this are right here in California. I wish I knew what I'm supposed to do."

"You'll think of something," Ellen whispered.

Over the next several days and weeks, U.S. law enforcement officials continued to find threads linking the suspects held by the Yemenis to bin Laden. President Clinton declared: "If, as it now appears, this was an act of terrorism, it was a despicable and cowardly act. We will find out who was responsible and hold them accountable."

It wasn't only Kyle who was uncertain about what to do next. With home healthcare about to run its course, Jenny was feeling the same indecisiveness about her mother. Jenny stopped by her friend Sherri's house on her way home, knowing she could count on her friend for some wisdom.

"This is getting harder," Jenny said. "I can't do it all by myself. But Mom is so determined she is going to get better that she won't let me bring in help."

"It was like that with my grandma too," Sherri said. "She was so independent."

"With Mom, it's more stubbornness. She still thinks she will be able to clean her house or go grocery shopping or take care of Earl or bathe herself . . . tomorrow. She'll let *me* do just about anything for her, but she won't let me bring in anyone else."

"What if you told her *you* needed the help, that you can't do it all by yourself. Maybe she'd do it for you."

"That just might work," Jenny pondered.

Jenny left Sherri's house and proceeded to her mother's for her regular morning stop. Sitting on the side of Ellen's bed, Jenny eased her way ever so gently onto the subject of hospice care.

"No, absolutely not! I don't need them," Ellen declared. "I don't need anyone! This is my house, and I have the right to run it the way I see fit." Ellen was more teary than angry. The subject was too close to home. It made her face the possibility that she might not get better.

Jenny understood her reaction. Thinking about Sherri's suggestion, Jenny chose her words carefully. "What about doing it for me, Mom? I can't do this all by myself. And even with Chad's help, I think we need a professional healthcare person to help us out."

Ellen didn't answer right away. "Oh, Jenny," she said with a sigh. "If it will make you happy, then okay. But I'm not ready to die. And that's what hospice is about. Dying."

"That isn't always true, Mom. But the last day for home healthcare is this Friday. Hospice will stay on for six months or longer, depending on our needs. Look, I'm determined to keep you out of the hospital. I know you don't want to be there. But to do that, I'm going to need some professional help."

After some research and help from Dr. DeWitt, Jenny selected a hospice group. At Jenny's request, staff members promised that they would not give their usual spiel to Ellen about comforting her while helping her prepare to die. However, when the hospice representative arrived to enroll Ellen, she was clueless. Addressing Ellen, but glancing at Jenny, the woman explained that they would not resuscitate Ellen under any circumstances, but would be there only to comfort Ellen through her illness. Jenny wanted to crawl through the floor. She couldn't even look at her mother. Ellen was truly shaken. It was too strong a dose of reality for her. Fortunately, the rest of the team did honor the promise. Jenny felt some relief; at least some of the responsibility was taken off her shoulders. It was comforting to have a nurse come in three times a week to oversee her mother's medications. A nurse's aide helped Ellen with bathing and changing the sheets and her diapers. The diarrhea from the C-diff was still alarmingly present.

Ellen resented having to wear diapers. Sometimes she refused, just to make herself feel that she really *was* getting better. During one of those times, Ellen had to make a mad dash for the bathroom but she didn't get there in time. When she came out, she went down on her hands and knees and tried to clean up after herself. Jenny grabbed a rag and immediately joined her in the effort. Still on her knees, Ellen dropped her head and began sobbing. Her spirit was losing the battle as her body grew weaker. Jenny stroked Ellen's hair and simply held her mother. It was the reverse of most images—daughter cradling mother in her arms. In silence, Jenny led her mother back to bed. Ellen allowed Jenny to put the diaper on. Neither of them said a word, and Jenny sat by her mother's side until Ellen fell asleep.

Shortly after that—maybe in part to prove she didn't need hospice—Ellen rallied. One morning Jenny walked in to fix the usual poached eggs, bacon, and toast for her parents. She greeted them both sitting at the breakfast bar, and they cheerfully greeted her back.

"It's a great day for the race!" Earl shouted as if he were a NASCAR announcer.

"What race?" Jenny asked with nearly equal enthusiasm.

"The human race!" Earl exclaimed, thrusting his arms into the air like a crusader.

What a change! It was like old times. "You both never cease to amaze me," Jenny said both delighted and hopeful. For the first time since her mother's illness, it appeared that Ellen was going to get well.

"I feel like my old self today, Jenny. After my bath, I'd like to go have my hair done. I'm long overdue."

Fourteen

The Last Supper

On the evening of November 7, Kyle and Jenny were cuddled on the couch watching the national precinct returns when they learned with astonishment that America was without a president-elect. In the days that followed, newscasters reported that George W. Bush and Vice President Al Gore were locked in an extraordinary political and legal contest to secure the electoral votes for the presidency of the United States.

One week after the election was Mike's 70th birthday. Jenny and Kyle celebrated the occasion with him at one of Mike's favorite hangouts down the street from his condo. Jenny felt like she was out with two celebrities. Mike stopped to hug the members of his usual crowd and others came over to Kyle to acknowledge him for his stance on gasoline pricing or to razz him about his soft stance regarding SOA Watch. From a health perspective, neither of the men was at their best. While Kyle struggled with his emotional health, Mike had spent the last few weeks recovering from a virus that his doctor hadn't yet identified. And there was little competitive tension between Mike and Kyle. If either felt any jealously, it wasn't evident to Jenny. It was time for succulent food, fine wine, and celebration with good friends. They ordered one of Mike's favorites—a Montevina Terra D'Oro 2003 Barbera. They all had a wonderful time.

Unfortunately, their sharing of bread and wine that night turned out to be their last meal together. Two days later, Mike's virus was determined to be liver cancer. Mike's doctor had also detected prostate cancer a few weeks earlier but it was in its early stages, and the prognosis was excellent for a treatable recovery. It was when Mike went in for the pre-op prostate work that the lab discovered abnormalities in the ducts leading to his liver and spleen. With that finding, the prostate problem suddenly became insignificant.

There was some paradox in Father Mike suffering a malfunctioning liver. He had a friend, Laurie Hampton, who needed a liver transplant, and he had put extensive energy into helping her get on the waiting list for an organ donor, all to no avail. About the same time, Kyle's office had initiated a regional organ donor committee, allowing neighboring states to work together to get more donors and prioritize those patients most in need. As a result of Mike's inspiring work with Laurie, and during one of their *on* times, Kyle had appointed Father Mike to the committee. But now Mike, anxious about his own liver problems, asked Jenny to accompany him to San Francisco to meet with a team of specialists whom Laurie had recommended.

The team of doctors outlined the treatment options available to Mike. Dr. Gish, the liver specialist at Cal-Pacific Medical Clinic and oncology surgeon Dr Cohen, studied Mike's medical records and ordered a CAT scan. Their primary concern was to see if the cancer was contained in the liver. If so, they recommended surgery. If not, they suggested that chemoembolization, a direct injection of selected chemo drugs through the groin and into the damaged organ, would be the next best option.

While waiting for the results, Mike didn't let any grass grow under his feet. Knowing that he would be returning to San Francisco for the final recommendation, Mike sought a third opinion with a liver specialist at U.C. San Francisco. He faced the seriousness of his illness head-on and put all of his energy into seeking solutions to fight the cancer. Again, Mike asked Jenny to accompany him and she was happy to go.

On November 18, the election counts and recounts continued, and the country still did not have a president-elect. It was the day of the annual fundraiser for Mercy General Hospital, to which Kyle was always invited. Jenny was thrilled to go with him. It was one of those wonderful chances to dress up formally and enjoy the evening with Kyle, dining, dancing, and visiting with friends. It had been a perfect weekend for the two of them. She spent Friday night with him at River House, where they had a night of gentle, prolonged love-making. Saturday morning they slept in, lingered over breakfast at the dining room table, and spent the afternoon by the fire reading each other favorite passages from books, and philosophizing about life. Jenny drove home briefly to dress in her floor-length, black sequined gown, and Kyle looked exceptionally debonair in his tux when he arrived at her door.

Just before the scheduled second trip to San Francisco with Mike, Jenny's world was thrown into more tumult. Kyle was hospitalized for a blood clot in his leg—probably brought on by the almost non-stop dancing he and Jenny had done during the fundraising party. Because Kyle had experienced something similar more than 20 years earlier, the doctors wanted him thoroughly examined and tested. Concerned about his twin, Josh flew out to be with him. Jenny picked him up at the airport, and they headed straight to the hospital.

"Thought you needed more attention, huh, bro?" Josh said as he entered Kyle's room.

"And I got it! You flew all the way out here, and Jenny took time off from her other patients to be with me."

Josh sensed that Kyle's retort about Jenny was a bit weightier than the flip way it came across.

After a day spent with Kyle at the hospital talking about world affairs and their careers, Josh and Jenny went out for a bite to eat.

"So, Jen, aside from the blood clot, how's Kyle's state of mind?"

"His mania and depression seem to be under control. He's working really hard and has some heavy issues weighing on him. But, Josh, that doesn't explain the blood clot. Do you think there could be any correlation between this and his bipolar medication?"

"I don't know. I wouldn't rule it out. I had a small blood clot a few years ago. I didn't think it was any big deal, but maybe our genes are susceptible to them. I'm sure that's why the doctor is going to such extremes to keep this one from advancing above his knee."

"I hope it's not serious," Jenny said.

"Well, just take care of him, Jen. I wouldn't want anything to happen to my brother. He's got important work left to do with his time on earth."

"You two are so close. In fact, I still have trouble telling you apart." Jenny said as they waited for the check to come.

"But he and I are two sides of the same coin. He makes decisions more thoughtfully, with his intellect, whereas I am all emotion and spontaneity."

"That may be true of him in his professional capacity. But in his personal life, believe me, he decides with his emotions too."

Josh laughed.

As the waiter arrived with the check, one of the state's senators approached their table. "Mr. Attorney General," he said to Josh. "How nice to see you."

Josh didn't miss a beat. "It's nice to be seen, especially with the love of my life."

Josh introduced Jenny as she extended her hand to the senator.

As he walked away, Jenny teased, "You two always step in for each other, don't you?"

"All our lives. And we probably always will."

Due to his job, Josh had to fly right back out, and Jenny drove him to the airport, and from there her car found its way to her mom's as if on automatic pilot.

Ellen was spiraling downward again. Earl was growing more blind from his diabetes and, with Ellen unable to care for him, Jenny felt his growing dependency. Now Kyle lay in his hospital bed, frightened that this bout with diverticulitis might be something extremely serious. Plus, Jenny had already committed to going back to San Francisco with Mike to get his final results. She felt the weight of the world on her shoulders. *Dear God, guide me*, she silently prayed. *I am only one person. I can't be with all of them at once. Lead me to be where I am most needed at this moment.*

Jenny reasoned that if she kept her commitment to Mike, she would only be gone for 24 hours, but still she felt apprehensive about leaving everyone else. Explaining to her mother, Ellen assured Jenny that she would be fine, and Chad promised to check in on Ellen double-time during Jenny's absence

Jenny then made her way back to see Kyle. She crawled into his hospital bed with him. They snuggled and said night prayers together. Jenny stayed until he drifted off to sleep, and then she went home and packed, slept lightly, and got up at six the next morning. She dropped by the hospital to see Kyle one last time before picking Mike up and hitting the road to San Francisco. By now, Kyle's medication, Coumadin, was beginning to thin his blood, and he was recovering nicely. But the doctor wanted to keep him there a few more days for observation.

Jenny had made her decision to go with Mike, but she found it hard to explain to Kyle. "I feel bad about leaving you like this, sweetheart."

"It's okay. I understand," he said. But his tone wasn't convincing.

Of course he's hurt, she thought. *I'm leaving him in the hospital to take another man to the doctor in another town.*

"I'll be back as quickly as I can," she promised. "You know if this weren't so serious for Mike . . ."

"I know. Don't worry, sweet pea. You're doing the right thing."

"I'll call you when I know something. And in the meantime, you can reach me anytime on my cell. I love you."

"I love you too," Kyle replied as his eyes followed her to the door.

As Jenny left his room, she felt uncomfortable with her decision. But she knew she wouldn't have been comfortable reneging on her promise to Mike.

Jenny struggled to keep her mind on the road as she and Mike rode to San Francisco. Arriving at Cal Pacific, they found bad news waiting for Mike.

"We have your test results, and I'm afraid it isn't what we hoped for," the doctor told him. "The cancer has spread from the liver to the portal vein. That means I can be of no use to you."

"I don't think I quite understand," Mike said. "Is their no treatment available for that?"

"Father, if the cancer was contained in the liver, it would be relatively easy for me to excise it. But because it's gone into the portal vein, that option isn't open to us. What I would recommend is that we have our oncologist perform a chemoembolization. Essentially, that means that we will inject chemo treatment into the cancerous areas throughout your groin. You'll need to stay in the hospital for a night so we can watch you, and then you'll go home. We'd probably need to redo this procedure again in a few months."

They left somewhat encouraged, but Jenny knew Mike was scared. The news was grave, but the treatment option gave Mike some hope

Jenny called Kyle to see how he was doing and to share Mike's prognosis. At first Kyle was a little cool with her, still, she assumed, struggling over her choice to go with Mike and not stay with him. He mentioned friends who had stopped by to see him, and how happy he was to have the boys and Jo visit him. He let Jenny know that he couldn't wait to see her. She promised that the minute she got back in town, she'd be heading straight to the hospital. Exhausted, Jenny and Mike drove to the furnished rental condo owned by one of his friends where he had arranged for him and Jenny to stay the night. They went to sleep early, and awoke refreshed to the dawn of a new day overlooking the bay and the dazzling Bay Bridge. Mike expressed a desire to say a private Mass with her before they headed out to see the other doctor. Over breakfast afterwards, they both acknowledged they had no doubt that, whatever challenges lay ahead, God was journeying with them.

Feeling both physically and spiritually nourished, they left to get a second opinion from a specialist located across town, Dr. Vanook. He had already reviewed Mike's records and the scan done at Cal Pacific. The doctor walked into the office where they were seated looking anxious.

After a peremptory greeting, Dr. Vanook explained the options. By now, they were familiar with the list. He came to chemoembolization and enlightened them on the pros and cons of this procedure.

"It's very dangerous," he said. "In radiating the bad cells, we also would be killing the good cells. And you can't afford to lose the good cells in your liver. I wrote the first article on this procedure and have studied it as thoroughly as anyone. Believe me, if this method were right for you, I'd be the first to recommend it."

"So what do you recommend?" Mike asked cautiously.

There was a pause. Then the doctor slowly replied. "I recommend that you go home and get your affairs in order."

The chill of the news filled every particle of air in the room. Jenny looked at Mike, but he didn't return eye contact. He was stoic, containing his emotions.

"How long do I have?" Mike asked.

"Your chances of survival are, at best, fifteen percent. I would give you three months. Six at the outside."

They left the office in silence. The pendulum of their moods had dramatically shifted from the early morning. Mike's faith was being severely tested. They began the drive home, stopping only for lunch. They said very little . . . and ate even less.

They began the drive home in silence, but Mike quickly perked up, his fighting Irish spirit in full overdrive.

"I'm not ready to roll over yet, Jenny. I want to check out more hospitals that specialize in cancer treatment like M.D. Anderson in Houston. Maybe Scripps down in San Diego or Mayo in Phoenix. And I want to explore alternative treatments. If traditional medicine can't help me, then I want to explore other less conventional approaches."

"There are several people I know who might have information. We'll call them when we get home," Jenny encouraged.

Mike's spirits appeared to bounce back for the rest of the trip. Despite all the pressures back home, Jenny thanked God that she had made the decision to go with him. No one should have to receive this kind of news alone. It was obvious that having her with him gave Mike enormous comfort. Plus, he seemed to feel hope.

After dropping Mike off, Jenny went straight to the hospital to see Kyle. He was thrilled to have her back yet sad to hear the news about their friend. Jenny needed to be with Kyle as much as he obviously needed to be with her.

Kyle was discharged from the hospital just in time to celebrate Thanksgiving. He was still under close observation. He had regular blood tests and wore a stocking on his leg to prevent the clot from moving upward toward his heart. But Jenny was thankful to bring him home for the holiday.

Thanksgiving was not quite as upbeat as the year before. All the same people were gathered, but with Ellen still mostly bedridden, the celebration was moved to her house. Kyle was limping, his left leg slightly enlarged from the clot; Mike was trying to keep up his spirits, but his heart was heavy; and Earl was fighting some depression brought on by his failing sight and his wife's lingering illness, but he was in fairly good spirits. Chad helped cook, and Jenny teased him that he was doing such a good job, he should consider opening a restaurant. Father Jeff had also come, and he added his hands to the kitchen help along with Mike. When the garbage disposal became clogged with potato peels, Mike put on his plumber's hat—one of his many hidden talents—and fixed the problem. Ellen rallied enough to come downstairs to join everyone for dinner. Conversation around the table was lively, and Kyle entertained everyone with his perspectives on the presidential election. The country still did not have a president-elect, and predicting the outcome and talking about the absurdity of the electoral process made for great discussion.

"I never want to go through a holiday like that again," Kyle abruptly declared after he and Jenny returned to his place. "It was awful for me. I just can't share you with other men, even if they are priests. Both Mike and Jeff fawned over you all day, and it was all I could do to stand it."

Jenny was taken aback by his sudden mood swing, and she took a cautious approach.

"I thought you had a good time, Kyle. I did. I was so happy that you were there with me. And I really appreciated Mike's and Jeff's help preparing dinner."

"But Jeff didn't have to be there."

"But Jeff is Mike's friend, and my friend. And Mike is our friend! You've no need to be jealous."

"Well, I'm handling what you're doing for Mike. After all, he's dying. But I'm having trouble dealing with the threesome of Jenny,

Mike, *and* Jeff: the three amigos. They are priests, Jenny! For God's sake, they're not supposed to have close friendships with women. Jeff wants to be your bosom buddy, just like Mike. You have to tell him no. There isn't room for him. You have Mike and me, not to mention your parents your son, and your zillion friends. You have to draw the line somewhere. You have too many balls in the air."

Kyle was exasperated and, although Jenny was at first put off by what Kyle claimed, she realized that he had a point. "All right, I'll concede that I do have a lot of friends. Maybe I do need to draw the line there a bit more."

"Sweet pea, I do understand your loyalty, and I admire it. But I need you to know it's hard for me to have to share you with so many people. I don't know if you realize it, but right now Mike is all you talk about. What about *our* life? What about *us*? Don't we count anymore?"

"You know we do," Jenny said as she moved closer to him. "And you know I love you. But you still have a lot of things to work out, too. It's only been a year since your divorce was final. That's not very long after twenty years of marriage. Getting over a divorce isn't as simple as replacing one woman with another one."

"Please don't change the subject," he said. "One thing at a time. What I need from you right now is the promise that you'll put me and your family first, that's all."

"And Mike," she said. "I won't turn my back on him."

"And you shouldn't, sweet pea, but he has lots of friends besides you. Let them help him too."

"You have a point," she said.

He kissed her forehead and pulled her closer to him. "Sometimes it scares me how much I love you, Jenny. You're becoming my whole life."

"That's the part that concerns me. I want you to have other parts to your life and be okay with me having other parts too. Obviously, right now Mike and Mom are a priority. Just know that my being there for them doesn't take away from my loving you."

"I know that," Kyle said. "I do. But . . . I don't want to lose you." A single tear ran slowly down his cheek.

"I don't want to lose you, either, Kyle. Don't you understand that I need you now more than ever?" Jenny touched his cheek and brushed away the tear. "I guess you know I tried to put a lock around my heart to protect myself. But you found the key. I'm vulnerable to you, and that scares me."

"Same here," Kyle said, stroking her hair. "So let's promise that we'll never leave each other."

"That sounds good to me. I know I'm not going anywhere."

"I'm not either. Life is all about making choices. And I keep on choosing you."

Over the next two weeks, Jenny helped Mike explore his treatment options. He discovered an alternative cancer treatment program called immune augmentative therapy, offered in the Bahamas. At Mike's request, Jenny spoke with several people from Sacramento and nearby areas who claimed to have extended their lives as a result of the Freeport program. Once Mike had enough testimonials to capture his attention, he phoned the director, Dr. Clement.

The doctor told Mike that, while each cancer is unique to the patient, everyone who has the disease has the common ground of a deficiency in the immune system. Ordinarily, a strong immune system should keep cancer from getting out of control.

"What our therapy does is treat the immune system, not the cancer, by bringing the body's natural defense system back into balance," Dr. Clement explained, adding that the body's own complex tumor-fighting system may well be the first, the best, and the last line of defense against cancer.

Mike prayed, consulted the sisters at Carmel, and sought the advice of Gene Vechio and other close friends before finally deciding to give it a try. He left for Freeport on December 11, convinced that it was his best chance at combating his liver cancer. He was excited and hopeful.

Shortly before 10:00 PM Eastern time the following evening, Josh sat in his den watching a news broadcast that the U.S. Supreme Court justices had reached a decision regarding George W. Bush's lawsuit—a decision that would decide the presidential race against Al Gore. In their battle for the White House, the two sides had argued about hanging chads, disputed ballots, manual recounts, extended deadlines, and a lack of unified standards in counting votes. In certain regions, blacks had ostensibly been turned away from the polls. The entire issue had bounced between the Florida and U.S. Supreme Courts.

After 35 days of anticipation, this moment of closure should have called for a ceremonial celebration, Josh thought, *perhaps someone appearing on an imposing balcony to intone solemnly to a hushed crowd, "Habemus ducem"—"We have a leader."* Instead, he and the rest of America watched a swell of TV reporters squinting to the camera lights and rummaging through 65 pages of a court opinion, searching frantically for a sentence that summed it all up. But, like the election itself, the opinion was long, complicated, and messy. After much journalistic hemming and hawing, the meaning of it finally seeped through—the election recount was over. By determination of the United States Supreme Court, George W. Bush was appointed president.

"This is outrageous!" Josh shouted to Kyle on the phone. "Do you realize this election win was based on 537 votes from only one state?"

"If Bush really won it at all," Kyle replied. "This election is only the third time in this country's history that a candidate has won the presidency while losing the nationwide popular vote. The other times were in 1876 and 1888. This so called 'election' was more like that of John Quincy Adams in 1824, who didn't win either and was *appointed* by the House."

If Mike had still been in town, he and Kyle would have agreed that the appointment of George Bush was a travesty, a misuse of American democracy. Kyle pictured oil interests and U.S. corporations dancing a jig at the prospect of one of their own in the White House.

Jenny basically sleepwalked through the Christmas season that year. Ellen was still mostly bedridden; Chad was spending the holiday away with a girlfriend; and Mike was in the Bahamas fighting cancer. Her usual high energy was depleted, and Kyle did his best to keep Jenny's spirits up.

Inviting her for an intimate Christmas Eve dinner, Kyle arranged a candlelight feast, soft music playing in the background. After they dined, he presented Jenny with an exquisite emerald necklace, with matching bracelet and earrings. She was speechless. Quietly, she held the necklace up and turned so that Kyle could help her fasten it around her neck.

"You're so beautiful," Kyle said adoringly as he fastened the clasp.

"Thank you for ... everything, Kyle. Most especially, thank you for standing by me through all of this."

Jenny had generously gifted Kyle with a unique dining room set. The table was colorfully hand-painted with philosophical writing scripted around the edge, and the words "love, dream, hope, and share" written on the backs of each chair. The moment she spotted it, Jenny knew it was meant for him.

However, Christmas day was a lonely one for Jenny. As part of Kyle's commitment to his new Christian calling, he had joined the bishop, who was saying Mass at outlying areas. Jenny had pushed to complete her remodeling in time to celebrate this day with her family and loved ones. But with everyone gone or sick, her house was empty; her Christmas table setting looked surreal as it sat untouched for days.

Finally, just before the end of the year, Ellen felt strong enough to open presents. They celebrated Christmas in her bedroom—Ellen, Earl, Kyle, Chad, and Jenny. Kyle took pictures, and Jenny later framed two of them: the four of them crowded around the bed with her mother, surrounded by wrapping paper, and the other of Jenny embracing her mother at her bedside. Ellen was smiling behind an oxygen mask; she had rallied one more time.

Fifteen

Making Better Choices

Shortly after the New Year, Mike asked Jenny to join him in Freeport. Mike was there for his ten-week treatment. He told her that his chances were slim, but if these turned out to be his final weeks, as Dr. Vanook had predicted, he wanted her to be near him. She prayed that Kyle would understand and that her mother would be in good hands while she was gone.

Before she left, Jenny called Kerry to wish her a happy New Year.

"As much as you care about Mike, don't let him come before Kyle," Kerry counseled. "Mike is your past, and Kyle is your future. Try to keep them in balance."

"Where do I draw the line?" Jenny asked. "I'm trying to make the best decisions I can, but it's so difficult."

Prompted by her conversation with Kerry, Jenny talked with Kyle about how they would handle her absence. He promised not to add to her anguish by laying a guilt trip on her. She let him know that she understood that this would not be easy for him, and they agreed to keep in touch by phone or email. More than anything, Jenny wanted Kyle to feel her presence from three thousand miles away.

Jenny had an overnight layover at JFK Airport in New York, and Josh and Emmy met her for dinner. They discussed Josh's Amnesty International projects and Jenny's mother's health, but their conversation focused mainly on Kyle.

"How is he handling this trip to the Bahamas?" Emmy asked as their appetizers were being served.

"As well as can be expected," Jenny answered, reaching for a piece of fried calamari. "He's being very supportive."

"Well, I hope his disposition lasts the length of your trip, Jen," Josh responded.

"Me too. But Mike's doctor predicted that he has only a couple of months left. What else can I do?"

"Just what you're doing," Josh said. "It might help you to realize something I've come to understand about my twin. He didn't choose to be bipolar. He really means what he says when he's at either end of the spectrum. Some people think the solution to manic-depression is simply a matter of snapping out of it. But it's not. It's every bit as much of a disease as what your friend, Father Mike, is experiencing. Cancer is just easier for people to accept as a disease. I'll do what I can to help Kyle see your trip in perspective. Every once in awhile, he actually listens to me."

"It is a hard call," Emmy added. "But you love Kyle and he knows it. That's what matters."

"I do love him, Emmy, more than he knows. This isn't the first difficult choice I've had to make in our relationship, and I doubt it will be the last . . . especially with Mom so sick, too."

"I'm facing a serious choice of my own right now," Josh said. "As you know, Colin Powell was appointed secretary of state."

"Yes, I heard that on the news," Jenny responded. "He's a great choice for that position."

"Well...he's asked me to serve on his staff."

"Josh, that's phenomenal! I'm so happy for you. I'm thrilled that Colin Powell will be serving in that capacity, and I'm even more reassured knowing that you will be there, too."

"I've given Amnesty notice, and I'll be starting the same day Powell takes office. I'm moving to Washington right away, and Emmy will come soon after."

"I'm excited about it," Emmy said. "It's always been my dream to live in the District and get involved in politics on some level."

Jenny shared their happiness. When they dropped her back at her hotel, Josh and Emmy wished Jenny well and told her to stay in touch. They had both grown fond of her.

"I sure hope my brother behaves himself while she's away," Josh told Emmy as they drove away.

"Me too," Emmy replied. "Me too."

When Jenny arrived in Freeport and saw the way Mike's face lit up when he saw her, she banished any regrets about her choice to make the trip.

As they drove into the city, they stopped at the market center where they had a lunch of conch, the local delicacy. Jenny marveled at how comfortable Mike was with driving on the left side of the road. Afterward, he drove Jenny back to his place, a two-bedroom bungalow right on the beach and only minutes from the clinic. Mike sat in his favorite chair by the window, overlooking a sweeping view of the ocean, and drifted off to sleep. Up until now, Mike had experienced no pain from the cancer; he only showed mild signs of fatigue.

The next day, Jenny accompanied Mike to the clinic to learn more about the program. The first thing she noticed was that, unlike a room filled with typical chemotherapy patients, there was an atmosphere of hope and pleasantness. She spoke with a patient, a man in his forties, sitting next to her. He, too, had been given only a few months to live by the traditional medical world but had been coming to the clinic for 17 years. He was there for his annual checkup.

While Mike had blood tests, Jenny chatted with June, the woman who handled public relations for the clinic.

"What is your success rate?" Jenny asked skeptically.

"Some people are unable to receive any help from us," June told her. "In those cases, the disease has spread too far and, regrettably, we have to send them home. But many people are able to extend their lives by several years because of our treatments; our longest survival on record is nineteen years."

"What exactly does Mike do here every day?" Jenny asked.

"In the early mornings, he comes for his blood tests so that we can evaluate and measure deficiencies in the immune system. We're looking for data that will reveal the relative activity of the tumor kill process and the immune response to what we're giving him," June explained. "The treatment is individualized to the patient. Later each morning, he returns to receive his serum for the day, which is uniquely designed to fight his deficiencies. Then, several times throughout the day, he injects the shots himself."

As Jenny was engrossed in conversation with June, Dr. Clement walked out of his office with Mike. After introductions, June brought the doctor up to speed on what she had explained to Jenny. "I was just about to describe what's in the serum," June said.

"Well, that's a bit complicated," Dr. Clement began. "Based on years of study and experimentation with other patients who've had a similar condition, we create formulas of cancer vaccine, adding the formula to blood that has been extracted from the patient. All of this makes up the serum that Mike injects into his body."

"Kind of like a flu vaccine?" Jenny asked.

"Not exactly. Flu vaccine contains pieces of the flu virus and stimulates the immune system to make cells that fight the illness. Flu vaccines add an element that is foreign to the body, and they are designed to prevent the syndrome from occurring. Cancer vaccines are different in that they are not preventive. They are used to actually *treat* the disease. Cancer vaccines have to rely on other substances or cells to help the immune response along."

"What kind of substances?"

"There are substances in cancer vaccines that can help alert the immune system to information about the cancer cells. This alert helps certain immune cells—those that are more sensitive to the cancer cells— to divide. This new army of cells will kill any cancer cell it comes in contact with."

"What about side effects?" Jenny inquired. "From the patients I talked to, this procedure seems to be nothing like traditional therapy."

"That's our experience. Unlike chemotherapy, cancer vaccines generally have few side effects. Of course, the results vary with the type of tumor and stage of disease."

"So no vomiting, no hair loss?" Jenny asked.

"No, none of that," Dr. Clement responded.

As Mike and Jenny walked out of the clinic together, Mike looked to her as if for reassurance.

"I think you've made a good choice in coming here, Mike. Some of your friends at home wish you were there to spend these days with them. But the program here seems genuine, and if it gives you a longer life—even a few months—every quality day you have is worth it."

Later that day, while Mike lay sleeping in his chair, Jenny tried to get online to check her email, but Internet access from Freeport wasn't working. For the next few days, she was frustrated at being unable to send or receive email. And the few times she tried calling Kyle or Chad, a recorded announcement stated, "All circuits are busy."

Finally, Jenny was able to access her email. Pleased to finally be on line, she scanned her email, and there were messages from Kyle.

-----Original Message-----
From: Kyle
Sent: Mon 1/08/01 12:24 PM
To: Jenny
Subject: To my lover in paradise

Someone said, "Life is paradise, if we only knew it." Given where you are today, it is easy to believe that life is paradise. I have no idea whether the treatment at the clinic can save or prolong Mike's life. But your journey has already taught me two things:

1. You are the best friend a person could ever have.
2. Whatever the treatment does or fails to do, your visit will make Mike's life much happier. This time together will glow in both your memories as the rarest gift of friendship and love.

I can't conceal my frustration that you are there and not here, with Mike and not with me. But know that everything is fine here, and I want this trip to be a guilt-free experience for you. You both have my love and blessings. I know I will see you soon and, until then, I will see you in my dreams. I love you very, very much.

What a sweetheart, Jenny thought. *The fact that he could put his frustration into written words is healthy.* She was grateful for his understanding and tolerance of the situation. She read his next message.

```
-----Original Message-----
From:    Kyle
Sent:    Tue 1/09/01 1:42 PM
To:      Jenny
Subject: To my silent lover in paradise
```

I haven't heard from you since you left. My first email I sent got no reply. There's nothing in my in-box from you and no telephone message at home or the office. Maybe I should just leave you alone?

I know your relationship with Mike is a deep, long, and devoted one. I also know that emotional monogamy (or whatever it's called) is important to me but apparently impossible for you. The paper boat of our relationship is new and fragile. It can't survive rough waters unless we pay attention to it. We have to keep closely in touch and share our thoughts and feelings as they develop, or we're sunk. So, what now?

The second he clicked the Send button, Kyle regretted it. His first email to Jenny expressed how he felt, even that he was frustrated that Jenny was with Mike and not with him. That was honest. So why didn't she respond? *More importantly*, he thought, *why did I send the second one? Why not just think it or write it in a journal? Do I intentionally want to hurt her? God as my witness, I don't want to cause her pain. God, I am a major fuck-up.* He immediately began crafting a third email.

Feeling let down, Jenny signed off Microsoft Outlook. *Despite his promise, he just can't share me at all,* she thought. *How can a serious relationship survive this drama?*

Jenny felt she was paying the price for her choice to be with Mike. She desperately wanted to talk to Kyle. Responding by email just didn't seem like it would convey the feelings in her heart. Jenny crossed her fingers and dialed his home number, and the call connected.

"I'm so glad I finally got through to you," she told him with relief.

"I was beginning to think the world really is flat and that you had dropped off the edge out there," Kyle said. His sarcasm was evident.

"At least I've got you now," Jenny said. "I've been trying to get a line out for days. Is this a good time to talk?"

"As good as any. How's Mike?"

"He's doing what he needs to be doing. He goes to the clinic twice a day—once for blood work and then back to pick up his serum for the day. He gives himself injections anywhere from eight to eleven times a day. He's a real trooper about it, even says it doesn't bother him being a human pincushion. He seems stable. At least, he isn't any worse than when he left."

"That's good to hear," Kyle said.

"Definitely, but I didn't call to talk about Mike. I finally got an Internet connection a few minutes ago, and I read your emails. I want to talk about us."

"I'd like that, too. I miss you, Jenny. And I miss you lying next to me at night."

"I miss you, too," Jenny said, "but I think it's harder to be the one left behind than the one who goes away. When you talked about making this 'a guilt-free experience' for me, I really appreciated it."

"I'm trying, but it's hard," Kyle said. "I had great resolve, but then I didn't hear from you, and I sent that second email. I backslid a little, but then I don't talk to you and . . ."

"It's okay, Kyle. We're talking now, and that's what matters. As for me, I know I'm a little distracted and anxious. About Mike and Mom. I haven't faced a lot of losses in my lifetime. But I'm facing them big time right now. And I'm scared."

"I know, sweet pea. I'm just a little worried about where you'll draw the line."

"Well, I've done my best to be there for you this past year," she told him. "The way I see it, this is going to be the year I need you."

"I want to be there for you," Kyle said. "I'm really trying but I'm also counting the days until you come home. I miss you so much."

"I miss you, too. I love you. If I can get a line out, I'll call you again tomorrow. Talking really helps." Jenny hung up the phone feeling more assured that Kyle and she would survive this. She needed his understanding. She then got through to Chad and learned that her mother was doing as well as could be expected. Chad assured her not to worry.

Kyle placed the phone on the receiver feeling more peaceful after talking with Jenny. He had to admit that he admired her friendship and willingness to go the distance for Mike. But at the same time, he envied Mike. He recalled his brother's advice: *Get over it, man. For christsake, she loves you.*

With Jenny gone, he had brought his dog, Winky from the family house to live with him. Winky had dirty-white, longer-hair with a mane that drooped in his eyes and brown floppy ears that encased his face. It was just too painful to be alone. It felt so much better to have his dog here with him, curled up by the fire sleeping peacefully. Before long, Kyle, too, fell asleep peacefully.

In the Bahamas, Mike had found a parish, Star of the Sea, where he could say Mass. It was a small church, nothing fancy. It seated about 200 and had a choir that sounded twice its size. The congregation was nearly all locals, and they were grateful to have a priest volunteer his time to celebrate the liturgy with them. As a token of his appreciation, the local pastor, Father John, invited Father Mike and Jenny over for lunch to officially welcome them to the island. Wherever they went, people from the parish would wave to Mike. He'd been there less than a month and already, typically, Mike had won his way into people's hearts and lives.

Jenny was aware that Mike had started sleeping more since she arrived. And he was complaining of back pains. She thought she noticed a little swelling in his stomach. But he managed to keep going. He was losing his appetite, and yet his belly kept getting bigger. Jenny knew something was wrong but was not sure what it meant.

On the next afternoon, just before heading to the airport, Jenny met with Dr. Clement and raised her concerns. "I'm supposed to go back to the States today, doctor. My mom is ill, and I need to get home to her. Can you assure me that Mike will be okay if I leave him? He seems to be struggling more now."

"He's in good hands here and, as I'm sure you've noticed, he has already made a lot of friends. As far as the distention in his belly, we'll keep an eye on him."

Jenny spent the night at a hotel in Orlando, waiting for her Southwest connecting flight to Sacramento. Back in the States, she had no trouble getting through to Kyle with her cell phone, but when she called his house there was no answer. She went to sleep and was awakened by the phone ringing at 2:00 AM. It was Kyle. He had an excited tone in his voice, and Jenny wondered if he was manic.

"Hi!" Kyle exclaimed. "How are you?"

"A little sleepy but happy to hear from you."

"Oh, I'm doing great. Really fine. I'm over at Ann's house right now. We're talking about opening a law firm together and doing some big business with settlement work. It has all kinds of possibilities."

"Ann who, and what time is it anyway?"

When Kyle explained, Jenny realized Ann was an old acquaintance of them both. *But what is he doing at her house at this hour,* Jenny thought, *and why is he calling me from there? And what did he mean about going into business together? He already had a job—a big one!* Their conversation seemed incoherent and spacey, but she was too foggy to ask any more questions.

By the time Jenny boarded the plane to go home the next day, she was struggling over the late night phone call. Usually it was Kyle who was jealous. But this time, she was. *Maybe it's the pressure of death and dying surrounding me,* she thought. *Maybe it's my hormones acting up. Maybe it's Kyle calling me from another woman's house at such a late hour.* During the few minutes that her plane was on the ground in Dallas, Jenny placed a cell call to Kyle. During the conversation, she sensed that he found it comforting that she wasn't so self-confident and cool about his relationships with other women. Kyle assured her that his being at Ann's house late at night was innocent. *Innocent but mighty manic,* Jenny thought. Even so, he fully understood her insecurity with the situation. They both agreed that they had been apart too long.

Jenny arrived home just in time to celebrate Chad's 25th birthday the following day. Ellen was feeling well enough to attend the party at Jenny's house and, along with Earl and Kyle, they had a wonderful celebration. Ellen was still using an oxygen tank but otherwise in good spirits. Kyle was the life of the party, taking pictures and making everyone laugh. For Jenny, it was a moment of family time at its best.

Jenny admired Kyle as he continued to conquer a yin-yang battle within himself regarding her friendship with Mike. Kyle was drawn to Mike but also put off by Mike's love for Jenny and her loyal and loving support of him. Despite this, Kyle kept reaching out to Mike and, when he did, Jenny loved him all the more.

-----Original Message-----
From: Kyle
Sent: Tues 1/16/01 3:44 PM
To: Mike
Subject: A Message of Healing

Dear Mike,
When I read today's meditation by Chiara Lubich, I thought of you. She describes how believing in God's love does not mean helplessly entrusting him with the solution to our problems. She acknowledges how much struggle is involved in order to overcome sickness, suffering, and unfairness. "The balance found in Christian life, in fact, consists in uniting a filial abandon to what God wishes for us together with our own personal initiative."

To me, that means we ultimately entrust everything to our Father in heaven, but on earth we fight like hell to overcome ills and evils. That is what you have always done and what you are doing now.

It is lovely to have Jenny back home. It is obvious from her glow of peace and happiness that your time together was beneficial for you both. She believes that being there for you is one of the truly great honors of her life, and I know she is grateful to you for the retreat she made with you in your temporary island home.

I have been remiss in expressing to you how much you mean in my life, too. You brought me to the communion, which is the center of my faith. You completed a process I know was begun years ago by my brother, carried on by Sister Marsha and Brother Anthony, and brought to full membership in the Body of Christ by you. Now I look forward to more meetings with you and our friends when you return shortly. Jenny reports that you are pleased with the program. I am so glad.

What reverberates over and over in my mind is my knowledge that the Catholic Church and Jenny, whom you love so much, are the gifts of love you gave me. Love really does grow by what it gives.

My love and blessings to you,
Kyle

Jenny had been home less than a week when the phone rang early one morning around 4:00 AM. She barely missed answering, and checked her messages to find that it was Mike who had called. He had phoned from the emergency room in Freeport's Rand Memorial Hospital, and he'd had a major setback. In a weak voice, he said he was being flown by private plane to Northridge Hospital in Fort Lauderdale. She called back immediately but missed him and had to wait to reach him until he arrived on the mainland. The wait seemed an eternity.

Jenny finally spoke with a hospital staffer who explained that Mike's esophagus had burst. His liver had malfunctioned, and everything backed up in his system. With no place to go, the backup had burst the weakest part of the chain: his esophagus. *That's why Mike's belly was distended,* Jenny realized. In Fort Lauderdale, Mike was in surgery having bands placed around his esophagus to repair the damage and strengthen the organ.

Mike called Jenny later that day, after the doctors had completed his procedure. He sounded like death warmed over. His voice was a whisper. "The experience was too awful to even describe. Maybe someday I'll be able to talk about it. I know I'm lucky to be alive."

"Mike, I'm so sorry I left when I did."

"Don't be silly, you couldn't have known this would happen," he said. "But I feel like I'm in good hands here. They want to keep me for a few days to be sure the banding will hold. My niece, Sarah, is flying in this afternoon to be with me."

"Good, it'll be like having your own daughter there. Get some sleep now. And we'll talk tomorrow."

The next day, she learned more of the story from Mike. He told her that he'd called Father John of the Bahamas rectory to come to his aid and that he had driven him to the emergency room. He'd been doubled over in pain as Father John drove him to the emergency room.

I should have been there, Jenny thought.

On January 20, 2001, George W. Bush was installed as the 43rd president of the United States. On that same day, after being unanimously confirmed by the U.S. Senate, Colin Powell was sworn in as the 65th secretary of state. With less hullabaloo, Josh Anderson began his first day on the job on the sixth floor of the State Department, where Colin Powell and his top aides had their offices.

His first week on the job, Josh caught sight of an allegedly classified memo: "We *urgently* need . . . a top executive-level review on the al Qaeda network." The memo, from Richard Clarke, counterterrorism coordinator, was addressed to National Security Advisor Condoleezza Rice. Clarke's memo requested an immediate meeting of the National Security Council. He wanted the principal's committee to discuss strategies for combating al Qaeda, including giving counterterrorism aid to the Northern Alliance and Uzbekistan, expanding the counterterrorism budget, and responding to the USS Cole attack.

The proverbial shit is about to hit the fan, Josh thought. But over the next several months, Josh was dismayed to see no response to Clarke's "urgent" request.

Sixteen

Mike's Fight for Life

JANUARY 26 - FEBRUARY 13, 2001

Nine days after arriving at the Fort Lauderdale hospital, Mike was finally discharged. He couldn't face going back to the Bahamas, even though he was only five weeks through the ten-week program. The thought of going through a medical emergency again in a place so ill equipped to handle it frightened him. He was also still associating the cancer treatment with the bleeding episode, even though there was no relation. But he was determined to do whatever he could to continue to fight the cancer.

While in the Bahamas, Mike and Jenny had learned about a light treatment therapy that has been known to help cancer patients. The clinic in the Bahamas had been in the process of entering into a relationship with a cancer treatment facility in Tempe, Arizona. Dr. Clement recommended that, under the circumstances, Mike would be better off picking up the pills and equipment needed for light therapy from the U.S.-based clinic and taking it home to carry out the treatment. Dr. Clement made arrangements so that Mike had only to stop in Tempe and learn how to use the apparatus before going home to Sacramento to self-administer the regimen. Dr. Clement also offered to ship Mike the serum he'd used in the Bahamas.

The trip was obviously going to be rigorous for Mike, but his spirit gave new meaning to the term "Fighting Irish." Now that he had the esophageal rupture under control, he was determined to focus solely on his battle against the cancer. And he could do so while still within range of a hospital. His nephew, Joe, flew to Fort Lauderdale to relieve Sarah. When the day of discharge came, the plan was for Joe to get Mike from the hospital to the airport, transferring from Dallas-Fort Worth to Phoenix, where Jenny would be waiting to take over.

Jenny packed enough clothes for three days. That was adequate time to go to the clinic, pick up the equipment for the light therapy, learn how to use it, and bring Mike home. She stopped to check on her mother. Ellen was stable and her spirits rallying again, which took some of the pressure off of her daughter's concern for her. Jenny arranged with Chad to have him stop by more frequently to check on his grandparents while she was gone.

Jenny spent her last night before the trip with Kyle. They were the picture of the perfect couple, spooning as they slept, with Winky curled at the end of their bed. Kyle was mustering up his strength to support Jenny as she once again prepared to leave on Mike's behalf. He was determined to stand by her through these few days of separation as she again played Florence Nightingale.

When Mike and his nephew, Joe, arrived at the Phoenix airport, Jenny was waiting for them to come through the gate. As Jenny saw Mike being wheeled down the runway wearing his little brimmed hat, she was stunned by his weight loss, and he seemed to have aged 20 years in the two weeks since she'd left him in the Bahamas.

His face lit up when he spotted her standing there to greet him. Jenny leaned down and hugged Mike, and he weakly returned her affection.

Joe took care of the luggage, taking it to the rental car while Jenny wheeled Mike along. Then they all drove to the Mainstay Suites. Their lodgings were more like an apartment than a hotel room—complete with a bedroom, a hide-a-bed in the living room, and a kitchen with a full refrigerator.

Later that afternoon, Joe went with them to the Tempe clinic to meet Dr. Rubin and receive instruction on using the light treatment. Jenny was struck by how young Dr. Rubin was—maybe only five or six years older than her son. The depth of his knowledge about cancer indicated that he had dedicated himself to the research and ultimate cure of the disease. He explained that the light treatment was still an experimental process but offered some hope. The clinic would need a couple of days to get the equipment ready, and they could be on their way home to try the new process. The light therapy, together with the serum from the Bahamas, gave Mike the plan of action he needed to continue to fight for his life.

With work waiting for him at home, Joe headed back to the airport and departed for Sacramento. He looked worn out from the ordeal of caring for Mike and the responsibility of getting him to Tempe. Jenny was feeling fresh and ready to take over. With this plan in place, she could see Mike's spirits begin to pick up. While Mike slept, Jenny plugged in her computer and sat at the suite's kitchen counter to check her email. She was delighted to see a message from Kyle.

-----Original Message-----
From: Kyle
Sent: Mon 1/29/01 8:56 AM
To: Jenny
Subject: A Prayer for your journey

Dearest:
When I think of our relationship, I sometimes wish I could express myself the way C.S. Lewis did for his beloved Joy Davidman: "What can I say to you that is not already understood? What can any of us do for another except give a kiss or a handshake and a good wish, and hope to do as well when our time comes to be challenged in a similar way?"

Each day is a new journey as much as it is a short stretch of our larger journey. As you begin another journey of your own this week, I pray: Lord, stay so close to my darling Jenny that she is indeed the vessel of your love in the world she is about to encounter. Keep her close to you so that she may feel the ever-present guidance of your divine hand in her every thought and word and deed. Grant her, especially at this time, wisdom tempered by mercy to provide the gifts of sound judgment and consolation to her friend in the grip of disease. Return her to me and to all those who love her with deeper insight and renewed confidence that all is well in you. Amen Alleluia.

> Know that I am holding you in my heart as you are holding
> me in yours. Always. Wherever we are in the world. Be
> confident that I love and support you all the way, every
> day. My entire love and blessings accompany you. Kyle

God, how I love him, Jenny thought. *How could I ask for anyone to be more understanding and more supportive?* Jenny reread Kyle's email three times, each time thanking God he was in her life.

With Jenny gone, Kyle arrived at work earlier than usual and left later than normal. One evening as he busied himself with a recent case file, the phone rang, and a glance at the caller ID showed that it was Josh calling from his secured line. Kyle answered.

"Hey Josh, how's the fray?"

"Being part of a new administration is interesting to say the least," Josh said. "We're all newbies and still getting our feet wet here."

"Even the president?" Kyle questioned.

"*Especially* the president. He spent the morning addressing religious groups on his faith-based education plan, and the early afternoon at a nearby school, he talked about 'armies of compassion,' and how 'real change happens street by street, heart by heart—one soul, one conscience at a time.'"

"Interesting."

"Yes, but by half past three, he was in the Situation Room meeting with his national security advisors. His agenda switched from 'armies of compassion' to armies of an entirely different kind."

"I would expect that he would be focused on this terrorism threat I keep getting memos about, or maybe he was concerned about China or Russia," Kyle said.

"Wrong. He set his focus on three key objectives: get rid of Saddam Hussein, end American involvement in the Israeli-Palestinian peace process, and rearrange the borders in the Middle East."

"Huh? He's never been that interested in international affairs. He's been in office all of ten days. Powell must be going crazy."

"Paul O'Neill, the newly sworn in secretary of the treasury, was also at the meeting, along with Cheney, Powell, and Rice. O'Neill stopped by here looking for Powell afterward and was so frickin' pissed that he opened up to me. He said Powell was taken totally by surprise. Powell had long stopped believing that Iraq posed any serious threat to the United States. Since he was the only one in the room who had ever met Israel's current leader, Ariel Sharon, he tried to tell Bush that the consequences of a sudden reversal of our policy could be dire, especially for the Palestinians."

"Where did that idea come from?" Kyle asked.

"O'Neill said it was a policy that had been drawn up five years earlier by three long-time militaristic, neoconservatives: Richard Perle, Douglas Feith, and David Wurmser. It's a weird deal. Originally, they all served under the Reagan administration, then left and acted as a kind of American council to the Israeli Prime Minister Benjamin Netanyahu during his reign from 1996 to 1999, and now rumor has it that they are soon to be reappointed to senior administration positions under Bush."

"Why would he want men who advised a foreign government to now advise him? That's outrageous," Kyle exclaimed.

"Well, even more unsettling is the fact that they're recommending ways to masquerade the true purpose of these attacks from the American public. They know this is not going to be an easy sell."

"So you're thinking they are going to take the plan designed for Israel and bring it to us?"

"You got it. In their Clean Break plan, as they called it, the idea was for Israel to make a clean break from old policies that had failed, such as exchanging land for peace with Palestine, and instead promote Western values and traditions. And for that to happen, they recommended launching a major unprovoked regional war in the Middle East, attacking Lebanon and Syria and ousting Iraq's Saddam Hussein."

"This plan makes some sense if you're Israel, but how is it going to help the United States? And how on earth would they ever sell Americans on this scheme?"

"That's all in the written report by these guys," Josh said. "They're so pro-Israel that they are frickin' anti-American in my book. They're as guilty as any traitor to our country. In order to cover this up, they suggested that a phony pretext be used as the reason for the original invasion of Iraq."

"Like what?"

"Two ideas: one, they would claim that the purpose of the invasion was to halt Syria's drug money and counterfeiting infrastructure going on there—a subject that holds almost no interest for Israel but would gain the sympathy of Americans—or, two, by drawing attention to Iraq's weapons of mass destruction. That way they could claim that Israel's war was really all about protecting Americans from drugs, counterfeit bills, and WMD."

"Josh, the American public will never fall for such bullshit."

"I hope your right, bro," Josh said. "God, I hope you're right."

Later that night, while an agenda of war was being discussed in Washington, a message of peace was being delivered in Sacramento. Father Mike had been instrumental in creating a millennium series in Sacramento, in which he and his board of directors, funded by the Wiegand Foundation, invited Nobel Peace Prize recipients to speak on the subject of forgiveness and healing. So far among the speakers had been Cardinal Cassidy from Australia, Archbishop Tutu from South Africa and, this evening, John Hume from Ireland.

Father Jeff called Mike in Tempe from the Sacramento Community Center Theater and held his cell phone up so that Mike could hear the introductions being made and his own video in the background. It was one that Mike had made in the Bahamas, knowing that he could not be present. Speakers commented on how much Mike was missed and said this series had been his brainchild. Lying in bed, he listened as the audience clapped, and Jeff said they were giving Mike a standing ovation. The applause went on and on. Jenny watched Mike's face and could see that he was deeply moved.

But the joy of his accomplishment was soon overridden by the acute back pain Mike was experiencing. Along with the pain, Jenny could see the distention beginning in his belly again. During the night, Mike and Jenny walked the hallways of the hotel. He couldn't sit. He couldn't lie down. He couldn't sleep. Finally, with nothing helping, Jenny asked the hotel receptionist for directions to the nearest hospital.

Fortunately, Tempe St. Luke's was close by. Jenny grabbed Mike's medical file and they headed to the hospital.

From the moment he was admitted, Mike's treatment there was humane. Jenny signed him in and the staff didn't keep him waiting in the reception area. Jenny completed the paper work while Mike was rushed into an examination room. By the time she had completed his admission and joined him, a doctor was already present. He introduced himself as Dr. Patele and briefed Jenny on Mike's condition.

"The x-rays show that Father O'Malley's esophageal bands broke. We need to go in and add more right away. He's got bleeding varices, which means swollen veins in his esophagus. These varices are fragile and can rupture easily, resulting in a large amount of blood loss. I'll be placing several rubber bands onto the bleeding sites. It's not a difficult procedure but there is no guarantee that the new ones will last either."

"You'll need these," Jenny said as she handed Mike's medical records to the doctor. "He has been diagnosed with hepatic cellular carcinoma and is here getting cancer treatment."

"That explains a lot. This is a serious problem. He can't last much longer like this."

"Are there any other options open to him?"

The doctor thought for a moment before answering. "There is one procedure that you may want to consider. It's called TIPS, which stands for Transjugular Intrahepatic Portosystemic Shunt. It's a radiological procedure in which a tubular device, called a stent, is placed in the middle of the liver. The stent connects the hepatic vein with the portal vein. This procedure is done by placing a catheter through a vein in the neck. The TIPS relieves the high blood pressure that has built up in the liver. I'll give you more details later. In the meantime, I'm going to arrange for the rebanding of these esophageal varices."

Jenny stayed with Mike until the procedure was completed and she knew he was out of immediate danger. By six o'clock the next morning, Mike was back in his room and sleeping peacefully. The nurse suggested that Jenny go home and get some sleep.

After a few hours of rest, Jenny called Kyle to let him know what had happened. She promised him she'd call again as soon as she knew

anything more. Before returning to the hospital, Jenny logged on to the
Internet and typed in TIPS. Jenny quickly scanned several articles, all of
which said the procedure was a sensible solution when the esophagus
was bleeding due to a malfunctioning liver. It sounded like the right
step for Mike to take next.

When Jenny arrived at the hospital, she asked for Dr. Patele.

"Which patient are you here for?" the nurse asked politely.

When Jenny told her, the nurse explained that Dr. Patele was the
emergency room doctor. Father Mike would have one of two other
doctors in charge of him now, but she would let the doctors know that
she and Father O'Malley would like to meet with them.

"How's the patient?" Jenny asked the nurse.

"Much better this morning. But Dr. Patele did recommend that he
be kept here for observation. It might be a few days."

Jenny thanked her and headed to Mike's room.

"Hello, love," Mike greeted Jenny as she walked into his sterile
hospital room.

Jenny noted how pale and tired he looked. She leaned over and
kissed his cheek. "How are you feeling this morning?"

"Remarkably better. I can't even begin to describe the difference."

"Do you hurt anywhere?"

"A little where they put that scope down my throat. But it's
nothing in comparison."

"I guess the doctor told you he wants to keep you here for a little
while to be sure these bands are holding."

"I can be patient," Mike said. "I need this to be fixed so I can get
on with the cancer treatment."

"I spoke with Dr. Clement and he offered to send the serum here if
we want him to. How do you feel about that?"

"I don't know. I'm having a hard time disassociating what
happened from the treatment at the clinic there."

"I can understand how you feel, Mike," Jenny said. "But from
everything that I've read and learned about what happened to you, it
was inevitable. It wasn't caused by your treatment. You need to stay
on the program. It may or may not be helping. But I'm sure it isn't
hurting you."

Mike agreed. He trusted her judgment. He said to go ahead and have the serum sent. He was beginning to nod off even as they spoke.

Jenny stepped into the hallway and used her cell phone to call her mom. Ellen said she was doing okay and not to worry about her. She encouraged Jenny to stay with Mike for the moment. Jenny marveled at the way her mother was concerned about someone else even as she battled her own serious illness.

Next Jenny called Kyle. It was going to be hard to tell him that she didn't know when she was coming home. He was disappointed but, under the circumstances, he understood. After all, she couldn't leave Mike alone in the hospital. He also mentioned that a lawyer friend of his was in Phoenix settling a case and, if they needed a private plane to bring them home, he could help arrange it. Jenny was grateful, knowing that if they were to come home anytime soon, it would be nearly impossible for Mike to take a commercial flight.

Jenny called a few more people to update them on Mike's condition: Sister Marsha, Father Jeff, Gene, Joe, and Sarah. They all said they would pass the word on to everyone else.

A couple of hours later, a doctor came in to see Mike. He took his vitals, checked him over, and said everything seemed to be holding fine. Jenny brought up the subject of the TIPS procedure that the emergency room doctor had mentioned. "I looked it up on the Internet this morning. I read several articles about it, and it does sound like it could help Father Mike."

"Well, I would recommend against it," he advised in a grim voice. "It is much too dangerous in Mike's condition. But you'll need to take that up with one of our radiologists. I'll ask one of them to stop by and talk to you."

"What a chipper guy he is," Mike said sarcastically, rolling his eyes. "Tell me more about the procedure, Jenny."

She told him what she knew and said that she would do some checking with doctors at home to see what they thought of it.

Then the radiologist came in. "I understand you're inquiring about TIPS. I've looked over Father's medical records, and I definitely would not recommend it. The risks involved are way too high for him."

How much riskier can life get than impending death? Jenny thought. *What does he have to lose? I would rather see him die of cancer than drown choking on his own blood.*

"If not TIPS, are there other alternatives?" Jenny asked.

"Not really. Nothing that I can think of at the moment. But we can buy him a little time by getting these bands to hold." He said he would be back to check in on him tomorrow.

"Well, the doctor and that radiologist were the classic Dr. Doom and Dr. Gloom, eh? Such chipper guys," Mike said with a chuckle.

After several days, Mike was released. Jenny drove him back to their Mainstay Suites, and Mike fell asleep immediately. Jenny called a doctor friend at home who described to her the pros and cons of the TIPS procedure. Then she called Father Jeff to ask him to check it out with doctors in his parish. Jeff reported back that it was a reasonably common procedure and that, given what Mike was facing, two doctors in his parish agreed that it was in his best interest to do the procedure.

Several days had passed without Jenny checking her email. Completely preoccupied with Mike's unexpected hospitalization, she had let everything else go. She logged onto the Internet and found a message from Kyle.

-----Original Message-----
From: Kyle
Sent: Thurs 2/8/01 6:47 PM
To: Jenny
Subject: Be Still Inside

Dear Jenny,
We talked about your setting limits on how far you would go to stand by Mike. A three-day trip has turned into ten days. Day and night by his side, in his room, racing from place to place, consult to consult, cure to cure. In the meantime, your mother, stepfather, son, friends, house, business, and boyfriend are all in abeyance. Enough is enough. This is not healthy for you or anyone else.

This time, I really believed your trip was a joint project for both of us. I deeply believed that seeing Mike through the last days of life and my helping you to do it would be a spiritually deepening experience for both of us. Then what happened? You abandon me. If I am out of the picture when you get home, then you can continue with Father Jeff or Sherri or someone else. No loss to you, just to me. Then the evening calls, which we have shared for so long have also stopped.

I applaud his and your heroism in trying to find a cure anywhere at any cost, but Mike is dying of liver cancer, Jenny. I see no evidence that either one of you understands the most fundamental spiritual lesson of all: leaving the most important things of our lives in God's hands.

I've held on as long as I can. Even as I think of letting you go, I reflect back on what we have shared in so short a time: sunrises, sunsets, books, thoughts, prayers, laughs, dances, dinners, trips, walks, friends, music, sex, sights and smells, sleeping sweetly like spoons, silly and elaborate "breakfast dinners," the Holy Eucharist, my baptism and confirmation, my first public prayer and scriptural reading, tears, fierce fights, hot tubs and massages and mud baths, sensuous scents and lovely scenes, formal ballroom dancing and dancing in parking lots, kissing everywhere and every way in every public and private place we have been.

But without communication, we have no relationship. There are no words to express how grief-stricken I am that our relationship is over. There will always be a hole in my heart where you once were. It will not be my lot to so completely love another human being again. I will not ever abandon you as a friend. Even if I am with another hundred women after you or you with another hundred men, it will not change. They can never find the secret chamber of our hearts we reserve for each other. In every single thing we have said and done together, even through the fights, we have brought each other closer to love everlasting and, therefore, closer to God. I am grateful that I experienced it once and fully before my time on earth was up. Kyle

Jenny closed her laptop, already crying. She was too shaken to respond. She sat and sobbed until there were no tears left to cry. Jenny thought about Kyle's advice to be still inside. She was convinced that every human being on the face of the earth has a dam inside which can be open or closed at will. If lifted up, all the secret thoughts that have been building up for years are exposed. It is a rare opportunity to look clearly at oneself. The real troubles in life, she thought, happen when that dam stays closed too long. Jenny longed to go home, to check in on her mother, to open up completely to Kyle in hopes that it would salvage their relationship. Jenny imagined the two of them holding each other and talking long into the night. But for now, that was not possible. She knew of no other way to deal with the challenges she faced except to handle those directly in front of her, but her resolve didn't ease the pain of Kyle's rejection. She cried herself to sleep.

The following day Mike's back pains returned. His stomach began to swell again and Jenny called the hospital. She reached "Dr. Doom," who told her that there was little that could be done.

"And don't be surprised if the banding breaks again," the doctor added. "It's not uncommon for that to happen."

It seemed to Jenny that she had spent every Saturday for the past month either taking Mike to the emergency room or sitting by his hospital bed. As Saturday rolled around, she felt anxious. Mike wasn't hungry. He would frequently nod off, but then the pain in his back or stomach would wake him soon after. As evening approached, Jenny saw him making his way to the bathroom. Before he could shut the door, she was shocked to see blood gushing from his mouth into the toilet. Only a few steps away, she ran to him and stood helplessly by. While Mike hung his head over the toilet, Jenny went to the kitchen sink to wet a washrag for him. Thinking this episode was over, he walked the few steps to the kitchen, but suddenly he began to fall. Jenny caught him, and they tumbled to the floor together as he lost consciousness. She crawled to the phone and dialed 911. Within a minute, a staff member from the hotel was at the door verifying her emergency call. Within another few minutes, an EMS team was at the door.

One of the team members placed an oxygen mask over Mike's mouth. The paramedic pressed on Mike's chest, waited, and pressed again. And again.

"I've got his BP up to seventy over twenty," the paramedic said to one of the others. "Let's get him into the ambulance now. And we need to hurry."

Up to seventy over twenty? What was his pulse before that? Jenny thought as she grabbed her purse and followed the gurney down the hallway. Standing in the elevator next to Mike, she held his hand and could see that he was conscious again. He looked up at her but didn't try to speak. Jenny stayed by his side until he was load into the ambulance.

Once the door was closed, Jenny jumped in the rental car and followed behind. She was sure that this was the end for Mike. From the car, she used her cell phone to call Sister Marsha at the monastery. No answer. She called Father Jeff. He answered on the first ring, and as providence would have it, he was with Sister Marsha. Jenny told them that it didn't look good. Prayers were needed now even more than medical treatment.

The hospital staff members skipped the admission protocol. It had only been a few days since Mike had checked out of the hospital. Mike was wheeled to a cubicle filled with high-tech equipment in the emergency room. A team of nurses and doctors quickly went to work doing a blood transfusion and inserting an IV. Within half an hour, Mike's blood pressure was up to eighty over forty.

Jenny left a voicemail message for Mike's niece, Sarah, about what was happening. Sarah called back, and the hospital put the call through to Mike in the emergency room. He said his goodbyes to his niece.

When Jenny was allowed in to see him, he told her, "This is it, love, and I'm ready for the Lord to take me." Mike seemed more accepting of his imminent death than Jenny had seen him before.

Jenny stood by his side, holding his hand, with tears streaming down her face. She had never been with anyone at the moment of death. She felt helpless, yet she didn't want Mike to have to endure such pain anymore. But she wasn't ready to let him go. She prayed the only prayer that made sense: *Dear God, not my will but yours be done.* Jenny swallowed the lump in her throat and found the words to ask Mike if there was anything he wanted her to do for him after he died.

"Yes, there is a locked trunk at my apartment. The key is on a nail in the bedroom closet. I have some personal letters and files in there.

Shred anything that you think would be hurtful to anyone. Give the rest to Sarah."

"I'll do it, I promise." Jenny wiped her tears off of his face.

"I don't know what I would've done without you, love," Mike added. "You have been a Godsend to me."

"I love you, Mike. You've been the best friend anyone could have."

"Likewise," he whispered. Then his eyes closed, and he drifted off, his chest barely rising and falling with each breath.

By midnight, with countless blood transfusions, the team succeeded in reviving him. His blood pressure stable, they moved Mike to the intensive care unit, where he had been only a few days earlier.

Relieved, Jenny went to the hotel for a brief nap. Then she arose, showered, dressed, and went downstairs for breakfast. She called Father Jeff and gave him an update on Mike's condition.

"Praise the Lord," he said. "When you called last night, the nuns started praying for him even before the ambulance arrived at the hospital. I guess there are no more powerful prayers than those of Carmelite prayers."

"It's a miracle he's alive," Jenny said. "There is no way he should have lived through that ordeal. But he did. I guess God still has plans for Mike on earth."

"I'm just heading over to say Mass right now," Jeff said.

"The bishop is covering the later Masses for me so I can get away sooner." Monday and Tuesday are my days off, so he hoped I could offer you a little relief for awhile. By the way, the bishop is most appreciative of all you are doing for Father Mike." He gave her his flight arrival time, and right before they hung up, she asked Jeff to phone Kyle and let him know about Mike. Jeff promised he would.

Jenny made her usual round of calls, letting everyone know that Mike had experienced a serious setback but, for the moment, he had pulled through. It was only after that when Jenny allowed her thoughts to settle on Kyle. She wanted so much to share this with him. Actually, she just wanted to feel his arms around her. *Please, Kyle,* she thought. *Don't give up on me. I have to see this through. I can't quit on Mike now. But I promise to make it up to you. Just hold on. Please, hold on.*

Arriving back at the hospital, she found Mike awake but groggy.

"I got the patient-of-the-month award," Mike was joking to one of the nurses. "They invited me back just to give you all a hard time." He was obviously feeling better but he drifted off to sleep soon after. Jenny phoned her mother, and Ellen said she was feeling great, and sent her good wishes to Mike.

Finally, Jenny couldn't stand it anymore. She dialed Kyle's home number. needing to hear him tell her that everything would be all right.

But the call was a terrible mistake. Kyle was viciously angry. "How can you abandon me and your family? Your mother and stepfather need you. What kind of a daughter are you that you can leave them in their time of need? And for what? For some wayward priest who lives a frivolous life?"

Jenny was horrified by his anger yet fearful that part of what he was saying was true. *What kind of daughter was she?* She couldn't stand to listen anymore and hung up on him. She was shaking. It felt as if her heart had been ripped from her chest.

After a sleepless night, Jenny met Father Jeff at the airport. On the drive to the hospital, she told him how anxious she was to meet Mike's newest doctor and get his recommendation on what to do next. As they walked into Mike's room, seeing Jeff, he broke into a big smile.

Soon a new doctor made his way to Mike's room. "Father's bandings are holding together nicely, but I have to warn you that they could burst again at any time."

"Dr. Patele suggested a procedure that we might consider called TIPS," Jenny said. "What do *you* think about it?"

"I think it's his only hope. Our best guy here for this procedure is Dr. Christianson. I'll tell him about Father Mike and send him down to talk to you."

What a difference from the advice of Dr. Doom and Dr. Gloom, Jenny thought feeling more hopeful.

While Mike slept, Jenny and Jeff talked.

"It's hard to see Mike like this," Jenny said.

"Yes. He's always come across so full of energy, coming up with new ideas, and brimming with passion. His mind was quick and alert. Even though he's ten years older than me, he never seemed old . . . until now. He looks so weak and frail."

Late in the afternoon, they met Dr. Christianson.

"Father, I've examined your MRI and your ultrasound, and it's not good news. Because your liver is malfunctioning, you're experiencing blockage in the blood flow throughout your body. This causes everything to back up, putting pressure on the portal vein, the vein that carries blood from the digestive organs to the liver, as well as on your stomach and esophagus. A chain is only as strong as its weakest link, which, in this analogy, is the esophagus. That's why the veins in yours have burst and, despite the banding, will continue to burst unless we can find a way to reroute the blood flow and bypass the liver. That's the purpose of the TIPS procedure, which allows us to place a shunt in the malfunctioning liver and drain blood from the digestive tract into the general circulation."

"So what seems to be the problem?" Mike asked.

"In order for the procedure to work, we have to be able to make a complete loop in your system. But, in your case, some of the arteries are clogged, and we can't find an opening to complete the circuit," the doctor explained. "I know this is really hard to hear."

"So what now?" Mike asked.

"There is nothing left to do. Now we hope that your esophageal bandings will hold a while. That's all we can do."

"How long would you expect them to last?" Father Jeff asked.

The doctor shrugged his shoulders as he looked at Jeff. "Who knows? But not long."

Desperation filled the room. None of them was ready to give up. "What would you do if this were your dad?" Jeff asked the doctor.

"I don't know that I can do anything more than what we've done," Dr. Christianson replied.

Jenny felt lightheaded as she listened. She didn't want Mike to die the way she had seen him Saturday night. "Doctor, isn't there some other way? There must be someone else you can talk to."

The doctor sat facing Mike, and Jeff and Jenny were standing, holding on to his presence as if to a lifeline. He sat silently for a minute. "There is one person I can call who teaches at Cornell University. Maybe he can think of something I haven't thought of."

Dr. Christianson got up, touched Mike's arm gently, and left the room. Mike, Jeff, and Jenny sat staring at each other. Mike and Jenny felt the same way they had at that moment in Dr. Vanook's office just a couple of months earlier—hopeless. They prayed together and Jenny called Sister Marsha to ask the nuns for their intercession. About an hour later, Dr. Christianson called. He said that his friend had an idea, a special vena MRI that involved putting dye in the veins surrounding the area in question. Even if the scan couldn't see an opening, the dye would confirm one. It was a long shot, but Christianson was willing to give it a try.

That evening, a nurse came to escort Mike to the lab for the dye test. She was spunky—just what Mike needed to lift his spirits. Jeff and Jenny headed back to the Mainstay Suites and, before going to sleep, Jenny checked her email.

-----Original Message-----
From: Kyle
Sent: Mon 2/12/01 3:44 PM
To: Jenny
Subject: Service and Love

You have told me many times that the most frustrating thing is to be unable to help someone you love. Well, I wanted you to know that I understand completely. The root source of my frustration, anger, sadness, and alienation from you is simply this: The person I most wanted to help in the world wouldn't let me help her.

My idea on Saturday was to get to Phoenix as soon as possible so that if something traumatic happened to Mike, I would be there for you, and I could console you and help with the work to be done. But the person you chose to be with you was Father Jeff. I should have seen that coming. So, this is to let you know that, in the future, I will offer my service only where it is needed and truly wanted.

Jenny didn't know how to respond. She hadn't chosen Jeff. He just came. Kyle could have done the same. She would have loved to have him by her to love and nourish her so that she could replenish herself and continue her role of caregiver. But Kyle's feelings toward Mike were like a yo-yo. One moment he was grateful to him. The next moment he was jealous of him, and Jenny hadn't wanted anything to cause Mike upset, even if it meant she couldn't be near Kyle. And at this precarious stage of Mike's life, negative energy alone could kill him. She sighed and turned off her computer.

By 6:00 AM the next morning, Jeff and Jenny were back at the hospital waiting with Mike for the test results. They waited and waited. And waited. Finally, around 3:00 PM, a nurse entered the room with a file. "I have some papers for you to sign, Father," she announced.

"Dr. Christianson needs your permission to do a TIPS procedure on you. A nurse will be in soon to prep you for surgery."

Jeff and Jenny jumped up in the air and gave each other high fives, and Mike let out a weak whoop as they went to the bed to embrace him. For the first time during the ordeal, Mike broke down, sobbing with relief. Father Jeff also started to cry, and Jenny grabbed the box of tissues off the bed stand and passed it to them. She comforted the two men and they reveled in the good news. Mike quickly signed the permission form, and he was soon on his way to surgery. Jeff had to get to the airport for a late flight, and by the time Jenny got back to the hospital, the surgery was over. It had been a lengthy and arduous procedure but it was a success.

Jenny headed down to the radiology department to leave a letter of thanks for Dr. Christianson but, as she turned, she found herself facing him. They barely knew each other but she hugged him acknowledging his courage at attempting what seemed an impossible procedure.

He stood back shaking his head and explained, "I've never experienced so many miraculous openings to blocked veins in my entire life. At least four times I was ready to give up and out of nowhere, came an opening."

Jenny knew that the Mike was given a little more time on earth due to the doctor's skill coupled with the power of so many prayers, especially Carmelite ones. When she arrived back at the suite, she collapsed onto the bed and slept better than she had in weeks.

After checking with the hospital the next morning and learning that Mike was still doing fine, Jenny lingered in the suite, treating herself to a long, hot bath. As she soaked, she contemplated answering Kyle's last email. She wanted to share Mike's good news with Kyle but she wasn't sure what else she wanted to say. Jenny composed several responses in her head, and, after drying herself off, she poured herself a cup of coffee and sat down at her computer.

-----Original Message-----
From: Jenny
Sent: Tues 2/13/01 12:30 PM
To: Kyle
Subject: RE: Service and Love

Dear Kyle,
I thought you would want to know that Mike had surgery last night and the procedure was a success. He'll be getting better now, and I thank God that everything will be all right.

Regarding your last email, I am sorry for your frustration and anger, and that you felt alienated. But you must understand that, from my perspective, you have alienated yourself. If you had wanted to be here for me, you would be here now. Instead, you have chosen to blame me for your own inaction. Father Jeff came because he wanted to come, not because I asked him to come. He did not need my permission to lend me or Mike support, and neither did you.

However, only those people who unconditionally love and honor Mike should be around him, and so it's probably best that you didn't come. I have missed you and I still do, and I love you with all my heart. But I will respect the fact that you want me in your life only as a friend.

Jenny

Jenny reread what she had written. It wasn't very loving. But, with Kyle's dark side coming out so caustically, it was the best she could do at the moment. Reluctantly, she clicked Send, but there was so much more she wanted to say.

Seventeen

Valentine's Day Slips By

FEBRUARY 14, 2001 - MARCH 13, 2001

Mike was discharged from the hospital feeling more ready than ever to tackle his cancer. Arriving at the Mainstay Suites, he fell quickly into bed and asleep.

Jenny opened her laptop to check email. Chad had sent her a quick note that her mother was doing fine, but Jenny hadn't noticed the day's date until she read Kyle's reply to her email from the previous day.

-----Original Message-----
From: Kyle
Sent: Wed, February 14, 2001 6:58 PM
To: Jenny
Subject: Happy Valentine's Day?

You didn't ask what I'm doing tonight. I suppose if you wanted to know you would have asked, at least slyly. Just as if you had wanted to know these past two weeks how my leg or health or anything about me was doing, you would have asked about that.

By the way, your Valentine from me is in your mailbox at home. I will not churn the misery we have dished out to each other. And before I climb into bed, I will pray that you and I will have happy new lives on our new paths.

One more thing everyone must say to the one (or in your case, the many) he or she loves on Valentine's Day: I love you. Kyle

Kyle's attitude broke Jenny's heart. But she owned her part in it. Right or wrong, she had made her choices, and each choice led to a new set of choices that kept moving her in the direction where she now found herself. She hit the reply button with a one-sentence message: "I love you, too."

Still staring at her computer screen, Jenny wondered if Kyle was discussing his dark mood with Dr. Monroe. Even though Kyle had said goodbye, she wasn't going to give up on him. There was no point in trying to reason with him, no gain in hopeless attempts to talk this through right now. All that Jenny could do now was to take small steps to improve the situation. She wished she had sought outside help for Mike sooner so she could find a way to split her time between caring for her mom, Earl, and Mike, and spending time with Kyle. Somehow, she had believed she could juggle all those balls in the air at one time.

When Jeff returned to take over caregiver duties for Mike, Jenny felt relieved. By Friday, after weeks away, Jenny was on a plane heading home. Chad met his mom at the airport and took her straight to Ellen's house. In the time that Jenny had been gone, Ellen had deteriorated more than Chad had let on. Her mother looked much weaker and had been spending more and more time in bed. The hospice team and Chad had done a good job of holding things together, but now it was time for Jenny to spend some quality time with her mother. Earl gave Jenny a warm embrace and was clearly relieved that she'd returned.

Jenny sat on the bed next to her mother and gave her a prolonged hug. She felt Ellen's fragile body in her arms and was careful not to squeeze her too tightly. But neither did she want to let go. It was obvious how much Ellen had missed her daughter. Jenny felt guilty for having been away too long.

"It's so good to see you," Ellen said, smiling feebly at her daughter. "How is Father Mike?"

"He's much better. The TIPS procedure definitely bought him some time. Now, it's just a matter of whether the alternative cancer treatment can turn things around for him. I don't know. It's hard to tell. At least he's out of pain for the moment. How about you?"

Brilliant sunlight beamed through the window and lit up Ellen's face. "I'm going to get better. I have to get better. Earl needs me."

"I know, Mom. Do you feel like you're making any progress?" Jenny asked.

"Some days I do. I want to start walking around a little more. I think that will help." Ellen paused for a moment and seemed hesitant to say what was on her mind. "Jenny, something strange happened to me while you were gone."

"What, Mom?"

Ellen paused again before she spoke. She looked up at Jenny with wondering eyes. "Mother came to visit me. I saw her sitting in that chair." Ellen pointed across the room.

Jenny absorbed what Ellen was saying before she spoke again. Her grandmother had passed away about eight years earlier. "Did she say anything to you?"

"No, she just sat there." Ellen sighed. "She was wearing the polka-dotted navy blue dress she was buried in. She sat there just like she would if she had come to visit me when she was alive."

"How did it make you feel?"

Ellen started to cry. "Scared. I thought she was here to help me make the transition from this world to the next. But I don't think I'm dying. I'm going to get better. I just have to get better."

Jenny held her mother and, for the next few minutes, they were silent, eyes locked onto one another's.

Ellen soon got a hold of herself and changed the subject. "How are you and Kyle doing?"

"Not so well. He broke up with me. Being gone so long really jeopardized our relationship. I can't tell you how much it hurts. I'm hoping that I can make it up to him but I don't know . . ."

"You have been gone a long time, Jenny. You know I'm fond of Kyle but...well, he's a lot to handle"

"He's high maintenance, that's for sure. And he is very critical of my friendship with Mike. And the O'Connors. And my politics. And my lifestyle. But I love him, Mom. He has so many good qualities."

Reaching out to touch Jenny's hand, her mother spoke softly. "I want you to be happy and I just don't know if this can ever turn into a relationship that's good for you."

"Let's face it. No one is perfect. When things are good between us, they're very good. And when things are bad, they're horrible. But I love him and I really want to try to put things back together between us. Some of this is my fault."

"Kyle can be very controlling. While you were gone, I guess you asked him to make sure I ate. Believe me, he never left from one of our visits until he saw me eat *something*."

They laughed. "Yeah, he can be bossy. He would run every little detail of my life if he had his way, but that's what makes him so good at his job. Somehow I think we can work those things out. Right now, the problems we're having I have helped create. I don't know of anyone who would have put up with my going to the Bahamas and then to Arizona to care for another man."

"Oh, Kyle loves you, Jenny, there's no mistaking that."

"We've had some rough times, but he does make me happy, Mom. I love him so much. In many ways, he and I are more suited for each other than Don or Matt and I were."

"Kyle is struggling with a lot of things right now," Ellen offered. "He visited me a lot while you were gone. He's worried about his boys, and that stirs up tension with his ex-wife. He misses you. He's jealous over your relationships with Mike and Jeff."

"Yeah, he has tunnel vision about that. Father Jeff took my place with Mike so I could come home. I wish Kyle could know that."

"Well, there is a lot going on for Kyle. He has talked to me some, and the rest I can read between the lines in the newspaper."

"Like what?"

"Apparently his involvement with the SOA Watch protests is a no-win situation for him politically," Ellen said.

"I read that School of Americas was changing its name, but it seems like just a cover up to get the opposition off its back."

"Well, Kyle is in the thick of it. I understand our need for training military leaders but if it is true that we are training people who can become a threat to our own country, I don't understand it. Why would our government do that?"

"I don't know the answer. Those who support the school say they are teaching democracy. Those who oppose the school say they are training assassins. I've missed talking to Kyle about it."

"I think he's doing a courageous thing, trying to get the base closed. But when you get in the middle of something like that, you can't please all the people all the time." Ellen smiled, knowing that Jenny could relate. "I think he could use your support on this right now. His political career may be in serious trouble."

"See, Mom. This is an example of why I love Kyle so much. He has such strong ethics."

"I thought if you knew what he's struggling with, you might better understand his moods. This might be one way you can be there for him. I've had to learn to do that with Earl."

Jenny headed home and, before even unpacking, she called Kyle. He was detached, but agreed to get together with her for dinner the next evening. When he arrived to pick her up, he was cordial but cool. Over dinner, they kept the conversation light. Jenny was eager to resolve the tension between them. Much to her delight, after their meal, he suggested they return to his place to continue their conversation in private.

Kyle flipped the switch on the gas fireplace as soon as they arrived. They made themselves comfortable on pillows in front of the hearth.

"As much as I love you, Jenny, I just can't take the continuous rejection," he said once he had settled in. Winky was lying nearby, keeping a protective eye on them both. "I need close companionship. This whole ordeal of your being in Arizona with Mike has been more than I can handle."

"Kyle, I got so caught up in his fight for life that I went overboard. I know it. But when someone is dying, where do you draw the line?"

"Well, I admit that I might have the same problem," Kyle said. "You have pointed out, and you're right, that we are alike in so many ways. We're both gregarious, warm people, and others are easily drawn to us. And we both have a tendency to want to save the world."

Jenny nodded, recognizing that he had articulated one of the struggles she had lived with throughout her life.

"I think we'd both like more simplicity in our lives," he continued, "because, although we can handle more complexity than most people, the number and depth of our 'causes' sometimes becomes a greater burden than we can handle."

Kyle had obviously given a lot of thought to how he was going say
that to her. He wasn't evidencing any anger, either, and he wasn't
putting her down. He was simply sharing his insights with her. With
this tone prevailing, Jenny relaxed. Kyle had hit the crux of a
significant part of their problem. With him owning it, he made it easier
for her to own it, too.

"You're right," Jenny said. "Since my divorce from Matt, you know
that I've had this concept of having an inner circle of friends.
Somehow, in my vision of it, we would all get along, all be on a similar
journey. Through our mutual support, we'd all be drawn closer to God.
I really believed it could work."

"Maybe it could if we weren't sexually involved. Somehow that
changes the equation. But if I step out of the way . . ."

"Let's keep exploring this with you in the picture. I love you, Kyle.
Despite what I emailed, I'm not ready to give up on us."

Kyle looked longingly at her. She held his gaze. "I do believe that,"
he said. "But just when I'm convinced you're willing to substantially
'rearrange' your life so we can grow closer, something comes up which
confirms that you haven't made any significant changes at all. I want to
mean more to you than Mike, Jeff, or any man. Period."

"I know you think they are more important to me than you are . . .
but it isn't true," Jenny said. "It's just that I'm on overload right now. I
have more than my share of people who are depending on me. I don't
know how to take care of all of them and give our relationship priority
as well. I am open to suggestions, sweetheart. Really, I am."

Kyle could sense the sincerity in her voice. He believed that she
truly did want to elevate his importance in her life, and she was asking
a fair question. "Okay, here is one way. So far, you've been unwilling to
give up your Sunday dinners with Mike and his friends. I'm not sure
why they are so important to you. But you have to understand that it's
hard to justify socializing on that level with another man—I don't care
if he is a priest—when you and I have a committed relationship. Can
you imagine any of the men we know in relationships dining out once a
month with another woman or two and their significant partners not
getting upset?"

"I hadn't looked at it that way. I've been having dinner with Mike on Sundays long before you came into the picture. It never occurred to me that I should stop once I met you. I don't know how to explain it, sweetheart. All I know is that I didn't have a father growing up. I didn't have a brother. I was raised only by women and by nuns. Other than my high school boyfriend, who played a critical role during those years, I didn't have any men in my life at all. Except for priests. They were my male role models. They were wholesome, beautiful, spiritual men. So for me to be close to priests is as normal as you making friends with female lawyers."

"But what about all of this from Mike's perspective?" he asked, pressing the subject. "Why doesn't he have the decency to back off?"

"I don't want whatever I say next to turn into an argument. So if I say something difficult for you to hear, are you open to hearing it?" Jenny asked.

"You're just going to look for ways to justify this whole thing, aren't you, Jenny?"

"No. I've never been more eager to resolve this with you. And I want to figure out what my part is in this so I can fix it. But I'm going to give you some feedback that you need to hear if you are ever going to have a successful relationship with a woman—me or anyone else."

Jenny gazed at the fire for a moment before she spoke. "When I first met Mike, it was I who was needy and he who was able to help me through the emotional down time I was experiencing with my divorce from Matt. He also shared a lot of personal things with me, and we even talked about how close we felt to each other. But talk was as far as it went, for both of us. There's no question that Mike loves me deeply, but—"

"And that's the problem. He's a priest, for godsake. He is not supposed to love a woman."

"He's human, Kyle. Priests may take a vow of celibacy, but it doesn't put a fence around their hearts. You know Mike was out of the priesthood for about ten years. I asked him why he didn't get married while he was out. He told me that he missed preaching the Gospel, both in words and by his lifestyle. Mike is a good priest, Kyle. But that doesn't mean that he doesn't have feelings. What matters is how he *acts* on those feelings. Mike has always remained true to his vows. He has never crossed that line and never would."

"That's really hard to swallow, Jenny. Maybe it's because I'm a convert to Catholicism, but it just seems unbelievable."

"This is the part that's hard for me to tell you. Partly, it's because of your . . . because of your mood swings and erratic behavior. Mike loves me and, I believe, truly wants what's best for me. But your angry outbursts, your mood swings, your obsession with me, your need to control my every move, your always putting yourself first over me—Mike doesn't want to see you hurt me. He's concerned that, in my moment of need, you won't be there for me. He is terrified that, in the end, I'll one day be devastated by your behavior. Does he love me? Yes. Does he care deeply about my well-being? Yes. Does he enjoy my company? Yes. But at the very core of it, he is afraid that you won't stand by me when I most need you. In part, I think he's hung in so that he can be there to pick up the pieces when you abandon me." Jenny stopped talking and took a deep breath.

His response both pleased and surprised Jenny. "Am I really that bad? Does he see me as some kind of monster out to destroy you?"

"No, and this is as hard for me to talk about as it is for you to hear. But you have some issues. I think you won't deny that. With Harvey's help, you are attempting to control the mood swings with medications. But sometimes your moods get away from you. One moment you respect Mike and are grateful to him. The next moment, you describe him as the most disdainful man on the face of the earth. Apart from his feelings for me—if you can separate that out—how do you feel about Mike? I mean, really? That's what has prevented me from having you join me in caring for him. When you're down on him, you are *consumed* with hate. He's scared of your behavior. And, in those times, I'm scared to have you around him."

"You're right," Kyle said. "This is hard. What I need is a woman to love who will love me back. She would go to work, come home, and have no other serious friendships in her life but me. Maybe I need to keep it that simple. I don't know if I have what it takes to deal with all of this other stuff."

"Okay, total honesty here. Do you think that part of the problem is that you are threatened by the way Mike loves me? I mean, look at this, sweetheart. You love me but want to control me. Mike cares about me but isn't trying to be in charge of me. You're critical of so many aspects of my life. He accepts me the way I am. You seem to love me when I make *you* happy. Mike seems to love me and want *me* to be happy. Maybe this is what the competitiveness is all about. From your side, it's the fear that you can't love me as unconditionally as Mike does, and from his perspective, that he will lose precious time with me if I give in to your demands."

Kyle was reflecting on Jenny's words. After a minute, he responded. "Do you love Mike? I mean, do you love him the way you love me?" There was vulnerability in his voice as he asked the question.

"I love Mike. It's obvious by my actions. We're exceptionally close friends. But I've never been physically involved with him. Kyle, I'm *in* love with you, not Mike, and I keep growing more in love with you every day. I missed you terribly when we were apart. I want to blend my life with yours and, to do that, I am willing to make some adjustments—like my Sunday dinners. But I'm not willing to give up my friends entirely to have a life with you. Obviously, my friendships will change over time, but do you really want me to relinquish them all together? Most of all, I want you to trust me, to believe that I really do love you even when I'm not with you."

"But when you're with Mike or Jeff or Sherri or Kerry, you really love them, too. That's the problem, Jenny. You give yourself so completely to whomever you're with."

"That's me, Kyle. That's who I am."

"Maybe part of your bond with Mike is that he's safe."

"I do feel safe with Mike," Jenny said. "I know he cares about me and would never abandon me."

"Except for dying. Death is a form of abandonment."

"I hadn't thought about that. But you're right," Jenny acknowledged. "Even though it will not be his choice, I will experience abandonment when he dies. And even more so when Mom dies. There is no worse kind of pain for me. Fear of being abandoned goes so deep with me."

"And with me, too. Josh and I were both abandoned by our parents, whoever they are."

"So maybe you and I are too much alike to be able to complement each other's needs."

"Maybe that is the root of your bond with Mike," Kyle said. "You trust him completely. With me, you feel vulnerable."

"It's true. You could leave me anytime your mood swings in that direction. Maybe I hold on to my inner circle because if I fall, I know they will catch me. But if I fall with you, I'm not sure you'll be there. Maybe that's why I hold back with you."

"Would you have ever married me . . . I mean, if we worked out this trust issue?"

"It is a trust issue, isn't it? On both our parts. You're afraid that I'll love others more than I love you. And I'm afraid that you'll leave me. We love each other, but we haven't learned to trust each other yet."

"So what happens if we ever mastered both at one time?" Kyle asked.

"I still don't know that I want to be married in the traditional sense again. You know how hard I worked at both my marriages. At this stage of my life, I'm just not sure that is what I want or need. I've told you how I feel. It all seemed simple before you came to matter so much to me."

"Why? Do you think I've complicated it?"

"Ogod! Let me count the ways," Jenny teased.

"Okay Ms. Browning," Kyle mocked as he pulled Jenny closer.

"I love you so much, Kyle," Jenny whispered.

"I love you too, sweet pea," Kyle said as he squeezed her tighter.

"There are so many reasons why we should go our separate ways. But do you understand why it's hard for me to let go of you?"

"Because I'm so handsome and even-tempered and understanding . . . and steady in your life?" Kyle grinned.

Jenny poked him in the ribs. "I wish!" Winky perked up to join in. He licked Kyle's face, then Jenny's, and settled back down in front of the fire.

"Seriously, Kyle, I trust in our ability to grow together. There aren't many men out there like you. Even though we may not be where we should be yet, I believe in our ability to get there eventually."

"You've already helped me grow," Kyle said. "I'm a Catholic now, for starters. And you got me through one of the worst depressions I've ever known. But your need to be so emotionally involved with other people won't change, Jenny. And I can't go through the same unhealthy cycle with you again. I secretly suspected we'd pick up as usual when you returned home. And I knew we'd fall right back into our old habits until the next time. But the truth is, I do want marriage and everything it entails. We are just two people hopelessly in love but destined to walk different paths."

Jenny started to cry. She was exhausted from all that she had been through in Mike's fight for life. She was distressed at seeing her mother and facing serious doubts about her winning her fight for life. Kyle held her as her tears turned into sobs.

"I feel a bright spot in my heart for all the wonderful experiences we've shared," Kyle whispered. "No one has ever made me happier. I have no regrets and neither should you. I want us to be at peace with each other."

His seeming detachment from her made Jenny want him more. Hearing him confirm their breakup devastated her. She couldn't meet his eyes, nor could she speak.

He recognized that she was feeling the depths of abandonment she had just described. If only he could take her pain away without bewildering her. He felt separate from her and yet one with her all in an instant. Jenny continued to cry, and he rocked her until she finally quieted down.

Jenny thought of the paper boat analogy Kyle had used to describe the newness of their relationship months earlier. She felt like that boat had just drifted away from shore and was being carried out to sea, tossed about by massive currents.

Jenny rose quietly and offered her hand to Kyle. When he took it, she led him upstairs to the bedroom. Her stormy tide had turned, and she was going to steer it toward calm water. Silently, they undressed each other, and then lay quietly in each other's arms.

Her love revealed itself through the softness of her touch and her gentle looks as she gazed adoringly into Kyle's eyes. He held her in his arms and stroked her body. There was no need for words.

As their lips met, she was surprised by his tenderness. Kyle pulled her closer, comforting her, and she felt his love. Their movements were natural—Kyle kissing her breast, her hand caressing his chest and nipples, his body moving on top of hers as she opened herself to receive him. Jenny pressed longingly against him. For the first time since they had known each other, she felt completely safe in his embrace. Tonight he *was* there for her. She wanted time put on hold and the world to stand still. For this moment, she felt reassured that he would not abandon her in her time of need. She was losing too many people at once. She could not endure the possibility of losing him, too. Never before had she made such passionate love.

The next morning Kyle awoke early with his arms still wrapped around Jenny. He slipped a numbed arm out from under her without her waking and watched her as she slept. He felt Jenny's deep, committed love for him. If only she could sustain it. He recognized that his wavering was much more about him than about her. He loved her with every ounce of his being. So why was it so difficult for him to trust in her love? *Was it a natural outflow of being given away at birth?* He wondered. He made a mental note to discuss it with Harvey. He was convincing himself that, once he found such a deep and mutually shared love, it was far better to stay with the person and work through problems than to begin the search for real love all over again. Despite his resolve to end their love affair the previous night, Kyle realized that he was not ready to give up on Jenny.

The next day was Earl's 86th birthday. Slowly making her way down the stairs, Ellen joined Jenny and Chad for the celebration, a bit lackluster with all the illness surrounding them. The previous year Jenny had given Earl a talking calculator so that he could use it with his failing eyesight. This year, she gave him a talking watch. Every hour on the hour, it announced the time. And at certain set times of the day, it would make the sound of a rooster crowing.

As Jenny walked her mother back upstairs and tucked her in, she sat on the edge of the bed. "Mom, I'm so worried about you."

"I'm going to get better soon, Jenny. I have to. As you can see, Earl needs me. But let's not talk about me. How are you and Kyle?"

"I've put our relationship to the ultimate test, but I think we're going to survive all of these crises."

"All that matters to me is whether he makes you happy."

"He does, Mom. He can make my life miserable but overall he makes me very happy." Jenny reflected on the night before and felt more secure about her relationship with Kyle than she had since she had been gone so much.

As she walked downstairs, Jenny glanced toward the dining room at the old grandfather clock, an heirloom that had been in their family for more than 150 years. It was one of her mother's most prized possessions. For the first time ever, Jenny noticed no sound coming out of it. The symbolism was ominous to Jenny.

"What's happening to our life, Mom?" Chad asked walking up behind her. "Everything seems to be falling apart around us. I hate it."

"I know," Jenny said, "but it doesn't just seem that way, it *is* that way. And it's scary." Ellen, Earl, Mike—the life they'd known was coming undone, and there was nothing they could do to stop it.

At least, Jenny thought, she and Kyle had revived their relationship. She was grateful that they were back together, and talk of their breaking up had dissipated. In fact, she felt they had worked their way to an even deeper level of understanding. Before it was time to part again, they both wanted to seal the fragile bond between them by spending as much time together as they could.

Over lunch the next day, Jenny brought up the subject to Kyle of his meeting with SOA Watch. "Dealing with these military issues must be hard on you, Kyle," Jenny said.

"More than I thought they would," Kyle answered. "Closing down a military base isn't that easy. And especially with all the military-related issues coming across my desk every day. Terrorism throughout the world is quietly on the rise. Although few government officials seem to be taking it very seriously, I have reports that something could happen in our country any time. And, of course, New York, Washington D.C., and California are the most likely targets. I feel such a responsibility. The governor has a business background. Even though he and I have different political views, he relies on my judgment, especially in regard to legal issues, threats to our state, and the role of the military bases in our state.

"You really think something might happen, don't you?" Jenny asked, seeing the fear in his eyes.

"With the reports I'm receiving, yes, I'm very worried. Did you know that ten years ago, a group of academics and historians compiled this startling information: Over the past 5600 years, the world has known less than 300 years of peace. During this period, there have been more than 14,000 wars, in which more than 3.5 billion people were slaughtered in the name of peace?"

Jenny loved the depth of Kyle's knowledge. "Have you ever discussed 'respect for life' issues with the governor?"

Kyle rolled his eyes. "Jed's beliefs in that area are inconsistent. He's pro-life but contradicts that by being pro-war and pro-death penalty. My stance is just the opposite, although I do believe in a woman's right to choose termination under extenuating circumstances."

"You are doing good work, sweetheart, but you definitely have your work cut out for you with the governor."

The next morning, Kyle drove Jenny to the airport and kissed her farewell. "I love the pilgrim soul in you and, this week, you have shown me 'the sorrows of your changing face.' Come back to me soon."

For the next few weeks, Jenny divided her time between Tempe and Sacramento. Mike was finishing up his cancer treatment with Dr. Rubin. The next decision needed to be made: Where would he go? He didn't want to be alone, even with a professional caregiver on duty. After much discussion, Father Jeff offered to have Mike stay with him at the rectory.

On St. Patrick's Day weekend, Kyle made plans to go to Santa Monica with the Irish Consulate. Kyle asked Jenny to join them for the parade and weekend festival sponsored by the Irish Congress of Southern California. Once again, she felt a familiar tension in her heart as he made the request. *I need to get Mike home and settled,* she thought *and I need to check on Mom.* But Jenny also knew she needed to be with Kyle.

Eighteen

Dying and Death

With Mike's Tempe treatments complete, Jenny and he flew together from Phoenix to Los Angeles. From there, Mike was to fly on to Sacramento where his nephew, Joe, would meet him and get him settled in his old room at the rectory. Jenny was planning to stay on for the three-day weekend with Kyle.

On the plane at LAX, Jenny made sure Mike was comfortable in his seat. She had ordered a wheelchair to be waiting for him in Sacramento and asked the stewardess not to let him off the plane there until his nephew arrived. It was hard to say goodbye to Mike. They had just lived through an unforgettable chapter in his life.

"I will be indebted to you for the rest of my life for what you've done for me," Mike said. He could barely say anything sentimental anymore without crying.

"I'm glad I could be there for you. I love you, Mike."

"Likewise," he said as Jenny hugged him, and she exited the plane. Rarely had she heard Mike say, "I love you too."

As Jenny headed down to claim her luggage, she thought of her mom. Something told her she should have stayed on the plane and gone home to see Ellen. *Stay in the present*, she told herself. *I am where I need to be at this moment. I really need this time with Kyle—for both of our sakes.* Jenny had only precious minutes to make a radical change—from the world of Mike and cancer treatment to the world of Kyle and the St.

Patrick's Day parade. Her mind was still drawn back to her mother, but she was trying to let it go.

As Jenny waited at the LAX baggage claim, Kyle approached with the Irish Consulate and his wife. His eyes lit up when he spotted Jenny, and she rushed to his open arms.

Kyle had reserved a beautiful room for them at the Huntley Santa Monica Beach Hotel, just two blocks from the beach. After they had settled in, they went to O'Brien's Irish Pub for dinner. When they got back to the room, Jenny checked her cell phone messages. Ellen's hospice nurse had left a voicemail telling Jenny that Ellen was not doing well. Jenny immediately called her mother's house but got no answer. Then she called Chad, but he didn't answer either. Jenny shared the news with Kyle, and he suggested she remain calm until she knew exactly what was happening.

Jenny slept fitfully. She called Ellen the next morning, but her mother was sleeping and Earl didn't want to wake her. She asked if Chad had been over. Not yet, Earl said. Jenny felt better having at least spoken to Earl, and she got ready for the biggest event of the weekend—meeting Kyle's mother.

As Kyle drove them across town to meet Glennys Anderson, Jenny felt anxious.

They pulled into the driveway and, as they walked toward the house, Jenny spotted Glennys standing behind the screen door, watching them approach. Jenny noted how tall and stately Glennys was for a woman in her nineties. Opening the door, mother greeted son with a warm hug, and then she embraced Jenny.

Inside, Glennys served juice and homemade fruitcake, and then she brought out the family photographs to share with Jenny. It was a good visit. Before leaving, Jenny and Kyle posed for pictures with his mother. With the digital camera, they could look at each photo. Jenny could see Kyle's pride and joy as he stood between his mother and Jenny with his arms around each of them.

From his mother's house, Kyle drove them to the parade. Along the route were Irish fanatics watching Irish dancers and bagpipers, and Irish and Celtic organizations were in heavy attendance. Jenny and Kyle rode the float with the Irish consulate and his wife, tossing green-wrapped candy to the crowd. Waving to the people along the parade route, they felt like celebrities. Kyle could tell that Jenny was a bit preoccupied, but he chalked it up to her concern for Ellen. However, he felt a distance between them.

The moment Kyle and Jenny arrived back in their room, Jenny nervously called Ellen, but she was still sleeping. As much as Jenny wanted to be with Kyle, she knew she had to get home. She hung up the phone and booked a flight home. As she began to pack, she explained the situation to Kyle.

Kyle was openly disheartened, and feeling his familiar head-heart battle. He understood that her mother needed her and she had to get home. But she had been gone from him so much, always taking care of others. It was his turn now. He needed her to be with him.

On the way to her flight, Jenny finally reached Chad and asked him to pick her up at the airport. Kyle offered to come with her, but she knew he had appointments to keep. She kissed Kyle goodbye but saw the forlorn look in his eyes. Once again, Jenny's heart was torn.

Earl was sitting at his desk when Chad and Jenny walked through the door. She could see relief written all over his face when he saw her. The three of them walked upstairs together and found Ellen sleeping and breathing heavily. Jenny pulled back the covers and was sickened by what she saw. Ellen hadn't been to the bathroom nor had her diaper been changed in at least 24 hours. She was lying in her own excrement; it was all over her legs and all over the sheets.

Jenny didn't know where to start in cleaning up her mother. After getting over the shock, she woke Ellen. She revived slowly, and Jenny spoke quietly with her while she gained consciousness. She told her that she and Chad were going to help her out of bed. Jenny guided Chad to begin running bath water in the tub. A bed bath was out of the question. Ellen seemed aware of the situation but shyly hid her embarrassment. Chad brought his mom several warm washcloths, and Jenny cleaned up the worst of it. The two of them helped her sit up, put her legs over the side of the bed, and got her to a standing position. With Chad on one side and Jenny on the other, they guided Ellen toward the bathroom. Ellen was limping, and when Jenny asked her about it, Ellen remarked that she had fallen a few days ago. But even a potentially broken foot was incidental at the moment.

Once they got her to the bathroom, Jenny removed Ellen's diaper and washed her legs while Chad supported his grandmother. Then they guided Ellen to sit on the toilet. Jenny sent Chad downstairs to get Ellen a glass of water while she cleaned out the tub, but he didn't return for at least 15 minutes. Then she stripped her mother's bed and, as she was making it up with fresh linens, Chad returned.

"Are you all right?" Jenny asked. The color had drained from Chad's face.

He nodded. "This is really hard for me, Mom. I threw up downstairs. I've never seen anything like this before. I'm sorry."

"Hang in with me, sweetie. I can't do this without you. We need each other to get her through this."

Together, Chad and Jenny got Ellen from the toilet to the tub. She had lost over 40 pounds, but what was left was dead weight. When they lowered her into the warm water, she let out a sigh of both relief and joy.

"This feels so good," she moaned.

Chad cleaned up the toilet while Jenny knelt over the tub and helped her mother bathe. Earl had appeared at the door and was watching helplessly. Jenny couldn't imagine how he had dealt with this the last 24 hours. He may be nearly blind, but he still had his sense of smell. For a split second, Jenny felt angry at him, but she quickly realized that he had his own health issues to deal with aside from watching his wife of over 35 years become an invalid.

After the bath, Chad and Jenny helped Ellen out of the tub. Jenny dried her off, helped her into a fresh nightgown, and slowly guided her back to bed. As they lay her back on her pillows, Ellen seemed relaxed.

"I don't know what I would do without you both," she said, smiling up at her daughter and grandson.

Chad asked if Ellen was hungry. The answer was no, but he went down to fix her something anyway. Jenny slipped into the bed beside her mother, staying until she fell asleep only moments later. Then Jenny eased out of the bed and went downstairs where she found Chad crying at the kitchen table. She held him while he cried aloud

When Jenny finally arrived at her own home, there was a phone message from Kyle. "I'm sad that you had to leave. After dropping you at the airport, I cried all the way back to the hotel. It feels like you are always leaving me. I know you had to leave, but I'm having a hard time dealing with this. I'll call you when I feel better."

Jenny went to bed in tears. Her world was falling apart. Her mother was not going to get better. *Please, God, don't let her die*, she silently prayed. *I'm not ready to let her go. I need her. Please.*

Kyle called the next morning and they said prayers together. A good night's sleep helped him put things in perspective. Kyle reassured Jenny that she had done the right thing by returning home early. He repeated how sorry he was that he had obligations in Santa Monica, but he was winding things up so he could get home to help her.

When Jenny picked Kyle up at the airport the next afternoon, he wanted to see Ellen right away. Kyle was concerned about her foot and said that he had a doctor friend who could see her immediately.

"But how will we get her there? She is so weak and frail. Can't we bring the doctor here?" Jenny asked.

"He can't X-ray her foot here. I'll just pick her up and carry her. We'll do what we have to do."

The next morning, Kyle made room in his busy schedule so he could help get Ellen to the doctor. But when he arrived at the house, Ellen was sleeping deeply. Jenny didn't try to dress her. She would take her in her robe. But she couldn't rouse her. When Kyle leaned over to pick her up, Ellen moaned. After a couple more futile attempts, they realized that their desire to get her foot examined was more for themselves than for her—their last effort to demonstrate to themselves that Ellen would get better. Moving her might be more painful to her than helpful. In deciding to let go of getting her foot X-rayed, they were admitting that the end was near.

Over the next week, Jenny spent every waking moment with her mother. Ellen's bedroom carried an odor of death. Earl seemed lost. Jenny moved into the guest room so she could take care of Ellen during the night. She would frequently crawl in bed next to Ellen. Lying as close to her mother as she could, Jenny thought back to when she was little, how she and her mom often shared a bed when they were together. They didn't always have the luxury of two beds. It was comforting to Jenny now to be that close to her mother again.

Throughout her illness, Ellen had insisted to Jenny that she was going to get well. But the night arrived when Jenny knew that the end was nearing.

"Mom, do you still think you're going to get better?" Jenny whispered, knowing the answer.

"No," Ellen replied in a faint voice.

"It's okay. I'll take care of Earl. You don't have to worry. Mom, I love you so much."

There was a pause, and then Jenny heard Ellen say ever so softly, "I love you, too, sugar."

Sugar. Jenny's mother hadn't called her that since she was a little girl. It was a southern expression. Now tears were streaming down Jenny's face, and she could barely stifle her sobs. She crawled out of bed, heading downstairs, where she could lie back in the lounge chair and cry out loud. Opening her eyes, she found Earl standing over her. Jenny told him there was no mistake that Ellen was dying. For the first time in all the years he had been her stepfather, Earl shed tears. Standing together, they held each other and cried.

Knowing that Jenny was uncomfortable leaving the house for even a quick errand, Kyle brought lunch over the next day. He tried to comfort Earl, who was no longer the macho man but was visibly shaken. He made Jenny take a brief walk with him to get her some fresh air. He felt helpless as Jenny's tears continued to flow. Before leaving to return to work, Kyle lay with Jenny across Ellen's bed doing the best they could to comfort her.

Jenny was stroking her mother's face as she asked, "Can I get you anything, Mom?"

"Un-uh," she uttered.

"Mom, we are taking care of Earl. I can't do all that you did for him, but I will do my best. I promise."

Kyle held Ellen's hand as he added, "And I'll take care of Jenny. Thanks to you, Ellen, we've worked a lot of things out with each other. I will be there for her."

"Okay," Ellen whispered, barely audibly.

"I'm going to the store to get a few groceries for you and Earl, Mom. I'll be right back. Kyle will stay here with you."

At the grocery, Jenny hurriedly filled her cart and was approaching the check-out stand when her cell phone rang, "Get home quickly," Kyle said. The line went dead. Abandoning her shopping cart, she drove back to her mother's home at lightening speed. If a police car had tried to stop her, she would have outrun it.

Arriving, Jenny ran up the stairs and into the bedroom and found Earl and Kyle sitting by Ellen's bedside. She looked at Kyle and he shook his head. Realizing this was the end, Jenny knelt next to the bed and stroked her mother's face and hair. Ellen opened her eyes, smiled faintly and sighed. Within moments, she had taken her last breath. Jenny closed Ellen's eyes and kissed her on the cheek. She sat next to her in silence and prayed.

Over the next couple of hours, Jenny felt numb. All that followed Ellen's death seemed surreal. The hospice nurse arrived and Ellen was officially declared dead. The nurse called the coroner's office and Kyle called the mortuary. When the morticians arrived, they asked if Jenny needed any more time with her mother. She shook her head. She had said her goodbyes. Ellen's body was carried out and placed in the back of the hearse. Kyle put his arm around Jenny and stood with her as they stood in the street watching the hearse drive away.

A childhood memory suddenly flashed through Jenny's mind. It was one of her mother standing on a curb, waving goodbye as a young Jenny was being driven away. Only this time it was Jenny standing on the curb as her mother was being driven away. She continued staring down the street long after the hearse turned the corner, experiencing a moment of complete and utter emptiness. She was so grateful that Kyle was there. They stood and held each other and let the tears flow. Then they walked back inside to comfort Earl.

When Jenny arrived home later that day, she read the framed card Mike had given her years ago: "Nothing can make up for the absence of someone we love. . . . For the gap, as long as it remains unfilled, preserves the bond between us. . . . God does not fill it, but . . . keeps it empty and so helps us to keep alive our forever communion with each other even at the cost of pain." Jenny knew it was true. The pain would never completely go away.

Jenny went through unconscious motions the next day when meeting Chad and Earl at the mortuary for the viewing. Kyle had meetings all day and promised to meet her later. As the threesome walked into the viewing room, Jenny was immediately aware how peaceful her mother looked lying in the coffin, more so than she had on her deathbed. Earl held onto the coffin to steady himself and Jenny stood between Chad and Earl with her arms around their waists as all three looked down at Ellen—grandmother, wife, and mother—aware how different their lives would be without her. As Chad and Jenny turned to leave, Earl hung back. Tears filled his eyes as the elderly man leaned down to kiss his wife's cheek for the last time. Softly, he whispered to her: "It won't be long. I'll be joining you soon."

The days that followed were filled with cremation, funeral, and burial preparations. Jenny chose to have the service at Carmel with Father Jeff and Father Mike helping to decide on Scripture readings and prayers. Jenny stayed with Kyle but she was too teary and restless to get much sleep.

Although Mike was growing weaker day by day, he was determined to participate. But even the preparation for his homily exhausted Mike. Jenny saw him sitting in the dining room at the rectory, his notes to one side, and his forehead resting against the table. Though very ill, nothing would stop him from speaking at Jenny's mother's funeral.

On the day of the service, Jenny had Earl's flower arrangement placed to the right side of the altar: yellow and white roses—Ellen had been his "yellow rose of Texas"—mingled with lilies of the valley, small white blooms that looked like tiny bells. On two easels to the left, Jenny positioned two enlarged poster-size photographs of Ellen—one when she was about 25, with jet-black hair just covering her ears, and the other at 75, when she had gray hair cropped around her ears. Fifty years apart but, to Jenny, Ellen was just as beautiful at an elderly age as she was as a young woman. Both photographs captured the sweetness in Ellen's eyes that was always characteristic of her.

During the service, Kyle read from Corinthians: "Love is patient, love is kind. It does not envy, it does not boast, it is not proud. It is not rude, it is not self-seeking, it is not easily angered, it keeps no record of wrongs. Love does not delight in evil but rejoices with the truth. It always protects, always trusts, always hopes, always perseveres."

When it came time for the homily, Mike stood unsteadily, leaning heavily on the podium. "When I look for an expression that sets the Christian belief about the mystery of death apart, the word that comes to me is exaltation!" he began, extending his hands upward.

As Mike faltered for a moment, Kyle, on the edge of his seat near the podium, was ready to steady him. But Mike recovered his balance. "Exaltation means that, through this life passage, God is doing something magnificent now—not in the past and not in the future. It means that we are being exalted now in such a way that all of us who share in that person's life experience a major transformation—a transformation that sees a God who is acting, revealing, and bringing joy, peace, tranquility, and hopefulness to us in a way that we have never experienced before. As Jesus described in First Corinthians, Chapter Two, Verses 9 and 10, 'The eye has not seen, and the ear has not heard, nor has it entered into the heart of man, what things God has prepared for those who love him.'"

Jenny was the last to speak and trusted with God's help that she would be able to hold her emotions in check. She began with a recitation of her mother's favorite song, *The Bluebird of Happiness*.

"In a very real sense, this was her life philosophy," Jenny said as she pulled out a sheet of paper and began to read:

> Be like I, hold your head up high
> Till you find a blue bird of happiness.
> You will find greater peace of mind
> Knowing there's a blue bird of happiness.
> And when he sings to you
> Though you're deep in blue,
> You will see a ray of light creep through.
> And so remember this, life is no abyss,
> Somewhere there's a bluebird of happiness.

Jenny then described the conversation she and Ellen had while lying next to her mother the night before Ellen died. "'I love you, sugar'—that was the last full sentence Mom said to me." Jenny paused again gaining control of her emotions and sending a silent prayer to God to help her through this. "I love you, too, Mom. I'll miss those morning phone calls asking how my world is going. I'll miss our mealtimes together and having you there when my world isn't going so well. But I know you're at peace. No more suffering, no more illness. I'll miss you terribly." Jenny choked. No more words would come.

While the gathering headed to Jenny's home for the wake, Kyle helped her load up the pictures, flowers, and the urn to carry them back to her house. Jenny felt comforted and grateful to have him by her side. When she walked into the house, she felt slightly overwhelmed that so many had come to pay their respects to her mom and to offer their comfort to her family. Jenny made her way from group to group, doing her best to be cordial and welcoming. After a few minutes, Kyle whispered to Jenny that he needed to get back to work and would stop by afterwards to check on Earl who had gone straight home after the funeral.

While the guests enjoyed the food and lingered visiting with one another, Jenny showed Mike to her guest room where he desperately needed to rest after the service.

By late in the afternoon, the gathering had dwindled. Jeff returned from his parish to pick Mike up and take him home. As they stood in the doorway, the phone rang. It was Kyle.

"Is everyone gone?" he asked.

"Mike and Jeff are just leaving," she said.

"They're still there?" Kyle's voice was loud and sharp.

"They're leaving, sweetheart," Jenny said again, perplexed at Kyle's disapproving tone. "Jeff has the car running and Mike has one foot out the door." More than any time since she'd known him, Jenny needed Kyle *not* to be angry with her, today of all days. "Please come over. I need you."

"Well, I don't see how," Kyle retorted sarcastically. "Seems to me like you don't need me at all. I'm sure Mike and Jeff have seen to your needs very well."

"Kyle, please, I—" But Kyle had already hung up.

Mike saw the distress on Jenny's face and stepped back inside. He offered to stay, but Jenny insisted she just needed to be alone. She began to cry as she walked toward Mike. He opened his arms to her and she fell into them, crying with both anger and disappointment. Minutes later, they were still standing in the entranceway when the door flew open and Kyle came barging in, almost knocking Mike over.

"Thought you said he was leaving," he told Jenny with abruptness. "Didn't think I'd catch you in a lie, did you?" Then he turned and went back outside. Jenny was in shock. She'd said that Mike was leaving, and he was until Kyle's call. Suddenly, Kyle blasted back in the door, picked up a book he had left earlier, mumbled an expletive, and left again. Mike looked at Jenny and shook his head. Telling him she'd be all right, Jenny told him to go home and get some rest. He left, albeit reluctantly.

Jenny was hurt but furious. She felt like a knife had gone through her heart. This was the day of her mother's funeral. On this day of all days, Jenny's need for Kyle was magnified. She called Kyle and begged him to come back and spend the night with her. But he refused. Exasperated, Jenny took a sleeping pill and cried herself to sleep. She cried the tears of a little girl missing her mother and of a forsaken woman missing her man. She felt completely abandoned by the two people who mattered most in her life.

Around 11:00 PM, the phone woke her up. To her disappointment, it wasn't Kyle. It was a woman's voice.

"I'm trying to find Kyle Anderson," she said.

"So am I," Jenny said. "I don't know where he is."

"Well, tell him that his son is in jail."

Jenny realized that it was Kyle's ex-wife calling. She sounded greatly distressed. "Jo? Oh, my God, I'm so sorry."

In a choked voice, Jo said that their younger son, Marty, had been arrested for driving under the influence. For a brief moment the two women shared heartfelt exchanges, mother to mother. Jenny empathized deeply as she recalled a similar situation she had experienced with Chad. Anxiously, Jenny called Kyle's house. No answer. Even if he were there, he probably wouldn't take a call from her in his current state of mind. She got up, got dressed and, with barely enough of the sleeping pill worn off, drove to his house. Her eyes were swollen from so much crying. She rang his doorbell. No answer. She looked in the garage. No car. It was now nearly midnight. Where could he be? As she was leaving him a note telling him about his son, Kyle pulled into his driveway. As Jenny explained about his son, the new crisis of the moment took the focus off of their issues.

They went inside, and Kyle phoned the jail. By law, Marty had to be held overnight. There was nothing more he could do until morning.

At first, Jenny empathized with Kyle. When Chad was still in his teens, he had gotten a DUI and spent the night in jail. But through the wee hours of the morning, the shared moment slipped into an argument as their focus returned to what had happened earlier.

"Why did you lie to me?" Kyle asked.

"I didn't lie to you! Why did you abandon me?"

"Because I wasn't needed," he shouted. "You had Mike!"

"For God's sake, Kyle, 'Love is patient; love is kind; it does not envy.' Remember?"

Kyle flinched at her comment. "Jenny, you already have enough people who are there for you. I refuse to compete anymore."

"Why does it have to be a competition, Kyle?!" You're not running for office here. This is about my mother dying and you being here for me. Don't you get it? I may have others but it is *you* I needed *and* wanted tonight."

Kyle started to come back with an angry retort but her words rang a bell in his heart and he was silent.

"Apparently, I'm not the only one with 'others.' You have *others,* don't you Kyle? Where have *you* been tonight?" Jenny asked.

"With a friend. . . ."

"What's her name?"

"I don't have to tell you. It was just a friend. Of course, you know all about friends."

"I needed you," Jenny said.

"If you really needed me, why didn't you let me know?"

"I didn't think I had to. For godsake, it's the day of my mother's funeral! I shouldn't have to ask! You should have known and stayed with me."

They continued arguing. By 7:00 AM, they were worn out from fighting. Jenny's eyes were swollen and her face red and puffy from crying. Kyle's feelings were a collection of emotions: sad for his son; hurt at Mike's being allowed so much presence in Jenny's life, angry at Jenny for having 'lied' to him, and upset that they were fighting again.

"Go upstairs and get some sleep?" he finally told her. "I'll be back as soon as I get Marty out of jail and take him home to his mother." Then he left. When he returned, he crawled into bed with Jenny and they slept until late afternoon, arising barely in time for Saturday evening Mass at Carmel. They both knew that they needed spiritual help to get them past this hurdle with each other. At the "kiss of peace" during the service, they seized the moment to heal their rift. In place of the usual handshake and "peace be with you," they hugged, whispering words of forgiveness to each other.

A few days later, on April 2, Jenny carried her mother's ashes to her hometown of Dallas. Earl felt unable to make the trip, and Jenny knew that these first few weeks after Ellen's passing would be difficult for all of them. Chad felt he couldn't take time off of work, but he would be in Sacramento to watch over Earl, who definitely needed looking after.

As Jenny arrived at the checkpoint in the airport, the security agent looked suspiciously at the urn. Even though Jenny had authorization papers, the agent passed the urn to the next agent to have it examined more closely. Jenny burst into tears.

"It's my mother, for God's sake. Please . . ."

The agent's supervisor came over, inspected the urn and the papers accompanying it, and waved her on. Jenny realized in hindsight that perhaps they thought she was smuggling heroin or something. The security guard was well within his rights, but she would have been arrested before she would have let them open the container with her mother's ashes.

Ellen was to be buried next to her mother at Calvary Hill Cemetery. Family members were there, along with Kerry and another high school friend of Jenny's. Afterward, the cousins gathered for a family reunion at the home of Jenny's Aunt Patsy, her mother's only remaining sibling. It was comforting for Jenny to have them all there.

Jenny stayed with Kerry for a few days, allowing herself to be nurtured by her friend. Kerry had been there for Jenny many times over the years. Beyond losing her mom, Jenny shared her sadness over Mike's impending death, how worried she was about Earl, and her distress over Kyle's unpredictable outbursts. Kerry reminded Jenny of their past conversation about narcissistic personality tendencies. Until that moment, it had slipped Jenny's mind.

"Remember, when a hurtful situation comes along, they can only experience it internally," Kerry told her. "Isn't this exactly what had happened with Kyle? His pain of feeling that others were there to care for you left him feeling insignificant and unneeded, overshadowing his awareness of your pain of losing your mother."

Jenny realized that, in that light, Kyle's behavior made some sense. It wasn't justified by any means, and it didn't alleviate the pain he had caused her, but it was the best explanation she had.

Understanding Kyle was one thing, but knowing what to do was another. Jenny knew that, at his very core, Kyle was someone who *had* to be needed and appreciated. How could she let him know that, now more than ever, she needed him? But she was relying on him because of her own unhealthy abandonment issues. She had just lost her mother. She knew she would soon lose Mike. She couldn't, just couldn't, face losing Kyle, no matter how dysfunctional he could be.

Kyle picked up Jenny at the airport when she got back from Dallas. He took her straight to Earl's house. Earl and Jenny were grieving in different ways. Earl's style was to go through the house getting rid of things. Kyle helped Jenny dig through boxes and bags, retrieving family memorabilia before Goodwill came to pick up the donations. Among the many things Jenny saved were a favorite statue of Ellen's, parts of a train engine that Earl had let Chad play with when he was young, and a toy Buckingham Palace guard whose tall black hat and red suit were careworn.

Kyle tried with all of his inner strength to be supportive of Jenny as she mourned. Clearly, Jenny was depressed and withdrawn, and it took all of her strength to get out of bed in the morning and perform her rounds for Earl and Mike. Kyle knew that she had little left over to give to him. Within days of Jenny's return home, despite all resolve, Kyle felt those earlier feelings of being ignored creeping back inside of him. *I don't know how to love her. She cares about the needs of Mike and Earl and Chad*, he thought, *but doesn't seem to even notice I'm here for her.* Feeling her emotional distance from him was pure torture for Kyle. He had just gone to court with his younger son, Marty, to face the consequences of the DUI. Jenny hadn't even thought to ask how it went. He was burdened with mounting responsibilities at work: stress, memos from Washington, threats of terrorism hovering over his state, military issues, mounting differences with the governor. He desperately needed to come home to a woman who cared about him and who appreciated his caring about her. He felt like he didn't have that in Jenny and wondered if he ever would.

The tension between Kyle and Jenny continued to grow and, by early April, they reached an impasse and officially separated. It didn't take Kyle long to make a girlfriend out of the "friend" he went to see the night of Ellen's funeral. Substantially younger than Kyle, she was a legal assistant hired as needed by the attorney general's office.

Instinctively Jenny knew that Kyle dating this woman wasn't important. What mattered is that he *wasn't* with her. On the phone with Kerry a few days after they broke up, Jenny asked, "Why is this happening? I feel so alone. I don't know how to cope all by myself. I need Kyle to help me."

"Girlfriend, don't you understand why he can't?" Kerry asked.

"No, not really," Jenny said with a sigh. "It seems so little to ask for him to stand by me."

"If my sense about this is right, you both suffer from abandonment syndrome, but you each had different childhoods. You knew your parents, and he didn't. He was raised by two parents, and you were missing a dad. So you have both reached adulthood with differing spin-offs of your childhood issues. He seems to have had the security of a stable upbringing but still has the emotions of a self-centered child. I see you as the opposite. You are insecure. Your security depends on finding someone to be protective, loving—I guess you might say 'parental,' toward you. You missed out on that and can't quite give up looking for it in your life. But you have matured beyond the self-centered child to lead a life that is quite other-centered."

"So you think that Kyle and I keep repeating the patterns we experienced in childhood—whether it was abandonment or abuse or some kind of deprivation. That would mean neither of us is to blame. It is what it is."

"You're going to be fine, but you'll probably feel the pain of all of this as a helpless little girl. That's not all bad, you know."

After the call, Jenny crawled into bed. With only her eyes peeking out from under the covers, she curled into a fetal position. It was the only way she could feel comforted.

Mama, she thought. *Where are you?*

Nineteen

Caring for Mike and Earl

Out of necessity, Jenny shifted her focus to taking care of her stepfather and Mike. Earl was a handful—much more demanding than her mother. Jenny was grieving the dual losses of Ellen and Kyle but still had to get up each morning and face her remaining responsibilities. Jenny wondered how she had kept it all going before, when she had twice the load. Now it was only two and she felt overwhelmed.

Jenny had convinced Earl that for the present, it was best not to make any dramatic changes in his life. But he was hell-bent on whittling down what he called "all the paraphernalia" in the house, selling furniture, and throwing countless things into garbage bags. He wanted Jenny there when he wanted her. And God help her if she was 20 minutes late. He was grieving and lonely . . . but so was Jenny. Their shared loss helped them become closer.

At the beginning of Holy Week, the final days leading up to the feast of the Resurrection, Mike joined Jeff and several other priests of the diocese in hearing confessions at the Lenten reconciliation service. It was a time of cleansing and healing for Catholics, a time to break away from everyday distractions and seek forgiveness for things they had done or failed to do. The priests scattered themselves around the church so that parishioners could select one of them to hear their confessions. Although Jenny could talk to Mike anytime she wanted, she took this opportunity to have Mike administer the Sacrament of Healing to her.

"Bless me, Father, for I have sinned," Jenny began. She acknowledged how caught up she was in self-pity. She was tired of being the caretaker and longed to be taken care of.

"You've been through a lot, Jenny," Mike said softly. "Give yourself time to heal from your dear mother's passing. Be patient with yourself." Mike made the sign of the cross as he gave her his blessing. Tears flowed down her face as Jenny returned to her pew for the closing prayer and hymn.

Holy Thursday, Good Friday, Holy Saturday—the tritium leading up to Easter Sunday—represented the most sacred days of the liturgical year in the Catholic Church. Much to his sadness, at the most important time in the liturgical year, Mike was becoming too weak to celebrate at these services. But he couldn't stand the thought of missing out, and he pushed himself to stay active. However, on Good Friday, like Jesus, Mike fell three times. That evening, he became delirious, climbing over the guardrails of his bed. Jeff was awakened by a loud crash as Mike fell to the floor. Running to Mike's aid, Jeff helped him up and back into bed. But losing coherency, Mike kept trying to climb over the rails. Jeff found a comforter and pillow and spent the rest of the night sleeping on the couch in Mike's room.

Throughout Holy Saturday, Mike spiraled downward. He slept continually and was breathing with great difficulty. Jenny and Jeff alternated watching him. On Easter evening Mike's sister and nieces and nephews arrived from Carson City, Nevada, to be with him. They were surprised at how fast he had gone downhill. Mike's brother, Jimmy, made arrangements to fly out from New York and join his sister in saying goodbye to their brother.

Since the TIPS procedure, Mike had been pain-free. But now his pain was intensifying. Preoccupied with his impending death and how to alleviate his suffering, Jenny kept exploring ways she might get a hold of some kind of painkiller for him. Father Jeff had had oral surgery recently, and she vaguely remembered that he was given Vicodin for the pain. Jenny went to the living room where Jeff and Mike's family were sitting to ask him if he still had any of the painkiller.

But being under such stress, Jenny's thoughts got tangled. "Jeff, do you have any of that Viagra left?" Jenny asked intently.

The room went quiet—very quiet. After a prolonged pause, Father Jeff answered, "Moi?"

Still not grasping what she had said, Jenny repeated it. Mike's hospice nurse appeared at the door from his bedroom and said, "Hey, Viagra's a great idea. It's about the only kind of pill we haven't tried." Realizing her faux pas, Jenny's face turned beet red, and the entire group burst into uncontrollable laughter.

During Mike's few waking moments, his family and close friends gathered around him and prayed with him. The next two days were like a living wake; Mike was barely conscious, but people filed through Jeff's quarters at the rectory in droves, each one taking a few minutes to say his or her goodbyes. One of Mike's visitors stopped Jenny at the door to thank her for all that she was doing for Mike.

"Don't fret, he's going to be fine," the elderly woman said calmly.

"Yes, I know. It won't be long now," Jenny replied.

"No, I mean he's going to pull through all of this. Really. He's going to be fine." Jenny wished she could have as much blind hope as the woman did.

Friends had organized food to be brought in each day for the family while they were gathered. One good friend brought over a homemade bunt cake for dessert. Throughout his illness, Jenny was careful to avoid sugar and give Mike only healthy food. Jeff, finding Mike momentarily awake, cut a small piece of the cake and sneaked it back to Mike. He devoured that piece and asked for seconds. As he continued to enjoy what everyone came to call "the miracle cake," Mike rallied once again. It wasn't a gradual rally. It was instant and all the more miraculous. The elderly woman's prediction had come true.

Family and friends gathered around his bedside and cranked the head of his hospital bed up so he could sit and face everyone. He was bright-eyed and smiling. Someone put his Redskins cap on him, and it made him look even more like himself again. When Jenny brought in Mike's pills, he looked at her mischievously and asked, "Is that little blue one Viagra?"

Mike's appetite came back, and he was even taking little walks around the house. *And* he was talking about officiating at Gene's wedding, which was being celebrated at the governor's mansion. No one took him seriously but, by Saturday, he was still planning on going. Jenny contacted Gene's daughter and she made arrangements with the security staff at the mansion to bring Mike in through the back door. Early Sunday morning, when Jenny arrived at Mike's, he was raring to get up and get dressed in his Roman collar and full priestly regalia.

Gene had asked Father Jeff to fill in for Mike at his wedding. While Jeff went early to prepare for the marriage ceremony, Jenny arrived later with Mike and pushed him in his wheelchair through the kitchen entrance of the governor's mansion. They stayed hidden in a back corner while they waited for the moment for Mike to make his entrance. But his presence wasn't a well-kept secret. One by one, people made their way back to say hello: the governor, the first lady, Gene's bride, and several friends. The governor expressed his condolences to Jenny. She wondered if he intended them to be for her mother or Kyle or both. Everyone seemed to know that Mike was there—everyone, that is, except Gene.

As the service got underway in the entryway of the mansion, Gene and his bride stood on the stairs. The governor and his wife flanked them on either side. As Jenny guided Mike closer, she heard Father Jeff say, "And now, for a very special wedding blessing . . ." That was her cue. Jenny wheeled Mike into the midst of the gathering. Gene started to cry. Mike was supposed to stay seated in his wheelchair and administer the blessing. But he was too excited. He stood up and took several unsteady steps toward Gene and his new wife. As he gave them his blessing, making the sign of the cross in the air, tears of joy flowed around the room. He warmly embraced Gene and his wife. But Mike wasn't finished. Like a politician running for office, he continued to make his rounds, person by person, hug by hug. Terrified that Mike was going to fall, the governor grabbed the wheelchair from Jenny. With every step Mike took, the governor was right behind him, pushing the wheelchair like a wheelbarrow ready for the catch. Watching the scene, Jenny could see that she was not alone—torn between laughter and tears.

With the blessing given, Jenny and Mike made their way out the back door and into the car. They were no sooner on the road when Louie Armstrong's voice came on the radio singing "What a Wonderful World." And the song mirrored exactly how Mike felt. It was a wonderful world when he could surprise his friend with such a special gift. Clearly, he had willed himself to have the strength to accomplish his mission but, once he was home, Mike fell into bed, exhausted.

Jenny, too, returned home tired but happy with the day. As she walked in the house, she heard a strange sound, something like the distant ticking of a bomb. She crept through each room, tentatively following the noise. She made her way to the family room and, there, to the right of the stairs, was the family grandfather clock she had taken from her mother's house. It had stopped ticking when her mom's health was failing but now the pendulum was once again in full motion. Jenny was astounded. How could a wind-up clock just start up again on its own? *Hi, Mom. It's nice to know you are here with me.* Jenny fell peacefully asleep.

Kyle, however, was not feeling so serene; he missed Jenny. He had talked the situation to death with Harvey, who had once again adjusted his medications. Sitting at his desk after work hours, Kyle picked up the phone and dialed his brother.

"Hey, bro, what's happening?"

"I just needed to hear your voice," said Kyle.

"You sound down," Josh replied.

"I can't live with Jenny, and I can't live without her. I don't know which way hurts more. You and Emmy don't seem to have these kinds of problems."

"We worked our stuff out a long time ago," Josh said. "I can't tell you exactly how we did it. We had our near moments of breaking up but, thanks to her, we just kept talking it through. She wanted marriage and I didn't see the need for it at our age. She wasn't sure whether she wanted a child. I told her I'd make a good child for her but I knew I wouldn't be a good parent."

"Maybe that's my problem. I want to be the child getting all the attention," Kyle laughed. He noticed that his brother didn't join him. "So how did you two work it out?"

"You know how much Emmy loves politics. I promised her that one day we'd live in Washington. And since she landed her job with the Center for American Women in Politics, she seems fulfilled ."

"I don't know how to compromise with Jenny. We're just so far apart with what we want out of life. I know she needs me. She's doing the best she can to keep up the care of Mike and her stepfather. But when I call her, all we do is fight. We even argue in emails. I've tried seeing someone else just to get over her."

"It doesn't sound like that's working very well. What does Jenny want from you?"

"In a word—support," Kyle said. "She feels that I let her down on the day of her mother's funeral, and maybe I did. She's losing everyone and wants to be comforted."

"That sounds reasonable. What do you need from her?"

"I need Jenny back—the one who adored me and loved spending time with me. But for the last couple of years, there has always been someone else who comes first. And it's obvious this situation isn't going to change."

"Why can't you just be there for her? It doesn't sound like too much to ask."

"She has so many others who are there for her. Josh, it's like I have to get in line. Everybody loves Jenny, especially her male friends. I want to be *the one* but . . ."

"I understand what you mean," Josh said. "Emmy makes me feel wanted and she fills that hole that was left ever since our parents gave us up. Down the road, I think Jenny could do the same for you, but the timing is tough now."

"Yeah, ever since we met, one or the other of us has faced a crisis."

"How's your depression?"

"Depression does a funny thing to you," Kyle replied. "It clouds the joyful parts of your life and focuses you on the parts that are missing. I miss Jenny. But I can't figure out how to make things work."

"Give it time, bro."

There was a pause as Kyle swallowed the lump in his throat. "So how are things going at work? Are you on your secured line?"

"Yeah. Weird things are happening. There was a meeting this week in the Situation Room with a bunch of the lower-echelon, sub-cabinet officials. They were working through key issues before the big shots confer. You remember Richard Clarke?"

"Of course. He's been around since Reagan's time and highly respected as I recall."

"He's respected because his politics cuts across party lines," Josh said. "He led this meeting laying out a case for putting military pressure on the Taliban and al Qaeda forces in Afghanistan and going after Osama bin Laden. This is not a new direction for him. He was one of the first senior officials to suggest military action against al Qaeda during the Clinton administration."

"Based on the information I'm receiving out here, that advice sounds wise," Kyle said.

"Well, remember Paul Wolfowitz was one of my instructors? I took a summer class from him when he was dean of International Relations at Johns Hopkins."

Josh described a meeting he sat in between Wolfowitz, the new deputy of state, and Clarke. " . . . So he takes Clarke on in the meeting, asking why we would waste everyone's time focusing on bin Laden, and suggesting there are other more serious threats such as Iraqi terrorism. At that point, John McLaughlin, the deputy director of the CIA, says that the intelligence community has no indication of *Iraqi* terrorist activity directed at our country. Wolfowitz gets all worked up saying that they're giving bin Laden too much credit, that he couldn't act on his own without a state sponsor."

"Do these 'intelligence' guys have their heads up their asses?"

"Wolfowitz knows his stuff, but he's stuck in that same old neoconservative thinking just like Cheney and Rumsfeld. They're still holding onto the belief that Ramzi Yousef, the leader of the group that carried out the 1993 bombing on the World Trade Center, was actually an *Iraqi* intelligence agent. But Clarke, the CIA, and the FBI have all concluded that the group was tied to al Qaeda."

"I don't understand," Kyle said. "Why are they so determined to make this link to Iraq?"

"Damned if I can figure it out."

Things weren't going well for Jenny, either. She sank into a deeper depression. She had no energy. Taking care of Earl and Mike was becoming harder and harder.

Jenny called Harvey and reached him on his mobile phone, sitting in his plane on the ground in the Sky Harbor Airport. He had flown to Phoenix in his small, self-built bi-plane and would be staying overnight.

In response to his query about how she was doing, she responded: "Mike is dying. And, no matter what I do, I can't make Earl happy."

"Right now your role is to be with these two men," Harvey said. "What you do with your time is irrelevant. Sitting with them, getting them food, it doesn't matter. It is merely another way to say 'you matter to me and I love you.'"

Jenny admitted how badly she wanted Kyle back in her life. "It would be nice to have him stand by me through all of this. But I'm afraid the same things will happen all over again."

"Romantic relationships may be the most prevailing, weighty, distressing, excruciating, volatile, heart-wrenching subject for human beings. Most of us, me included, have been taught to love in such dysfunctional ways. You know, Jenny, as long as you believe that you *have* to have Kyle in your life to be happy, you're really just an addict using another person as your drug of choice. I don't know what the future holds for you two, but for now you both need this time apart."

That wasn't what Jenny wanted to hear. She remained quiet.

"Hang in there, my friend. I'll check in on you when I get back."

On Saturday, May 10, Chad and Jenny went together to take Earl out for the day. He didn't answer the doorbell, so Jenny used her key. As she and Chad entered the foyer, she noticed a manila folder in the middle of the floor just beyond the front door. Bending over to pick it up, Jenny saw with horror what was written on the cover in heavy black, felt-tipped marker: "I'm sorry, but I miss Ellen too much. Please forgive me."

"No," Jenny whispered. "Dear God, no." Her legs almost gave out from under her, and Chad moved to steady her. He quickly saw what had caused Jenny to falter.

"You stay right here, Mom, I'll go . . ."

"No, Chad, no. We'll go together."

Going up the steps was the longest walk of their lives. Reaching Earl's bedroom, they rounded the corner to see Earl lying on his mattress, his head covered with a pillow. Blood was splattered on the headboard and all over the bedding. His old service revolver was lying close to him.

"Oh, Earl," Jenny whispered. Chad tentatively checked Earl's wrist for a pulse. Nothing. The room reeked of blood and alcohol. Chad put his arms around his mother, and they stood holding each other in silence for several minutes.

Jenny's first call was to the coroner. Hanging up from that call and with the receiver still in her hand, she hesitated. Who should she call for help—Kyle or Mike? She dialed Mike's number.

By the time Mike and Jeff arrived, Earl's body was being bagged. They all watched together as he was carried out.

Then they gathered in the living room where Jenny answered questions from the coroner as he filled out his paperwork. Her cell phone rang, and it was Kerry calling to check on her. She regretted she was all the way in Texas but promised to be there in any way she could. The next call was from Sherri. When Jenny told her what had just happened, Sherri said she'd be right over. *How do friends just sense these things,* Jenny thought, *these moments when we really need someone?*

After the coroner left, Mike and Sherri stood on either side of Chad and Jenny as they looked down at the bloodied bed. Jeff stood in the doorway. The bullet had gone through the pillow, spreading feathers everywhere. Many were flecked with blood. Jenny shivered at the sight. Mike led them in prayer as they asked God to take Earl into his embrace and allow him to be with his wife once again. The room felt cold and empty.

Jenny struggled with the suicide. She felt angry. After all, it had only been five weeks since her mother had died. She felt guilty for not being there for Earl the previous week like she had before. She found it difficult to reconcile such a violent death with the concept of heaven. Mike softened Jenny's resentment, reminding her of Earl's extreme loneliness without his wife.

Jenny chose to have a simple service for Earl at the mortuary. He had no religious background, so she would not have anything too liturgical. Much to everyone's amazement, the morticians had done such a good job of masking the wounds on either side of his head that they were able to lay him out in an open casket. Chad and Jenny arrived first to pay their respects. They were followed by three of the sisters from Carmel, along with Father Jeff and Father Mike. Mike was even weaker than at Ellen's funeral. About a half dozen of Ellen and Earl's neighbors came. It was with great restraint that Jenny did not invite Kyle.

Over the days that followed, Jenny found herself anxiously checking her phone messages. After the funeral, she regretted that she had not told Kyle about it. Arriving home from Mike's one afternoon, she saw the light blinking on her answering machine. It was a message from Kyle. He had just learned about Earl's death and left a sweet message of condolence. It was also Kyle's birthday. Jenny gave in to the temptation to call him back.

"I couldn't let today go by without letting you know I was thinking of you," she told him.

"It doesn't take a special day to make me think of you," Kyle said. "I think about you every day." He said that, though it was wonderful to receive calls from his mother, his brother, and his office associates, this call from Jenny made his day.

"Well, your birthday made for a good excuse to call. I do miss you but . . ."

"Maybe we could try to be friends," Kyle proposed.

"We both know that'll never work."

"We could try," Kyle said. "Anything is better than not having you in my life."

They chatted for a few minutes, neither of them wanting to end the conversation. Jenny ended by wishing him a happy birthday and agreeing that they could be friends, but only friends.

Setting down the phone, Jenny picked up the newspaper and scanned it and saw an article referencing Kyle. The School of Americas had finally closed but, in the same bill that closed it, Congress established the Western Hemisphere Institute for Security Cooperation. *What a mouthful of a name,* she thought. While some provisions were written into the bill to make this newly named military base different from the School of Americas, for all practical purposes, it looked like the same agenda. The secretary of defense was authorized to operate the new school, while SOA had been commanded by the secretary of the army. The bill, however, also permitted the secretary of defense to designate a military department to carry out these responsibilities. As she continued reading, Jenny learned that the Department of Defense had selected the secretary of the army as its executive agent. Thus, the newly named base was still essentially operated by the secretary of the army, just like SOA.

"I am convinced that this military base must be closed down," the article quoted Kyle as saying. "If I have to fly to Washington myself and address Congress, I'll do it. I have to take some action."

This was the side of Kyle that Jenny loved. But at the same time, she was concerned for him. He was taking dramatic steps in his political career. She couldn't help but wonder who or what was moving him in this direction.

Word of Kyle's bravado reached Washington. Josh called his brother for their weekly update. "Getting a little bold, aren't you, bro? You coming out here."

"I thought you might need a little help to whip some of these Washington guys into shape," Kyle joked. "How are our nation's leaders holding things together these days?"

"Oh, about like you would expect. Larry, Moe, and Curly have taken their respective places as part of our senior staff."

"Who?"

"The three neocons who authored the Clean Break platform for Israel: Perle, Wurmser and Feith."

"Are you telling me that they are in a position to drive American policy based on concepts they designed for Israeli security and Israeli interest back in '96?"

"Mm hmm."

"Is Bush being led by a nose ring, or what?"

"The kindest thing I can say is that he's not very smart," Josh replied. "I think he just doesn't get it."

"Where are these guys being placed?"

"Douglas Feith is being appointed to the highest policy position in the Pentagon, the Undersecretary of Defense for Policy. His responsibilities include the formulation of defense planning and guiding the DOD's relations with foreign countries. David Wurmser moved into a top policy position in the State Department as Special Adviser to Undersecretary of State for Arms Control and International Security. That way, Cheney can have access to his expertise in Middle Eastern affairs. And Richard Perle has been moved up as chairman of the reinvigorated and powerful federal advisory board that Rumsfeld called the Defense Policy Board. So, believe me, they've got their bases covered."

"It sounds like they are setting up the neoconservative foxes to watch over the DOD's henhouse," Kyle said. "These guys are now positioned to have major control over any plans to invade the Middle East. It makes me sick."

"Me, too. With the three stooges in place near Rummy and Cheney, oh yeah, and good ol' Paul Wolfowitz," Josh said, "we are in for some interesting times."

To help lift Jenny's spirits and get her focusing on her future without Kyle, Kerry and two other school friends encouraged Jenny to put her picture and bio onto a singles website. But upon reflection, she just wasn't ready to meet anyone new. She was still too raw with pain and too intimidated by the idea of meeting men online. Besides, the only man she wanted was Kyle. She thanked them and never looked at her account or even thought about it again.

Not long after Kyle's birthday, their "just friends" status slipped into something more. They both wanted it that way. Jenny's weight of caregiver's responsibility was only for Mike now. She and Kyle drifted into spending most of their nights at River House, much the way Kyle had envisioned. What care-giving Jenny did for Mike was during the day. By evening, when Kyle got off work, she was there preparing dinner or ready with a suggestion of where they might go out. They took walks along the river with Winky and talked about their days. Kyle loved sharing the numerous challenges facing him in his job and appreciated her intelligence and insights. It was a peaceful time for both of them.

A few weeks later, Kyle's ex-wife discovered Jenny's account on the singles website. She shared it with Kyle and he went ballistic. He left Jenny an irate message on her answering machine. *Not again*, she thought. But she could understand why he was upset. Without knowing the facts, if the tables were turned, she might have been just as offended. Knowing that he probably wouldn't take a call from her, Jenny hurried to his house at 9:45 PM, anxious to set the record straight and not go to bed on yet another round of anger. She felt confident that she could resolve the matter quickly.

Jenny rang the doorbell. The house was dark inside. Soon the porch light came on, but a woman answered the door. Jenny was stunned. She had awakened with him in his bed that very morning. *How could he be going to bed that night with another woman?* Jenny demanded to speak with Kyle. The woman shut the door, leaving Jenny standing on the porch. Jenny could hear her running up the stairs yelling, "I'm not leaving! I'm not leaving!" *What am I doing here? What kind of fool am I?* Jenny quickly got in her car and began backing out of the driveway just as Kyle came out in his bathrobe and flagged her to stop.

He climbed in her car and began yelling about the singles site as Jenny screamed even louder about the woman. Jenny backed out and drove down the street as they continued to shout at each other. She offered her explanation about the website, but Kyle didn't seem to hear her and, if he did, he must not have believed her. He offered no explanation for the woman's presence—only that she just *happened* to call. Getting nowhere with their communication, Jenny stopped the car and let Kyle out. She was shaking with rage and then, without warning, her anger turned to hysteria. She found herself laughing uncontrollably as she imagined the California attorney general walking down the street several blocks from home, barefoot and in his bathrobe.

Two days later Mike asked Jenny to take him to his parish. He wanted to participate in the liturgy and say hello to his parishioners. Mike was beaming as he walked into his old sacristy. Jenny helped him vest for Mass. The priest who had taken his place welcomed him with open arms. As the entrance song began, the two priests walked back to the vestibule to prepare for the procession into church. Left on her own, Jenny walked down the aisle to find herself a seat. There, sitting on the far left, was Kyle. He looked startled to see her and motioned for her to join him.

As they waited for Mass to begin, Kyle whispered, "I know my behavior is really sick. I've been seeking help from Harvey. I know I need to do something serious. I'm considering getting shock therapy."

Jenny was horrified. She only knew of shock therapy from the film *One Flew Over the Cuckoo's Nest*, and that was enough to terrify her.

"There must be other options," she said softly.

"I don't know what they are. I feel like I've tried everything."

They sat in silence, each lost in their own worlds through the Liturgy of the Word. Kyle recalled his catechumen classes where he learned that this part of the Mass was the time to simply listen to God speak. But what touched Kyle more deeply was learning that he was not just listening to something God once said, but to the living God speaking to him here and now to address current issues in his life. From the podium, the priest announced that the reading that day was from Matthew 18. Two verses jumped out at Kyle: "Then Peter came up and said to him, 'Lord, how often shall my brother sin against me, and I forgive him? As many as seven times?' Jesus said to him, 'I do not say to you seven times, but seventy times seven.'"

As the priest delivered his homily, he gave examples of how as Christians we are called to forgive one another. "And sometimes we are called to forgive not just once but two times, three times, as often as is necessary." The priest's voice echoed throughout the church.

Kyle leaned over and whispered to Jenny, "Four times, maybe even five, six."

By the time the kiss of peace came, neither Kyle nor Jenny knew anyone else was present. They embraced and held each other for a very long time. Mike came down from the altar and extended peace to both of them as well.

After Communion, Mike stood up to address the congregation. Since he had been gone for so long, he began: "For those of you who are new, my name is Father Mike O'Malley." There was laughter throughout the church. Mike was so much a part of the lives of these parishioners that he was in their thoughts and prayers constantly. Mike shared with them how his illness has taken him down a path he hadn't anticipated. "My work on this earth feels unfinished. But that is not for me to decide. We must all be prepared for the unexpected in our lives, for those twists and turns that God has in store for us. Let us be ready to put our own plans aside and to say with heartfelt sincerity: 'Not my will but yours be done.'"

Tears flowed throughout the church, making Kyle's and Jenny's a little less noticeable. When Mass ended and the greetings had been exchanged, Jenny left Kyle's side to walk with Mike to her car. Moving gradually in the opposite direction from Kyle, Jenny looked longingly over her shoulder for one last glance at him. He was doing the same. From across the parking lot, their gazes locked into one another, steadily, tenderly, inescapably.

Kyle threw himself into his work the following week. He received a memo from the CIA alerting him that Osama bin Laden had just released another message: "The coming weeks will hold important surprises that will target American and Israeli interests in the world." To reinforce his warning, shortly afterward bin Laden released an al Qaeda-made videotape showing terrorist training exercises. The CIA report noted that just before the embassy bombings, bin Laden had spoken to a reporter from ABC News and offered a similar warning. This had George Tenet and his agency greatly concerned.

From the inspiring testimony of Mass on Sunday to the loathsome declaration of Osama bin Laden on Thursday, Kyle wondered if this could be the "unexpected in our lives" that Father Mike was referencing—those "twists and turns that God has in store for us."

Twenty

Kyle In Crisis

"Josh calling Kyle. Josh calling Kyle," he spoke into his twin's voicemail. "Come in, bro. Urgent. Get back to me. Ten four."

Kyle had just arrived at his office and received the message. He grabbed a cup of coffee and checked his calendar for his appointments. July 11. He was free until 10:00 AM. Picking up the receiver and dialing his brother, Kyle wondered what could be so important. "Kyle calling Josh. What's up?"

"I think the shit is about to hit the proverbial fan. There is so much 'chatter' going on around the intelligence circles, it's hard to sort out what is real and what isn't."

"What's it all about?" Kyle asked

"Apparently bin Laden's June 21 statement made the terrorism guys around here start taking him seriously."

"Do they have any idea what he's suggesting and where the 'surprise' he spoke of will take place?"

"They've been assuming that something might happen overseas, but now, as they connect the dots, it appears that it could be an aircraft hijacking right here on our own soil," Josh said.

"Well, yeah. Why else would the CIA be watching these goons Nawaf Alhazmi and Khalid Almihdhar sitting out here in San Diego?"

"That makes sense that, if these two guys are part of al Qaeda, they are in this country for a reason," Josh said.

"What worries me is that they are in my state for a reason. Why California?

"You have good reason to be asking that question. No one here has answers but everybody is scrambling to try to stay out in front of this, like a band leader looking over his shoulder to make sure the band hasn't gone off in another direction."

"From the communication I've received," Kyle said, "it sounds like the CIA is doing the best it can but George Tenet is in Catch-22."

"Well, Tenet's fed up and not taking it anymore. For months he has been urging Condoleezza Rice to establish a decisive counterterrorism policy so that the CIA can carry out covert procedures against bin Laden," Josh said, obviously exasperated. "*Finally* yesterday, he called her and demanded a meeting immediately and took his counterterrorism chief, Cofer Black, with him. He counted on the unscheduled request grabbing her attention."

"What did they tell her?" Kyle asked.

"Cofer told me they were frickin' blunt. They said that they had information that al Qaeda was going to attack the United States, possibly on its own soil, and that this was an issue that needed to be addressed *now*!"

"What did she say?"

"She was polite and listened, but Tenet and Black both felt the brush-off. She had other priorities on her mind." Some of Josh's frustration dissipated as he thought about how the CIA director handled the rebuff. "It's kind of funny, though. Tenet had his CIA's Counterterrorism Center prepare a briefing paper anyway and issue it to all senior Bush administration officials. Without mentioning the reporter's name who had been the intermediary, their account presented the exact same information he had revealed as if it were a brilliant piece of intelligence work."

"Well, you can't blame Tenet. He had to do something. He couldn't just sit on information like that. . . . Josh, I'm worried for the people here in California—especially those in L.A. and San Francisco. Whatever form the attack takes, it could happen here in our state."

"Or here in Washington," Josh added. He promised to keep his brother informed if he learned anything new.

Mike had reached the point in his illness where he needed round-the-clock care. Jenny turned to all of Mike's family and friends for help. She booked herself in for a time that she could not otherwise fill—from 8:00 PM to 8:00 AM. When Kyle realized that Jenny was staying overnight at Mike's, he again went ballistic. He showed up banging on Mike's door, yelling and screaming questions about whose girlfriend she really was. Jenny let him in, and he stood fuming in the doorway.

Moving protectively toward Mike, Jenny tucked his blanket in closer around him and calmly told him she'd be right back. He looked confused. She patted his cheek and walked back toward Kyle. Grabbing his arm, she jerked him out the door. All she could think about was getting him away from Mike's as quickly as she could.

In the parking lot, Jenny exploded. "I don't *ever* want to hear again that I put Mike over you. EVER! I'm too angry to talk to you right now, so just leave!"

"But Jenny—"

"No buts! What you did tonight was abominable! You can't treat people that way—and most especially you are never to treat me or my friends that way again. Now LEAVE!"

Jenny pushed him toward his car. He pulled open his car door and climbed inside as if in a trance.

Jenny hoped Kyle didn't notice she was shaking, upset with both anger and fear. As soon as he drove away, she went back in to check on Mike. He was shaken up, and by focusing on calming him, she calmed herself.

"Mike, I'm so sorry for what happened, but it will never happen again. I promise."

As he drove away, Kyle slowly came back to himself and began to realize the magnitude of what he'd just done. Even he recognized that his behavior was deplorable. Manic depression had the capacity to deceive even someone as intelligent as Kyle. Using his cell phone, he called Harvey and told him what had happened.

"Get help, Kyle. Pick a place, go there, and surrender yourself to the professional staff. I know without a doubt you're finally at the place where you're ready to work on changes in yourself." Kyle was weeping so heavily that he had to pull off the road.

The next day he called Jenny but got her voicemail. He apologized for his behavior and told her that, upon the advice of Harvey and Josh, he would be seeking treatment at a facility. He faltered for words, wanting to say more. He made no excuses and offered no defense. He closed as he began: "Jenny, please forgive me. I won't blame you if you give up on me . . . or already have. But, please, give me a chance to get better and promise you'll meet with me when I get back."

When Jenny listened to the message, she felt heartsick, but she didn't return his call. Kyle had crossed the line.

After dozens of calls over the next couple of days, Kyle finally chose a treatment center in Tucson, Arizona. He knew that this treatment was critical to his health and to his future. Harvey accompanied Kyle to get him settled and to provide the moral support he needed. After returning, Harvey phoned Jenny to let her know where Kyle was and to brief her on the program. She was glad to have the news; her own grief and sadness was over the top, and she confided to Harvey that she felt she needed help with her grief. Harvey told her that the facility offered a satellite workshop in Sacramento and, without hesitation, Jenny enrolled.

In Arizona, Kyle committed to a month-long program. Other patients included top-level professionals such as Kyle, all receiving medical care and behavioral therapy for various emotional dysfunctions. After a few days, Kyle settled into his new living arrangements and particularly enjoyed the company of his roommate, a doctor.

In Sacramento, Jenny was one of eight in a more intimate non-medical group. The people in her group were a diverse, upscale assortment of individuals—a banker, a homemaker, a student, and an actor. They were all serious about working through the obstacles to their emotional happiness. The challenges they faced were just as varied: two were weighing divorce; one was a man abused by his wife;

one man wanted to learn to be open with his wife; a woman wanted to learn how not to be controlled by her husband; another felt hopeless.

It was exactly what Jenny felt she needed and, by the second day, she experienced a major breakthrough in her grieving. Their leader conducted a psychodrama, asking each of them to prepare to enact a significant moment in their lives and bring one person with them on the journey. Jenny chose her mother. Once her own session was underway, Jenny began talking to her mom in the present moment, telling Ellen how much she missed her and how hard it was to live without her. Unconsciously, Jenny began changing roles. Her communication became that of a child—a little girl talking to her mommy and telling her how sad she was that she couldn't live with her. *Can't you please find a way to support us where you don't have to leave me? Stay with me, Mommy. Please don't leave.* Jenny's sobs were so deep that her outcry was like a primal scream. She couldn't remember ever crying with such wrenching in her gut. She was grateful to be under the guidance of a professional. The intensity of prolonged weeping frightened her as much as it cleansed her. Jenny felt as if that painful lump had been building inside of her for more than 50 years. In one dynamic morning exercise, the cancerous knot of abandonment that had consumed her since childhood seemed to drastically diminish. The relief she felt was as healing as anything she had ever experienced.

Jenny shared her experience with Mike.

"I don't know how to describe it, but some tightly wound-up ball of pain and fear and loneliness just exploded inside of me.

"I'm so happy for you, love."

"I came to understand that Mom didn't leave me when I was a child because she loved me less. In order to support us during an era when single parenthood was virtually unheard of, Mom made the best choices available to her. Somehow in coming to that realization, I felt less abandoned. I was able to let it go."

"It sounds like the tears you were shedding were less about losing her now and more about feeling separated from her when you were little," Mike said.

"I think so. It freed me, and now I'm less afraid of taking risks where I might face being abandoned."

One of the workshop assignments was "list work" and Jenny chose Kyle as her subject. She dove into the task like an enthusiastic student. In between sessions, she spent two days on her list work, following a well-defined format she had been instructed to use. All workshop members were given the opportunity to vocalize their script out loud in Gestalt fashion, sitting facing an empty chair, imagining their partners sitting opposite them. When Jenny's turn came, she imagined Kyle walking into the room, charming everyone as he often did in real life. She mentally had him sit down across from her with their knees nearly touching. Once she visualized him settled in, she began.

"These are my thoughts, feelings, and perceptions about you." She took a deep breath and then began her list as the group looked on. Gazing straight ahead at the imaginary figure of Kyle, Jenny described how consumed and possessed it made her feel when he depended so completely on her to fill his time and meet his needs, or when he wanted to shut out everyone and everything else in her life in order to keep her isolated for himself. She told him how frightened, sad, misjudged, demeaned, and completely hopeless she felt when he passed judgment on her, criticized the people in her life, or lost his temper so violently, especially when he barged in on her at Mike's, scaring them both with his behavior. She concluded: "And when you felt imaginary hurt, you put your own pain ahead of mine regardless of the circumstances (and I'm sorry for giving this example, but I'm not over the pain of it yet) like when you spent the evening of Mom's funeral with another woman rather than staying with me when I needed you more than I've ever needed anyone in my life, I felt devastated, angry, and abandoned."

Jenny shifted in her chair as she wiped her bangs from her face and recomposed herself. Then she began the easier part of conveying the things she most appreciated about him. She described how grateful she was when Kyle read her passages from his favorite books, talked about his feelings, and sent her cards with sweet messages. "I am hopeful you'll be able to assess your own behavior and see when it is out of perspective. But of every good thing you've ever done, I most appreciated your kindness to my mother when you spent time with her when she was so sick. These were the times I loved you more than I can say."

Jenny knew that if she could accomplish this milestone of setting limits on the demands and expectations he and others made on her, she would be a much healthier and happier person. She ended by telling him that she was moving on with her life.

Jenny's group watched as she tearfully shared her feelings with the empty chair. At the end, the leader asked them to describe to her how this experience made them feel. One by one, Jenny heard that her communication with Kyle made them sad and that they understood why she was choosing to move on.

The workshop experience was one of the most valuable of Jenny's entire life.

In Arizona, Kyle was making excellent progress. The medical staff had adjusted and readjusted his medications, and he was faithfully taking them.

During Kyle's treatment, Josh stayed in close touch with his brother. He was proud of him for making his own health such a priority at the risk to his career. Josh kept him up to date about politics and life in the outside world.

"The mess is escalating, bro. Cofer Black, speaking out as director of the CIA's Counterterrorism Center, has joined some of the others in sounding the terrorism alarm. He's convinced that this could be the big one and said so publicly: 'We *are* going to be struck soon. Many Americans are going to die, and it could be in the U.S.'"

"Is anyone listening to him?"

"No. That's what upsets him. He says top leaders are still thinking it will be overseas and they're unwilling to act unless they're given indications that an attack is coming within the next few days and told what the terrorists are going to hit."

"Has any of this made its way to the president?" Kyle asked.

"Finally, yes. About nine days ago, on August 6, the president's daily briefing had a headline that was intended to grab his attention. It said, 'Bin Laden Determined to Strike U.S.' It warned that the FBI had intelligence indicating that terrorists might be preparing for an airline hijacking in the United States and might be targeting a building in lower Manhattan. Powell called a meeting in our office. He's beside himself with concern."

"I've been worried about L.A.X. There were rumors about this airport . . ."

"Yeah, there were references about it in the PDB," Josh confirmed.

"The what?"

"The president's daily briefing. It says that a convicted plotter named Ahmed Ressam admitted to the FBI that he conceived the idea to attack Los Angeles International Airport himself and that bin Laden and Lieutenant Abu Zubaydah encouraged him and helped facilitate the operation. Ressam assured the FBI that bin Laden was aware of the Los Angeles operation."

"So there is strong reason to be concerned about an attack in California?"

"Bro, from everything I'm seeing come through this office, I think there is reason to be concerned about something happening in New York, Washington, D.C., and California," Josh said. "They even seem to be able to recruit U.S. citizens to their cause."

"Remember the CIA report I received about two guys they're watching in San Diego? I haven't received any information since March. Do you have updates on them? Their names are Nawaf Alhazmi and Khalid Almihdhar."

"Hold on a minute, and I'll look up what I've got." Josh shuffled through some papers in his desk file. "OK, here they are. They're still there and are using their own names on everything: their rental agreement, their driver's licenses, their Social Security cards, credit cards, car purchase, and bank account. They're even listed in the phonebook. They don't act like they have anything to hide."

"Yes, I knew all that. But is there anything that arouses your suspicion?" Kyle asked.

Continuing to read the file in front of him, Josh said: "This says that another Saudi, Hani Hanjour, joined them for a couple of weeks. Neighbors noticed some odd behavior: They have no furniture; they are constantly using cell phones on the balcony and playing flight simulator games. Oh, here. This is interesting. On April 10, Nawaf

Alhazmi took an hour introductory lesson at the National Air College in San Diego. Eight days later, he received a $5,000 wire transfer from Ali Abdul Aziz Ali in the United Arab Emirates. In May, Alhazmi and Almihdhar arrived at Sorbi's Flying Club, a small school also in San Diego. They announced that they wanted to learn to fly Boeing airliners. They're there with this same guy, Hani, but only the two of them go up in an airplane. This report says that instructor Rick Garza noticed an unusual lack of any basic understanding of aircraft in these two. When he asked Almihdhar to draw the aircraft, Almihdhar sketched the wings on backward. Both spoke English poorly, but Almihdhar in particular seemed impossible to communicate with. The two offered extra money to Garza if he would teach them to fly multi-engine Boeing planes, but Garza declined. He's quoted as saying: 'I told them they had to learn a lot of other things first. It was like Dumb and Dumber. I mean, they were clueless. It was clear to me they weren't going to make it as pilots.'"

"Sounds like something you'd say, Josh. Are these guys on the TIPOFF watchlist yet?" Kyle asked.

"Hmmm, no. No mention of them anywhere that I can see."

"Keep me posted. Even if I'm tucked away here, I need to know if there is anything I should do to protect Californians."

"If I know about it, you will too. You know I love you, bro, and I'm so proud of what you're doing for yourself."

"Josh, have you…have you heard from Jenny?"

"We've been in touch," Josh answered.

"I really blew it, didn't I?"

"It appears so," said Josh. "She still loves you, Kyle, but not your errant behavior."

"I can't blame her, Josh. I wish I could turn back time."

"Well, just use this time to learn how not to blow it with somebody else, eh? I'm here for you, bro."

After Kyle's outburst, Mike turned to Sister Marsha for support. Her wisdom, listening skills, and prayerfulness drew many to seek her counsel, especially Kyle, Jenny, and Mike. Still shaken emotionally from the disturbing confrontation, Mike cried as he described the scene to her. Marsha cried with him and prayed with him. It was painful for her to see him so deeply hurt. And the sad part was that she knew Kyle hadn't a clue how deeply he had wounded Mike. Kyle's emotional disorder only allowed him a narrow, single perspective—his own.

Mike was also getting physically weaker. He had a second CAT scan, and the results indicated that his cancer was spreading. It had been more than the projected six months since he had had the TIPS procedure. It was time to find out what follow-up, if any, should be done. He was going to die, but Jenny hated the thought of him dying of esophageal bleeding. Jenny called the radiology department and asked to speak to Dr. Christianson, the doctor who had performed the amazing procedure.

"It's great to hear from you," he exclaimed. She could feel his genuine enthusiasm through the phone line. "How's the padre?"

"Still hanging in," she said as she caught him up on the highlights of what Mike had been through.

"I can't believe he's still with us," Dr. Christianson said softly.

"That's why I'm calling. We've passed the half-year mark. Does he need to be checked?"

"To tell you the truth, it never occurred to me that we'd have to face that possibility. It was beyond my imagination that he would still be around. There really isn't any practical follow-up. It would be far more dangerous to tamper with the shunts that are in place. And if it was failing him, you'd have seen signs by now."

"If it ain't broke . . ." Jenny began.

"Exactly. My advice is to leave well enough alone. But I will tell you that I have Father Mike's card under the glass on my desk. I keep it there as a reminder, whenever I have a request from a patient that I think may be too risky or arduous, that it is worth taking a second look. For that person, I could make a difference."

"We won't ever forget you, doctor. You definitely made a difference for Mike."

Jenny reported the conversation back to Mike.

After they discussed Mike's health, he changed the subject.

"You are so special, love. You deserve someone who will recognize that and treat you with kindness and compassion. This illness has taught me something about purifying my love for others, loving people in my life because I truly want the best for them. It's about their happiness and not so much the happiness they bring to me. I think I am as close as I can be to feeling that for you."

It was clear to Jenny that Mike was getting ready to go home to his Heavenly Father. He seemed more peaceful, more accepting of God's will for him. In the doctor's opinion, Mike was no longer responding to any of the alternative treatments they were doing for him—the enemas, the injections, and the countless pills. Upon the advice of hospice and this new doctor, Jenny and Jeff gradually backed off some of these things and, surprisingly, Mike's fog seemed to lift. He wasn't quite the old Mike, but he was more coherent. The hardest part of going through the dying process with Mike was seeing him lose his ability to converse on the level he once had.

As Mike grew closer to the end, the next challenge was dealing with the disapproval of family and loving friends who had different ideas about how he should be treated during this stage. Jenny understood their concerns but still felt the pain of their criticism. While the guidance she was receiving from both Mike's volunteer doctor and from hospice was to let Mike and his body dictate how often he should be fed, others were distressed that they had stopped many of the medications and were not feeding him sufficiently, even if this required some force-feeding. Mike's medical advisors recommended that Jenny and Jeff could do more damage by trying to transport him to the tub and should rely on bed baths from now on. Everyone had an opinion and wanted to help. Tension mounted as Mike became weaker and less able to fight his disease.

Jenny was determined to implement some of the advice she gained from her workshop. She needed to make more time for herself. She scheduled some tennis and began working out at the club. As another part of her own recovery, Jenny found a therapist, Dr. Elizabeth McFarland, whom she began seeing once a week to get help with her grieving, her facing of Mike's death, her prior relationship with Kyle, and how she could learn to set boundaries in her life.

A few days after Kyle returned from Arizona, he phoned Jenny. "I've learned so much about myself and I talked ad nauseam with my personal therapist there about us. I blew my marriage. I don't want to make the same mistake with our relationship. I know this is a lot to ask, but would you come with me for my appointment with Harvey this week? It would mean so much to me."

What relationship? Jenny thought. At first she was reluctant but she reasoned that there could be no harm in supporting Kyle in his transition back home. She was proud of him that he had the courage to seek help and, in truth, she wanted to see him.

They met at the Old Spaghetti Factory in Old Town. Nothing romantic—just a favorite hangout with excellent Italian cuisine.

"Thank you for coming. I didn't know if you would for sure."

"Neither did I," Jenny said matter-of-factly. But I do want to hear about your program and how you fared."

"The medical evaluation pretty much confirmed everything Harvey had done for me—especially the lithium. And they got through to me that I may *think* I know more than all the doctors but I can't trust myself to be my own doctor. I definitely can't skip my meds like I've been known to do."

Jenny gave him a knowing glance, thinking back to the night at Mike's front door.

"But most of the work I did was related to behavior changes in myself. The staff helped me feel understood but wouldn't take any of my bullshit. Mostly I learned that I can't carry over my professional behavior into my private life. In my work, I do have to take charge and be in full control of my actions and those of my staff. But I discovered how wrong that can be in my personal life."

Jenny nodded indicating how well she related. "Change takes time but you know how strongly I believe that human beings can change and grow."

"That is one of the many things I love about you. And I do love you," Kyle added, looking directly into her eyes. "Do you have any love in you left for me?"

"You know I love you. No matter what happens, I always will."

"But, Jenny, do you think we can give it another go?"

Jenny said a silent prayer before she spoke. "Let's ask Harvey. He knows more about us than we may know about ourselves."

"I see no reason for your relationship not to work," Harvey said. "I have no doubt that Kyle loves you and, from what he tells me, that you love him. The most important advice I would give both of you is this: Kyle, let go of trying to control her life. Jenny, if he should slip, set boundaries and keep them. You are both spiritual people. Put God and each other first in your lives."

They talked about Kyle's return home and what changes they would make with each other. They did the list work with each other. Kyle used exactly the same format that Jenny had been taught to use. His list of negatives with her that had caused him so much heartache included: not being able to trust her when she was not with him, her lying to him, her attachment to Mike, her lack of emotional monogamy, her inflexibility at not wanting to live together or get married, the lack of structure to their relationship, and her desire for some nights apart. Jenny listened carefully. She wasn't mentally negating his comments but really taking them in. There was so much earnestness as they shared the parts of their relationship that had caused so much anguish for each of them.

When Kyle had completed the negative list, he began to express undying appreciation for her standing by him during his dark times, for her having literally saved his life, for the beautiful moments that they shared when they were by themselves, for the many nights of cuddling and lovemaking, for the depth of her love for him, and for having given so much of herself to him. Jenny thought deeply about this. She had given herself as completely as she knew how in her marriages to Don and Matt. But she was certain that she had never given with her whole being as she had to Kyle. With age and maturity, she had more to give than in earlier times. She knew that his appreciation was well founded. Through all of the crises, she had continued to love him.

Kyle stated convincingly that he was committed to continue getting healthier and bring renewed stability to their relationship. His boundaries were well thought-out. He promised to take time out if they got into an argument and to allow himself time to think before reacting to situations. Harvey devoted himself wholly to the couple throughout the afternoon. As he led them out of his office, Jenny and Kyle both felt fortified.

They celebrated that night with an intimate dinner at River House. After the meal, as they were sipping cognac in front of a cozy fire, the atmosphere became sexually charged. It had been over a month since they had slept together, and both of them felt starved for the other's touch. They began holding and touching and kissing. Jenny unbuttoned his shirt and nuzzled her face against his chest. Soon, they were both disrobing. Skin to skin, he pulled her close to him and laid his face next to hers. She felt his warm tears. He kissed her cheek, her eyes, her nose, her lips. Jenny wanted him more than ever. She was damp and ready for him. He slid inside of her and told her in every conceivable human way, "I love you." With their lips and their hands, they made love again and again throughout the night.

During his program, Kyle had come to grips with the fact that he had left Jenny alone to deal with both of her parents' deaths. "I will never leave you again. I promise," he whispered. Wrapping her legs around him, her only response was to embrace him as her hips rose up to take him inside of her. It was as if they were discovering each other for the first time. They searched for ways to express their passion that left them bewildered and euphoric. Slowly they brought each other to a place of ecstasy, holding back until they could not hold out another moment. In a stream of pleasure and joy, they came together. Exhausted, they fell asleep in each other's arms.

The next morning they awoke feeling well-loved and prepared for the future. Concerned about Kyle's transition, with his permission, she encouraged him to make a retreat at Carmel. He spent his first few days there reading, taking walks, meditating, and praying with the sisters. Jenny joined him for Vespers, and they spent evenings together. She was there no longer because he made her feel obligated. Her love for him was so much stronger than anything she had known before.

Months ago, Kyle had received an invitation to teach a weeklong workshop to politicians from the South Pacific nations. To celebrate their new beginning, Jenny agreed to go with him. But once again, she felt torn between wanting to go and being worried about Mike. "What if he dies while I'm several thousand miles from home? After all we've been through, I couldn't forgive myself if I'm not with him when he passes away," Jenny asked Sister Marsha.

"You have done all that is humanly possible for Mike. Enjoy your time with Kyle. You deserve it. And trust God that this will all unfold as it should."

When Josh called to welcome his brother home, he told him, "I'm so proud of you. You have sounded different for the past couple of weeks. And you and Jen?"

"Back together, and it's never been better," Kyle said. "I think we're going to be fine. And how is everything on the home front? Any more indication of a threat?"

"After our last conversation about your two goons in California, I passed along some information to the FBI about their activities last January in Kuala Lumpur. To his astonishment, the agent discovered photographs of two suspected al Qaeda men—would you believe Almihdhar and Alhazmi?—and the fact that they had been issued multi-entry U. S. visas allowing them to come and go."

"But the CIA knew that a year and eight months ago," Kyle said. "And my office contacted the FBI and made further inquiries about them."

"Dumb and Dumber aren't only residing in San Diego," Josh joked. "They must have namesakes right here in our nation's Capitol. Anyway, the next day, your two guys were finally placed on the TIPOFF watchlist. The FBI alerted the U.S. Immigration and Naturalization Service just in case."

"A little late, wouldn't you say?"

Part II

After 9/11

Twenty-one

Dinner With the Governor

Exactly six days after the 9/11 attacks, President Bush signed a classified, two-and-a-half page directive that laid out his strategy for war on Afghanistan. He had support from most countries around the world for this action as well as strong backing from Americans. What bothered Josh was that, at the same time, the document also ordered the Pentagon to begin planning for a military invasion of Iraq.

Two days later, Richard Perle called a meeting of his Defense Policy Board, which Defense Secretary Rumsfeld attended. The topic was not Osama bin Laden; it was Saddam Hussein. Ahmed Chalabi, who headed the Iraqi National Congress and was opposed to Saddam, was also invited by Perle and Wolfowitz. They wanted Chalabi to lead Iraq once Saddam Hussein was removed.

Josh reported to his brother that all efforts at the Pentagon were converging toward one effort—building a credible case to convince the American public that Saddam was tied to the 9/11 attacks. These strikes provided the pretext they had been seeking to justify an Iraqi invasion to the American public. Rumsfeld, Wolfowitz, Feith, and Perle chose David Wurmser to arrange a stealth intelligence unit that would skirt the normal channels and report directly to Feith. Josh watched with dismay as the three stooges, his pet name for them, were reunited in their common cause to wage a preemptive war on Iraq.

On September 20, military planes and ships left the United States for Afghanistan, and the president thanked the world for its support.

Josh bristled at the conclusion of the president's remarks: "From this day forward, any nation that continues to harbor or support terrorism will be regarded by the United States as a hostile regime."

Josh was incensed. *How can Bush say this publicly while it is a known fact that most of the hijackers were Saudis and the funding was Saudi?? And he continues to protect Saudis currently in our country with federal militia and provide them with chartered planes to leave the United States!* Josh shook his head in total disgust.

Four days later, on Monday morning, while getting back to his routine after returning from Bali, Kyle watched with his staff as President Bush addressed the nation. In light of the shocking crisis, President Bush was facing within his first year in office, Kyle told them, "I bet right now he's wishing he'd agreed to a recount."

Bush announced that he had signed an executive order to immediately freeze the assets of terrorist organizations and leaders.

"Good for him," Kyle said. "That's one action I can agree with."

At that moment, Kyle's secretary motioned to him that there was a call on the line. Kyle stepped back into his office and punched the blinking button.

"Hey, what's happening, bro?" asked Josh.

"I can't believe how much there is to do after being gone so long."

"You and Jen okay?"

"Absolutely. We're much more open with each other. No secrets. No avoiding telling each other the truth about how we feel. It's amazing how much healthier I feel living this way—you know, trusting her, believing that she really loves *me*, and being totally open with her."

"I think our top leaders in Washington need to enroll in your program," Josh said. "Things are just the opposite around here. It's a web of secrets and lies. You wouldn't want to be playing defense on this team. The neocon offense is tackling anyone who stands in the way of their goal."

"Iraq."

"Yep, in his newly appointed post, David Wurmser has just one job to do, namely, to produce evidence to justify attacking Iraq. He is commissioned with the task of coming up with some basis to contradict the CIA's findings and uncover or invent a credible link between al Qaeda and Hussein. You should hear what this guy has to say about the level of competence of George Tenet and his agency. He knows Tenet knows the truth so he *has* to undermine him."

"Among the countries that pose a threat, wouldn't Iraq rank way down the list of those most likely to be an active state sponsor of terrorism?"

"Absolutely," Josh said. "Iraq would come after Libya, as proven by the 1988 bombing of Pan Am 103 over Scotland. And after Syria, which attacked Israeli targets and ended up killing a bunch of Americans. And after Iran, which bombed the Khobar Towers in Saudi Arabia in 1996. Making Iraq the frickin' ogre is absurd."

"Has Perle made any moves yet with his board?"

"Oh, yeah. A letter just came into our office that blows my mind, even if it doesn't completely surprise me. Perle and his cohorts had written a similar letter to President Clinton in 1998, but he wasn't impressed. It's dated September 20 and written to President Bush by Perle and a bunch of his neocon buddies. Listen to this part. You frickin' won't believe it.

> ". . . It may be that the Iraqi government provided assistance in some form to the recent attack on the United States. But even if evidence does not link Iraq directly to the attack, any strategy aiming at the eradication of terrorism and its sponsors must include a determined effort to remove Saddam Hussein from power in Iraq . . . .

"I mean, it's crazy. These guys aren't even trying to conceal what they're doing, Kyle. They're bulldozing over every bit of information that has been gathered by other intelligence agencies and pushing their resolve to go after Iraq. The only value in coming up with links that don't exist is to persuade the American public and the world at large. The three stooges, along with Cheney and Rummy, are running the whole goddamn show."

Kyle hung up the phone sickened by what he was hearing. He was putting in long hours after returning home. He found most of his correspondence depressing, with little or no solution that pleased him. But once in a while something uplifting appeared. He shared a letter with Blake that particularly touched him. It was addressed to all the nation's attorney generals from a peace organization called Heaven on Earth Project.

> Maybe it's too raw at this point, but we would like to float the following idea: Why not declare September 11 as International Peace Day? It could be a paid holiday for the world. A day of peace and quiet. No parades, no gift-giving. People could send peace cards or choose to make peace with someone in their life that they have been in conflict with. A day, not unlike Thanksgiving Day (a day that some call the perfect holiday— little shopping or hassle) where you could be with those you love and care for and indulge in comfort foods. We haven't sorted out exactly how this could come about, but it's a proposal worth thinking and talking about. This would not be a denial of what happened, but rather an antidote—a way of honoring our loss by choosing peace.

Kyle was enthralled with the concept. He thought of President Kennedy's words: *"Our most basic common link is that we all inhabit this planet. We all breathe the same air. We all cherish our children's future. And we are all mortal."* But if it couldn't be an international or even a national holiday, at least he could be instrumental in making it a day of honor in his own state. After all, much of the western half of the nation followed the precedents set in California.

Kyle received a written invitation to a dinner at the governor's mansion for Sunday evening, September 30. It was to be an informal evening in honor of a senior staff member of the White House, Harry Sheen, who was in California for business and pleasure. Wives were invited, and the invitation included a hand-written note from Jed suggesting that Kyle bring Jenny.

"Yes, I'd be honored," she told him when he asked her to attend. "How intimate a dinner is it?"

"Just six of us, I think. A Washington big shot, along with his wife and the four of us."

In her best imitation of Scarlett O'Hara, Jenny drawled, "Oh, Rhett, *whateva* shall I wear?"

"How about what you have on now?" he suggested.

Lying next to him in her black lace bra and bikini panties, she tackled him and pinned him down on the bed. He rolled on top of her, and their lively wrestling match soon turned into gentle love-making.

Afterward, Jenny decided to wear her black dress pants with a turquoise chiffon blouse. She felt comfortable with the way the slacks fit around her hips and hung, loosely pleated, down to her ankles. Her shoes matched her top. She felt elegant, and Kyle reaffirmed how classy she looked. Marilyn, Jed's wife and the first lady, greeted them at the door and escorted them to the living room. After Marilyn and Jed introduced their guests and served them cocktails, they led them to the dining room, a rectangular area with silk wallpaper. On the left wall were double French doors that opened to the porch.

Despite their different political parties, Jed and Kyle had always worked well together. But as the country was becoming entrenched in war, their differences began to show, and their bantering was more intense than before. As Jenny glanced around the room, she realized that five of the six present were Republicans, assuming that Kate was the same party as her husband. Granted, Jenny was not a party loyalist, but still she was a *registered* Republican. Jenny decided to let go of her concern. When it came to debating, Kyle could hold his own . . . even outnumbered.

While the antipasto was being cleared, Jenny talked to Marilyn. She could hear Jed and Harry talking about what most people around the country were talking about: President Bush and his handling of matters since 9/11. "We warned the Taliban to turn Osama bin Laden over. We had no choice but to go after him," Harry said to the governor. "This man must be found and killed."

"There is no question about it," Jed agreed. "As Americans, we'll not feel safe again until we put an end to this man and those who jeopardize our way of life."

They continued along this vein for a few minutes until Kyle offered another perspective. "I agree that we need to go after him, but what concerns me is that we are sending thousands of troops into Afghanistan without even knowing where he is. And in the process, we'll take the lives of many innocent people. It seems to me that we in the West have to find a way to reach a treaty with Islams on such issues as democracy and human rights."

"We didn't make the first attack," Bradley said. "Ours is merely a response to their outrageous and despicable behavior."

"But try to stand back and look more objectively at what's happening here. They see their actions as a response to our behavior, our injustice," Kyle retorted. "In war, it is always the other side that starts it. We can't hold ourselves completely free of responsibility here. If we're going to find any kind of resolution, we have to look at our own past actions and see what we may have done to incur their wrath."

"That's absurd," Harry responded. "Are you justifying what bin Laden and his al Qaeda forces did to us?"

"Hardly," Kyle said. "Killing is wrong for either side. But we have to search for other means of going after him than wiping out a lot of innocent lives."

"We can't reason with these people," Harry replied. "We're never going to change the extreme, radical, Muslim mentality. Their attitudes go back thousands of years. We have to take the Islamic reign of terrorism out of power and, unfortunately, the only way to do that is through warfare. This is hardly a time for turning the other cheek."

There was a lull in the conversation while salad was served. Jenny asked Harry's wife, Kate, how she liked living in Washington. She learned that, for years, Kate had served on the Board for the Center for American Women and Politics. Describing Emmy as Kyle's sister-in-law, Jenny asked Kate if she knew her. She explained she had just begun working at CAWP a few months earlier. Kate promised to look her up and make her feel welcomed. From the excitement in her voice, Jenny could hear how much Kate enjoyed her work with the center; from Kate's description, it was non-partisan and rather laissez-faire in its philosophy. It became clear to Jenny that Kate and her husband were not joined at the hip in their politics. Jenny was thrilled that Emmy was involved with such a worthwhile group and might have the benefit of working more closely with Kate.

Before long, Harry picked up where the conversation had left off. "These terrorists leave us no alternative. They're not only terrorizing us. They're slaughtering their own countrymen as well. We owe it to ourselves and to those who look up to us to stop these groups from further acts of violence."

"I thought our goal was to introduce democracy to these countries and liberate those who are living in fear," Marilyn offered.

Jenny admired the governor's wife for speaking her mind. Kate remained quiet but appeared to agree with Marilyn's comment.

"Exactly. It isn't easy to instill democracy. It may take years, but our only hope for real change is with a democracy," the governor said.

"No country has ever been liberated by destroying it," Kyle said. "You don't help a country by going in and killing thousands of innocent people. There has to be another way. When the U.S. invaded Panama, we went in during the middle of the night and plucked out Manuel Noriega. He is in prison today. Why couldn't we do that with Osama bin Laden?"

"This is much more complicated," answered the governor. "Bin Laden is well-hidden. And his loyal followers are so committed to their cause that they are willing to sacrifice their own lives. These are ruthless terrorists, and we have no choice but to go after them. And that means conducting warfare on their soil."

"I'm not sure that I understand what drives them," Jenny said. "What have we done to cause this degree of hatred?"

Putting his arm around the back of her chair, Kyle reinforced his appreciation for her raising that question. "That's exactly what we as Americans should be asking," Kyle declared. "It isn't possible for any of us to bring peace to any situation until we assume responsibility for our part in what brought about the friction."

Jenny caught Kyle's eye to see if he picked up on the profundity of his own words. *Hadn't this been part of their own growth experience in working through their relationship?*

"Assume responsibility for what?" the governor asked with mild annoyance. "These hatemongers attacked us for no reason. All we've tried to do is help Afghanistan. We came to the country's rescue when it fought Russia. We've supported its economy with our oil trade. What have we ever done wrong?"

"We say we are protecting *their* interests," Kyle responded, "but we have a knack of going into a country, consuming its resources, and leaving the country in ruins. Sure, we provided the weapons and assisted the Afghan people in their war against Russia. But why did we do that? Because there was something in it for us in our own cold war against Russia, that's why. And when we left, we did nothing to rebuild the country. We have given the bin Ladens of the world plenty to fuel their fire of hatred."

"That's just a lot of bleeding liberal bunk," the governor said. "Kyle, these men are evil. That's all there is to it."

"Damn it, Jed. You are such a reasonable man on so many issues. Why . . . ?" Kyle took a deep breath before he continued. "Dostoevsky wrote, 'While nothing is easier than to denounce the evildoer, nothing is more difficult than to understand him.'"

Jenny looked on with fascination. Kyle was one of the most well-read men she knew, and she often heard him quote people to gain power in a debate.

Just then, the entree was brought into the room. Once the plates were served, Kyle resumed his point with greater restraint. "We make up five percent of the world's population and consume forty percent of the world's resources. We have made ourselves the great nation that we are at the expense of many of these third-world countries. As long as there are haves and have nots, as long as there are people whose bellies are full and those who are starving, there will never be peace in the world. And that isn't liberal anything. That is just the plain and simple truth."

"That's nonsense," Harry retorted. "There's a liberal body in this country that wants to blame the U.S. for everything that happens that isn't to their liking in the world. America has a responsibility to protect and defend our people and those in Afghanistan. And it isn't just about us. Look at the plight of the Afghan women. They're treated like chattel; they can't go to school; they can't have careers; and they can't escape. What kind of people would we be if we let them continue to have meaningless lives? We are there to capture these terrorists and to help the country rebuild as a democracy. I can't see how anyone could disagree with what we're doing there."

"I agree with these reasons for our presence in Afghanistan. But why didn't we do that ten years ago when we were 'helping' them?" Kyle asked. "We saw the abject poverty and dire oppression of the Afghan people then. But we didn't stay around to do anything about it.

Just look at the difference between how we dealt with the aftermath of World War II and the aftermath of the Afghan war against Russia. In the former war, we were seen as a nation who stood with the Jews during the Holocaust and with the West Germans against the Russian blockade. We were saviors to them. After the war, we stayed to help reconstruct countries like Germany and Japan, and today they are our allies. They have no hatred toward us."

"Those were different times," Harry responded.

"And we were a different America in the forties," Kyle countered. "If we dealt with both situations in the same compassionate way, maybe there wouldn't have been the intense swell of hatred that resulted in the bombing of the Twin Towers."

"You're going back to the past," Harry said. "We have no choice now but to stay on the offense against the enemy. I see us doing something noble in Afghanistan and, until we have captured this evil man and the rest of his terrorist followers, the world will not be safe."

"Today, other countries, especially third-world countries, see us as a people who will step in to 'liberate' them when there is something in it for us. They see America as a country that stands for profit for ourselves at any expense and that uses our military to achieve this," Kyle said. "Why do you think the U.N. won't cooperate with us?"

Governor Bradley was becoming noticeably worked up. "The U.N. is a corrupt but necessary organization. We have to do what we know is right. If there is any cause for people hating us, it is jealousy."

Kyle appeared equally agitated. "If we can go across the world and drop bombs, why can't we go across and drop food? Look at the poverty, starvation, and destitution of these people we're purportedly going to free. Thirty thousand children under the age of five die every single day of malnutrition and disease."

"That's just a bunch of liberal gibberish. It sounds good, but the reality is that we have to be the aggressor," the governor stated firmly as he lightly banged his fist on the table. "It's been proven time and time again that appeasement encourages aggression by the terrorists as it did with the Nazis and the communists. We have two world wars and a long series of terrorist attacks that show the fallacy of pacification. This is not about root causes, poverty, starvation, or U.S. arrogance. It is about eliminating the terrorists before they kill us."

"Do to others before they do it to you—not exactly the golden rule by any religious standard," Kyle said with a twinkle in his eye, attempting to lighten the conversation. Jenny nudged his foot with her own to let him know how well he had timed changing the tone of the discussion.

On the drive home, Jenny told Kyle how proud she was of him. "You're not afraid to say what you think, even with the odds stacked against you. I love that about you."

"Do you think any of us came any closer to hearing each other tonight . . . or, more importantly, to understanding?"

"Well, there is at least one of us who came closer to understanding *you* tonight," Jenny said softly as she reached for his hand and held it tightly for the remainder of the ride home.

As the weeks unfolded, the pressure on Kyle continued to escalate right along with the war itself. His time with Jenny, however, was relatively stress-free. He thanked God everyday that she had not totally given up on him after the incident with Mike. Jenny's unconditional love continued to amaze him. Above all else, he loved her because he knew their relationship had been on the brink of failing and it was Jenny's belief that, with outside help, he could work through the problem that had saved it from utter destruction.

Kyle picked up the makings for dinner on his way home from work. He greeted Jenny with a warm kiss as she joined him on the patio. As he flipped the hamburger patties, he talked about internal struggles he was facing. "I used to be a basic, down-the-middle Democrat. But over this past year, something is happening to me."

"I see you becoming more distressed about the war and more caught up with matters involving human rights and human dignity. You've helped open my mind to some of these issues," Jenny said as she stood behind him and put her arms around him.

"Thanks, sweet pea. It's reassuring to know that I have a positive influence on you."

As they crawled into bed for the night, Jenny kissed him and then touched her forehead to his. "You're so special, Kyle Anderson. Our state is fortunate to have you protecting it. And I feel blessed to have you watching out for me."

They lay together in silence for a moment before Kyle began speaking again. "I find myself reading things I wouldn't have given the time of day to a year ago—things that come across my desk like this." He sat up and grabbed a *Workers Party* newsletter from the nightstand, pointing her to a headline that read, "The U.S. Government Keeps Escalating Its War Against the People of Afghanistan."

Jenny scanned the article.

> For more than two weeks, U.S. bombs and cruise missiles have rained down on people, especially targeting the major cities of Kabul, Khandahar, and Jalalabad. Savage bombardment has destroyed airports, electrical installations, and other vital infrastructure. As many as 900 civilians are reported killed and thousands injured. U.N. and other international relief agencies have repeatedly condemned U.S. bombardment as the cause of impending humanitarian disasters, including a massive refugee crisis and the possible starvation of seven million people.

Jenny skimmed the rest of the article, learning that the Bush administration anticipated that the war was only the first round in a long-term war against international terrorism. Top U.S. officials were openly calling for an all-out war against Iraq and, the previous week, had begun talking about extending the war into neighboring countries. "In summation," the article concluded, "the U.S. war in Afghanistan will only create greater tensions and new wars throughout the region and the world." Jenny looked at Kyle and saw the sadness in his eyes.

"It sounds like the beginning of World War III, doesn't it," Kyle whispered. A tear slipped down his face. "With all of our sophistication as a nation, I don't understand why we're choosing such an extreme means of addressing the problem. I supported going into Afghanistan. But I had hopes that we'd go in, get bin Laden and his al Qaeda network, and get out. Why are we killing so many innocent Afghans? We are doing exactly what they did to us, and that makes us no better than them. And as long as I work in the government, I feel I am an accomplice to this."

"Do you want out of government?" Jenny asked, turning onto her side and facing him.

"The party is asking me that," Kyle responded quietly. "I have put off giving them a direct answer as long as I can. I've been a public servant for a long time now. Maybe I need a change."

"What would you do?"

"I'm not sure . . . but something worthwhile." Kyle spoke with more power in his voice. "I'd find a way to make a difference."

Jenny was still going with Kyle to see Harvey, who had become more of a friend while remaining very much Kyle's doctor. He was supportive of Kyle going for treatment but from the very beginning had expressed concern about the follow-up when Kyle returned home. If one had a drinking problem, there was always Alcoholics Anonymous. But if one suffered from bipolar or narcissistic tendencies, there were no organized support groups.

"So now what?" Kyle asked him one afternoon.

"Well, the challenge with your unique personal struggles is that they can crop up any time, Kyle. I spoke with your doctor from the program and I'd like to share some information with Jenny."

Kyle nodded his approval.

"Sometimes the needs of one twin are satisfied by mirroring the identical twin," Harvey told them. "If this happens, it can interfere with normal bonding and gradual separation from the mother."

"So my not feeling particularly close to my mother is because I had my twin and didn't need her as much?" Kyle asked.

"Something like that . . . but we are more concerned about the separation-identification experience. If anything happens that gets in the way of a child not seeing himself as a separate individual, there may be later signs of faulty development of the ego. In other words, too much early identification can sometimes prevent normal development of self-worth and can result in narcissistic character malformation."

Jenny thought back to her conversations with Kerry, who had predicted that Kyle had narcissistic tendencies. "So why isn't Kyle's brother fighting the same demons?"

"Good question," Harvey said. "Identical twins do have the same set of genes when they're born. But a recent survey showed that, shortly after conception, identical twins begin to differ increasingly in the normal chemical changes that occur in their genes. Differences emerge as the twins grow older and become even greater the longer they live apart."

"I've never believed that we're victims of our early childhood experiences," Jenny told Harvey. "Right or wrong, I learned to survive living without either parent mostly by developing my people-pleasing and helper skills. I just won't accept that any of us has to be stuck where we are. I have faith in the human ability to grow and work through any situation."

"I agree with you," Harvey responded. "And, hopefully, you both will spend the rest of your lives developing yourselves." Turning to Kyle, Harvey added, "My sense is that you and Jenny both share a fear of being abandoned. Anticipating this, in an all-out effort to avoid it, you precipitated it. Maybe your subconscious reasoning was that by being the cause of your own abandonment, you were in control of your relationship."

"So I'm the pleaser and he's the controller," Jenny reasoned. "Are those compatible dysfunctions?" Jenny joked.

"I'm afraid not if your apprehension is being abandoned. If I'm reading this correctly, Kyle doesn't want to be abandoned again, either. So he's likely to say to himself, 'If anyone will do the leaving, it will be me,'" Harvey said.

Kyle appeared forlorn. The last thing he wanted to do was leave Jenny. "What can I do to keep working through my own stuff?"

"I would like to see you in a support group. But it may have to be one that you create. Do you have some guys in your life that you can open up with?"

"It's hard with the visibility I have in my job. I don't know . . ."

"The best thing you can do is to be in some kind of work where you are serving people," Harvey said. "Get out of yourself and make a difference in the lives of others."

"What can I do to help?" Jenny asked. "I'm so happy with our relationship now, and I don't want to lose what we have."

"Stop being the helper. It seems to me you have already helped plenty," Harvey said.

Kyle agreed. "She's the best. I don't know what I would've done without her."

Determined to follow up in every way possible after their respective programs, Kyle offered to join Jenny for her weekly visit with her therapist. Sitting across from Dr. McFarland, holding hands, they both acknowledged that everything with them was going well and they wanted to keep it that way by continuing to work on their relationship.

The doctor observed how they looked at each other when they spoke to or about the other. They addressed each other with kindness while still being honest about their hurdles.

Kyle was forthright with Dr. McFarland, bringing up his difficulty with the priests. "I'm handling it much better now, but I know it isn't going to be easy. I also want to give Jenny more space and be less demanding but . . ."

"But what?" the doctor probed.

"Why," he asked sincerely, "shouldn't I be able to be with her most of the time outside of working hours? At our age, and after nearly two years of dating, what's wrong with wanting to live together or . . . or get married?"

"These seem like fair questions." Dr. McFarland turned to Jenny and asked, "So what holds you back?"

Jenny thought about the question carefully before speaking. "It's complicated, of course. And I'm not sure that I know the answer. I know that I want Kyle to have all the time he needs to rediscover himself after his long-term marriage. A big part of it is that I need to see him able to hold steady for a while. I need him to get things more settled with his ex-wife and his boys."

"You're making this all about Kyle. What about you? Are you ready to fully commit to Kyle? And if not, why not?"

Jenny didn't answer immediately. "I don't know. It's not because I don't love him."

"Do you trust that he will be there for you, no matter what?"

Jenny shook her head from side to side as she teared up. "I want to trust him. But . . ." Desperately, she tried to sidestep the directness of the question. "What's the hurry? What's wrong with what we have now? We're together almost all the time anyway. Let's give ourselves a little time to live the commitment we've made before we rush into anything more."

It was apparent that Kyle and Jenny were in different places on the subject of the next step in their relationship. Dr. McFarland was careful not to take sides and didn't make either of them feel that their point of view was inappropriate. Kyle was ready to move forward, and Jenny was happy where they were.

After all the work Kyle had done in Tucson, he was dedicated to taking this time for serious evaluation of himself—whether he was making advancement in his personal growth, and whether he and Jenny had, as Harvey put it, a "compatible set of dysfunctions." He knew that if his desire for her was primarily to satisfy his own needs, then she was replaceable. There were numerous others who undoubtedly could be more accommodating. He was conscious about how much he wanted *this* relationship to evolve to its full capacity. But for that to be, he had to find within himself the ability to love her enough to want what was best for her. He prayed that he could be a genuine spiritual partner to her.

Relationships had never been easy for Jenny. She had always worked hard at them and was in awe of people who said they were with someone with whom they'd never had a misunderstanding or a disappointment or an argument. She found it hard to believe this was really possible. From her experience with Don, Matt, and now Kyle, some heartache just went with the package. Was she willing to give herself so completely to another man for a third time? What held her back? What was she afraid of? These were questions for which she was determined to find answers.

Twenty-two

Overcoming Fear of Trust

NOVEMBER 1 - DECEMBER 14, 2001

"Kyle wants us to get married . . . or at least live together," Jenny told Mike. "Like he says, we've been together for three years, and it's time to move on one way or another. Why am I so resistant to this? Am I afraid of marriage or of Kyle's instability?"

"Perhaps a bit of both, love," Mike responded. He was propped up in his bed, and Jenny sat on the edge. For this moment, he felt more energy than usual and he treasured all his time with Jenny.

She too loved these discussions with Mike and was grateful that he still had the mental capacity to discuss deeper subjects with her. It had always been such a core part of their friendship.

"You know, marriage began as a pagan event," Mike said. "It may have been to further validate women's subservient role to their husbands. Your idea of spiritual partnership is really taking the paganism out of it. At the Vatican Council back in the sixties, marriage was presented as a commitment not so much to physical security as to spiritual growth between two equals."

"Exactly," Jenny said. "In Gary Zukav's *Seat of the Soul*, he developed some strong beliefs that I've just begun coming to on my own over the past several years. He points out that marriage tends to place more emphasis on the couple's shared financial and physical union, while those in a spiritual partnership are more committed to their own and one another's spiritual growth. He sees spiritual partners assisting each other in the discovery of what he calls their 'authentic power,' which he describes as 'the alignment of the human personality with the soul.' Every hour of every day, we're confronted with choices, each one leading us to follow one avenue and not another. We can actually measure our growth by our awareness that we *are* making more responsible choices with a greater realization of their consequences."

"It certainly makes for a better opportunity to grow when that kind of inner work is done with someone else who's doing the same thing," Mike said. As he looked at Jenny sitting on his bedside, he added, "That's one of the roles you've played in my life."

Jenny squeezed his forearm. "That's the whole idea. It's what leads us beyond ourselves to a spiritual relationship."

"I don't hear you confused at all about where you stand on the subject of marriage," Mike said. "You want what you have just described. But does Zukav make any distinction between married partners and spiritual partners?"

"Well, he says it's possible for married partners to also be spiritual partners," Jenny explained, "but he indicates that it's special when that happens. Generally, he describes married partners as couples intending to have children and to merge their finances so as to build a home and life together. Spiritual partners bring a different consciousness to the relationship. They're less focused on the outer parts and mutually agree that their primary reason for being together is to help develop the 'soul' part of each other. I especially like the emphasis he places on trust, which he indicates is essential in a spiritual bonding."

"For this kind of intimacy to work," Mike observed, "it sounds to me like you would have to have two reasonably well-rounded, self-assured individuals who value each other's needs as much as their own. What I see holding you back is that you're still wondering if you have that with Kyle."

"Or with me. Do I have the capacity to trust one man that much? Gary says that spiritual partners are so committed to growing that they must create a safe space to say the things that really need to be said, that they can't be afraid to say things that they most fear would destroy the relationship. That's the part I have to overcome with Kyle. We're making headway but . . . ."

"Let's come back to the question about what you're looking for in your life now."

"I don't know if I want to get married again in the traditional sense," Jenny said. "I'm not even sure about living together, but I'm happy living separately and spending an exorbitant amount of time with Kyle . . . just like we're doing now. Maybe it's because I want to make sure that I remain fully responsible for myself so that I can reach beyond those comfortable places I've settled into in the past."

"So you've answered your own question. It's not marriage that you seem confused about. You can be married and have separate residences. You sound like you're afraid to let Kyle fully into your life."

"More than anything in the world, I want a normal life with Kyle. I love him so much, Mike. I know there are a myriad of reasons why I should let go of him, but I don't think we have a choice about why we love one person and not another. We just do. He's full of challenges, but my recent life hasn't been easy for someone to put up with, either. Both of us are the product of our life circumstances. The question is: has Kyle's made him too unstable for me to trust, or has mine made me incapable of placing that much trust in one man?"

"It sounds like a little of both," Mike said. "Neither of you has reached the point of unconditional trust in each other. And, without unwavering trust, you have only a façade of a relationship."

"I try to visualize myself falling backward, believing with absolute confidence that Kyle will catch me in his arms. But instead my head hits the floor. Mike, if I can't picture the trust in my mind, how will I ever achieve it in real life?"

"Is there anyone whom you can picture catching you?"

"You, Mike. And beyond you, I have absolute confidence that others will if I am surrounded by a circle of close friends. That is what I've experienced in my life. Men leave and friends are forever."

"You know that isn't healthy for you."

"I know. I know. That's what I need to work through if I'm ever to succeed in a long-term relationship. But maybe God doesn't intend that for me. Maybe I'm more likely to find the kind of trust and spiritual partnering I want with a circle of friends. That's the part about me that worries Kyle the most."

"Ideally, you should have both—a close bond with one special man *and* a close circle of friends all on the same journey. But I think you know, Jenny, that if God decided that I should live longer, it would be impossible for you to have both Kyle and me in your circle."

"Because I am sexually involved with him."

"Partly. But also because of Kyle's nature. That is his internal struggle. He isn't secure enough that *his* love is enough for you. If any other man loves you deeply and unconditionally, Kyle will be threatened. It won't ever be enough that you choose him as your primary partner and lover. He's extremely vulnerable when it comes to loving and being loved. He needs the exclusive love of one woman with no outsiders to jeopardize the relationship. There's nothing wrong with that, but it is clearly in stark contrast to what you want."

Jenny handed Mike his water. He took a sip and handed it back to her. She noticed his hand was shaking a bit. They had always loved these penetrating conversations about the human condition and about those who were closest in their lives. Setting the water down on the side table, Jenny spoke reflectively. "To me, human sexuality is such a mystery. Why are we drawn to one and not another? And how do we attach a definition to it when, in reality, a glance can be sexual? Holding hands and touching in a soft and gentle way can be sexual. Embracing, dancing, even thoughts can be sexual, while the act of intercourse itself can be a mechanical, programmed response. I can see myself becoming close to people on more than one level, but I would always want to be monogamous with Kyle. I want him to trust that without making a prisoner of me. No matter how many people are in my life, I will always choose him."

"And you, love, want to know that, when you face painful times, you can trust that he will be there, no matter what."

"It all comes back to trusting, doesn't it, Mike? And you have always reminded me that everything relates back to understanding— understanding why each of us has evolved with our own unique and personal challenges."

"And without understanding, there can be no forgiveness . . . no healing. Jenny, love, keep working on understanding each other. If you can do that, God will take care of the rest."

In the days that followed, Mike's health began to plummet. "I think the Lord may be ready to take me, love," Mike whispered to Jenny as she stopped by for her daily visit.

"Are you ready, Mike?"

"I wish I could stay longer. I haven't gotten Laurie her liver. And I haven't finished the work on several people's marriages."

"You did bless Gene's marriage. The rest may be things you'll have to finish from the other side," Jenny said, smiling at him.

"What about you, love? Are you going to be okay?"

"Things seem to be better for me. I'm stronger now. And Kyle is being an angel."

"Wherever I am, you know I'll be watching over you."

"I know, Mike. You've done that since we first met. I'm just grateful that I got my turn to take care of you."

Mike had little interest in food and was living almost exclusively on Ensure and soup broth. Father Jeff kept a monitor nearby, listening expectantly for any movement coming from Mike's bedroom. Gradually, their walks by the river slowed down, and they could only push him in a wheelchair until, finally, he became mostly bedridden. Jenny enjoyed sitting by his bed and reading to him or talking when he felt up to it. His recall of names was failing, but he could still remember certain people: Sister Marsha and his "girls," several of his priest friends, Gene, his brother and sister and nieces and nephews, the many who asked for his prayers, like Laurie. Mike clung to life as he struggled to retain some independence. Occasionally he fell and seriously bruised himself. The family wanted to bring in their own nurse, and Jenny was put in the uncomfortable position of insisting that they stay the course they were on. Their job now was to make his final days as painless as possible and to help him prepare for his transition from this life to the next.

Jenny shared her care-giving challenges with Kyle. He was pleased to see Jenny more accepting of the inevitable with Mike. For months, he believed her fight for Mike's life was not just for him as much as it was a protection against her own lack of readiness to accept his dying. How well he understood this as he recalled his own struggle with the deaths of his father and sister.

November 14 was Mike's birthday, and Jenny planned a small afternoon party for him. Kyle called and invited Jenny to dinner that evening. She agreed but asked if he could be flexible about the time. She expected the gathering to end around 7:00 PM, but she couldn't be sure that everyone would be gone by then. He hung up the phone, appearing to be perturbed with her answer.

A few minutes later, Kyle called back. "Let's just let this evening go," he said matter-of-factly.

"I don't want to let it go. I'm looking forward to having dinner with you. Can't you hang a little loose? Please."

"It's too hard, Jenny, just sitting here not knowing when you're coming. I don't like putting myself in that place. It's not healthy for me. I need to set boundaries for myself, just like you do. I'd rather know you're not coming at all than be left wondering when you'll finally get here."

Jenny's unwillingness to bend when it came to Mike vs. Kyle was the core of the problem for Kyle. *Why can't she hear my need*, Kyle thought, *and set a definite time to meet me? Let someone else say goodbye to the guests. Let someone else clean up the kitchen.*

Jenny felt guilty not doing what Kyle was asking. As much as it pained her, Jenny let go of plans with Kyle that evening.

Kyle then offered to pick Jenny up around noon the next day for the Cal State football game. She and Kyle almost always welcomed in the weekend together. Even the fact that he wasn't suggesting breakfast together bothered her. She hung up the phone feeling sad. The tables were turned. With Mike's approaching death, it was she who felt clingy. She needed to be with Kyle after the party.

Jenny rejoined the birthday crowd and made every effort to keep herself in the present moment. The rectory was filled with balloons and flowers and people coming through the door to wish Mike well. Mike tried to stay up for all the festivities but, before long, he asked to go back to bed. After a few minutes, Jeff went back to check on him.

"How're you doing, Mike?"

After a moment, he responded, "They're sure having fun out there." He couldn't stand to be missing a party. With great difficulty, he got up and rejoined his friends.

Jenny stayed to help clean up afterward and then headed home. She was still miffed at Kyle. More than anything, she wanted to crawl into bed with him and feel his arms around her. She was wearing down from the care giving and could use a little nurturing herself tonight. She thought about driving straight to his house and surprising him. But she realized that, after her previous experience, she was afraid of what she might stumble upon. *How strange,* Jenny thought. *If things are so great between us, why am I feeling this way? I shouldn't be afraid of going to Kyle's home unannounced.* But she was. Jenny drove home and climbed into bed alone.

The next day, Kyle picked Jenny up, and they headed for the game. Jenny knew that Kyle loved the Hornet games, but he was being somewhat aloof.

"What's up with you, Kyle? You seem . . . distant."

"Maybe more like detached. I'm working on being more removed from your time spent with priests."

Jenny could feel a fight coming on and wanted to do everything she could to avert it. She recalled everything she had learned at her program. She changed the subject. "What did you do last night?"

"I went out to dinner and a movie."

"By yourself?" she asked.

"With a friend."

"Why do I have the feeling it was a woman friend?"

"Maybe because it was?"

"Are you going to tell me who?"

"No. But don't worry," Kyle said. "I explained everything to her so she wouldn't get the wrong idea. She knows where you and I stand with each other."

"So where do we stand? I'm not sure I know."

"Look, Jenny, this whole thing with Mike is getting to me. It's always Mike first and then me. I can't go on living my life around when you are finished taking care of Mike. Harvey tells me I need to detach my emotions from all of that. I need to live my life and not always be waiting around to see when you can fit me in. That's all I did last night. There was nothing more to it."

Something told Jenny that there was much more to it. The evening would haunt her over the next few weeks. But for the moment, she let it go. Mike was dying, and she needed Kyle's support to get through it. She definitely didn't feel like arguing with him.

Over the past several weeks, Mike had been experiencing hallucinations. One day he thought he had been abducted. He insisted that his nurse tell Jenny so she would find him and bring him home. His vision no doubt was indicative of death approaching. During another visit, he told Jenny that his mother had come to visit him. From her experience with her own mother, Jenny believed that it was no hallucination. Mike described his mother standing in the doorway. She had spoken softly to him: "You'll be fine, Mike. Just keep up what you're doing, son." Despite the fact that he had come to accept that he was dying, he took her words to mean that he was going to get well.

Thanksgiving was approaching and soon after that would be Christmas. Jenny was dreading the holidays. Nothing would be the same this year. She had tentatively planned to go back to Dallas to bury Earl's ashes with her mother's and then travel to Cancun with Chad for the Thanksgiving holidays. She couldn't face celebrating the day sitting around a table with so many empty chairs. But Jenny was still worried about leaving Mike.

The shared tombstone for Ellen and Earl was finished and ready to be set in the ground. Jenny notified her family in Dallas, and most everyone was available on the Saturday before Thanksgiving. As her plans were coming together, Kyle offered to come and, when she asked him to join her and Chad in Cancun, he eagerly agreed. Burying her parents' ashes together in a single plot was going to be a momentous and emotional event for Jenny. She was elated that Kyle *and* Chad were coming with her. Chad had not seen the family in years, and Jenny was eager to have Kyle meet all of them.

Jenny checked in on Mike before she left. As he lay there weak and helpless, he told her not to worry about him. He said he would be fine and promised not to leave the world while she was gone. Jenny gave him a hug but pulled away and turned before he could see the tears running down her face.

It was November 22 when Jenny, Chad, and Kyle arrived in Dallas. It was a typical autumn day—in the mid-sixties and overcast with a bit of gloom in the air, enhanced further by the memorial honoring the 35th anniversary of the assassination of President John Kennedy. At Calvary Hill Cemetery, many of Jenny's family and friends gathered again around the plot that held her mother.

As they placed Earl's ashes in the ground next to Ellen's, Kyle read the Prayer of Committal.

"In sure and certain hope of the resurrection to eternal life through our Lord Jesus Christ, we commend to Almighty God our family members, Ellen and Earl Emerson, and we commit their ashes to the ground, earth to earth, ashes to ashes, dust to dust." Everyone gathered around the grave and, holding hands, they recited the *Our Father* prayer. Jenny knew her mother would have liked the service.

The weather was perfect as the threesome landed in Cancun. They were shuttled to their hotel located on the peninsula stretch of the island and, like in Bali, they were given rooms overlooking the ocean. Chad had a connecting door to their suite. Jenny was delighted to be with both her son and her man. They were a family enjoying the beautiful ambiance, the warmth, and the holiday together. They spent their days parasailing over the ocean, swimming with the dolphins, and being serenaded by mariachis while they dined. They devoted countless hours to reading and sunbathing. In the afternoons, they created a ritual of going in the expansive hot-tub bar, where they sipped margaritas while the warmth of the whirlpool swirled around them.

Just a few months before, Kyle and Jenny could have walked away from each other, could walk away still. But they were inexorably drawn to each other, as if by some divine ordinance. Peacefully, each night, they fell asleep in each other's arms to the sound of waves rolling onto the beach.

While they had been in Bali, Kyle had wanted to get matching rings as a symbol of their commitment. At that time, it was too soon for Jenny. But now, pleased with the direction their life was heading, she told him she was ready. They spent hours wandering through jewelry shops, looking at rings. They found the process of searching for them to be enlivening. Chad teased them about how much time they were taking to make their selection. Finally, they settled on simple matching silver rings.

With the rings in hand, Kyle led Jenny down to the beach at sunset. *Keep it simple*, he thought. *Don't make a big deal out of the exchange.* He had been ready for this moment far longer than Jenny. So many times Kyle had asked where their relationship was going. Now, at last, it was taking a direction of its own. Not a wedding—just a simple commitment of their love symbolized by an exchange of rings . . . on their *right* ring fingers.

Jenny was also ready to seal their bond. The very act of placing rings on each other's fingers was a huge step forward. For her, the exchange meant they could count on each other, knowing that they were fully committed. She felt she could melt into his arms at this moment, or better yet, fall backward into them, knowing that he would be there to catch her. His lips gently touched hers in the softest of kisses. The simplicity of the exchange and the quietness all around them said it all. "I love you and I always will. I go on choosing you."

As they walked away from the beach, they found Chad, and Kyle chose Ruth's Chris Steak House for their Thanksgiving dinner. Kyle ordered a special bottle of wine, Opus One, to celebrate the day and the new step they had taken.

Jenny had never had Opus One before. For that matter, neither had Kyle. She knew enough to appreciate that it was expensive and probably more so if it was imported. In his excitement, Kyle quietly ordered the wine from the waiter, paying no attention to the correlation of Spanish pesos to American dollars. When the bill arrived, showing the wine had cost several thousand pesos, Kyle was more than a little shocked.

"What's a few dollars compared to what we have to be thankful for this Thanksgiving?" Chad joked with Kyle. "Well, okay, maybe a few *hundred* dollars!"

On November 30, they headed home. Chad was ready, but Kyle and Jenny longed to stay in their fairytale world. Kyle had a heavy workload to face with all the ramifications of 9/11, and Jenny had to return to care for Mike, and look death squarely in the face once more.

Arriving back in Sacramento, Jenny made her way immediately to see Mike. The smile on his face showed how delighted he was to see her. "I can't thank you enough for all you've done for me," he said in a faint voice.

"I love you, Mike. And I will always be grateful to you for being there for me through my hard times."

He didn't answer. Tears simply streamed down his face.

Sister Marsha continued to visit Mike several times a week, and Jenny often joined them when she was there. Jenny felt she had much to learn from listening to Marsha and Mike talk in his last stage of life. Sister Marsha drew him out to talk openly about his feelings related to dying—the sadness of leaving all of his loved ones behind and the joy of being with the Lord and with his family and brothers and sisters and friends who had gone before him. Even though he was a priest and had counseled countless individuals about death, Mike admitted his own apprehensions about dying. Holding his hand, Sister Marsha assured him that the transition from this life to the next was nothing to fear. The beauty, the glory, the oneness with God would be so beyond any ecstasy he had ever known that his sadness and trepidation would be overshadowed. The loss and the grieving would rest with those he left behind.

"Our peace will come in knowing that you are no longer suffering, no longer sick, no longer feeling sadness of any kind. Our peace will come in knowing that you'll continue to be with us and watch over us and that our time to join you will come soon enough." Marsha's words brought comfort to Jenny as well.

It was only a few days later that Mike quietly drifted into a coma. The doctor continued to stop by. Hospice arrived three days a week. Father Jeff was with Mike night and day. Sister Marsha came every day to pray with him. His nieces and nephews stopped by often. Jenny was there by his bedside. While everyone watched, Mike was slipping away.

Meanwhile, in the hills of Tora Bora, Osama bin Laden was also slipping away—from his refuge in Afghanistan to create a new safe haven in Pakistan. As Josh sat at his desk reading the report copied to the Secretary of State's Office, he was outraged. Here it was December

2001, and the most wanted man in the world was cornered in a mountainous region along the Afghan-Pakistani border. The intelligence chief for the Eastern Shura, which controls eastern Afghanistan, testified that he was astounded that Pentagon planners didn't consider the most obvious exit routes and send in U.S. infantry ahead of time to block them. If bin Laden was not captured before he crossed into Pakistan, there was little or no chance of capturing him at all. Scanning the report, Josh noted that three of the most senior officers on the Joint Chiefs of Staff recommended opening another front to the south to halt the fleeing al Qaeda forces. The general in command, Tommy Franks, resisted being told what to do by anyone other than his direct chain of command, Secretary of Defense Rumsfeld. Josh read that Franks did open a second front by deploying a small unit of Marines, but they were so outnumbered by the 800 al Qaeda and Taliban forces that on the night of December 12, bin Laden appeared to have slipped away.

Too little, too late, Josh thought. *We knew right where he was. How could he escape? How could the Pentagon not redirect all its efforts to the most important mission of the war?* Josh found the answer as he read on. The U.S. military chose to outsource this part of the mission to Afghan troops purportedly because they knew this mountainous region better. But their failure to secure critical areas may have been intentional in order to aid bin Laden's escape. The report proposed that relying on local troops rather than more experienced and reliable U.S. troops could come to be seen as the gravest mistake in the war against al Qaeda. Josh set the report down on his desk as a tear ran down his cheek.

Besides receiving daily copies of the *Los Angeles Times* and the *San Francisco Chronicle*, Kyle continued to read offbeat publications to gain a well-rounded view of the Middle East conflict. In an issue of *Common Dreams*, he found an article by James Jennings titled, "U.S. Wages Overkill in Afghanistan," reporting how the U.S. military was using excessive tactics in their bombing of this small country.

> Polls and anecdotal evidence make it plain that Americans overwhelmingly favor the war in Afghanistan. But there's something terribly disquieting about TV images of an impoverished country filled with acutely suffering, starving

people being bombed daily while millions of Americans cheer.

Bombing Afghanistan has meant overkill from the beginning. The stark fact is that the world's richest and most powerful nation has for the past two months bombed one of the poorest and weakest. That's nothing to crow about. If a humanitarian catastrophe, such as is now looming, follows the war, then instead of celebrating a victory, the United States will suffer a strategic setback.

It was exactly what Kyle had feared from the beginning. Even though *Common Dreams* was considered far to the left of mainstream, he found its facts and perspective extremely accurate and sensible.

The total number of war victims in Afghanistan equals or exceeds those killed on our own soil on September 11. Only a handful of them could possibly have had any involvement with or responsibility for the September attacks. A realistic count shows that hundreds of civilians have been killed unnecessarily, people as undeserving of death from the skies as were the victims of the World Trade Center and Pentagon attacks.

Kyle set the publication down. So many thoughts tumbled through his head as he gazed out the window.

The next evening while Kyle and Jenny were having dinner at home, he suddenly announced, "I've decided I'm not going to run for office again."

Jenny looked apprehensive but said nothing.

"I'm sickened by the choices being made by our country," Kyle continued. "I can't be part of this government anymore. I'm too out of sync with what's happening. I have to find something to do where I *can* make a difference."

"You sure about this?" Jenny asked.

"I'm sure about needing to move on. What I'm not sure about is what to do next."

"Well, you have my support in whatever you decide."

"I hope so," Kyle said.

Jenny looked at Kyle and, for just a moment, felt afraid for him. She saw in him both vulnerability and strength, uncertainty and determination.

Beyond all else, she saw in him a man she loved and admired. She didn't care what title he held, she just wanted to see him fulfilled by his work.

The following evening, Kyle and Jenny attended the annual Christmas party given for the California Legislature and state employees. Kyle looked dashing in his tux, and Jenny wore the emerald jewelry that Kyle had given her the previous Christmas, a perfect contrast to her red velour skirt and lacy white blouse. At times they were the only couple on the dance floor, allowing Kyle to whirl and twirl Jenny across the floor. They laughed. They kissed. They held each other close for slow dancing. With his arms around her, Jenny felt a strong sense of security. As she looked at her right hand resting in his, Jenny noticed her ring sparkling in the soft light of the ballroom. She was grateful for the joy of these recent months together. Whatever career decisions he might make, she felt at peace with their relationship and. more confident than ever that it was on solid ground.

"You know how often I've looked back at the Mercy gala event," Kyle reflected on their drive home, "and how much I loved our time together that night?"

"How could I forget?"

"This evening topped that," Kyle said. "I love you so much."

"I love you too."

Reveling in their happiness as they walked into River House, Kyle took a moment to check his answering machine. There was a message from his brother-in-law in Santa Monica that Kyle's mother had taken ill and had been rushed to the hospital. Kyle called the hospital and was immediately connected to his mother's room. Kyle spoke with Glennys for 15 or 20 minutes while Jenny stood by nervously. He assured Glennys that he was jumping on the next plane and would be there first thing in the morning. Closing the conversation with "I love you, Mother," he placed the phone back on its cradle and turned helplessly to Jenny.

"She sounds awful, Jenny," Kyle said as he began to cry. Jenny held him while tears streamed down his face.

Kyle spent the next few hours manically making calls and packing. He even phoned Harvey and, because of the obvious pressure Kyle was under, the doctor increased his medications. Kyle and Jenny had almost no sleep, but what little there was they spent holding each other. Long before dawn, the alarm sounded, signaling that it was time to get Kyle to the airport. As they waited in the lounge, having coffee, Kyle's cell phone rang. It was his brother-in-law calling to tell Kyle that Glennys had just passed away.

Thank God he spoke to her last night, Jenny thought. She held Kyle close and promised that she would join him for the funeral.

After his flight left, Jenny drove back home and caught a few winks before officially beginning her day. With Kyle out of town and Mike so close to the end, she spent a quiet day by Mike's bedside. Throughout the day, she read passages to Mike from his favorite books. Even though Mike lay in a coma, Jenny hoped he could hear the words and be comforted by them. One of Mike's favorite passages was from Thomas Merton's *Dialogues with Silence,* and Jenny slowly recited that part, a prayer, as it described how difficult it was to know the road ahead and where it will end.

" . . . Therefore I will trust you always though I may seem to be lost and in the shadow of death." Jenny closed the book as she read there is nothing to fear for God will "never leave me to face my perils alone."

Mike was holding on to life by a thread. *Who of us knows for certain what lies ahead in our lives? Not I,* Jenny thought. *Not Kyle. Maybe Mike's future is more evident.*

By nine in the evening, Jenny was exhausted and, with so little sleep the night before, she headed home for a while. She asked Father Jeff to call her if anything changed.

Twenty-three

Farewell Dear Friend

DECEMBER 14 - 22, 2001

Jenny had barely returned home and slipped into her bathrobe when Jeff called.

"You'd better come back right away," he told her. She hung up the phone, threw on a warm-up suit, and ran out the door. Her car was on automatic pilot as it made its way through the streets it had traveled so many times over the past year. Jenny's thoughts wandered back to the many experiences she had shared with Mike since they first met. She came out of her reverie just as she was pulling into the rectory parking lot. She hurried upstairs, let herself into Jeff's quarters, and headed straight to Mike's bedroom. A candle she had lit earlier in the day flickered in the darkness. Light from the nearby bathroom spilled softly into the darkened bedroom, and Jeff was sitting on the edge of Mike's bed, his face and eyes red from crying. Jenny sat down on the opposite side of the bed and slipped an arm under Mike's head while Jeff held one of his hands. Mike was fighting desperately for each breath of life. Though he remained unconscious, Jenny hoped he could hear her as she reassured him.

"It's okay, Mike. God is finally calling you home," Jenny said as tears ran down her cheeks.

"You're going to be fine, buddy. I love you," Jeff added.

They continued conversing with him just as they had so many times before when he was awake. Jenny thought back to how often she had said goodbye to Mike: in the ER in Tempe, the week after Easter, and again in October. But this time she knew his time had come.

Father Jeff got out his prayer book and found a litany to recite. In between each one, Jeff and Jenny sang in unison a modified version of a haunting song that was usually sung at Good Friday services. "Jesus, remember Mike as he comes into your kingdom. Jesus, remember Mike as he comes into your kingdom."

Everything seemed to be happening in slow motion. Mike's spirit was slowly, slowly leaving his body. His breathing was slowly, slowly stopping. Tears slowly, slowly slid down Jenny's cheeks—tears that were more for her loss than for his. Her faith reassured her that this was a moment to feel jubilance. Mike would soon be at peace, blissfully joining his family and friends who had gone before him all united in some cohesive and illuminating beatific vision. *But I am losing my friend,* she thought. She felt the loss as more tears spilled slowly, slowly down her cheeks. *Don't be sad,* she heard a voice speaking in her mind. *Mike will continue to watch over all of us with even more presence, more love, and more influence than he ever could before.* Suddenly, she began to feel a joyfulness overtake her.

Mike's breathing dwindled until finally, there was only silence.

"Father, into your hands we commend Mike's spirit," Jeff prayed.

With Mike's head cradled in the crook of her arm, Jenny sat very still. About a minute passed, and suddenly Mike expelled another breath. Frightened by the unexpected sign of life, Jenny's body jerked. She then realized it was the final discharge of air from his lungs. She looked up at the clock. It was 11:11 PM.

With an overwhelming sense of Mike's spirit leaving his body, Jenny whispered, "I love you, Mike." The candle's flame flickered, and then went out.

Hospice arrived and officially announced Mike's death. Shortly afterward, the mortuary arrived to take his body away. For the third time in a year, Jenny felt helpless as a body was being bagged and carried away. The cumulative effect weighed more heavily on her than her heart could bear. By 1:00 AM, a sense of emptiness filled the room. Oxygen seemed to have been replaced by some noxious substance that made it arduous to breathe. The finality of it all tore at Jenny's heart.

Jeff and Jenny made a few calls to Mike's family members, leaving the bulk of the calls for the next morning. The days that followed were all too familiar for Jenny.

Kyle and she were in communication two or three times a day. She had been worried about how he would handle Mike's death *and* his mother's. She felt close to Kyle even though they were apart because they were going through exactly the same ritual: arranging the funeral date, coordinating the service time with the bishop, getting programs and prayer cards printed, notifying family and friends, taking clothing to the mortuary, and arranging the viewing, cremation, and burial.

Mike's vigil service was set for Tuesday, his funeral on Wednesday, his cremation on Thursday, and his burial on Friday. In Mormon fashion, Kyle's mother's viewing, funeral, and burial would all be on the same day, Thursday. So Jenny could be present for all the events in Sacramento, join Kyle in Santa Monica on Thursday, and still make it back in time for Mike's burial service on Friday.

On Tuesday, about 150 family and close friends gathered for Mike's vigil with his "girls" at the Carmelite monastery, the same place where Jenny held her mother's funeral. Everyone had an opportunity to say their personal goodbyes to Father Mike, who was laid out in an open casket. Many of his friends came from out of town, each one explaining that he or she had a very, very special relationship with Mike. Sister Marsha turned to Jenny and whispered, "Boy, are they going to be surprised to discover the other two hundred of us." He'd had a way with people—everyone in Mike's life felt they shared a special closeness.

Father Jeff led the service and several people shared humorous stories and touching memories about Mike. One of the priests with an exceptionally beautiful voice sang an a cappella version of "Danny Boy." Mike had planned most of the service, so there was little question that it was to his liking.

The next day there would be a formal service, but this evening was an informal gathering of most everyone close to Mike. Jenny chose this time to read a portion of Mike's will as he had dictated it to her in the hospital. Although it was a legal document, it read more like a prayer and a testimonial to his family, his friends, and his God. Jenny could hear his niece gasp when she read the part that mentioned her and her two daughters: "Sarah will always be the daughter I never had. And I will regret it if I am not able to dance at Nicky's wedding or watch Maggie receive her advanced degrees."

When Jenny reached the part where he thanked her personally, she momentarily broke down, and Sister Marsha came to her rescue and read it for her.

> Jenny Roberts has become the closest person to me in my life and in more ways than one saved my life during periods of extreme danger during my bout with cancer. Her willingness to sacrifice and change her plans for me is something I could never dream of repaying. Having come through so much together, all I ask is that the Lord will allow us to spend many more years together, and when he finally comes to call me home, I will pick a place for her as well.

The crowd milled around afterward not quite ready to accept that Mike would no longer be in their lives.

Among Mike's diverse friends, some were students of numerology. Commenting on the time of Mike's death, one woman shared with Jenny that the number eleven is considered to be a master number.

"It represents such qualities as idealism, visionary insight, intuition, and revelation," the woman told Jenny. "But the number repeated is even more powerful: 11:11 is seen as a key to unlock the subconscious mind and a reminder that we are primarily spirits having a physical experience—not merely physical beings embarking on a spiritual experience." The woman's words brought Jenny comfort.

When Jenny arrived home, fumbling with her keys, she raced in to the sound of the phone ringing. It was Kyle. She fell on the bed, revived just hearing his voice.

"How did your day go?" he asked sweetly.

"One down and the rest of the week still to go. Emotional trauma is so much more fatiguing than running a marathon. I can't begin to tell you how totally drained I am."

"I can relate. I didn't think I'd feel the loss of my mother this much."

"I think it's much better that you're feeling it rather than stuffing it down. It's hard to believe all of this is happening to us at once."

"Well, that must be God's plan," Kyle said. "Perhaps we're meant to deal with these deaths, and then put them behind us so we can get on with our lives."

"I have one small thing I need to deal with in order to put this to rest. I need to make amends with Mike's family. They've been distressed during this last month of his life about not continuing the same regime with his food and pills and I think pretty upset with me for not letting them bring in their own nurse."

"Well, that seems rather normal," Kyle said.

"I agree. Everyone deals with death in different ways. But as the end neared, it was hard for them to accept some aspects of our care-giving. They didn't all approve of the vigil service this evening. Some of them wanted a rosary at the vigil tonight."

"I thought Mike laid out the services just the way he wanted them." Kyle said.

"He did. But that still doesn't take away their hurt," Jenny said. "I need to clear this up before they all head out of here."

"How do you plan to do that?"

"I'm leaving here to be with you immediately after the funeral, and I won't be back again until Friday for the burial," Jenny said. "I thought maybe I could do it over dinner after the burial. That is the only time I can foresee having with them. Will you go with me?"

"I don't know, sweet pea. To be honest,,, I don't really want to spend time with Mike's family. "

Jenny sighed. *It seemed so little to ask.* But she said nothing more.

"I'm so glad you're coming down here," he said, changing the subject. "It means more to me than I can ever tell you."

"It all worked out so nicely, didn't it? Obviously God is in charge of all of this."

"I'll be there to meet you, and I have a nice evening planned. By the way, when are you returning? I'll schedule myself to come home with you."

"On Friday. I land around 1:00 PM."

"You'll miss the ladies' Christmas luncheon at Mandy O'Connor's."

In all the distractions of the week, the event had completely slipped Jenny's mind even though she had attended the gathering for more than twenty years. *Is Kyle being thoughtful, suggesting that it would be good for me to take out a couple of hours to celebrate Christmas with Mandy? Or is he being cynical about his ongoing disapproval of my "rich Republican friends"?* Jenny wasn't sure, but she wanted to believe the former. Unsure about clarifying his statement, she sidestepped the question.

"I have to call the airline to confirm my reservation," Jenny said. "Let me call you back with the exact time and the flight number. Will you be home for a little while?"

"I'll be here." He hesitated and then added, "I'm so glad you're coming down."

"Me, too. I'm glad it's all working out."

"That's for sure." After a pause, he added, "I love you, Jenny."

Jenny hung up and called Southwest Airlines to inquire if there was an earlier flight. There was one that would get her back by 11:00 AM instead of 1:00 PM, and that would allow her to be present for all the events for Kyle's mother in Santa Monica and squeeze in the luncheon before Mike's burial back in Sacramento. With the flight confirmed, she called Kyle back to give him the time, but his line was busy. She kept trying, but to no avail. Gradually, she drifted off to sleep.

Jenny's phone rang early the next morning. "Well, I see that you changed your flight home." Kyle's voice was perturbed.

Jenny couldn't believe that an airline would give her flight information to him. "What do you mean?" she responded, uncertain what to say and wanting to avoid an argument.

"You know damn well what I mean. The airline agent told me you had moved your reservation up from what you had originally scheduled."

"Is that time all right for you?" she asked, evading the issue.

"Yes, I booked myself home at the same time, but I guess some things just don't change."

"Sweetheart . . . please."

"Damn it, Jenny, you just can't miss a party, can you? Especially an O'Connor party."

If she had any doubts about his intention in mentioning the party, there was now no mistaking how he'd really felt.

"Sweetheart, after all I will have been through this week, I really wanted to do something uplifting—something that will remind me this *is* the Christmas season. This time of the year is not supposed to be all about death but also about new birth."

Kyle was quiet for a moment and then said in an agitated tone, "Is there Monday Night Football this week or are you done with that?"

"I'm not sure." She really wasn't sure and had given it no thought.

"Ten thousand dollars says you'll go."

"With ten thousand dollars riding on it, I can absolutely guarantee you I *won't* go."

"You know, I keep hoping against hope but, the fact is, you'll never change, Jenny."

"Kyle, I don't know what you want from me. What is the big deal about my going to a ladies' Christmas luncheon for a couple of hours? I've been going for years, and I enjoy it. We have finally reached the place of having things the way you have wanted them for so long. All my care giving responsibilities are over now. I'm yours. We can make our life whatever we want it to be. Please try to think of it that way and don't be so hard on me. We've both been through too many losses. We don't need to be fighting." Jenny let the silence linger and then asked: "You still want me to come down?"

"Of course I want you to come."

"Then I'll be there," Jenny said.

In Santa Monica, Josh arrived before Emmy to help with the funeral arrangements. He was still keeping in close touch with his office, and had that morning learned from an intelligence agent that U.S. military leaders had committed too few ground troops to the Tora Bora campaign. Consequently, Osama bin Laden had escaped through a mountain pass.

In the fact-finding missions that followed, it was learned that other al Qaeda leaders were dispersing by different routes, but bin Laden and his men were journeying on horseback directly south toward Pakistan. All along the route, in the dozens of villages and towns on both sides of the frontier, the Pashtun tribes were lighting campfires along the way to guide the horsemen as they slowly continued through the snow toward the old Pakistani military outpost of Parachinar. Considering the season, Josh thought, the scene conjured up something quite ethereal . . . not unlike the scene of the magi on their way to visit the Christ child.

In Sacramento, a crowd had already begun to gather for Mike's funeral when Jenny arrived at the church. The mortuary had moved Mike's body from the monastery to the vestibule and opened the casket for viewing. As it came time to begin the service, the coffin was closed and Jenny joined the procession into the church. When it was time, Jenny followed the master of ceremonies to the podium and, looking out at the eight or nine hundred in attendance, she read: "For everything there is a time . . . a time for laughing and a time for weeping, a time for living and a time for dying . . ." She managed to get through the entire reading without weeping and to communicate the message with all the love she could project.

Father Jeff gave the homily . . .

> Gaudete, Rejoice! Seventy-three years after God gave life to Michael Joseph O'Malley, he called him home to the heavenly kingdom. Gaudete, Rejoice! Forty-three years after being called to the priesthood, Father Mike took his place in the heavenly liturgy. Gaudete, Rejoice! Thirteen months after the doctors told him that he had advanced liver cancer with only three months to live, Mike O'Malley gave up his spirit among us to enter the fullness of the kingdom of God.
>
> In the Gospel for Gaudete Sunday, Luke tells us that even tax collectors, who were held in low esteem, and soldiers, whose job it was to keep the chosen people subject to Rome, were all welcomed. It is as if Luke were saying, "If you think the Lord is interested in preaching only to the already converted, think again." And wasn't that Mike? You may remember the ad he placed in the *Sacramento Bee*: "Former Catholics, resigned Catholics, cultural Catholics, angry and disappointed Catholics, collapsed Catholics, retro-Catholics, pre-Vatican II Catholics, questioning Catholics, survived-Catholic-school Catholics, never-darken-church-doors-again Catholics, wanna-be Catholics, missing-in-action Catholics, never Catholics—we

extend a warm and cordial welcome." Father Mike went out into the highways and byways—which, for him, meant football games, weddings, social events, political functions, fundraisers, dinner parties, any kind of party—and welcomed everyone into the wedding feast of the Church. A died-in-the wool Democrat, an unwavering Redskins fan, a devoted Catholic priest, Mike touched lives from the South Sea islands to a little church in the Bahamas, and most especially in our community, always making a difference in so many lives. All considered themselves members of Mike's inner-circle: wealthy, homeless, mainstream, upper-echelon, and even those most would consider a bit wacky.

Father Mike gave his last sermon just a few months before his own passing, at the funeral of the mother of one his closest friends.

Jenny's eyes welled up at the reference to her mother, and she said a silent prayer for both Ellen and Earl. She shifted in her chair uncomfortably as she remembered Mike's valiant delivery of his homily.

In the eulogies that followed, Mike's niece and nephew recalled how fully their uncle involved himself in their lives and that of their children. As Gene Vechio choked back his tears, he acknowledged that he had never confided in another man the way he had with Mike. There was something about Mike that drew everyone out. Sister Marsha recalled when Father Mike first volunteered to be the chaplain at Carmel. She expressed how he truly lived the meaning of priesthood through his lifestyle of reaching out to many diverse people. She concluded by sharing how privileged all the sisters felt to have Mike buried at Carmel, where even his silent counsel could be sought.

"That was the most beautiful funeral for a priest I have ever seen," one priest commented during the Irish wake afterward.

"Father Mike should be pleased," Jenny replied. "After all, he chose each participant and outlined his final celebration of life right down to the last hymn."

Before heading for the airport, Jenny went back to the sacristy to pick up Mike's chalice. In his will, Mike had left this to her in gratitude for her love and caring for him. She had already chosen a place for it on her mantle.

Leaving from the church for the airport, Jenny arrived at the check-in desk with just enough time to spare. She needed to put Mike's funeral behind her and refocus her attention on Kyle and his mother's funeral. *So much bereavement in one short week*, she thought.

As Jenny came through the gate in the Los Angeles airport, Kyle's smiling face greeted her. They grabbed a hold of each other as if to cleave to life itself with their embrace. She glanced down at his right hand, and the ring that matched her own was still on his finger.

They stopped by the mortuary on their way to dinner. According to Mormon custom, Kyle told Jenny he needed to put a handkerchief in his mother's hand.

Oh, and doesn't everybody stop by a mortuary on their way to dinner? Jenny thought with perverse amusement.

As they stood beside his mother's coffin and paid their respect, Kyle voiced displeasure with the way Glennys' lipstick had been applied. He accepted Jenny's offer to help, and she touched Glennys' lips with her fingers, gradually smoothing and reshaping the lipstick lines. But the lipstick smeared horribly. Under the stress of the situation, they began to giggle. And giggle. The mortician entered the room and offered to repair the damages. He didn't appear to share their humor.

Afterward, they drove to Ruth's Chris, a chain of the same restaurant where they had dined in Cancun during their Thanksgiving holiday. Despite a wonderful meal and glass of Rombauer chardonnay, Jenny felt a subtle shift in Kyle's attitude. She broached the subject of his mood, but that only seemed to irritate him more. He wasn't able to talk about what was troubling him. It wasn't clear that even Kyle knew.

It had been an exhausting day, and Jenny just wanted to lie in Kyle's comforting arms. But he was in a different place. He was angry with her, and she didn't know why. *Is this how he deals with death? Perhaps he has no built-in immune system for handling crises*, she thought. *Or maybe he's still angry over Mike and all the care and attention I gave him.*

They went back to his mother's house and climbed into bed. But before long, Kyle got up and went to a different bedroom in the house. Jenny didn't know where she mustered the strength, but she followed him into the other bedroom and crawled into that bed with him. She told him that they needed each other right now and whatever it was that was bothering him couldn't be more important than what they had to face the next day.

"Do you want to go through tomorrow without me?" Jenny asked.

"No."

"Do you want me to stay?"

"Yes," he whispered.

"Then act like it. You aren't the only one who's had a tough week. Do you want to tell me what's bothering you? Or do you want to fall asleep in my arms and let go of it?"

He didn't answer but curled his body up next to her. That was answer enough.

Jenny fell asleep thinking of a line from the movie, *As Good As It Gets*: *"Why can't I have a normal boyfriend? Just a regular boyfriend, one that doesn't go nuts on me!"* And the response had been, *"Everybody wants that, dear. It doesn't exist."*

The following morning, Emmy arrived from New York and they all fondly embraced. Kyle and Josh were the perfect sons at the funeral home, warmly greeting Cassie's family and longtime friends of their mother's. Kyle introduced Jenny to each person and seemed proud and comforted to have her by his side. Even when Kyle's former wife, Jo, and their two boys arrived, everyone managed to deal with the awkwardness with little tension.

Glennys was placed in the viewing room, and everyone gathered there during the first hour and a half. Then the crowd slowly moved to the chapel, where the Mormon bishop conducted the service. Kyle did a beautiful job of eulogizing his mother and celebrating her life story of 90 years. Out of character, Josh was more reserved but added his own comments. To his own surprise, Kyle was experiencing the agony of losing his mother even more deeply than when their father died. Pulling out his violin, Kyle closed the service by playing "Come Come ye Saints" for his mother. The gathering drove in procession to the cemetery and remembered Glennys through prayers as she was lowered into the ground. Josh and Kyle each placed a rose at her graveside. Kyle went second and arranged the stem of his rose to touch that of Josh's so that it looked like two roses blooming from one stem.

Back at the church, many of the mourners gathered for food and punch. In Mormon fashion, there was no alcohol. The spirit of the wake was more reserved than Jenny's Catholic experiences. But then, she had just come from Mike's Irish Catholic wake where wine and emotions flowed freely.

Josh had arranged for Emmy and him to stay with family friends. The couples agreed to meet for dinner at a neighboring restaurant. Kyle was fidgety and somewhat distant. Even Josh noticed his brother's uneasiness.

Arriving back at Glennys' house after dinner, Kyle picked up the previous night's discussion where it had left off. This time, Jenny's assertiveness failed to calm him down. She could not get him to talk about what was bothering him. They both had a sleepless night and ended up in the TV room watching an old movie, Jenny lying on the couch and Kyle on the floor with a pillow and blanket. As the romance in the movie began to build, Jenny gradually moved down to the floor and joined him. They lay together as she rested her head on his shoulder. As the scene in the movie escalated, so did the passion between Kyle and Jenny. They made love as intensely as ever before. Their bodies enveloped each other like vines that entwined and wove together through misty rainfall until they became completely entangled. Exhausted, they spent what was left of the night dozing on the floor.

The next morning, Kyle was in a better mood. He went to his mother's closet and pulled out a mink coat and held it out for Jenny to slip on. It fit beautifully. She took this as a gesture of him making up with her. Jenny was grateful and, to show her appreciation, she wore the coat on the trip home. Jenny wasn't just thankful for the coat but for its symbolism that the strife between them, whatever it was, appeared to be over.

Arriving back in Sacramento, Kyle insisted on going to get his car, which, of course, Jenny had parked. She tried to describe where it was but, while she got the baggage, he was unable to find his vehicle. Twenty minutes later, as he walked back toward her standing at the curb, she could tell that he was beyond frustrated and was fighting to contain it. She left him with the baggage while she went to get the car and pulled up in front of him. He loaded the bags and climbed into the driver's side. The silence was deafening.

Jenny asked if he wanted to drive her home or to Mandy's luncheon. He didn't seem to care, so she asked to be dropped at the O'Conners and offered to catch a ride home with one of her friends.

"Sweetie, I'll call you sometime between 1:30 and 2:00," Jenny said as they pulled up to the luncheon. "We can meet at my house or yours and go to Mike's burial together."

Kyle didn't answer.

Jenny could hear laughter and gaiety coming from inside the house. She leaned over to kiss Kyle, but he pulled away.

"I can't believe you. I just can't believe you," he said, grimacing as Jenny exited the car. He leaned over and pulled her door shut while she knocked pleadingly on the window.

"Please, Kyle. Please don't leave like this," she pleaded.

Jenny watched his car speed away, leaving tread marks in its wake. The fumes of his anger co-mingled with those coming out of the muffler. *Oh, dear God, this can't be happening again,* Jenny thought, feeling abandoned and alone as she was left standing in the road. With no way home yet, Jenny couldn't leave but she was embarrassed to go inside. Another guest was approaching in her car, and Jenny had to make a move. She darted in the front door and took an immediate left to the guest bathroom. She washed her face, regained control over her emotions, and touched up her lipstick. She could barely distinguish between her distress over what just happened or what lay ahead.

Mike's burial service was scheduled at Carmel for four o'clock and Jenny didn't know if she could make it through one more public acknowledgement of loss, especially with Kyle so blatantly missing from her side. Over the months, he had wavered whether he would or wouldn't attend Mike's funeral and burial. Surely he would come around and realize how vital it was that he be with her at this time.

But no, apparently that wasn't going to happen. He left three messages on Jenny's cell phone: one angry, the next angrier, and the last angriest. He wanted to set the record straight. It wasn't *he* who abandoned her. It was *she* who abandoned him on the day after his mother's funeral. And why? To attend a stupid luncheon. How could she? And how dare she ask him to join her for dinner with Mike's family! He certainly didn't want to spend the night after his mother's funeral with Mike's family. If she had problems to work out with them, she could handle it on her own.

Jenny was devastated. She couldn't stifle her sobs when she read a prayer as Mike's ashes were lowered into the ground. She disintegrated in tears as the mourners each took turns shoveling dirt onto his grave. Jenny was drained both physically and emotionally. As she walked with Sister Marsha back up from the graveside, they spotted most of the family gathered in a circle.

"There's something I need to take care of, and this may be my last opportunity," Jenny told Marsha. "I need to muster my strength for this."

"I'll go with you," Marsha answered quietly. Sister Marsha stayed with Jenny as they went to the parking lot and over to where most of the nieces and nephews were gathered.

"While all of you are here, I just want to take this moment to acknowledge that I'm sorry for any hurt that I may have caused you during the final month of your uncle's life," Jenny said.

"We weren't ever upset with you," one of them said. "We just wanted to be sure that everything that *could* be done *was* being done to make Uncle Mike comfortable in his final days."

"It isn't easy to deal with the death of someone we all love so much. I just want you to know that Father Jeff and I did the very best we could and were following the best guidance we had."

Jenny felt relieved as she walked back with Sister Marsha to the monastery door.

"That was one of the most beautiful reconciliations I've seen," Marsha said as she hugged Jenny. "You accomplished exactly what you set out to do. I'm so proud of you."

Jenny told Sister Marsha what had happened with Kyle earlier in the day. "I don't think I can survive all that has happened without him." Jenny broke down in unrelenting sobs.

"I'll pray for both of you, my dear, that God works this out in his own inimitable way."

"But I could have considered him more," Jenny said. "I wonder how much of this was Kyle going through his bipolar mood swings as he faced another death in his own life. I'm the stronger one. He doesn't deal well with this kind of crisis. I should've known to skip the luncheon and stay by his side. Maybe, just maybe, he would've reciprocated and stayed by mine."

"I'm not sure you could have changed the outcome," Sister Marsha said as she tried to comfort Jenny. "Kyle may have needed more of you than you could give him. But one thing I know—you both love each other deeply."

Jenny drove home, emotionally spent. As she walked into her bedroom, she saw that Kyle had brought in her suitcase and his mother's mink coat was lying across the chaise lounge. No note. No message. No Kyle.

Jenny slept little that night. The next morning, December 20, she called Harvey to see if he had heard from Kyle. They had breakfast together and then drove to Kyle's house and knocked on the door. No answer. No car in the garage. They drove past his ex-wife's house. He wasn't there, either. Harvey promised he would let her know as soon as he heard from Kyle.

It wasn't long before Harvey called back. He said Kyle was fine. But he had asked Harvey to deliver a message to Jenny.

"All of your plans for Christmas with Kyle are cancelled." There was little else he could say.

Jenny was stunned. She could barely breathe. Harvey stayed on the phone with her while she tried to regain her breath. *Please God, don't let this be happening. No Mom, no Earl, no Mike, and now no Kyle.* When she could speak, Jenny asked Harvey as a professional, "Didn't it please him that, in the midst of all the morbidity, I flew to Santa Monica to be with him?"

"Yes, but he is upset about the luncheon. With the passing of his mother, he felt abandoned by her, and because you went to the luncheon, he now feels abandoned by you."

Jenny was speechless . . . breathless. "Harvey, has he been skipping his meds again? I can't believe he'd be so upset about a luncheon!"

"Well, he is upset, and he's coming in this afternoon so perhaps I can get to the bottom of it all. But I advise you not to contact him right now. Just let him be."

Jenny hung up feeling as if she had been kicked in the stomach. She was sad but she was also extremely angry, both at herself and at Kyle. That night she ran the gamut of emotions, and finally fell into a troubled sleep.

The next morning, staring at the empty seats around her dining room table, Jenny thought about the invitations she had extended to Kyle's boys for Christmas Eve and to Harvey for Christmas day. As she stood pondering the consequences, Harvey called and she discussed it with him.

"What does this do to our plans?" Jenny asked him solemnly.

"I guess it means that Kyle has cancelled us, too. We certainly couldn't have dinner under these circumstances. You remember—I am his doctor."

"Oh, boy," Jenny muttered under her breath. More silence. She had never felt so utterly and completely abandoned and empty inside. Jenny ended the conversation with Harvey by thanking him for his support and promising to call if she needed him.

Jenny was in a state of shock. She could hardly believe this was happening. Three days before Christmas, she took her bookkeeper, Julie, out shopping. Since Julie had taken over as her bookkeeper, this had become a holiday tradition for them. Afterward, they went to dinner at P.F. Chang's in Roseville, a favorite eatery of Kyle's and Jenny's. After their meal, they exited the restaurant to find Kyle just outside the door. He appeared to have been waiting for Jenny.

"At Mass this morning, they handed out Mike's prayer card. It was lovely," he told Jenny, knowing that she had written it.

Falling back on their longtime friendship, Kyle and Julie chatted while Jenny just stood silently by. Julie bragged to Kyle about what a wonderful boss Jenny was to have gotten her wonderful clothes for Christmas and then headed to the car ahead of Jenny. Once Kyle and Jenny were alone, he put his arm around her shoulder.

"You have a wonderful week," he said, kissing her on the forehead. Then he turned and walked inside the restaurant.

Jenny just stood there in amazement. She stayed there for several minutes before she could remember where she had parked. *Why did words fail me?* Jenny thought. *I should have told him how much I needed him. Told him I was wrong to leave him that day. We could have worked it out. Why didn't I run after him?*

But Jenny knew why she hadn't pursued him. She was afraid he wasn't dining alone.

Twenty-four

Christmas Alone

Jenny chose to spend Christmas Day at home alone. Friends had invited her to join them for the holiday, but she declined. She was in too much emotional pain.

Remaining in bed, tucked safely under the covers, Jenny watched a movie called *Silent Night* about American and German soldiers both inadvertently taking refuge out of the storm in a German woman's house on Christmas Eve. After several skirmishes, the woman insisted they leave their firearms outside her door. After sharing a meal on Christmas day and coming face to face with the enemy in such a personal way, none of the soldiers could return to the battlefield. By the end of the film, Jenny was sobbing uncontrollably. So many thoughts raced through her mind. She thought about her empty dining room. She knew it would have been meaningful to share this holy day with others. Instead she lay in bed feeling completely abandoned.

"After Mike's death, I will be there for you. I promise," Kyle had repeated many times over. Jenny had believed him. And she was sure he meant it at the time.

She crawled out of bed around noon to check her email. Completely nude, she wandered in and sat down at her desktop. Just then she heard the front door open.

"Yo, Mom, are you here?"

Jenny looked around for something to put on and grabbed the first thing within her reach—the mink coat from Kyle. There she sat as Chad walked into the office.

"In here," she called to Chad.

"I found a deli open," he said cheerfully as he walked through the door. Ignoring the fact that she was sitting at her computer wearing a mink coat, he extended a white sack and said, "I thought you might like a turkey sandwich." Without cornbread dressing, cranberry sauce, or any fanfare, she and Chad shared Christmas turkey together. Chad had felt the loss of his father and his stepfather. Now he, too, felt the loss of Kyle. After visiting with his mom, Chad left, reassured that she was getting through the day.

Jenny's thoughts wandered to Harvey. *What had he decided to do with his day after Kyle cancelled their plans?* She picked up the phone and called his cell.

"What are you doing?" she asked, attempting unsuccessfully to swallow the lump in her throat.

"Working at my desk, cleaning up the office, answering email," Harvey responded, trying to sound as if these were normal activities on Christmas day. They both allowed the silence to linger. "So how are you holding up?" he asked with genuine concern. "You sound like death warmed over."

"That about describes it. I guess I'm doing as well as anyone would be after a complete annihilation of almost everyone in my life. I think this is the most alone I've ever felt."

"Where is your son?" Harvey asked.

"He's been over and brought turkey sandwiches from a deli. He's been so supportive. He doesn't believe this is the end for us."

Harvey let that pass. "You're probably doing the best thing you can do for yourself right now."

"What about you? I feel badly that, because of Kyle and me, you're in the office . . . alone," Jenny said.

"Well, this isn't my favorite way to spend Christmas. I'll do a little better planning next year."

"I hope we both will." Jenny couldn't imagine what next Christmas might hold. A year out was far beyond what she could let in. Even an entire day was too much. One hour at a time. Yes, maybe that.

Two days passed, and Jenny had not moved from her self-imposed confinement. She was still spending most of her time in bed. Depression was frightening. Remembering Mike's encouragement to journal her feelings, she got out her laptop and began to write.

> Every end is a new beginning? It sounds so simple, and yet I find it so complex. I have no interest in a new beginning. I just want my old life back.
>
> Dear God, be with me on this journey. Let me feel your presence as I walk the stations of my own crucifixion. I've been through crises before, and you have seen me through them. I thought divorce was heartbreaking but it was a bump in the road compared to the emptiness surrounding me now. I have never known this depth of loneliness. I know I was blessed to have my mother as long as I did, but my heart feels ripped out without her. I miss that morning phone call from her asking how things in my world are going. And I feel responsible for having failed to take care of Earl like I promised. I miss all of us—Mom, Earl, and Chad—gathered together around a meal.
>
> And Mike, I knew I was going to lose him, but I hadn't bargained on losing him and Kyle at the same time. For the last few years, Mike has walked by my side through all my crises. Please let me feel his presence now. I know he would have had something wise and comforting to say to me at this moment.
>
> And Kyle, dear God, what can I say about him? In my heart I want to ask you to make him healthy and send him back to me. But "be it done unto me according to your word." Help me to believe in your omnipotent and all-seeing wisdom. Any rational person would tell me I am better off without him. But I feel so lost. Help me to work through the sadness and to place my trust totally in you. I feel such need for human comfort. Guide me to build my reliance on you. God, I am so weak. Have compassion on my weakness and help me to become strong. Help me to remain open to whatever you have in store for me. Amen.

Jenny's worldview was darkened by gloominess and hopelessness. She knew she had to do something, or she feared she would spiral further downward and never come back. A friend told her about a New Year's tennis clinic in Palm Desert. A quick phone call let her know there was still an opening. With all the strength Jenny could muster, she forced herself out of bed and out of her house and boarded a plane for southern California. For the next few days, she played hours and hours of tennis. She played until she fell utterly exhausted into bed each night. At the encouragement of one of the coaches, she worked on changing her grip. After more than 35 years of using the continental style, the new eastern grip was not so easy. Jenny believed the change would improve her stroke but, more importantly, she saw this as a constructive way of proving to herself that it was possible to change old, well-grooved habits. Change. That was one of the things Kyle seemed to appreciate about her—her belief that human beings could change and grow.

This year had undoubtedly been the worst year she had ever lived through. So many losses both in her own life and, with 9/11, throughout the world. Jenny joined her tennis group for New Year's Eve and survived the evening without crying until the moment that the crowd began singing "Auld Lang Syne." Halfway through the song, her tears flowed, and she prayed that the transition would symbolize a closing out of sadness and an opening up of joyfulness to come.

At the end of the week, Jenny instinctively knew she wasn't ready to return home. She was frightened of the solitude there. She didn't trust herself to keep away from Kyle, and there were too many opportunities for them to run into each other in Sacramento. But where should she go next? With the encouragement of another friend, Jenny chose Rancho La Puerta in Tecate, Mexico, as her next retreat.

The ranch, located on 3,000 acres of mountains and meadows beneath Mount Kuchumaa, was dedicated to helping visitors experience healing through classes, physical exercise, and spiritual awareness. It was the perfect next step in Jenny's recovery. She felt the support of people around her while also having the space to spend time alone. She began each morning around six with a three-to-four-mile group hike up the mountain. Watching the sunrise from the mountain top was breathtaking.

After the hike, she had breakfast, then a stretching class followed by a tennis lesson. Then she had lunch and quiet time. When the sun was out, she enjoyed lying by the pool and reading. Kyle had inadvertently left a book behind: Wally Lamb's *I Know This Much is True*. She found it a fascinating novel in its depiction of two brothers, identical twins. The book helped her to better understand Kyle and find some of the missing pieces of the puzzle regarding her relationship with him.

With plenty of time for reflection during the week, Jenny realized that, with Kyle's departure, she was relating everything in her life to the way it had been with him. The present seemed to hold little for her; the past was the only place she chose to dwell. She was afraid of the present. It only served to remind her of the loved ones who were missing. *What can the future hold besides yet more reminders of the emptiness?* She didn't need a therapist to tell her that this kind of thinking was pulling her further into the depths of depression.

One evening near dusk as Jenny walked to the spa for her massage appointment, she stopped as she heard a "chirp, chirp." She listened and then saw a bluebird jump from a hidden branch into view. Suddenly, a second bluebird joined the first. She immediately thought of Ellen and Earl. The birds happily chirped at Jenny for a couple of minutes. She could imagine her mother saying, "How are things in your world today? I love you, sugar, and I'm right here with you. You're not alone." And Earl saying, "Dry up; this guy isn't worth it. You can have your pick of the litter. Why are you crying over this one for christsake? And, incidentally, your mother and I are fine. You don't have to boohoo over us." As quickly as the birds appeared, they flew off together. For a moment, just for a moment, Jenny felt lighter.

As the week neared an end, Jenny rented a condo for ten days on Imperial Beach near Chula Vista. Living right on the sand overlooking the ocean had always brought Jenny comfort. She used the time to begin keeping an in-depth journal about her feelings after all her losses.

Jenny created a new regimen at the beach house. After saying morning prayers, she dedicated hours each day to writing in her journal. She lost herself in reliving parts of the past year, gaining a new and better perspective on certain events. It was strange to her to have no one for whom she was a caregiver, but she began giving herself the care, and her confidence grew.

When Jenny had gone through the breakup of her marriage to Matt, Mike had urged her to keep a journal of her healing. With the wisdom of hindsight, she came to understand that she had a pattern of recovery. Like the sacred biblical number, she discovered that she had gone through seven stages of grieving: *sadness, anger, seeing reality, seeking understanding, rediscovering self-worth, forgiveness, and risking new beginnings*. She recognized that healing doesn't necessarily take place in this order. Usually, the first and the last steps are in place but the ones in between can happen in just about any fashion. Jenny's recovery from her divorce had taken a year. She began to wonder how long it would take her now to recuperate from all of her recent losses. What did it matter how long? For the moment, she accepted that she was still in the first stage and was prepared to spend weeks working through her deep sadness.

Before all the illnesses, when Jenny was still on the speaking circuit, she often shared with her audiences that success was not necessarily reaching the end point of a goal. As long as people were taking steps toward the goal, they were already successful. She now consoled herself with the belief that it was the same with recovery. As long as she was taking steps toward healthiness, she was already in recovery.

With this in mind, Jenny wandered into a small bookstore and, searching through the shelves, discovered a book called *The Grief Recovery Handbook* by John James and Russell Friedman. Each day, she read a few pages from it and performed the assignments. The first step they recommend in the process of grief recovery was examining all the myths that she had learned about recovery and determining to which, if any, she may have fallen prey. Like a student with a new assignment, she carefully examined each one.

Despite the admonition to "not feel bad," Jenny was not falling victim to this illusion. Rather, she was allowing herself to feel the feelings to her core. She did somehow believe that "time would heal" but, unlike the myth, she knew that would happen only if she took the right steps to recover. For now, it was acceptable to fall apart. And Jenny was not "keeping busy" for its own sake but was pleased with her choices to stay active in a constructive and healing way. After some thought, she recognized that there might be two areas where she was not making the most of her recovery time.

The first was a feeling that surfaced from time to time of impatience with the speed of her recovery. After all these months—and only a month since the loss of Mike and Kyle—she was expecting to see more visible signs of improvement. She was as teary now as she had been a month earlier. Some days she felt that she was walking on a precipice, barely hanging on, coming close to going over the edge.

The second was even unhealthier than the first; she had made no progress in getting over Kyle. Despite everything, she still wanted him to come back to her. Thoughts of him entered her head about 50 times a day. Intellectually, she understood that, even with all the good in him, all that she found so loveable, he was not able to be steady as a partner and was unable to give her what she needed. She poured out her feelings in her journal.

> When I was most down, when I needed him more than ever, he left me. He would say that it was I who abandoned him but it doesn't feel that way to me. How could I possibly want him still? But in my heart, I do. As hard as I have worked at moving past him, all I want is for Kyle to come back, even if only for a little while, to put his arms around me and make some of the pain go away. I'm sure that, with his help, I could have worked through all the deaths. But the fact that he added himself to the list of losses is more than I can handle. I can't bear the weight of losing him, too.

Journaling helped heal Jenny's soul. Taking active steps toward recovery was cathartic as well. After nearly a month of staying away, reluctantly, Jenny faced that it was time to return to Sacramento.

Her first full day home was dreadful. Each morning, she awoke to Kyle's absence. His scent was missing. When she got up to go the bathroom, his robe was no longer there, and in its place was the infamous mink coat.

Kyle had helped her purchase many items when she remodeled her home. Now, everywhere she looked reminded her of him. There was the painting of a front porch they had found together at a craft fair with fuchsia, deep purple, and forest green colors blending together in a radiant ambiance. The lamp on her writing desk was a Christmas gift from him from the year before. The arrangement of the pillows on her couch evoked the way they had left them the last time they lay there together. Kyle had helped her select the shade of maroon for the kitchen cabinets.

Jenny cried through her entire first 24 hours home. She cried over coffee with a friend. She cried on the phone with another friend. She cried through her workout at the club. She cried with a friend she met at the store. She cried through her visit with her therapist. She had little to explain when she was asked how her recovery was coming along. It was self-evident.

During her second therapy session after returning home, she and Dr. McFarland discussed getting her some medical help. Jenny was resistant but, after a month away, she admitted that she had tried almost everything short of medication. She told Dr. McFarland her fantasy of going to see Kyle and simply asking him to come back and help her through this. Even Jenny had to admit it was a bad idea. Finally, Jenny agreed that taking an anti-depressant was preferable to continuing on the way she was.

Jenny stopped by Harvey's office that evening to ask his advice. He recommended an anti-depressant and reassured her that the drug would not mask her emotions. More than anything, she did not want a temporary bandage for her pain. She wanted to recover and come through this a renewed whole, healthy person. Not wanting to confuse her friendship with Harvey or create a conflict, she agreed that she would call her general practitioner, who could officially prescribe the drug for her.

Harvey continued to be Kyle's support as well. He saw him weekly and sometimes more. Kyle acknowledged to his therapist that work was his salvation. He was grateful that he had so much to distract him from this breakup. It deadened some of the pain.

Of course, thoughts of Jenny still popped into his head. He went back and reread every email they had ever exchanged. It was all there—the love, the friction, the ups, the downs. God, he did love her. He still loved her. But loving by itself—however deeply and passionately and even mutually—was not enough to make their relationship work. Even Harvey agreed with him on that.

Ending his relationship with Jenny after three years was one of the most difficult decisions Kyle had ever made—right up there with ending his marriage after 20 years.

"Why is that?" Harvey asked him. Out of character, Kyle stumbled over his words looking for an answer.

Maybe it was the timing of their meeting. She came into his life when he most needed someone to be there for him. Maybe it was sharing their journals. He loved getting to know her innermost thoughts *before* he reconnected with her in person. Something about it created a deeper bond right from the start. Physically, she was easy to fall for. She was a knock-out! But it was her personal strength along with her quick mind and multifaceted emotions that first drew him. It was her gentleness and caring spirit, he admitted in his therapy sessions, that attracted him the most.

"But that was the very part of her that came between you," Harvey reminded Kyle. It was true. She cared for everyone. He needed her to care more for him than for all the others, to *need him* more than anyone else. But Jenny was too independent—not just financially but emotionally. She could enjoy being alone and he hadn't mastered that yet. Kyle thought back to her world of friends. For him, that was the heart of the problem. She was not emotionally faithful. She had a deep relationship with too many others. And she invited it, for godsake!

And there had to be shared goals, he realized. He wanted marriage. She did not. With all of her spirituality, why couldn't she see that marriage is a good thing, as a sacrament blessed by the Church. As Kyle attempted to delve into the very essence of Jenny, he tried to understand her resistance to marrying him. He blamed it on her childhood, her previous marriages, her abandonment issues. They were all tapes replaying in her head and they stood like a fortress barricading her from wanting to marry again. By ecclesial rules, he was free to get married in the Church since his baptism came after his divorce. Jenny could have gotten an annulment. But she claimed not to believe in the annulment process. Wasn't that just an excuse? The truth was she was afraid of marriage. She was afraid of trusting a man. And this was never going to change. He needed a partner who would want a life primarily with him. It was that simple.

From however many perspectives he looked at the situation, he kept coming back to the same conclusion—he had to break it off. Yes, ending this insanity was the right thing to do. He thanked God he'd had the courage to do it. For him, the pain of their relationship had become greater than the joy. He was tired of the endless knot that kept flip-flopping in his stomach. And that stabbing ache in his chest. At last those godawful feelings were all but gone now.

Kyle definitely had his own support system. Not only Harvey, but Josh was always there for him.

"Hey, bro, it's your wise and witty twin calling."

"Just the man I wanted to talk to," Kyle said after he grabbed the receiver in his office.

"Are you okay?" Josh asked. "I've been thinking about you a lot."

"I'm okay," Kyle said. "Surprisingly, I don't feel as much pain this time. I had to let go of her, Josh. Right or wrong, I need something from her that she just can't give. There'll always be something or someone that takes her focus away from me."

"She's a good woman. I hate to see you give up—especially under the duress of losing our mom."

"I'm going out with someone now whose life is simpler. She isn't trying to keep up a hundred relationships. She seems happy just to be with me."

"You have to do what you have to do," Josh said, not convinced that Kyle was right.

"So, what's going on in your world?" Kyle asked.

"I just got through meeting with an intelligence guy here who says he's been given marching orders to find a reason to go to war with Iraq. He said there were about fifty people in the room when the official said to them: 'If Bush wants to go to war, it's your job to give him a reason to do so.'"

"Where did that order come from?" Kyle asked.

"It came directly from Alan Foley—you know, he's a longtime veteran of CIA internal politics and head of Weapons Intelligence. I think he's a loose cannon inside the CIA. He marches to a different drummer than most of the others."

I still can't believe someone could say that openly and get away with it," Kyle exclaimed. "I've seen my share of screwy politics, but I still don't believe the American people will fall for all this misinformation."

"What outraged the agent most was that there was no sign of outrage from the intelligence staff sitting at the meeting. They seem to be getting accustomed to being ordered to slant their intelligence reports. Some of the other office workers recalled Cheney also coming into their offices at the end of last year to tell them they needed to find something nuclear."

"It all depends on how much the media grabs hold of it," Josh replied. "Washington staffers can't risk their frickin' jobs to go public with what they're being told to do. But here's a memo that the media would love to get a hold of. It's dated today, January 25, and just came in from White House Counsel Alberto Gonzales. It warns that U.S. officials could be prosecuted for war crimes as a result of new and unorthodox measures used by the Bush administration in the War on Terror. It says that it might even apply to the highest officials themselves. To avert the problem, Gonzales urges President Bush to declare the war in Afghanistan, including the detention of Taliban and al Qaeda fighters, exempt from the provisions of the Geneva Conventions."

"Oh, my God!" Kyle shouted. "Has Powell seen the memo yet?"

"He's furious. The memo essentially says that Gonzales is looking for ways to allow the administration to keep using torture, and Colin Powell is opposed."

"Is anybody listening to your boss?" Kyle said. "He seems like the only one with his head on his shoulders."

"Yeah, bro, I'm afraid the rest of them have their head up their frickin' asses."

Kyle hung up the phone, saddened by his conversation with his brother. *There must be some way to stop another war from breaking out. With such inhumane treatment of those being captured in Afghanistan, one war is bad enough.*

Twenty-five

Recovery

Jenny was frightened as she looked at her gaunt face in the mirror. It reflected how close to the surface her pain remained.

She began seeing Dr. McFarland more often as she searched for positive ways to work through her grieving. "It's only been a few weeks since your life came undone. Be patient with yourself," Dr. McFarland advised.

Sitting on the couch across from her therapist, Jenny spoke between sobs. "I feel so useless. I'm not working. I'm not taking care of anyone. All I'm doing is sitting around feeling sorry for myself. I don't just *feel* alone. I have to face the reality that I *am* alone."

The doctor waited until Jenny blew her nose. "You are making progress. The work you're doing on your grief therapy is the most constructive step you can take right now. Keep going with it. You will get through this, Jenny. I have worked with many patients. And I can tell you from my own experience, you are moving forward."

Jenny trusted Dr. McFarland and was committed to staying with the program. She was exhausted from crying but accepted that this was part of what she must go through to reach the other side. She thought about what the other side looked like: Healthy, happy, standing on her own without Kyle, her mother, her stepfather, or Mike. This image seemed so unattainable from where she stood today. She couldn't feel even a tiny strand of hope for achieving these things yet. Faith. She would keep taking steps on faith. She thought back to Thomas Merton's words that she read to Mike on the day he died: that God will "never leave me to face my perils alone."

Jenny opened the grief therapy handbook to where she had left off. She was instructed to list and describe her feelings about the most painful losses over her early life.

> Age two, my parents' divorce: not terribly intense because I was too young; set the tone for the rest of my childhood; raised by a Baptist family while Mom worked out of town.
>
> Age four, earliest memory: riding in the back of the family car quietly crying because I was leaving this family; then crying on the way home because I was leaving Mom.
>
> Age seven, taken away from the Baptist family to be placed with a new family: somewhat traumatic; I didn't want to leave them; my mother and grandmother felt I needed to be with a Catholic family, now that I was in school.
>
> Age thirteen, left the Catholic family who had become my family to begin living with Mom: difficult to leave them but offset by the fact that Mom and I were moving into our own home together.
>
> Age eighteen, broke up with my high school boyfriend of four years in order for him to enter the seminary and me to go away to study at a convent school: the excitement of my studies offset some of the pain of separation; Mom went through the biggest trauma of her life over this event.
>
> Age twenty-five, the mother of the Catholic family who raised me died: I felt the loss of her because she was like my second mother.
>
> Age thirty, met my first husband: our relationship was erratic from the very beginning; a deep love relationship with all the joys and all the anguish.

Next Jenny was guided to chart a graph of these significant losses. The longer the line, the more intense the loss. After givingthis some serious thought, she began creating her diagram.

Chart of Significant Losses
Early Years

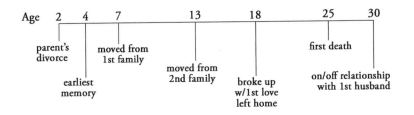

Next she was instructed to list and describe her feelings about the most painful losses over her later life.

Age forty-one, widowed: after eleven tumultuous years with my husband, this loss of him was the worst moment of my life at that time.

Age forty-five, Dad died: since I never lived with him as a child, this had minimal impact on me; when attending his funeral, the difficulty was realizing how he was recognized throughout his life for his work with children; I felt cheated; why them and why not me?

Age forty-seven, my grandmother died: since she was very involved in my upbringing, I felt close to her; she did not approve of my marriage to a former priest; I felt guilty that I had not stayed closer to her at the end of her life.

Age fifty, divorce: the ending of this phase of my life was devastating; it brought a screeching halt not only to my relationship with my husband, but to my speaking career with him and our partnership in business; left us in huge debt and caused me to move out of my home and lose the family life with our grown children.

Age fifty-five, deaths of mom, step dad, and dearest friend together with abandonment of my life partner: too many losses in too short a time; this has been, by far, the most critical down period of my life even beyond Don's death.

Again she was guided to chart a graph of these significant losses, the longer the line, the more intense the loss. Jenny was overwhelmingly aware how much longer the lines in her life were now than in her earlier years. She thought she had experienced crises in her life but they were nothing compared to now.

Chart of Significant Losses
Later Years

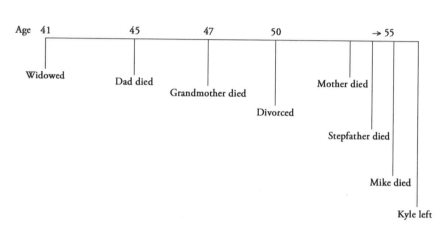

As Jenny looked over her graph, it was apparent how much divorce and loss of loved ones had shaped her life. Without a father, with her mother gone so much, and with marriages and key relationships that didn't last, she realized how abandonment issues continued to plague her life. As she looked over her chart, Jenny began to feel the first sign of an inner conviction that she could get through it. Creating the chart highlighted the devastating endings she had already come through. *And I survived*, she thought. She felt stronger, believing that she *would* get through this series of losses.

Jenny realized, however, that it was going to take time plus effort to heal. In the same way that a patient uses physical therapy to mend after a broken bone, so she was committed to emotional therapy to heal her broken heart. She resolved to treat her recovery like she would a job, knowing that she wouldn't be worth anything to anyone until she pulled through the hurt.

Jenny then retrieved her Henri Nouwen meditation book and began reading.

"We are all wounded people. Who wounds us? Often those whom we love and those who love us. When we feel rejected, abandoned . . . it is mostly by people very close to us: our parents, our friends, our spouses, our lovers. . . . That's the tragedy of our lives. This is what makes forgiveness from the heart so difficult. It is precisely our hearts that are wounded. We cry out, 'You, who I expected to be there for me, you have abandoned me. How can I ever forgive you for that?' Forgiveness often seems impossible, but nothing is impossible for God. The God who lives within us will give us the grace to go beyond our wounded selves and say, 'In the name of God, you are forgiven.' Let's pray for that grace."

As it was Jenny's nature to look for signs, the passage reinforced her yearning to communicate with Kyle. It had been six weeks since their split—six weeks of unadulterated anguish added to 10 tearful months since losing her parents. Jenny decided to refrain from contacting him until she spoke with her therapist.

During her next session, Jenny told Dr. McFarland, "I need to talk to Kyle. It's time. It's been too long already."

"What if he doesn't want to talk to you, Jenny? Can you handle another rejection?"

"I'm willing to risk it. If that happens, at least I'll know. Maybe then, I'll be able to move on. We never had any real closure. He hasn't returned my clothes and stuff from his house like he used to when we had an argument. Nor have I asked for them back. Everything's in limbo. I need to know where he stands."

"I don't want to see you hurt any more than you already have been," Dr. McFarland said. "Twice now he's let you down at critical moments—the day of your mother's funeral and the day of Mike's burial. And if you count Earl, that's three. How can you count on him not to do that again? When is enough, enough?"

"Believe me, I've asked myself that same question," Jenny said. "Yet when I do, I always find reasons related to his illness to justify his behavior. With a manic-depressive personality, reason isn't always part of the equation. And with a touch of narcissism thrown in, his inclination is to deal first with his own pain before he could ever consider mine."

"Is that what you want? Do you really want a man in your life who continually puts himself first and can't support you when you need it?"

Jenny paused before answering. "No." She felt tears running down her face again, and she started to sob. "But I think I understand him."

"What do you understand?" Dr. McFarland asked.

"One of my friends helped me comprehend what he feels. And I truly believe what she told me." Jenny related her conversation with Kerry when she had been in Texas. "People with this disorder take in things differently than the rest of us do. When I feel sadness and turn to Kyle for support, more often than not he can only experience the sadness within himself. He can't feel it from my perspective. It is as if he's unable to empathize with me. But I can't just write it off as self-centeredness. It's a genuine personality disorder. Like on the day of Mom's funeral, he couldn't put himself in my place and feel my sadness and my need of him. My pain was overshadowed by his sense of feeling left out and unneeded since I had so many others to take care of me. Or his outrage, when I tried to cover up Jeff's returning to pick up Mike, that rated higher than my neediness after losing my mother. In both cases, from his perspective, his pain outweighed my pain. And for those of us who haven't experienced this, it makes no sense. We can't begin to understand what it's like to have that kind of block."

"Your friend described it well, Jenny. But you may have more compassion than is good for you. I understand what you're saying, but I also believe you deserve to have someone who can empathize with *your* pain and be there when you need it. It can't be all one-sided."

"It all comes down to one thing: I love him. And I need him right now. I know he loves me, too, and he always will. But right now, he doesn't need me. I've learned that he isn't very good during crises. And I've really put our relationship to the test this year because my life has been nothing but one crisis after another. The events in my life this past year are more than almost anyone could put up with."

"There are men who could have been there for you," Dr. McFarland said. "You just didn't pick one of them. And right now, you're longing for comfort—and not just any consoling, but *his*."

Jenny nodded in agreement. "I am scraping bottom emotionally. I've tried everything I know to get better, and I'm not getting better."

"I think you are. More than you know. But you've got to give yourself more time. Grieving takes longer than a few weeks. And especially when it's stemming from compound losses."

"I'm obsessed with wanting him back. That's all I can think about."

"I'm sure it feels like you're stuck."

"Worse than stuck. I feel like I'm about to go over a precipice. I'm hanging on with my fingernails, but I'm slipping." Jenny began sobbing and she held her head in her hands.

Dr. McFarland handed Jenny a tissue, and paused while she regained control. "Have you considered the fact that your need for his love may be an addiction?"

"I don't know. Who knows the difference between being head over heels in love and being addicted to it? I'm a hopeless romantic. I know I have a strong tendency to be in love with being in love. It's an incredibly wonderful part of life, isn't it? But it can also be so painful."

"Yes, it can be. And when life hits bottom as it has for you, Jenny, your neediness and yearning for comfort takes over. The needier you are, the unhealthier you become. And the unhealthier you become, the needier you are. It's a vicious cycle."

"I need closure, Dr. McFarland. I need to talk to him. This silence is killing me."

"I'm not opposed to your talking to him, Jenny. Actually, I had hoped that I could hold you off from that for another couple of weeks or maybe even a month. But perhaps that isn't possible. Perhaps you do need to take some action now."

Jenny nodded. "I'm open to a better suggestion if you have one."

"No, there really is no other action save waiting. But if he rejects you and wants nothing more to do with you, what will you do then?"

"Go home. Fall apart some more. And then begin to deal with that reality. It'll hurt terribly, but I'll get over it. Anything's better than this limbo. If he doesn't love me anymore and has moved on, I need him to tell me that."

"How likely do you think it is that he'll reject you?"

"I don't know," Jenny said. "But if I ask for his help, I believe that he will be willing to reach out on some level, even if it's only friendship."

"What will you say to him?"

Jenny paused before she answered. "I'll remind him that the issue when Mom died, according to him, was that I didn't *ask* for his help. I thought it was obvious to him I needed it, but he felt left out. He told me then that he just needed me to ask for his help. So this time, I'll be asking for it."

"That's a good place to start: a simple, direct request. And that is being true to yourself. So, how will you ask him to help you?"

"I'm not sure. I'm so needy at the moment that I would accept almost anything on his terms. That sounds terrible, doesn't it?"

"Not if it's the way you feel."

"I guess I just want him back in my life in some form," Jenny said. "I'm willing to do a lot more compromising than I was willing to do before. I want to really listen to what he feels drove him away and what he needs from me to make him happy."

"You know, Jenny, if you always try to be what someone else wants, the one who winds up unhappy is you."

"But if I don't make *some* attempt to be what someone else wants, I come off as selfish and end up alone. Either way—too much compliance or not enough—the relationship disintegrates into something that isn't real. What I really want to do is leave here and go directly to his office."

Dr. McFarland gave Jenny her blessing, comparing her to Joan of Arc. A few minutes after she left McFarland's office, a cell call came from the doctor.

"I have cleared my 5:30 time for you today, Jenny. Just in case things go badly and you need me, I'll be here. No need to call. Just come over."

So Jenny wasn't completely alone. She has at least one backup in her crusade.

Jenny made her way straight to Kyle's office, asking God for guidance as she drove. When Jenny arrived and asked to see Kyle, the secretary said he was gone for the day. Jenny stood there not knowing what to say. *So much buildup for nothing*, she thought. She felt deflated and demoralized. As she took the elevator down, suddenly Jenny felt a surge of inner strength for having taken at least some action.

The next day, feeling a rush of anticipation, Jenny called Kyle on his private line at work, but she only got his voicemail. She didn't leave a message. On a whim, she called him at home, and he answered.

"What a surprise to find you home," she said.

"I'm waiting for the cable man. I finally decided it was worth it." Kyle and Jenny had watched very little television at his house. They always seemed to have other things to do with their time together.

"I need your help, Kyle," Jenny said. "I need to talk to you."

"What do you want to talk about?" he asked guardedly.

"Kyle, do you remember when we went through all the difficulties around Mom's funeral? You said then that the big problem for you was that I didn't come out and point blank ask for your help. You felt I had so many others there for me that I didn't really need you."

"Of course I remember."

"Well, now I'm *asking*. I'm really struggling. I've never been this depressed before in my life."

"Are you getting help?" Kyle asked.

"Yes. I guess you and I are kindred spirits now that I'm on anti-depressants, too."

"And they aren't helping?"

"Not yet," Jenny said. "I hope they kick in soon. I started on five milligrams. But, since I was feeling no effect, Harvey suggested I push it up to ten. I've tried everything—I mean, *everything* to pull myself together. But I'm not getting very far on my own. I have had too many losses in too short a time. It's more than I can handle. And that's why I need your help."

"Well, if you think talking to me will help, I'm willing to do that. I just want you to know, though, that I finally realized that we want different things in our lives. No need to kid ourselves; neither of us is ever going to change. If we got back together, we'd be arguing again by Sunday if not sooner."

Jenny didn't say anything.

"Don't you agree?" Kyle asked.

"Actually, no. But you have no way of knowing all that I've been through and how I've changed. That's why I wanted to reopen our communication."

Kyle was silent for a moment. "Okay," he finally said, "how about lunch tomorrow?"

"That sounds fine. I'll bring sandwiches."

Kyle agreed, and then suddenly added, "Do you want me to bring your clothes from the house?"

"No, I don't want to haul clothes out of the attorney general's office, thank you very much. I'll make other arrangements to get those. Clothes I can live without. It is *you* I need right now."

There was another short silence. Finally Kyle asked, "Do you remember that moratorium you made us take way back when?"

"Of course."

"Well, I'd talk to Mike about it, and he'd console me by telling me it was just temporary, that you needed a break. And he'd describe how well you were doing. For you, it was a relief and you felt great. But I was dying. I could hardly stand it, I hurt so much. I couldn't understand why you weren't feeling what I was feeling. Well, this time I feel relief. The knot in my stomach, the pain in my chest, the headaches—they're all gone. I feel relieved. My life feels like it's back on solid ground."

That was hard for Jenny to hear, but she could relate to his feelings. She wondered if he could relate to hers.

"Kyle, in that instance, we both knew it was temporary and that, at the end of it, we'd get back together to see where we were. That's what I need now. You see, I may have been able to get through Mom's death and Earl's suicide and Mike's passing. But I just can't get through the loss of all of them and you, too. Your rejection was the straw that broke this camel's back. I need you to hang in long enough for me to get through this. I can't hold up under the weight of this many losses so close to me." Jenny worried that she had said too much.

"Jenny, I want you to be realistic about this. I've come to accept that we just don't want the same things in life and, even though I love you and still think about you all the time, I realize that we're not compatible. I went back and reread all of our emails. We had the same issues over and over. I don't know how you kept so many balls in the air and kept me in your life, too. I couldn't have done it."

"What I tried to do was insane," Jenny said. "And each time one more person in my life became ill or needy, I just added them to my helper list until there was no time left for me . . . or us. I ran from one situation where I felt I was needed to the next to the next. And you weren't really a life partner. You were depressed and jealous and, therefore, one more person I was caring for. But, sweetheart, all of that's over now. It's history. I won't ever have to face those same choices again."

"There will be others to come along, Jenny. That's who you are."

"I don't agree. I have come through so much. All I ask is that you put this meeting to prayer and come with an open mind. I read something yesterday that gave me the courage to make this call. I'd like to email it to you."

"Sure." In the background, Jenny heard Kyle's doorbell ring.

"I'll let you go and look forward to seeing you tomorrow," she said. "I'll be there around noon."

"Okay, see you then."

Jenny hung up the phone and raised her eyes heavenward. *Thank you. Dear God, thank you.* She immediately pulled the Nouwen book out and sent the passage to Kyle.

Jenny then called Dr. McFarland and told her how the conversation had gone.

"And how do you feel, Jenny?"

"Neutral. I'm not feeling up but I'm not nearly as far down as I was, either. I'm glad I made the call. Taking some action was the right thing for me to do."

"Well, you have to see this all the way through. Either you'll be able to create some kind of relationship with him or you won't. He may turn you down. But you need to take it to the next step for your own peace of mind."

"You're right," Jenny said. "Taking a pro-active step is making me feel a little bit stronger. Doing nothing was killing me."

Jenny hung up the phone and sat staring out the window, wondering if she was meant to have a partner in life. Alone, she felt somehow set apart from the world. Her devotion to her spiritual life became less focused. She found it difficult to stay on course. Her idea

of complete joy was to live her life in God's presence with purpose and
dedication to what she was about, to have the freedom and capability
of being her own person and yet utterly safe in the knowledge that, at
the end of the day, the person she loved most would be there for her
and she for him. She thought, *Is that too much to ask?*

Jenny then took some time to put her thoughts into her journal.
She wanted to be prepared for her meeting the next day with Kyle.
Putting all the external issues aside—deaths, emotional disorders and
healthcare issues—at the very core, she asked herself, *What does Kyle
want from me and what do I want from him?*

Jenny knew that Kyle wanted structure and stability, a routine that
was set solidly in place. He came out of a traditional marriage. He was
happy having his job and his woman to come home to. He wanted to
give his love to her and have her love him in return. He enjoyed other
friends in their lives, but they were relatively low in importance.

Jenny wanted less structure—some "space in their togetherness,"
as renowned poet, Kahlil Gibran, so wisely wrote—but she also
wanted a great deal of stability. It was essential to her that she was with
someone who was growing and would support her growth as well. Life
had taught her that relationships come and go, but her friends had
always been there for her. She needed them to be high on the ladder of
significance in her life, but with her man coming first.

Their common ground was that they both wanted steadiness in their
relationship. The question was whether they could resolve the trust
issue. Could Kyle feel so loved by Jenny that he no longer felt jealousy
and mistrust when she was with other friends, male or female? Could
Jenny change her behavior in ways that would enhance his sense of
trust? Could Jenny trust that Kyle would be there for her, no matter
what? Could Kyle become comfortable with filling his time when they
were apart? In the past, Jenny had put Mike and her parents before Kyle.
Whether she was right or wrong in the choices she made then, they were
over now. Jenny closed her journal with a sense of anxiety and
hopefulness. If two people truly loved each other, surely they could
resolve these differences.

Feeling restless, Jenny walked over to Sherri's house and told her
what had recently transpired.

"I'm scared," Jenny told her, "but I know exactly what I want to say to Kyle. I understand what we both want. I believe it's possible for us to work things out. Sherri, I just can't stand to lose him right now."

"Based on what you've shared with me, it should all work out just fine," Sherri said.

"You think so?" Jenny sensed that Sherri wasn't saying everything she was thinking. "I need you to be brutally honest with me."

"Well, one of the problems is that he needs you to need him, and you didn't before," Sherri said, "but you do now. He also needed you to put him first. You didn't before, but you're free to do that now. So a big part of the old problem is gone."

"For the most part, my motives have been pretty selfless throughout my time with him. But now they are totally selfish. I want him back because I need him so much. Do you think that will please him or be a turn off?"

"I guess you'll find out tomorrow. He's in the power position now. And you're extremely vulnerable. What if he says yes, but issues an ultimatum: You give up your friendships with the O'Connors and Father Jeff. Would you agree to that?"

Jenny thought before she spoke. "If it all came down to that choice, I would choose him. I hope it wouldn't come to that, but if it did, I think my friends love me and would understand."

"Doesn't it matter to you that you may have to sacrifice more in this relationship with him?"

"I made some mistakes along the way. If I meet him more than halfway, that'll give me a chance to make things up to him."

"Now let's not get carried away," Sherri said. "He hasn't been exactly perfect either. You'd better keep your perspective about this."

"What do you mean?"

"Do you remember his 'friend' who turned out to be a girlfriend, after your Mom died?"

Jenny nodded.

"Think about it, Jenny. How do you think she ended up at his house and in his bed the night you went to him to clear up the misunderstanding? Didn't that strike you as strange? Did it cross your mind that, even after you got back together, he hadn't closed the door on that relationship . . . just in case?

"No, that didn't occur to me. Overall, I think he's been pretty honest with me."

"Maybe so, maybe not. He has his patterns. And what about the new girlfriend—the one he was having dinner with a couple of days after your last breakup? Don't you think she came into the picture pretty quickly after you? Was she the 'friend' he had dinner with the night of Father Mike's birthday? And where was she during those last weeks you were together? Were thoughts of her coming between you even as you exchanged rings in Mexico? Was he also keeping her in the wings . . . just in case?"

That had crossed Jenny's mind at one time but she'd dismissed it. Sherri was asking questions that Jenny should be asking herself. "I'll admit that I doubt he would have cancelled our plans for Christmas if he didn't have a back-up," Jenny confessed. "He hates being alone."

"Look, I'm not raising these questions to hurt you, Jenny. I just want you to be realistic. You both have things to forgive and to ask for forgiveness of each other. It's a two-way street. I don't want you going into tomorrow's meeting with the mindset that you're the only one who needs to ask for forgiveness."

Jenny thanked Sherri and walked home thinking about her meeting with Kyle the next day. She felt apprehensive but energized. Because of the depth of her pain, right or wrong, Jenny was more willing than ever before to meet Kyle's wishes. If Kyle wanted her unconditional love, she would give it to him.

```
-----Original Message-----
To:      Jenny
From:    Kyle
Re:      Morning Prayers
Date:    Tues 1/29/2002 3:02 PM
```

Dear Jenny,
Thanks for the lovely meditation thoughts. But about tomorrow: On reflection, I don't think it is a good idea to get together in person right now. I am moving on in my life, and I hope you are in yours. If you want to communicate in emails or letters, I'll do my best to respond to you. Kyle

Twenty-six

Facing Rejection

Dear God, help me, Jenny thought after reading Kyle's message. *My therapist warned me. My friends warned me. And they were right.*

Jenny was shaking. She immediately called Dr. McFarland and left word for her to call back. She sat down at the computer and began drafting a response. She had to get her feelings out. When Dr. McFarland called back, Jenny read her the email. Overall, Dr. McFarland felt her response was direct and honest.

-----Original Message-----
To: Kyle
From: Jenny
Re: Our Meeting Tomorrow
Date: Tues 1/29/2002 8:24 PM

Dear Kyle,
As you'll recall, I stood by you through your deep depression. I stood by you through your therapy and diagnosis. There were times you could barely talk or get out of bed and I stayed there through all of that with you. In the midst of the emotional week of burying Mike, I left here to come down to be with you to help bury your mother. For godsake, Kyle, it is my turn now. I am hurting and I need you.

I was hesitant to exchange rings with you, but when I finally did, you knew that it was a huge step for me. I knew that I loved you but I had to be sure that I could embrace you the way you are—including your mood swings. I took the ring ceremony very seriously. I was committed then and am still committed now. I have not removed your ring from my finger. I understood it symbolized that we would stand by each other, no matter what.

I can only attribute your behavior to your emotional struggles. I have to take them into consideration and believe that they distort your judgment. For anything I've done to cause you pain, I ask your forgiveness. But you claimed to love me more than anyone else in the world yet you abandoned me on the day of Mike's burial. You left me to face my first Christmas alone without both of my parents, without Mike, and without you. Where is your compassion?

My choosing to take care of Mike was a gigantic issue in our life. But now that he is gone, why won't you hang on to see what life might have been like for us now?

You promised my mother, minutes before she died, that she didn't have to worry, that you would take care of me. You told me that the mistake I made after Mom died was that I failed to pointedly ask you for your help. So, Kyle, I am asking you now. I need your help to get through this.

Please, let's keep our meeting for lunch tomorrow.
Jenny

Jenny felt as if her future was in Kyle's hands. The only thing that mattered to her was meeting with him and finding a way to work things out. As the time for the meeting grew closer with no response, she was reasonably certain that their lunch was off. Even so, she checked her email obsessively all morning. Finally, about an hour before noon, she received a message from him:

-----Original Message-----
    To: Jenny
From: Kyle
Re: Lunch Today
Date: Wed 1/30/2002 11:04 AM

Dear Jenny,
After my decision not to meet with you today, I made

arrangements to meet my son at the Cal State bookstore shortly after noon.

I do not believe it is in my best interest or yours to get together.

The issues you referred to in your email are the same old story: I abandoned you repeatedly in your hour of need and nobody could have treated you so horribly but you are willing to forgive me nevertheless.

If I revisited the same stuff, I would say: Nothing has really changed. I told you I couldn't tolerate your intimate relationship with Mike (and Jeff), and questioned why your social life was so all-important to you. I loved only a part of you: the warm, loving, spiritual person. The more I saw of your life, the less I liked it. The "you" I loved was the Jenny who loved me when we were together.

If you look back over our old emails, you will see that you either ignored them (by not responding) or turned the tables to talk about how I abandoned you. You never faced them honestly and squarely. How you kept all the balls in the air with me and your other suitors, family, and friends is beyond me.

Take the priests. This stuff about how I hurt you when you were merely caring for a dying man is bullshit, and you know it. Your relationship with Mike was long and deep. All you have to do is read Mike's will to understand the nature of the relationship. He wanted you and only you to be his number one person on earth. And you took care of him because you loved him, too. When I was in the hospital, you and Mike were traipsing around San Francisco to get his cancer diagnosis. Your choice. So I spent many long days and nights trying to understand. Now I do not want to revisit any of this old stuff. I am not defending or attacking. I am giving it up. I do not want some novel form of a relationship where the primary partners are not going to marry, do not live together, do not share finances, and suffer each other having whatever relationships they choose with other intimates.

As I have told you so often, I am a simple person. I want to love one woman who loves me. I want to merge my life with hers. To live in the same place. To put her above all others. And I expect the same from her. The world calls such a relationship "marriage"—something you avoid like the plague.

I have moved on, Jenny. I really have. I have a woman who meets my needs in my life now, and I am not going to dishonor that relationship by becoming entangled with you again, just as I hoped you would have ended it with Jeff or Mike or maybe a skipped luncheon or party once in a while.

Please do not communicate with me again. I love you. I always will. I am so grateful for the wonderful time we shared. That is what I will remember. I hope you do, too. But that is over, and I am moving on.

Jenny sat staring at the screen, her whole body numb. She could feel the tattered edges of her life unraveling around her. If she held any illusion that time had softened Kyle's heart toward her, it was dispelled. With no other choice, Jenny was forced to *face reality*, another necessary and gigantic step in her recovery. She had hit bottom and was emotionally wrenched.

Jenny desperately needed to meet with her therapist. After Kyle had canceled their meeting, Jenny scheduled an afternoon appointment with Dr. McFarland. She quickly printed out a copy of Kyle's email and put it into her purse. As soon as she sat down in Dr. McFarland's office, Jenny handed her the email.

"I think we should begin with you reading this," Jenny told her. "And do me a favor. Don't ask me how this letter makes me feel. First, I want to know *your* insights."

"Fair enough." Dr. McFarland read the letter in silence, making notations as she read. Tears began running down Jenny's face. Soon, she was quietly sobbing. And then she was bawling to the point that she could hardly catch her breath. When she quieted down, Dr. McFarland shared her thoughts.

"This email is from a very angry man who isn't inclined to forget or forgive. Everything he has ever believed about you or held against you is listed here with no interest in ever getting past them. I would feel very attacked if I received this letter."

Jenny nodded, still unable to get words out.

"Do you really want to be with someone who thinks so negatively about you?"

Again Jenny responded without words, shaking her head.

"He loves only a part of you, Jenny, the part that can give him what he wants. But he doesn't accept the rest of your life, and I doubt if he ever will. So *now* let me ask you. What are your feelings about the letter? What are your tears about?"

"Facing the truth about myself," Jenny whispered, choking on her words. "I'm horrified to look at my own reflection through Kyle's eyes. I don't like the person he is showing me. I want to believe that I'm basically a good person. But this woman whom he is forcing me to look at is not the person I want to be."

"I'm not sure that I see it that way. If I remember correctly, he has a couple of facts wrong. He seems to imply that you had more going physically with Mike than you did."

"But I never did anything to jeopardize Mike's priesthood and I never would have."

"Of course not, so what is upsetting you?"

"Everything else he said has truth to it."

"Some truth."

"Okay, but still, with all that I had going on, as hard as I tried, I couldn't keep up a relationship with Kyle."

"You weren't just keeping up a relationship with Kyle. You were a caretaker for him, too. That was what broke you. He implies that he's just a simple country boy. But I don't see him that way. He's very complicated. He's bipolar; he's high maintenance. Maybe you did ask a lot of him in putting up with this phase of your life. But some men would have pitched in wholeheartedly to help you."

"He did help with Mom and he did it well," Jenny said. "And he spent time with Earl, too. The truth is, I made some bad choices. I even lied to him. Several times."

"Why?"

"Because I was afraid of losing him," Jenny said. "I really loved him, and I wanted him to hold out for me, let me get through this, and be waiting for me when it was all over. But sometimes he would call on

my cell phone and ask where I was. And if I was at Mike's or the
O'Connors or in any situation that I thought he wouldn't approve of, I
would make up something just to avoid his wrath. See what I mean? I
don't like this person I became. I am ashamed of her. Kyle is right to
be angry with me."

"But if he loves you as much as he claims, he also should be able to
find forgiveness in his heart"

Jenny paused to wipe her eyes.

"I think you've been saved, Jenny, saved from future hurt. Can you
accept the fact that through all three deaths, he was not there to see
you through the aftermath of even one of them? What if you ever got
sick? What guarantee would you have that he'd be there for you? The
pattern is that he would leave you when you most needed him. Is that
really what you want in a partner? Is that what you think you deserve?"

Jenny shook her head: No. No. No.

Twenty-seven

Kyle Alone

Kyle's first appointment of the day was with Marion Barker, the woman who had made significant contributions to helping him update the *Women's Rights Handbook* a few years earlier. After serving coffee to both of them, his secretary closed the door.

"I'm surprised to see you back here," Kyle began. "I thought we'd done an outstanding job to improve women's role in the workplace."

"We did," she quickly assured him. "That's precisely why I'm here. Now we want to help our Afghan sisters and we think our handbook could serve as a model." Marion explained that the United Nations was marking this year's International Women's Day by focusing on the plight of women in Afghanistan.

Kyle was aware of the Afghan Women's Summit for Democracy that had been held in Brussels the previous December. But he acknowledged that he knew very little if any follow-up had occurred.

"They agreed to send a group of women to Afghanistan to help reopen the schools and evaluate medical needs. That's a start. But for twenty-three years," Marion elaborated, "Afghans have been living in the dark under Taliban rule. Two generations were illiterate; girls were banned from school; and boys were brainwashed to become extremists. All of this was bad enough *before* but, since our invasion of their country, thousands of Afghan women have lost their homes, they're not allowed to work, many have lost their husbands, and others have lost a child. The question we keep asking ourselves and now I ask you, Mr. Attorney General: Are their victims somehow lesser than our own lost in the World Trade Center?"

Kyle was silent as he felt the question fill the room and seep into every particle of air in his office. He could only imagine the devastation and broken hearts of these poor women. Innocent American lives were lost. And now, because of U.S. military actions, innocent Afghan lives have been lost. This woman was hitting him with hard cold facts . . . facts that caught in his chest. When he could speak again, he asked, "So what are you proposing we do?"

"We want California women to lead the way in improving women's rights over there just as we did here. We want to step out of our comfort zone and help the Afghan women whose very lives have been destroyed by America's military actions. Let's take the handbook we designed for us and introduce it as a basis for the new governmental regime being set up in Afghanistan. It could be the start for reasserting the rights of Afghan women—the right to participate actively in all sectors and levels of society and in all stages of the work to bring peace and development back to their country."

Kyle was drawn in to the persuasiveness of this woman. He reached in his desk drawer and pulled an article from one of his files. It was U.N. Secretary-General Kofi Annan speaking at the Afghan Women's Summit.

"Let me read you his quote that captured my attention," Kyle said. "'There cannot be true peace and recovery in Afghanistan without restoration of the rights of women . . . I offer my full encouragement to all of you here, and to your sisters inside Afghanistan, as you work towards a society that reflects that unbroken strength and spirit of its women, and the full and equal measure of their right.' I must have saved the article for a reason. Let your group know that this office stands fully behind your effort."

As Marion left offering accolades of appreciation, Kyle leaned back in his chair. His coffee had become cold but his heart felt warm as he thought about the possibilities and the difference he and this group of women could make.

Kyle had a few minutes before his next appointment. He picked up the phone and called Josh. After sharing what a gratifying meeting he had just had, Kyle asked, "So how's it going in the Washington zoo?"

"Let me call you back." After a moment, Josh dialed Kyle back on his secured line. "We're on a one-track plan around here," Josh said. "Iraq. Iraq. Iraq. I think they've forgotten that the man who heads the most wanted list is Osama bin Laden. As far as they're concerned, there is only Saddam Hussein."

"What's their logic?"

"There isn't any. It just doesn't matter. You won't believe the latest caper. Last fall a mysterious call was received at Italy's Military Intelligence and Security Service. Someone was offering to sell information on Iraq's efforts to regenerate its nuclear weapons program through the purchase of tons of uranium from Niger, a small West African country. They were apparently phony documents designed to create the impression that the true purpose of the Iraqi ambassador's trip to Niger in 1999 was to secretly arrange a large shipment of uranium to Iraq in 2000 and that he may have had something to do with the attacks of 9/11. Both were exactly what the Bush administration was trying to convey to the American public. The Italian Military Intelligence passed this information on, knowing that it would be of great interest to the U.S."

"But the CIA didn't back up this report, did they?" Kyle asked.

"Hell, no! They discounted the report on the grounds that it was third-hand information coming from unreliable sources. However, to satisfy the office of the vice president, in February the CIA dispatched former ambassador Joe Wilson to investigate the reports. Wilson had served as the senior director for Africa at the National Security Council, which brought him in close proximity to the Niger government. At the conclusion of his trip, he reported back to the CIA that it was 'highly doubtful' Iraq had sought to purchase nuclear fuel from Niger. The CIA put the matter to rest in its report, declaring that there was no substance to the Niger allegations."

"Yeah, but I bet what is fool's gold to the CIA is the real thing to the three stooges."

"You got it," Josh said. "The minute they got a hold of the Italian Military's phony report, they passed it onto Cheney. It was a matter of the vice president hearing what he wanted to hear. Prompted by his interest, today the CIA has issued an unclassified report to Congress with the headline, 'Baghdad may be attempting to acquire materials that could aid in reconstituting its nuclear-weapons program.' The CIA buried this information under a lot of other items, but they did introduce it to Congress."

"So they got to George Tenet," Kyle said dismally. "He's in an untenable position. "But where's Colin Powell in all of this? He brings such a down-to-earth outlook to these issues."

"You know he's my hero. But even he is having trouble withstanding all the pressure."

"But he knows the truth?"

"Oh yeah, but he's inches away from caving in," Josh said. "He can't stop this blizzard single-handedly. I can see where this is going. They will use him for whatever they can get out of him and then toss him aside."

Kyle flinched at the image as Josh abruptly changed the subject.

"So have you heard from Jenny?"

"Yes, and I may've just closed a door that can never be reopened."

"Are you sure that's what you want to do?" Josh asked.

"No, I'm not sure. She wanted to come see me and talk. But I'm afraid if I let her come through my door, I wouldn't want her to leave again. We'd pick up right where we left off and create the same old revolving door. I had to say no."

"What are you so afraid of?"

"I've never loved anyone like I love her," Kyle said. "But we want very different things in life. And neither of us will ever change. It makes me sad, but I don't see any hope."

"When something is that good, it may be worth digging deeper for a solution."

"There is no solution. I need her to be *my* woman, but she will never be that. She will always belong to others, too. I wanted her to marry me or at least come live with me. But she didn't want that either. I know she loves me, but she needs more than any one man can give her. It's just the way she is."

Sounding more serious than usual, Josh said, "Maybe you need to give a little, bro. In a relationship, it can't be only your way. Do you remember when Emmy wanted to live in Washington and get more involved in politics? I loved New York. There's just no city quite like it for me. But when I made up my mind that I was going to give on this point for her, it wasn't long after that when I got the call inviting me to go to work in the secretary of state's office. It's like I gave up something I wanted and got something even better in return. For me to take this job, we were going to be moving to the District anyway."

"Yeah, but it's different with us," Kyle protested. "Letting her go may be the most courageous thing I've ever done. I was pretty naïve when I came out of my marriage. I guess I thought I could just replace one woman with another and life would be great. I didn't know any other way of life, but I had a picture in my mind of how life with Jenny could be. Her way of life scared the hell out of me. She was so involved with her family and friends that I couldn't ever see her satisfied with having just me."

"When it comes to bacon and eggs, you know what they say about the chicken and the pig . . . Having laid the egg, the chicken is *involved* but having laid down his life, the pig is *committed*. Jenny may be involved with others in her life, but she seems pretty damned committed to you."

"Jenny and I do love each other, Josh. But it takes more than love for a relationship to work. Right now, I have to pursue what I know and understand. Our relationship left me in constant turmoil. I was always churned up inside. For my own inner peace, Josh, I had to let her go."

"You and I came into this world with more than a few challenges," Josh said intently. "Our parents dumped us. But another set of parents wanted us and took us in. Mother was the primary parent for me and Dad was for you. Now they're both gone and you never really got close to Mother. Maybe you need a little mothering, bro."

Kyle didn't speak. The lump in his throat blocked any words that might have come. And in truth, he had no response. He suspected there was something to what his twin was saying.

"Hey, bro, I'm sorry you're hurting," Josh said. "You know I'm here if you need me. I can't be your mother, but I can be your mother-frickin' twin. Just call anytime. I love you."

Kyle was shaken as he hung up the phone. He finished out his day and left work early. Carrying the mail in his hand as he walked through the door, Kyle was greeted by Winky begging for a walk along the river. After a quiet dinner of leftovers, Kyle picked up his violin and began practicing. After a few minutes, he put it down. It was no use. He couldn't concentrate. He sat down at his desk and absentmindedly sorted through his mail. He stopped short. There was a letter from Jenny. Slowly, he used his letter opener and carefully opened the envelope without ripping the edges.

March 12, 2002

Dear Kyle,

Nearly three months have passed since your mother and Mike passed away . . . and since you went away. But it feels like a lifetime ago. I am still in therapy with Elizabeth McFarland. I'm spending most of my time at home reading or writing or hiding under my covers. I feel sad, lonely, fearful, hurt, and shameful. It is the shame I want to address. In all the challenges that we faced during our time together, where could I have done better?

From the moment we met, we were on different tracks. You wanted to move our relationship along more quickly and I more slowly. I suspect that both of our motivations relate back to insecurities we faced in our lives before we met each other. For you to feel safe, you wanted us to move immediately into a close, committed, more exclusive relationship with as few outside people and distractions as possible. But I was in a different place and, to protect myself from being hurt again, I wanted to keep a broad circle of friends around me. Life had taught me that I could trust them to be there for me in times of crisis but, from painful experience, I was afraid to put all of my trust in one man. I doubt if either of us was conscious that these issues were underlying our personal struggles at that time.

Then came all the illnesses. I felt an overwhelming respon-sibility to take care of those close in my life. If I had it to do over, I would do it all the same save for one thing: I would have made sure that you understood that you were an equally important member of my family and that you knew how much you meant to me. Even though I was grieving in many ways, I thought I had the rest of my life fairly well in balance. Then *your* mother died.

When I made such an effort to get to Mandy's luncheon, I admit that I wasn't thinking of you. I was thinking only of myself and how I deserved a break from death. But for you, my leaving felt like the deepest kind of abandonment and I, of all people, should have understood that. I should have known. I, who fear abandonment more than anything in the world, should have realized how my leaving you, even for a couple of hours, would make you feel. Ironic, isn't it, that we both abandoned each other on the very day we most needed each other. I can't even begin to tell you how I wish I could relive that moment. I would have liked to be there for you fully and completely during that time. Had I chosen to do that, I believe you would have been inclined to go with me to Mike's burial service. And our story might have a different ending. I hope one day you can forgive me for not understanding all of this at the time. With the wisdom of hindsight, I could have made better choices.

The slate of my life has been wiped clean. I am letting go of you but it isn't easy. I still believe in you. I believe in your ability and mine to grow and to change. I believe that, even separately, we will both find our own solutions to our life struggles. I still love you more than I can say, and I wish we could be together. But I want you to be happy, and if that means I must live without you, then I will do so. But know that losing you will remain my greatest regret in life.

Jenny

Kyle laid his head on the desk and sobbed. Winky stood by his side whimpering as he rubbed his master's leg with his paw. Kyle could not even lift his arm to pat Winky and assure him it would be okay. Never before was he so unsure than anything would be okay—either in his personal life or throughout the world.

+++++++++++

Jenny was putting the box of cereal away after eating breakfast when the phone rang. It was Dr. McFarland.

"Have I caught you at a good time?"

"As good as any."

"Well, I heard from Kyle," Dr. McFarland said. "And I want to pass the information on right away."

"What?" Jenny asked hopefully.

"He said that he received a letter from you, and he asked me to tell you that he forgives you, he forgives you, he forgives you."

"Wow!" Jenny felt a sense of utter peacefulness wash over her. "Did he say anything else?"

"Yes, we talked for about fifteen minutes. He went back over the issues again. But he mostly wanted you to know that you are forgiven so that you can move on with your life."

"Did he say anything about asking for my forgiveness?"

"No, nothing like that." They both let that go for the moment. "Are you okay, Jenny?"

"Yes, I do feel better now. The point of my letter wasn't to try to get him back. It was to clean my part of the slate. It was a huge step for me. I feel like a weight has been lifted from my shoulders."

"Maybe now you'll begin to feel a greater sense of your progress."

"I think so," Jenny confirmed. "Now I think I can finally move on."

Twenty-eight

Moving On

Kyle realized that one of the continuing mysteries about the direction foreign policy was taking at the Pentagon was how seasoned politicians like Dick Cheney and Donald Rumsfeld could be led to believe that going into Iraq could be relatively uncomplicated. But it appeared that they were swayed by the influence of Iraqi exile Ahmed Chalabi. Although the CIA wanted nothing to do with Chalabi, the Defense Department—where the neoconservative movement was so well-represented by Rumsfeld, Wolfowitz, Pearl, Feith, Wurmser and others—continued to establish a close relationship with him. In fact, many believed the Defense Department planned to install Chalabi as a successor to Saddam Hussein. In the spring, Josh had found memos in which Wolfowitz and Rumsfeld were seeking Bush's intervention to grant Ahmed Chalabi ninety million dollars. The State Department argued that it would be throwing good money after bad, since Chalabi hadn't accounted for previous funds given to him to protect U.S. oil contracts. To Kyle, it appeared once again to be a case of the neoconservatives supporting whoever would give them the information that supported what they already wanted to do. He called his brother for confirmation.

"What's the story behind all this media hype?" Kyle asked Josh.

"Oh, it's just neocons at each other's throats. Wolfowitz is pushing Rumsfeld to go to war in Iraq. Rummy doesn't need much arm-twisting. He's already gung ho. Cheney is primed. We are going to war in Iraq. The only question is when."

"It won't take much to take Hussein out. But what then?"

"They think the aftermath will be a cakewalk," Josh said.

"Sure," Kyle said mockingly. "Just replace Hussein with Chalabi, and the Iraqis will greet us like conquering heroes paving our way with flowers and candy."

"Yeah," Josh said, "and after a brief occupation, democracy will thrive like a burgeoning wildflower." Josh began talking faster. "The deep-seated historical antagonisms among the Sunnis and the Shiites will be laid to rest; Iraqi oil production will be quickly doubled; and the invasion will create a kind of reverse osmosis in which one autocratic regime after another will topple in Iraq, Libya, Syria, and Iran, laying the ground for the emergence of a new democratic Middle East filled entirely with allies of the United States."

"Hello . . . does anybody in the Pentagon remember that we're looking for Osama bin Laden?" Kyle asked angrily.

"I guess you saw the president's response to that question on this morning's news."

"Yeah," Kyle retorted more bitterly. "Bush said, 'I don't know where he is, but I truly am not that concerned about him.'"

"Talk about having their frickin' priorities screwed up. The Pentagon has shut down the department whose job it was to be looking for Usama bin Laden—what they call the UBL unit. He's not even in their radar screen. We could have caught the s.o.b. in Tora Bora last December if the president and the military had kept their sights on him."

"I just wonder how such experienced guys can be that naïve. But then I guess we've all been there, haven't we?" Kyle said reflecting on his own questionable actions.

Over the next few weeks, Jenny did everything she could think of to continue her recovery. She increased her work-out routine to three times a week with her personal trainer. She began playing more tennis. And she kept up her journaling and daily prayer time.

As March 25 rolled around, Jenny wondered how she would handle the first anniversary of her mother's death.

Jeff called to check up on herherher knowing that this might be a difficult day. "Did you hear from your mom today?" Jeff asked wryly.

"*Hear* from her? Noooo," she answered, wondering where he was going with that question. "Why do you ask?"

"Because I heard from Mike last night."

"What?" Jenny asked incredulously. But then, the more she thought about it, the less surprised she was. "How did it happen?"

"He was very direct. I was working at my computer late last night and plugged my cell phone in to charge. It must have been about the time he passed away, shortly after eleven. Suddenly, my phone started blinking, indicating I had missed a call. But I knew I hadn't. I couldn't have. I was sitting right there. So I clicked on the button to see who had called. My screen said 'O'Malley, Mike'—just the way I have him programmed in my phone list."

Jenny laughed. "Mike always loved high drama. He'd be so upset with all of this talk of a preemptive war; he'd be leading protest marches if he were alive today. I don't understand, Jeff. Is war the only way these guys in Washington know how to solve problems?"

"I see Secretary Rumsfeld as one of the key leaders behind all of this," Jeff said. "He and his deputy, Paul Wolfowitz, and Vice President Cheney. Do you remember when Rumsfeld first took office? I remember reading how he insisted that the Office of Peacekeeping Operations be renamed the Office of Stability Operations and put under his control. After that, we never heard anything more about activity from this branch of government."

"I think Rumsfeld has an aversion to the word 'peace.'" Jenny said. "I'm worried about our country's values. These guys in Washington talk a good talk, but it just seems that everything we do is to preserve our supremacy and reinforce our greed as the world's richest country.

"It's a shame that this is always Washington's first line of attack. I don't think it's in their scope to consider that the rising anger toward the U.S. might be addressed by solving world hunger or helping young

Islamic Muslims who are displaced feel a greater sense of belonging. So many of them are isolated, poor, and feel no identity with their surroundings—so bin Laden offers them more answers than we do. Have you ever considered getting involved in the Peace Corp or some group like that? You'd be good at going out and helping resolve some of these issues."

"I've thought about it but I guess I've never really known how. When I'm ready to become more active again, I'm going to seriously consider it."

With the war heating up, Kyle became more concerned about the course that White House officials were navigating, and Josh kept him well informed.

"Did you read about the capture of Abu Zubaydah, Kyle? It's been all over the news."

"Yes. With his being such a key terrorist and a member of bin Laden's inner circle, his capture should prove helpful."

"Well, it has, but what's come out has less to do with bin Laden and more to do with the connection between *the Saudis* and al Qaeda."

"What are you talking about, Josh?"

"As a way to get him to talk, the CIA used two teams of interrogators," Josh said. "One consisted of undisguised Americans and the other Arab-Americans posing as Saudi security agents. Fearing the Americans, Zubaydah opened up to the Arabs and gave them the name of one of his allies that shocked his interrogators: Prince Ahmed bin Salman bin Abdul Aziz, one of the Saudis who, under U.S. protection, was flown out of our country right after the 9/11 attack."

"You're kidding," Kyle said. "Here our government tries desperately to make a case for Iraqi ties to al Qaeda and now they find a Saudi tie?"

"Zubaydah said that the royal family had made a deal with al Qaeda, promising that the House of Saud would aid the Taliban as long as they kept terrorism out of Saudi Arabia. He named Prince Ahmed of the House of Saud and two others as the ones he met with."

"The Saudis may have made a deal with al Qaeda *before* 9/11, but I can't imagine them collaborating with them afterward," Kyle reasoned.

"That's what his interrogators thought, but that's when Zubaydah dropped the real bombshell. He said that 9/11 didn't change anything because Prince Ahmed knew beforehand that an attack was scheduled on American soil that day."

"Why wasn't the information passed on?"

"Because bin Laden was safe knowing that the Saudis couldn't prevent the attack without more specific details but later they would be unlikely to turn on him if he could show that they knew before it happened," Josh explained.

"I understand the Bush family has a twenty-year relationship with the Saudi family, but I wonder if the president realized the implication when he went public saying"—Kyle switched to his best imitation of the president—"'We will make no distinction between the terrorists who committed these acts and those who harbor them.'"

"Obviously, with his longtime family ties, he will never go after the Saudis, but a lot of people have to be questioning why we're so frickin' alarmed about some countries and not others," Josh said.

"Exactly. Why isn't Saudi Arabia on our list?"

"The whole thing pisses me off, but it must have been hard for the president when *Newsweek* reported that Princess Haifa's charitable donations wound up in the bank account of a Saudi who aided two of the 9/11 hijackers. I'm sure that Bush couldn't even imagine that his longtime friend, Prince Bandar, the husband of Princess Haifa, could have been linked to the attacks on America."

"I can't remember an American president having such close connections to a foreign government that protects and supports our country's deadliest enemies," Kyle said, shaking his head in disgust.

After four months, Jenny was finally beginning to feel signs of progress. With dogged determination, she moved into the deepest and most significant stage in the recovery process. Through *The Grief Recovery Handbook*, she was guided to create a graph of the relationship with the person with whom she was still incomplete. The key to completing the loss of a relationship, they explained, was not to idealize it but to see it as it really was . . . for better and for worse. Jenny spent hours charting her memories of her time with Kyle.

Everything above the line represented positive memories and everything below the line negative ones.

Her purpose in this exercise was to release her emotional connection to those significant moments that were holding her captive to the relationship. She needed to reexamine those behaviors that were making her feel distraught and thereby making it so difficult to let go. Only then could she bring this relationship to completion.

What awareness it brought Jenny to chart out her and Kyle's relationship! She and Kyle had many beautiful memories, but it was unmistakable from the graph that they were on a never-ending emotional seesaw. She felt emotionally exhausted after the exercise. But what an incredible experience!!! For Jenny, this was the single most significant breakthrough so far. It was too easy for her to attribute many of their problems to his issues—his mood swings or his narcissistic tendencies. Jenny realized she had taken more than her share of the blame. But for the first time, she was narrowing down her own unwarranted patterns of behavior. If she was ever to have a lasting relationship, she knew she must recognize the importance of making changes in how she related to a partner. She felt overwhelmed with regret that she missed important opportunities that could have changed the course of their life together.

Jenny hoped that she was now taking two steps forward for every one step back. At one instant, she would find herself hoping against hope that Kyle would show up at her door, remorseful, ready to come back, whole, healthy, and fully committed to their relationship. Then she would level out and convince herself how much better off she was to not be relying on Kyle for support. While holding steady in that awkward state of balance, she would ruefully face her own shortcomings and mistakes that had contributed to their saga and begin to feel the first signs of detachment and facing closure. At those moments, she could feel admiration for Kyle. One of them *had* to draw the line and say, "Enough!"

As her birthday approached, Jenny was filled with momentary sadness as she let in thoughts of celebrating it without her parents, without Mike and, most of all, without Kyle. Friends planned a party for her in her backyard, but it felt more like a debut after her months of isolation. It was a warm spring day, and her yard looked like a botanical garden with each creek flowing into the crystal-clear ponds and day lilies and ice plants flaunting themselves between the rocks. After months of feeling as if she had lost her self-esteem, looking out and seeing so many friends mingling and sharing in the celebration, Jenny realized how much she was loved.

After the party, Harvey invited Jenny to stop by his office. He had a birthday present for her. Jenny followed him in her own car and entered through the back door.

"So," Harvey said, "you're not my patient and you're only on a mild dosage of Lexapro at the moment."

"Riiiight," Jenny said, drawing out the word.

"So you're coming alive again. I thought this called for a celebration between friends. This is a kind of 'rebirth' day." He walked over to his closet, searched around for a minute or so, and pulled out a bottle of Silver Oak. "Have you ever had this before?"

"No, is it special?"

"Well, maybe not as special as Opus One," Harvey said, smiling, indicating that he knew about the wine experience she'd had with Kyle at Thanksgiving in Cancun. As he opened the bottle, they let the shared memory linger in silence, a past event only they would have understood.

Jenny took her first sip and toasted Harvey for his good choice.

"I'm planning to take a case of this down to my son's wedding next month. I think this is suitable for the celebration, don't you?"

For the next couple of hours, Harvey and Jenny enjoyed their friendship and conversation, reliving some of their funny and painful experiences. Jenny expressed her gratitude for all he had done for Kyle and for her over their time together. "I don't know how you put up with us and all our high drama. I hope I'll have the chance to repay your kindness. You are a great friend, Harvey."

Twenty-nine

Letting Go

Jenny's message light was blinking. She hit Play and froze as she listened to Kyle's message.

I have some tragic news. Harvey is dead. He died in his plane. It was horrible, Jenny. He had his son in the plane along with his son's fiancée and her close friend. They were touring the Grand Canyon when the plane went down. As far as anyone knows it was mechanical failure—they think maybe the propeller. They were all killed. I wanted to tell you myself. I didn't want you to hear it on the news first." He paused and then added, "I hope you're okay."

Oh, my God, Jenny thought. *Oh, my God, this can't be happening.* Jenny felt numb. Then her thoughts turned to Kyle. No one knew better than she what a lifeline Harvey was for Kyle. There was little Harvey didn't know about him. There was *nothing* he didn't know about the relationship between Kyle and Jenny. He had heard it all, right down to the most minuscule of details. How would Kyle ever survive without Harvey? Then Jenny thought about what losing Harvey would mean to her. He was there so often when she needed to vent or question her own sanity. She thought about the Christmas lost and how Harvey and she each spent that day so alone. For a passing moment, Jenny felt rage at Kyle for destroying that day for them—a day that could never be relived with Harvey.

For the next couple of days, the accident was all over the news—on television and in the newspaper. The crash made the CBS Evening

News. Jenny watched several repeats on television over the next two days. She felt compelled to see it over and over, just to let it sink in that Harvey was really dead. He had traveled everywhere in that little aircraft and seemed happiest when he was flying. She hoped he'd been happy up until the end.

On May 20, Jenny attended Harvey's memorial service in Sacramento. The First Christian Church was filled with his patients, medical associates, flying and hiking buddies, close friends, and family. She looked for Kyle at the funeral, but he wasn't there. Jenny felt disappointment. Partly, she just wanted to see him. And, partly, she wanted to share this mutual loss with him. Knowing how this was affecting her, Jenny could only imagine how Harvey's passing was impinging on Kyle. *No more, please God. Please don't take anyone else away for a while.*

After reading Harvey's obituary in the *Sacramento Bee,* Jenny realized that she had paid almost no attention to the news these past few months. Flipping through the newspaper on the back page she saw that Kyle had just returned from a week at Mount St. Carmel Abbey in Santa Fe, New Mexico. *Good for him,* she thought. She was glad to know that Kyle was keeping in touch with Brother Anthony.

Just one week later, Jenny saw the headline: "State Attorney General Will Not Run Again." The filing deadline was the end of May, and Kyle was making his announcement at the last minute. Jenny wondered if the Democratic Party was forewarned of his decision since Kyle was a shoe-in for reelection.

Hearing the announcement stirred up a jumble of emotions for Jenny. She was not entirely surprised, but she found herself feeling happy for Kyle. She felt this was a step forward in Kyle's growth, but she was sure that most of his constituents would be taken aback. Republicans would already be weighing who might step in to take his place. His party would feel he was letting them down. Kyle was respected by both sides, but his anti-war sentiments of late had run the gamut of reactions.

"I feel strongly that our relationship with other countries is on the brink of disaster," Kyle was quoted saying in the article. "We have to get at the root cause of so much hatred in the world. There has to be a better way of dealing with our differences than going to war and massacring thousands of people. Whatever that direction might be, I want to be a part of helping make it happen."

The article concluded by stating that Kyle Anderson was not ready to go public with his plans, but he acknowledged that he was considering taking a major step in his career.

Could he be contemplating entering the monastery? Anything is possible, Jenny thought. *But, no, he couldn't handle celibacy. What work could be serious enough that he would refer to it as a major next step?*

Chad stopped by her house after he heard everyone talking about Kyle. He must have had the same thought Jenny did. "Yo, Mom, what's happening?"

"Mmm . . . just reading the headlines."

"Yeah, every station is carrying the news, too. People seem pretty upset. They're disappointed that he's stepping down." Chad had grown to love Kyle and held him in esteem as a mentor. He missed hanging out with him and felt Kyle's absence along with that of Chad's grandparents. All the recent losses had taken their toll on Chad as well. Lately he had been talking to his mother about what he might want to do with his life next. Although he had been in the workforce for five years, he felt that his career lacked direction, and he wanted to do something more meaningful. With their most recent discussions in mind, Chad cleared his throat as if to make an announcement,

"Mom, I don't know how to break this to you, but I guess I'll just say it. Kyle and I have been in touch. We didn't want you to know until we were sure. But we've decided to enter the seminary together. All of your influence has finally paid off."

Jenny hesitated, not sure what to say.

Before she could get words out, Chad dissolved into belly laughs. "Had you going, didn't I?"

"Well, I found it more believable that he might consider that option than you," Jenny said, feeling relieved.

Chad chuckled. "Me, too. But, seriously, what do you think our hero is going to do?"

"I knew he was thinking of not running again. But even he had no idea what he might do next. Whatever it is, I have to believe it's something where he feels he can do more good than where he is now."

"That's what I want too," Chad said. "I've been thinking, and I want to get your take on this. How do you feel about me going back to school? I'd like to take some more psychology classes and finish my degree. I checked with the department advisor, and I only have about twenty credits to go."

"Oh, sweetie, I'd love it. I always hoped you'd finish, but I never wanted to push the subject." Jenny gave her son a hug, and they held each other. "We've come through a really tough year, but we always come through it, don't we?"

"Yeah, Mom, you're a strong woman. I'm really proud of you."

"What is this—our mutual admiration society? I love you, baby."

Chad paused and then added: "I'm sorry about Harvey. I know the three of you were really close. Kyle doesn't have him to talk to anymore. And I know you're going to miss him a lot, too."

As the weeks passed, Jenny emerged from her self-absorption and found interest in the world at large again. She had had enough of living within the confines of her narrow parameters and was ready to broaden her horizons. Reading the paper and listening to the news, Jenny was becoming conscious of an interesting parallel. The healing process she was going through with Kyle appeared analogous to the course he felt America should take to resolve conflicts with other nations. She could be fighting with Kyle, but she had chosen not to go that route. Instead, she had devoted a great deal of energy toward understanding what angered him and why he left. She had owned her part in what happened. And she had asked his forgiveness. She was nearing a place where she felt at peace with herself and with him.

Were these the very steps Kyle was seeking on a national level? He didn't believe that continuing the war in Afghanistan or waging a new one in Iraq had any redeeming value. He recognized that terrorists were not confined to these two countries. They were cropping up in clusters all over the world. His reasoning was that if U.S. officials could understand what drove these radical extremists and what part America had contributed to their outrage, they might be able to find a solution. Many in her political circle would consider America free of blame, thinking that Americans were the innocent victims, the good guys, out to destroy the evil ones who have no rational reason for their anger. After all, the introspective work she had done on herself, seeking answers to these global questions made sense to Jenny. If America was to find resolution with those who threaten the country's way of life, Jenny saw Kyle recommending a more conciliatory approach. How often he had said to her: America could not and should not excuse what happened at the World Trade Center. It was a monstrous atrocity. But, despite the depth and breadth of wickedness in this act, Kyle felt it was essential for America's healing that the country look at what part it played to open itself to such animosity. America may not be able to change the mentality of fundamental, radical, Islamic terrorists, but by changing its own behavior, he had explained to her, the response of the world toward America would inevitably begin to shift as well.

Through all of her work toward emotional healing, Jenny had come to understand something new about forgiveness. It had nothing to do with recognizing the correctness or incorrectness of the other person's actions. She was just beginning to learn that forgiveness is an unfolding process. It changes the way we remember the past and helps us reach completeness quietly. Not with trumpet blasts heralding some grand entrance but with the weightiness of the anger slipping away almost unnoticed. It was not at all that she forgave or sought forgiveness because she had finally discovered that one of them was right and the other wrong. Rather, she recognized that there were offenses on both sides. Once she could own her part and stop blaming Kyle for all the transgressions, Jenny was permeated with a soft spirit that allowed her to let go of the ill feelings and to end the pain associated with the hurtful memories. The best part was that she could do this without losing her ability to reminisce about their unique connectedness. Jenny knew that the resentment and hurt she had felt toward Kyle was dissipating and being supplanted by an even stronger spiritual connection with him. The emotional part of their bond might fade with time, but there would always be that "secret chamber" of their hearts that they reserved for each other. Nothing could take that away.

Soon after, Jenny shared her epiphanies with Sherri.

"I'm so proud of you, Jenny. You've crossed over a threshold—I knew you would eventually. It just happened sooner than even I expected. You've left some heavy baggage on the other side and opened yourself to a whole new world."

"You know I still love him."

"Of course you do," Sherri said. "I'm sure you always will. And I know he will always love you."

"Letting go has nothing to do with ending the love we have for another person. It's all about shutting down the pain connected with loving that person. That's the main reason Kyle ended it—to shut down the pain. It took me a while longer to get there."

"Well, it's been inspiring to see you come through so much, Jenny. Do you realize how much I've seen you through in our short couple of years together? I think your faith has brought you through this quicker than it might have normally taken."

"God, friends like you, and a whole lot of intense work—that's what got me through this. Plus I have several connections up there," Jenny said, looking heavenward and thinking of Ellen, Earl, Mike, and Harvey. They had all invested a great deal of energy in her precarious journey with Kyle.

Sherri walked Jenny outside and started down the steps with her as Jenny sauntered slowly ahead to her car. Just at that moment, a bluebird flew over, circled around, and landed on the sidewalk between them. With only 10 feet separating the two friends, this would ordinarily be a risky move for a little bluebird. But there was nothing "ordinary" about this.

"Hi, Mom," Jenny whispered. "My world is better today. But you already know that, don't you? Where's Earl?"

Sherri looked to her left and saw another bluebird scavenging in the grass. "Hey, you. Still looking for cookies? You can have them with sugar now. No more worry about your diabetes, huh?"

For the next few minutes the two birds lingered and chirped. Jenny and Sherri enjoyed the moment as they watched.

Toward the end of summer, Jenny was at last beginning to experience a sense of peace about those she had lost in the past year. She enjoyed her alone time and kept up her journaling as Mike had encouraged her to do.

No matter how well we may think we are prepared, no matter how willing we are to accept the inevitable, we are still enormously affected when we face the death of someone close. The finality, the absoluteness of someone taking his or her last breath carries us into a whole new level of pain and of closure. And isn't a breakup just another form of death—and in many ways more difficult? It is the end of a relationship as well as the loss of all the accompanying hopes, dreams, and expectations. But because the person is still alive, there remains the inevitable hope that we will someday heal the wounds or that the other person will apologize for what we believe he or she has done to hurt us. Bereaving the loss of a special relationship might be compared to bereaving the loss of a child. The pain carries longer-lasting and more excruciating anguish. It gradually becomes less prevalent but never completely goes away.

Thirty

Build-up to War

While Jenny's world was growing more peaceful both within and around her, Kyle and Josh's work situations were just the reverse. The Pentagon was preparing to go to war. The SOA Watch was pressuring Kyle to shut down the California military base before any further human lives were destroyed. The governor, pressured by Washington, was insisting on keeping all his military bases open. The Secretary of State's Office was in pandemonium as they were taking on the Department of Defense. Richard Haass, the director of policy planning and a close aide to Colin Powell, dropped in on Condi Rice to discuss Iraq. Discouraged at the outcome of the conversation, he stopped in Josh's office afterward.

"How did it go?" Josh asked as he shuffled through papers.

Richard shook his head. "I raised the issue of whether we are really sure that we want to put Iraq front and center at this point, given the war on terrorism and other issues. And she said, essentially, that the decision's been made, don't waste your breath."

"Why hasn't the secretary of state been consulted?" Josh asked.

Richard shrugged his shoulders.

Larry Wilkerson, Powell's chief of staff and a former colonel in the Army, joined the conversation. "I'll tell you why. Since Desert Storm, everyone knows that the general is cautious about deploying troops. They know he has deep doubts about another war with Iraq and about our ability to see through the immense task of occupying the country and putting it back on its feet after the war and after decades of decay under Saddam's leadership. General Powell's view is that you'll be creating more problems than you're solving."

"Isn't that obvious?" Josh asked rhetorically as he picked up his briefcase and headed toward the parking garage.

Josh always looked forward to getting home to Emmy after work. Since moving from New York to Washington, they lived in a more homey setting: grass in the backyard, a garage to store their extra gear, even a basketball backboard and hoop attached over the garage so he could still shoot hoops with the guys. Josh opened a bottle of Bud and sat down on the patio for their usual after-work time together. He used the frosty bottle to wipe his brow. Washington was having its usual heat wave in August.

"You look like you've been through the ringer today," Emmy said.

"You know, honey, I wouldn't trade my job for anything in the world. I feel like I do something that really matters most of the time. But these idiots at the top won't listen to anybody, least of all to our office." He looked at Emmy and smiled. "Thank God I have you. You make me feel that my thoughts and insights matter."

She moved behind him and began rubbing his shoulders. "So, if I know you, you and the staff will come up with a plan."

Josh nodded. "We had one, but it just crashed and burned, too. We arranged for Colin Powell and his chief deputy, Richard Armitage, to go to President Bush's ranch in Crawford, Texas. In a more casual atmosphere, they hoped to be able to restructure the dialogue on Iraq. But Armitage said it just turned into a game of rope-a-dope."

"What?"

"You know, they threw out all the obstacles they could to Bush and Rumsfeld without seeming to be opposed to the policy. That's how the game is played. But Condi Rice was right. We are going to invade Iraq. There is no room for discussion."

Later that evening, Josh picked up the phone and then put it down. He sat looking out the window of his home office in silence. Then he picked up the phone again. He dialed Brother Anthony. After a wait, he heard the familiar, jovial voice of his friend.

"To what do I owe this unexpected pleasure?"

"I'm troubled about my work," Josh explained in an unusually somber tone. "All my studies and experience have been to help bring about peace in the world. Maybe I'm in the wrong job. Maybe I'm just frustrated. But I feel so helpless. Even my boss, Secretary Powell, seems weighed down by what we're up against. I don't know what I'm supposed to do."

"I have no doubt that God has placed you in Washington for a reason, Josh. We are all given a setting in life through which we have a chance to make our little difference in the world. It isn't always easy. It isn't meant to be easy. However fruitless our efforts may sometimes feel, we must keep putting them forth. It is serving in this manner—I in a monastic setting and you in a political one—that we can best learn the significance of liberation through love."

Josh received the encouragement he needed. As the movement toward war continued to escalate, Josh watched on with disbelief how far it appeared the CIA was willing to go, per orders, to find evidence to justify the war. He was determined to do all in his power to support the secretary of state's position that invading Iraq had no place in the war on terror.

Josh was asked by Cofer Black to keep track of Dr. Sawson Alhaddad, a woman in her mid-fifties who had defected to the United States from Iraq. She was one of several people the CIA had called upon to participate in a special program. As Josh read her background, he learned that she had escaped from Iraq in 1979 and settled in Cleveland as an American citizen, marrying and working as an anesthesiologist. She thought she had put her fears behind her until she received a call from the CIA asking for her to help the United States by going to Baghdad to undertake a secret mission.

Josh's assignment was to learn, for the Secretary of State's Office, the background of Alhadded's brother and the outcome of their visit. He was fascinated by their story.

Her brother, Dr. Saad Tawfiq, spent his entire career, starting in the early 1980s, as a member of one of the most secretive scientific teams in the world—the Iraqi Atomic Energy Commission that tried to build a nuclear bomb for Saddam Hussein. The day before he was to start work at the Tuwaitha plant, the facility was bombed by the Israeli Air Force in order to block Hussein from building a nuclear bomb that Israel's prime minister, Menachem Begin, feared could be used against his country. That attack led the way for the outraged Saddam Hussein to move into the covert world of developing nuclear weapons for self-protection. Saad's new employment soon led him to work under Ja'afar Dia Jafar, who had a plan for building a bomb that he promised Hussein would be impossible for the outside world to detect. The nuclear weapons program appeared to be oil-related work, even to the members of various subgroups working on the project. Despite the later fears and suspicions of the CIA, Iraq didn't need to buy uranium from Niger in order to provide fuel for this bomb. There was plenty of uranium already in the country. When Saad heard rumors about the infamous Niger report, he knew firsthand that the information was incorrect. In 1991, Hussein's nuclear program was permanently destroyed by an accidental bombing from an American aircraft over a complex of buildings in Tamiya, where Saad had devoted years of his life. Hussein sent out orders to destroy or hide all incriminating evidence and leave only the equipment that would appear to be dual-use technology.

When Saad's sister, Sawson, arrived more than a decade later, the nuclear program had been dead for years, and Saad's life had moved on. He was working for the Military Industrial Commission on a nitric acid plant for fertilizer production and teaching part-time at the University of Technology in Baghdad. Happy to see her brother after 13 years, Sawson went back with him to the home in which they had grown up. The house was located next door to the headquarters of the Mukabarrat, the Iraqi intelligence service. Sawson was depressed to see the house deteriorated by the bombing raids targeting the Mukabarrat building. Afraid to draw attention to his sister's visit, Saad did not take any time off from work, leaving his sister to visit with family and old neighborhood friends. Finally, on her second night there, Sawson was able to find time to be alone with her brother. She told Saad that the CIA wanted him to defect. He explained to her that it was impossible for him to get out of the country without being detected. Resigned, she began asking him the questions she had been sent to ask about the

Iraqi nuclear weapons program. How close were the Iraqis to having a nuclear warhead? How advanced was the centrifuge program? What process were they using for isotope separation? Where were the weapon factories?

Saad was stunned by the line of questioning. "There aren't any. There is nothing," he kept saying. "The nuclear program has been dead since 1991." Finally able to convince his sister, he suggested that the two of them had an opportunity to do something good and prevent an unnecessary war between America and Iraq. Unable to defect, he left it to her to carry the message back to the CIA.

Upon Sawson's return, Josh read her report to the CIA explaining that her brother had been unable to answer any of their well-prepared questions because there was no nuclear weapons program in Iraq. Period. Later, when the CIA came to deliver a gift to her for her bravery, she learned from her husband that the agents had concluded that her brother had lied.

Reportedly, the same strategy was used with thirty-some American families with Iraqi ties. They all testified that Iraq's programs to build nuclear, chemical, and biological weapons had been long-abandoned. Since that wasn't what they wanted to hear, officials chose not to circulate the reports from these family members to senior policy makers in the Bush administration. These statements from the families never reached the White House.

Josh continued to be open with his brother about his inner struggles with his job.

"I want to get this information to the right people. I've shared what I know with the main guys in my office—Richard Haass, Larry Wilkerson, and Richard Armitage. But we all agree that we'd be talking to a frickin' brick wall. If the CIA won't believe Sawson, the administration is not going to listen to us. I'm fed up, bro. I don't know how much longer I can go on doing this."

"You have to hang in," Kyle pleaded with him. "Don't give up now. There is too much at stake for our country."

"That's pretty much what Brother Anthony told me. But everybody around me is feeling the same way. I used to be the guy who pumped everyone else up, but I can't do that anymore. It all feels so hopeless."

Kyle paused before he continued. "Look, I don't exactly know what I'm about to say, but hear me out. In a way, I'm in the same boat here in California. I feel like I've run my course on a lot of different levels. The governor and I are more and more at odds over military base issues. Kevin is already off to college, and Marty will be leaving soon. They are both doing well now, thanks to their mother. I feel like I have so little involvement with them. I've broken up with the woman I was dating and have no interest in pursuing another relationship. My ties here are pretty well severed."

"What about Jenny?"

"I still think about her all the time, but we're so wrong for each other. It's not that I don't miss her. I do. It's just that we don't want the same things in life."

"Have you talked to her?" Josh asked.

"No. I don't know what I'd say. I wouldn't want to hurt her all over again by stirring things up when I have nothing new to offer her."

"Where is all of this leading?" Josh asked.

"Well, I'm thinking about getting a fresh start."

"Like what?"

"Like heading out your way once I see this term through."

"What would you do?"

"Something more meaningful, where I can make a difference . . . and be closer to you. I'm exploring some options right now. If this works out, we'd both have the support we're missing."

"Wow, man, I can't believe it. So . . . how soon can you get here?"

"Are things that bad?" Kyle asked.

"Well, Powell is getting creamed by Feith's secret Office of Special Plans. His most important responsibility is 'media strategy.' Once Feith's unit has cherry-picked the most derogatory items from the volumes of U.S. and Israeli reports, they are then turned into 'talking points' for senior officials."

"So, in other words, these officials would be using this bogus and embellished intelligence as ammunition when hard-selling the war to their reluctant colleagues . . . like Colin Powell."

"You got it."

"The White House has more secret operations than any boy's club I ever thought of having," Kyle said.

"You ain't seen nothin' yet. The latest covert group is the White House Iraq Group made up of a bunch of high-level administration officials that include Karl Rove, deputy chief of staff to the president; Condi Rice, national security advisor; Steve Hadley, deputy security advisor; and Scooter Libby, chief of staff to the vice president, among others. Their job is to sell the war to the general public. Everyone knows it's phony, but they're still clinging to that Niger report as if it were handed down by God to Moses at Mount Sinai."

"I told you a long time ago I didn't think the American public would ever buy this B.S."

"They're pretty convincing, bro. They've already set Cheney up for a series of presentations." Imitating Dick Cheney, Josh dramatized his words: "'There 'is no doubt' that Saddam Hussein 'has weapons of mass destruction.' And in another speech: 'We do know, with absolute certainty, that he is using his procurement system to acquire the equipment he needs in order to enrich uranium to build a nuclear weapon.'"

"Knowing what they know, doing what they're doing, how *do* these guys sleep at night!? Instead of using intelligence to help inform their decisions, they're cherry-picking through anything they can get their hands on, factual or contrived, and using it to justify an unjust war."

"With the intention of influencing the outcome of the September Congressional elections, Bush referenced 'new evidence' to a group of reporters at Camp David: 'A report came out of the International Atomic Energy Agency that Iraqis were six months away from developing a weapon. I don't know what more evidence we need.'"

"He's talking about that old Niger report? For christcake, why doesn't the CIA speak up and tell them that it's bogus?"

"George Tenet is off on the sidelines," Josh explained. "He nuzzled up to Bush and did every frickin' thing he could to give the president what he wanted. He promised that releasing information to the public to support the WMD issue would be a 'slam dunk,' but he couldn't follow through. Personally, I like Tenet but he's in the same boat as Powell. The higher ups have made puppets out of two good men. This thing is so out of control. Instead of speaking out, Tenet is quietly attempting to persuade the White House to stay away from the Italian Niger report. But the hawks aren't listening. Frankly, they don't care about the truth. Their only objective is to convince the public that going to war in Iraq is justified."

Kyle was home on Sunday morning, September 8. With his remote in hand, he switched from channel to channel. "It's now public," said Dick Cheney during his appearance on *Meet the Press,* "that Saddam Hussein has been seeking to acquire the kind of tubes needed for the production of highly enriched uranium, which is what you have to have in order to build a bomb." On Fox News, Colin Powell spoke out about "the specialized aluminum tubing that we saw in reporting just this morning." And as Kyle switched to *Face the Nation,* he listened as Donald Rumsfeld put a ribbon on the package by tying all of the day's presentations to the terrorist attacks: "Imagine, a September 11 with weapons of mass destruction. It's not 3,000; it's tens of thousands of innocent men, women, and children." Later that night, Kyle caught CNN's *Late Edition* with Wolf Blitzer in time to hear Condoleezza Rice say, "We don't want the smoking gun to be a mushroom cloud." Kyle shook his head, disgusted at the contrived tactic for Washington to get its phony message out. It further confirmed his decision to leave public office. He could no longer be a part of such a sham. There had to be a better way for him to spend his time on earth. But he was determined to accomplish what he could in the time he had remaining in office.

On the first anniversary of the September 11 attacks, and after all their political squabbling over the appropriate way to deal with national and state matters in its wake, the governor and attorney general jointly called a press conference. Before reading the proclamation, the governor stressed that this was a cooperative effort between himself and his respected colleague, Kyle Anderson. "You will note the greater than normal list of whereas-es in this decree," the governor said, laughing. "It is due to our attempt to reach consensus among two very strong-minded and opinionated leaders on a very controversial topic."

Summarizing the culmination of their efforts, the highlights ran on the evening news:

Whereas, on this day one year ago, September 11, 2001, terrorism threatened our country, and

Whereas, this is a day that should be remembered as one that changed our American way of life forever, and

Whereas, it is our desire to demonstrate by our example how people with differing outlooks can come together to find common ground, and

Whereas, we agree that world peace cannot occur in a single, sweeping moment of time but must be fostered person by person, state by state, political party by political party,

We therefore declare this day as the 9/11 Day of Remembrance throughout our state.

The announcer concluded that the proclamation encouraged the people of the great state of California—whether in the office place, the school yard, or the family—to use this day each year as an opportunity to resolve conflicts among themselves.

The proclamation was praised, blasphemed, called an absurdity, and honored as a concept that should spread throughout the world. Everyone watching had an opinion and stood firmly by their position. Further articles began appearing from the more liberal academics calling for the State University System to initiate a Department of Peace, possibly at the University of California at Berkeley. The department's objectives would include teaching conflict-resolution methods, peace tactics, alternatives to war, preemptive ways to avoid discord, and circumstances that call for taking action toward severance, self-assertion, and war. Kyle Anderson didn't care. Like the president of the United States granting pardons on his final day in office, he too had taken one last significant step to leave his mark. He was ready to take his leave and move on to another calling.

The news reported that one additional outcome of this proclamation was the formation of a Commission on Social and Criminal Justice, a group that would be chaired by Kyle's office and would exist for two reasons: (1) to administer fair methods for criminals who were trying to prove their innocence after their conviction, such as DNA testing, and (2) to investigate social justice issues that arose throughout the state, particularly vital matters that created divisiveness, caused riots, stirred up massive protests, or denigrated human dignity.

"It is my hope," Kyle was quoted as saying in the newspaper, "that, with the establishment of this commission, California will assume a leading role and serve as a model state for finding peaceful and just solutions to all levels of discrimination."

When Jenny read that news, she realized that Kyle was busy getting valuable precedents set as he prepared to leave office. She felt a surge of joy run through her as she saw unmistakable signs of Kyle's personal growth on human rights issues.

September 11 brought thoughts of Josh. Jenny hadn't talked to him since Kyle and she had broken up. Jenny called him the day after the one-year anniversary of the attacks.

"I'm sorry I haven't called sooner," Jenny said. "I couldn't stop thinking about you all day yesterday."

"Funny you should call, Jen," Josh said. "There's so much shit going on here in Washington. But I had a dream last night that made me feel better. Emmy's the only other person I've told about it. I saw myself falling out of the South Tower. I kept screaming, 'Oh, my God. I'm going to get squashed.' But I hit the ground and was like rubber. I just bounced up and walked away. I mean, it really wasn't a nightmare. I was a survivor!"

"You are a survivor, Josh. We have both recovered from one of the most challenging years of our lives. How do you think you got through it without emotional scars?"

"I think it had a lot to do with living through the experience with my concern focused on those who needed me along the way. When it was all over that day, after I got off the bus, I remember wandering into the nearest church and lighting a candle. I realized it was one of the few times in my life that I had witnessed something that I couldn't grasp. It was beyond my wildest imagination that those buildings could fall. There's no way to compare this with anything I have ever lived through . . . but they did fall."

"Like Kyle and me," Jenny said. "Once we got through everything, I never dreamed it was possible that we would fall out . . . but we did."

"I couldn't quite believe either one happened. You two were the 'twin towers' in my eyes. And like them, you had survived an earlier bombing and just about anything that came at you."

"It's inevitable for us to have recurring thoughts that take us back to the pain of it all," Jenny said.

"Emmy swears that what got me through that day was having several others who needed me on our 'exodus,' as she calls it, out of the building."

"What a lesson," Jenny said softly. "Having others to worry about is the answer to so many self-absorbing problems."

"Deep down, Jen, I knew you would come through yours, too. There were so many times Emmy or I wanted to call you, but we didn't want to overstep our bounds."

Their conversation lulled and finally Jenny said what was on her mind. "I'm almost afraid to ask but . . ."

"He's getting out of politics, Jen. To quote him verbatim, he said, 'There has to be more important things for me to do with my time on earth.'"

"Yes, I heard that on the news. But what's he going to do?"

"Kyle is joining an organization based here in Washington called the United States Institute of Peace which works closely with Congress," Josh said. "It fits with his world view. It is a perfect place for him to go. I can't tell you how glad I will be to have him close by. You can check out the group's website if you want to know more about it."

Jenny was already online as she told him to give Emmy her love and hung up. She found the homepage immediately.

Jenny scanned the site and learned that, as a result of the efforts of the National Peace Foundation, the U.S. Institute of Peace was an independent, nonpartisan, national organization established and funded by Congress in 1984. Its goals, Jenny read, were to help prevent and resolve violent conflicts and to promote post-conflict stability and development throughout the world. She found it of particular interest that the Institute provided on-the-ground operational support in zones of conflict, such as the Middle East. Jenny was pleased to see that Kyle wanted to continue in Washington the kind of work he had just begun in California. She was not surprised to see the headlines appear in the paper the following day: "California Attorney General to Assume New Post."

On September 14, President Bush repeated his nuclear charge during his weekly radio address. "Saddam Hussein has the scientists and infrastructure for a nuclear-weapons program and has illicitly sought to purchase the equipment needed to enrich uranium for a nuclear weapon."

In reality, Josh thought, there was no *new* report. Bush was again referring to the forged Niger documents.

Four days later, the husband of a 9/11 victim testified before the congressional 9/11 inquiry.

"If the intelligence community had been doing its job, my wife would be alive today." The victim cited the government's failure to place Khalid Almihdhar and Nawaf Alhazmi on a terrorist watch list until long after they were photographed meeting with alleged al Qaeda operatives in Malaysia. "Our loved ones paid the ultimate price for the worst American intelligence failure since Pearl Harbor." The gentleman suggested that the U.S. intelligence bureaucracy should be thoroughly restructured. "If it isn't," he said, "the next attack may involve weapons of mass destruction—and the death toll may be in the tens of thousands or even hundreds of thousands."

Josh filed these reports away, wondering if there was any hope of a restructuring with the neoconservatives in power. By the fall of 2002, he watched on as the Feith-Wurmser-Perle "Clean Break" plan came full circle. The Bush administration lied to the American people. The administration lied to Congress. The administration lied to the world. Despite the inaccuracies contained in the high-level briefings, the CIA succumbed to the pressure and reversed itself, sending a letter to the Senate Intelligence Committee, "We have solid evidence of senior-level contacts between Iraq and al Qaeda going back a decade."

While the insanity of Washington continued to broil, Jenny found herself continuing to revel in her newfound inner peace. Sitting outside in her yard early in the morning, she breathed in the fresh air and welcomed a new autumn day. The colors in the yard were yellows and oranges and varying shades of green. A resident squirrel nibbled on the flowers near her deck and scurried over the waterfall to hide behind the tree. She felt gratitude for life itself. She thanked God for having given Kyle such clear direction with his life and prayed that he would guide her as well. She missed Kyle, but at last she had broken free from the worst of the pain of losing him. Day by day, she was gaining new confidence and rediscovering her own strength as a person. She felt love all around her, the love of friends and the love of God all merged into one consciousness. She was truly a pilgrim soul who had come through an unforgettable journey. Kyle had loved that pilgrim soul in her. Now she was ready to embark on a new journey and to take the risk of new beginnings, the final step in her recovery. Somewhere in the not-so-distant future, she believed there would come a time when she could rewrite Yeat's verse in her own words.

> I long for one who sees my pilgrim soul,
> Close by my side through times of joy and strife;
> God's love revealed through harmony in life,
> As two hearts beat in cadence toward one goal.

Thirty-one

Move to Washington

OCTOBER 2002 - MARCH 2003

Kyle Anderson was in his final days of office. The November elections were right around the corner and Kyle was, of course, supporting the Democratic frontrunner, who appeared to have a good chance to win the office. Kyle would remain a lame duck until the new attorney general was installed in early January. Then, for the first time in 16 years, he would be free to do something with his life beyond politics: he had accepted the position as the new president of the U.S. Peace Institute in Washington.

Turning on the morning news in his office, Kyle caught a breaking story that stopped his heart. In the town of Kuta, on the Indonesian island of Bali, more than two hundred people were killed and another two hundred injured in a terrorist attack. *Oh, my God,* he thought, recalling his time in Bali with Jenny just over a year earlier. *That could have been us.* They had stayed in Kuta and spent their first evening in the Sari nightclub, the very place where the attack occurred. The attack was reported to be the deadliest act of terrorism in Indonesian history.

Instinctively, Kyle started to phone Josh but, as often happened, his brother beat him to the call.

"Hey, bro, did I catch you with your feet up on the desk?" Josh asked lightheartedly.

"Hardly," Kyle sighed. "I can't believe how much there is to do to close out my job and get ready to hand it over to someone else. I take it you've seen the news."

"That's why I'm calling. Isn't that the nightclub where you and Jenny were?"

"The very place. I can't believe it."

"Wow . . . that's really weird. Did you call her?"

"What would I say? 'Today's news made me think of you . . . and by the way, I'm moving.' If I have any decency, I won't call her. It's just not fair to her."

"I wonder what she's thinking about this Bali attack," Josh mused.

"Probably the same thing I did. It could have been us. In an odd way, it's symbolic of the ending that already exists between us."

Not fully believing that, Josh chose to change the subject. "You know that the U.N. Security Council just voted unanimously to order Iraq to admit weapons inspectors," Josh said. "I just ran into Larry Wilkerson and he indicated that Powell was troubled by the decision."

"Why would that bother Powell?"

"He said Powell remarked 'I wonder what will happen if we put half a million troops on the ground, and scour Iraq from one corner to the other, and find no weapons of mass destruction?'"

"My God. How did Wilkerson respond?" Kyle asked.

"He didn't. He said Powell left that rhetorical question hanging in the air and he returned to his office."

On a chilly December morning in Washington, Josh parked the car, said a cheery hello to the security guards on his way in to work, and sat down at his desk. Flipping through the documents in his inbox, his high spirits soon turned to anger.

Dick Cheney and Donald Rumsfeld were Colin Powell's two most challenging nemeses and, vicariously, Josh's, too. Cheney was a protégé of Rumsfeld's from their days in the Gerald Ford administration. They seemed joined at the hip on most of their militaristic decisions. Josh thought about Brother Anthony's advice. *You're in Washington for a reason,* he had said. To calm his mood, Josh picked up the phone and called his brother.

"Bro, I'm up to my ears in Guantánamo Bay prison camp issues. You won't believe what's going on there. It's so much worse than I even imagined."

"If I remember," Kyle said, "we've been leasing this facility from the Cuban government on the southeastern tip of Cuba since the early 1900s, but they aren't particularly happy with our occupying this site."

"No shit. They object to our presence *and* everything we're doing there." Josh explained that the Bush administration conceived of this as a place that could operate outside the system of national and international laws that normally govern the treatment of prisoners in U.S. custody. Right after September 11, administration officials argued that the Guantánamo site was not bound by the Geneva Conventions because terrorist suspects detained at the site were not ordinary criminals or prisoners of war. Rather, they would be given a new classification, "enemy combatants," and would not be tried in U.S. courts but in military tribunals.

"What bothers me," Josh continued, "is that they've held more than 600 detainees there for more than two years without charges."

"I remember last February when the story broke about the torturing going on in the prison camps and President Bush issued a directive that required American troops to treat detainees 'humanely,' in a manner consistent with the Geneva Conventions. Was Bush just covering up for what was going on?"

"I'm not sure but, if I give him the benefit of the doubt, he may not have known the extent of the tactics being used," Josh said.

"How bad is it?"

"Bad. Last June, the Pentagon released guidelines saying that health workers who care for detainees can't participate in interrogations. *But,* there's a loophole. You see, medical personnel who are *not* directly responsible for a patient's care *may* take part in interrogations. He has basically given a green light for medical personnel to use their scientific background for the purpose of helping suggest effective abuse techniques on the detainees."

"Let me get this straight," Kyle said, leaning back in his chair. "A detainee is not accused of a crime but is *held* for questioning. But aren't there fairly stringent rules for how long detainees can be held and what kind of treatment they receive?"

Still scanning the inbox document, Josh summarized it for Kyle. "A medical expert working under Rumsfeld is arguing that most of the detainees have never received better care than they've been getting at Guantánamo. They're getting more frequent medical treatment than most Americans. Blah, blah, blah. However, when I talked to the doctor, he did acknowledge that a number of medical and scientific personnel working at Guantánamo—including psychologists and psychiatrists—are not there to provide care for detainees. Rather, these 'non-treating' professionals have been using their skills to show our military commanders how to make these guys squirm and fess up what they know. It's brutal, and they stop at nothing."

"Hell, that's against everything the medical profession stands for. I've got a similar issue brewing here. The California Department of Justice is trying to demand that a medical professional be present to give the final injections to death row inmates. But to the credit of the medical community, hardly any of them will volunteer for the job. How can they? It's against the Hippocratic Oath. They're obligated to *care* for human beings and not to participate in their demise."

"That's the oldest ethical code around. Generally, society may've lost faith in *your* profession," Josh ribbed him, "but the medical profession is sort of the last gasp."

"I'd say that there's still a basic feeling about what doctors are supposed to do for their patients, namely, put *their* welfare first."

"Have you ever heard of a Pentagon-funded program known as SERE?" Josh asked. "It stands for 'Survival, Evasion, Resistance, and Escape.' You should know about it because it's taught right there in one of the military bases in your own state."

"I've heard of it. I think it's taught at the naval academy in Coronado, and I had a priest mention it to me a while back in connection with it being taught at the School of Americas. But I really don't know much about the details."

Josh explained: "The theory behind the SERE program is that soldiers who are exposed to nightmarish treatment during training will be better equipped to deal with this if they should ever be captured.

You know, they're hooded; their sleep patterns are disrupted; they are starved for extended periods; they are stripped of their clothes; they are exposed to extreme temperatures. The whole idea is that if a prisoner of war is trying to avoid revealing secrets to enemy interrogators, he's more likely to give in if he's been deprived of sleep or basic needs."

"So, as bad as it sounds, it serves a good purpose. I mean, our guys need to be trained in resistance techniques, right?" Kyle asked.

"Yes, but after September 11, several psychologists versed in SERE techniques began advising interrogators at Guantánamo Bay and other places. Some of these medical professionals essentially tried to 'reverse-engineer' the SERE program."

"The interrogators at Guantánamo adopted coercive techniques similar to those employed in the SERE program?" Kyle stood and began to pace around his office.

"Exactly," Josh responded, "and one component of the training program, called the 'religious dilemma,' really gets my skivvies in a twist. Trainees are given the choice of seeing a Bible desecrated or revealing secrets to interrogators. The Holy Book is torn up, thrown around, and trashed on the ground. They say they'll stop if the trainee talks. The goal is to make detainees react emotionally to the desecration. The guy who told me about it said that some of his colleagues became nauseated during the exercise. But then he read about the Guantánamo detainees describing something similar being done to the Koran by our interrogators, and knew the concept had come from the SERE training manual."

"God, that is so sick," Kyle said. "It also confirms something that the priest, Father Roy Bourgois, tried to tell me about what was going on at the School of Americas. He and many other protestors have even served time in jail in an effort to expose what's going on in these training camps."

"The feds just don't get it," Josh complained. "These tactics aren't only inhumane but they're vehemently turning those who're eventually released against us."

Josh then went on to describe another of the other SERE techniques, water boarding, a method in which the detainee is made to lie on an inclined board head down and water is poured up his nose, giving him a sense of drowning and asphyxiation.

"That sounds like something we use to do to each other when we were kids. Remember, with the hose in the backyard?" Kyle asked.

"Trust me. Their methods go way beyond anything we ever did with a garden hose." Josh described a few other SERE techniques, including the use of sexual embarrassment or a mock rape, where a female officer stands behind a screen and screams as if she were being violated. "The detainee is told that he can stop the rape if he cooperates with his captors. And if that doesn't work, another technique is to defile the detainee's national flag."

Kyle stopped pacing and gazed out his office window onto Capitol State Park where he saw people walking and lounging among the pristine landscaping, people utterly oblivious to what was being done half a world away in the name of peace and democracy.

"We're up against those who believe that all is fair in love and war, bro," Josh continued. "All they can think about is what the enemy has done to us—even though many of the prisoners are victims themselves. Being Muslims, they're viewed as guilty by association because they may know someone who knows someone who knows something related to 9/11."

Whoever fights monsters should see to it that in the process he does not become a monster, Kyle thought. *Nietzsche was right.*"Josh, this sounds a whole lot like the mentality of the Bloods and the Crips that I've had to deal with in south central L.A."

"Yep, and the really sad part is that many of the frickin' interrogators are convinced that all detainees are masterminds. But that isn't the case. Most of them are just plain dirt farmers in Afghanistan. The thinking now is that less than a quarter of the detainees have or had any intelligence value to us at all."

"One thing is for damn sure," Kyle noted. "If a detainee isn't a terrorist now, he will be by the time he is released."

"Sad but probably true, bro. And if that isn't bad enough, a rough, tough Texan and Guantánamo official named Major General Geoffrey

Miller is now making an official request to beef up interrogation techniques so as to break prisoners more quickly."

"How is the request being handled in Washington?"

"Like everything else around here. The FBI sees it one way and the Department of Defense another. You see, right after the Afghanistan war started, the FBI sent several of its top counter-terrorism agents to the Guantánamo prison to interview detainees. These agents generally believed that they were making progress with them by slowly establishing a dynamic of friendly rapport. It's not just a moral or ethical issue with them; they feel that more intense methods just aren't worth it. You get bad information from suspects when you use coercive force to get it."

Kyle reminded Josh that, even though there were many serious al Qaeda operatives who had been detained, Zacarias Moussaoui was the only man facing trial in the United States for the September 11 attack.

"The defense is bringing in witnesses that, quite frankly, amaze me," Kyle said. "They're made up of several relatives of 9/11 victims who claim to be testifying because they believe Moussaoui is the wrong man on trial and they feel that we as a compassionate people have a responsibility and an opportunity to show that we have more respect for life than al Qaeda. Bottom line, they think Moussaoui's role is relatively insignificant and would prefer to see some of these hardcore al Qaeda members stand trial instead."

"Well, that isn't going to happen with General Miller involved," Josh responded. "According to several sources at the FBI, when Miller assumed his administrative role at the prison camp, he became impatient with the FBI's mollycoddling methods of interrogations and insisted that harsher methods be used."

"Can't the FBI hold its ground?" Kyle asked.

"No, it's losing the battle. That's why the matter's in our office. A lot of guys here trust Powell to be the voice of reason. My FBI source said he thinks there's a major lack of knowledge about the mind-set of extremists. Torturing them just makes them more determined to hate us. Eventually they're going to be released and, when they are, they're going to talk and even exaggerate what happened to them in

Guantánamo. Ergo, they'll become heroes. Then we'll have even more extremist networks and more suicide bombers."

Turning from the window, Kyle resumed his pacing. "It's like a snake swallowing its tail, isn't it? And when the tables are turned and Americans are mistreated in the same ways…God, I don't even want to contemplate it. How can we stoop to the level of our enemies, Josh? It's only going to come back and bite us in the ass later on. Isn't *any* other government department concerned about this??"

"Actually . . . yes," Josh said. "This is what helps me hang in with my job here. Some officials at the Naval Criminal Investigative Service were also incensed by the use of these coercive techniques. They turned the matter over to the navy's new general counsel, Alberto Mora, who said he found the tactics to be 'unlawful and unworthy of the military services.' The Naval Criminal Investigative Service took it straight up the line of command inside the navy to the general counsel, who basically told Secretary of Defense Donald Rumsfeld that the navy might have to withdraw from the Joint Task Force in Guantánamo if they kept doing these sorts of things. After that, Mora contacted the Pentagon's general counsel and warned him that 'the use of coercive techniques' could expose the interrogators and threaten Secretary Rumsfeld's tenure and even damage the presidency."

"He's talking criminal prosecution. Hey, this Mora dude is my kind of man," Kyle said. "Where'd he come from?"

"His parents both fled totalitarian dictatorships to come to America. His father was Cuban and his mother Hungarian, and he has a great reverence for the law. He's a staunch Republican and a political appointee himself. He's not a bomb-thrower but just a loyal member of the administration. He put himself on the line and tried to tell the Pentagon that what they were doing was not only questionably legal but just plain unconstitutional. He tried to warn Alberto Gonzales and those giving legal advice to the administration that when they suspended the Geneva Conventions and allowed the maltreatment of the detainees in Guantánamo, they were breaking international law as well as American military law that states soldiers are not supposed to mistreat prisoners. He told them this was a complete and utter violation of American values. We haven't heard the last from Mora. He shakes off any heroism and acts like he's just doing his job and not afraid to render his honest opinion. Believe me, I'm planning to take him to lunch as soon as I can."

"You know, Josh, someone from the Justice Department is going to have to make a definitive statement about what our policy is on torture. They can't just sit on this. I'm afraid that the dominant image of America will not be the Statue of Liberty but the photographs of prisoner abuse."

Josh agreed. "One thing is for sure: Guantánamo is going to haunt us for a long time."

With the conversation winding down, Josh asked, "By the way, have you heard anything about Jen?"

"Nothing recently. I'm moving on, and I hope she is, too."

Josh held back from commenting. He thought about his last conversation with Jenny and how good she sounded. *Hopefully*, he thought, *she has moved on.*

On December 14, the first anniversary of Mike's passing, several friends processed by candlelight down to his graveside for a memorial service. Laurie Hamilton, Mike's friend who needed the liver transplant, stood next to Jenny. Laurie's skin was more jaundiced than ever. As everyone gathered around Mike's tombstone, Jenny whispered to Laurie, "How're you doing?"

"I have moved higher up on the list but, after nearly four years, I am still waiting."

Sister Marsha led the group in prayer and included Laurie's special need for a liver on the list of supplications. The group made a weak attempt at singing one of Mike's favorite church songs and laughed at their own vocal discord.

The next day, Jenny received a call from Sister. Laurie was at the hospital—at the University of California, Davis—awaiting surgery. The organ donor had come through—exactly one year to the day after Mike's death.

The day was also in Kyle's thoughts. It was the anniversary of Glennys Anderson's passing as well. He thought back to the irony of losing both Mike and his mother on the same day. He offered a prayer for both of them and felt a wave of sadness come over him. He missed his mother and he regretted not attending Mike's burial.

Going over final details with the newly elected Democratic attorney general, Kyle couldn't wait to complete his work in California and get to Washington, where he could begin his new assignment. Packing up the last of his things, he took one last look around at River House and closed the door. He felt he was leaving so much behind. But he was ready for a new start.

Josh had picked out a newly constructed condo for Kyle to rent, not far from the Tivoli Theatre, in the recently revitalized Columbia Heights area. Located in the northwest section, it was easily accessible to all parts of the District. Kyle loved the fact that it was one of the most ethnically and economically diverse neighborhoods in D.C. That suited him at the moment.

On his first night in the District, Josh and Emmy invited Kyle over for dinner. Emmy prepared the Anderson boys' favorite dish—meatloaf and mash potatoes. With the fireplace blazing in the background, Josh toasted his brother's arrival. "It's going to be great having you here. Watch out, world! Here come the Anderson brothers. Now we can really stir it up and watch it hit the fan."

That night President Bush was scheduled to deliver his State of the Union address. The trio gathered around the television and listened to the president speak about Saddam Hussein and his weapons of mass destruction.

"The British government has learned that Saddam Hussein recently sought significant quantities of uranium from Africa," Bush somberly announced.

"What?" Josh gasped. "Is he frickin' nuts? Why in the world would he say that knowing what we all know? Jeez, Louise." He started to turn off the tube in disgust when Emmy advised him to pay attention as Bush continued. "The United States will ask the U.N. Security Council to convene on February 5 to consider the facts of Iraq's ongoing defiance of the world. Secretary of State Powell will present information and intelligence about Iraqis illegal weapons programs, its attempt to hide those weapons from inspectors, and its links to terrorist groups."

This time Josh did hit the off button on the remote. He was speechless. With all the information he was privy to, he hadn't known that Powell would be the one to make the case to the United Nations. He had assumed it would be Cheney.

"I know I'm partial," Josh said after a moment, "but I feel terrible for my boss. Colin Powell is like the lion in winter. He may be waning but he's a regal statesman who embodies an era of great Republican reign that has all but vanished. He just can't hold out against all these frickin' chicken hawks."

"Quite frankly, I'm shocked that Powell's agreed to this," Kyle said. Then sensing how deep his twin's feelings ran for Powell, he added with some sensitivity, "One of his great strengths and his fatal weakness is his abiding sense of loyalty."

"You're right, bro, you're right. I'm sure it's his loyalty that keeps him staying on—at least through this term. If you were on the inside, you'd understand. He's caving in but almost anyone would under the pressure. He's trapped in an administration where he no longer has any influence except with the outside world. And make no mistake: we're going into Iraq. Powell's presentation is nothing but tokenism. The White House doesn't care whether the U..N. supports the U.S. or not. Bush is on the warpath."

In the days that followed, Josh listened carefully to the chatter around the White House about how the infamous sixteen words referencing Hussein's *recent* attempt to purchase uranium from Africa got into the president's speech. As deputy national security advisor, Steve Hadley acknowledged part of the blame. He said he remembered George Tenet telling him to take that reference out of the president's Cincinnati speech the previous October but by the following January he claimed to have forgotten. Tenet publicly took some of the blame saying that he only got the speech the day before it was to be delivered and passed it on to someone else to review. Josh learned that it was Alan Foley, the head of the CIA's weapon's intelligence, who once again pushed the envelope to give the president what he wanted. He approved those sixteen words on the basis that they didn't give away any secrets relating to the source of the information but then claimed he did not approve it for substance.

How can such seemingly intelligent officials screw up so horribly about something this important, Josh wondered.

Kyle spent the next weeks becoming familiar with his new job. The outgoing president was gracious in welcoming him and introducing him to the U.S. Peace Institute staff. Kyle didn't have the feeling that he was being sized up by the staff; he felt genuinely accepted.

It was a huge change of pace for Kyle. The general atmosphere was less frenetic and more orderly, more serene than what he was used to in California. It was as if the people working there had a personal life commitment to living peacefully.

It was a comfortable transition for Kyle to make his home in the District. He loved the excitement of living and breathing the political ambiance of Washington. He spent more time with Josh and Emmy. He had regular meetings with the staff and lunches with other peace organization directors who wanted to coordinate their efforts. Kyle instinctively knew that this was a good place for him to be, and he was glad he'd made the move. Even Winky had no difficulty adjusting.

On Feburary 5, while Emmy was going out to dinner and a movie with girlfriends, Josh invited Kyle out for a burger and beer.

"I'll pick you up, bro. I figured you've got your feet wet enough now that you're ready for a new scene." Josh took him to one of Pennsylvania Avenue's most daunting gathering spots, The Hawk 'n' Dove. It was Capitol Hill's oldest Irish bar and an archetype of the district, a place where staffers, both Democrats and Republicans, gathered to gripe about their bosses—always anonymously, of course.

Soon the brothers were engaged in political talk of their own.

"So is Powell ready with his pitch to the U.N. tonight?" Kyle asked.

"You can be sure the White House Intelligence Group has not only written his script but has been watching him rehearse to make sure he doesn't throw something out."

"Who're the watch dogs?"

"Condi Rice and her deputy; Scooter Libby, Cheney's chief of staff; and, of course, George Tenet, since it's in his conference room," Josh said. "But the general pulled in Colonel Wilkerson to be his right-hand-man, to help throw out all the misinformation and make a legitimate case for preemptive war against Hussein. Wilkerson had little time to undertake such a gargantuan task but he and Powell have worked together to make the best of a bad situation. They played excerpts of intercepted Iraqi military chatter, flaunted a vial of fake anthrax, and warned of mobile bio-weapon 'factories' and other doomsday machines—of course, none of which actually existed."

"How could that happen?"

"Wilkerson thought they had cleaned out the obvious garbage, but it turned out there was more."

"How did Powell handle it?"

"He did just what they thought he'd do. He'd say, 'I'm not using that.' Or 'This is not something I can support.' A lot of what he refused to use had to do with all the B.S. about Hussein's ties to the 9/11 attacks or the Niger report. And even after he'd throw stuff out, it'd magically reappear. The neocons wouldn't let up on Powell. Finally, he told Tenet that he's going to have to sit right behind him at the U.N. and put his imprimatur on it."

"Powell's trust in Tenet may lead to the greatest setback to his credibility in his entire military and political career," Kyle observed.

"Yeah, they're both being used, and they know it. Powell's been trying to find a way out of it. I think even Tenet wishes he could step down, but he doesn't want to appear like the guy who threw in the towel on the eve of the war. And since Powell started watering down his presentation, Cheney is chomping at the bit to give his own talk to the U.N. to include the information that Powell is throwing out."

"No way," Kyle exclaimed.

"Don't worry. It's not going to happen. You'll see in a few minutes. Tenet told the president that if Cheney delivers the speech, the CIA would not stand behind it."

"Thank God."

"Yeah, and wonder of wonders, Bush backed him on it." Soon all televisions in the bar were turned onto Colin Powell's presentation to the United Nations. The brothers munched on their hamburgers as they watched Powell take his seat at the round U.N. Security Council table and lay out the pro-war arguments to the world.

"My colleagues," Powell said, "every statement I make today is backed up by sources, solid sources. These are not assertions. What we're giving you are facts and conclusions based on solid intelligence."

"Bullshit," Josh exclaimed, grabbing a handful of chips. After years of NSA monitoring, he was shocked at how weak the backup evidence was.

Powell reminded the council that they had unanimously passed a resolution demanding that Iraq give up all weapons of mass destruction, that this country had been given one last chance, and that to date they had not taken it. Powell challenged the body to support a war effort by concluding, "We must not shrink from whatever is ahead of us. We must not fail in our duty and our responsibility to the citizens of the countries that are represented by this body."

"*I'm* shrinking from what's ahead of us," Josh said to Kyle, swigging the last of his beer and banging the empty mug on the table. "I'm just grateful you're here now, bro."

As Powell's speech progressed, Josh saw his own hopes and dreams crumbling.

The weeks following were pure torture for Josh. Everything he believed in was going downhill—especially Colin Powell. His U.N. speech was being perceived as a blotch on his record and on the office of the Secretary of State. Wilkerson felt that he had let Powell down. Powell himself could hardly hold his head up, realizing soon after that he had made a dreadful mistake. But a loyal soldier never turns back, so Powell didn't falter.

Josh was horrified when he learned that Rumsfeld had been placed in charge of post-war reconstruction.

"Can you think of anyone who knows less about what to do *after* a war than Rummy?" he had said to other staff members. But for a brief time, hope pervaded the Secretary of State's Office when Rumsfeld appointed Jay Garner to head up the post-war office. Garner was a three-star army general best known for having run a military humanitarian mission after the 1991 Gulf War. He was considered somewhat of a hero for rescuing thousands of Kurds in northern Iraq.

The only problem was that Garner was given no authority to go with his title. His plan was to have American and Iraqi contractors already established and ready to begin reconstruction work immediately after the outbreak of the war. But General Franks didn't want Garner in Baghdad until the invasion was over. Josh read Garner's reports, where he insisted to Rumsfeld that waiting would be too late. Garner believed that the Iraqis should have a strong stake in the new provisional government. Rumsfeld, on the other hand, wanted the Iraqi ministers chosen from his own hand-selected list. Garner could barely contain his frustration in the reports Josh read. "We have to have Iraqis as part of the new government. We can't impose our people and our ways on them." He disagreed with Rumsfeld on every key point about implementing a viable reconstruction effort in Iraq. There were bets being taken in the office as to how long Garner would last under Rumsfeld. His plan was far too favorable to Iraqis.

In another report, Josh read that on March 1, Khalid Shaikh Mohammad, one of the masterminds of the 9/11 attack and the one reportedly behind the bombing in Bali, was captured in Rawalpindi, Pakistan. Josh's thoughts briefly drifted to Kyle and Jenny. *If only my brother wasn't so stubborn,* he thought.

In the ensuing days, the air in the Secretary of State's Office was thick enough to be cut with a knife. A cloud continued to loom over the office and the White House in general, but few staffers felt free to discuss it. It was commonly felt that a U.S.-led war against Iraq launched without U.N. authorization would be seen by many nations and legal experts as a violation of international law. But President Bush had made it clear he would feel free to launch the war anyway if it proved impossible to win a U.N. vote. In the end, only four countries—the United States, Great Britain, Bulgaria, and Spain—supported a U.N. resolution to disarm Iraq by military force even if it was without U.N. approval. The rest of the world was not swayed by Colin Powell's presentation and remained in favor of continued WMD inspections in Iraq.

On the eve of the war, Josh and Kyle watched in dismay as the vast majority of public opinion around the world opposed the invasion. Nevertheless, on March 19—damn the torpedoes, full speed ahead—American troops invaded Iraq. Within three weeks, while Saddam Hussein fled into hiding, the multi-national forces toppled his regime. Rumsfeld's plan was to invade Iraq with the smallest possible number of troops. In its pre-war planning, the Pentagon estimated that, after the end of active combat, it could draw its forces down from the initial 150,000 to only 60,000 troops within six months and be out shortly thereafter, but that tactic would soon be proven woefully inept.

PART III

THREE YEARS LATER

Thirty-two

Saving the World

Over the three years since America had invaded Iraq, Josh had turned more to Brother Anthony for spiritual and personal guidance.

"Do you remember telling me several years ago that I was where I belonged doing my work on this earth?" Josh asked him during a conversation. "Because I think my time is up here, but how can I know for sure?"

"Listen as God speaks to you, Josh. It may come through prayer, through readings, even through signs."

"In that case, I think God is jumping up and down and screaming at me to get the hell out of here."

Anthony laughed. "So what is he, or *she*, telling you?"

Josh chuckled at Anthony's comeback. "For starters, nothing is the same around here since Colin Powell resigned along with his deputy, Richard Armitage, and his chief of staff, Larry Wilkerson. I miss our old team and feel like a dove among hawks and, believe me, Anthony, the few doves who still exist around here ain't cooing very loudly."

Daily news was not a regular part of cloistered monastic life. Anthony was aware of general world affairs so that he could keep them in his prayers, but he wasn't aware of some of the explicit details of the wars in Afghanistan and Iraq. For the sake of seeking his advice, Josh informed him of the basics. Instead of a quick reduction of troops as planned, the United States was engaged in a long-term guerrilla war. As of this month, over 2,300 American soldiers had died and thousands more wounded. Through lawlessness, badly managed government, and poor healthcare, an estimated 600,000 Iraqis had also died.

Anthony let out a sound of dismay at the sheer size of the staggering numbers.

"You probably know that Saddam Hussein was captured several months after the war began and is on trial for killings that date back to 1982. Of course, our main man, Osama bin Laden, is still on the loose. Well, about two months ago, bin Laden proposed a truce, but our government, in its words, 'refused to negotiate with terrorists.'" Josh explained to this saintly brother that two thirds of Americans not only believed that the war was not helping curb terrorism but that it had turned Iraq into a bloody training ground and operational base for a growing number of jihad terrorists.

"What about democracy there? I read that America had at least helped in this regard," Anthony asked.

Josh sighed. "You're right. Since nearly ten million Iraqi people cast their vote for a new constitution, the public image is one of a true democracy being formed in Iraq. But, Brother, believe me, that's not the reality. Few Iraqis could have known that the constitution they approved turned over all of their country's power to the United States. You see, we had this really good guy named Jay Garner who was the president's envoy to Iraq. But Secretary of Defense Rumsfeld replaced him with a guy named Paul "Jerry" Bremer who represented everything Garner did not. He was like a dictator in Iraq for nearly fourteen months from May 2003 to June 2004, and most of these U.S. self-serving decrees are still in effect today."

"I'm aware of Secretary Rumsfeld and have kept him in my prayers daily," Anthony said.

"It would be good for me to learn from you, Anthony, to pray for my enemies. Rumsfeld is sliding in popularity, and all I can do is thank God and hope he soon self-destructs. He was recently caught in a blatant lie on *Face the Nation* denying that neither he nor the president ever suggested that Iraq posed an *immediate* threat to the nation. Even several retired generals are calling for him to step down from office."

"Let's continue to pray that God's will be done with regard to Secretary Rumsfeld," Anthony said. "I take it he is the reason you feel you can't stay in your job anymore."

"Not only him. Just about everything going on under this new Iraqi constitution is immoral from my perspective. Due to Bremer's manipulations, extraordinary advantages now exist for U.S. corporations. While we're ensured long-term U.S. economic reward, there is little, if any, recompense to the Iraqi people. It's wrong, Anthony. It's just plain wrong, and I can't stand the anguish of being unable to do anything about it."

"So, my dear Josh, has God sent you a sign?"

"Well, maybe not a sign but a definite hazy inference. There's been a huge turnover in the administration, and I would hardly be missed if I left compared to the dozens of significant people who have stepped down from office. I was thrilled to see some guys leave, like Paul Wolfowitz and Doug Feith, who were part of the neoconservative movement that got us into this war. But some I'm sorry to see go, like counter-terrorism advisor Richard Clarke. I don't know if you saw the State of the Union address," Josh said, "but Clarke stepped down shortly afterward, bitter after being dragged into a public argument over who allowed the flawed information about the Niger report to get into the president's speech."

"Yes, I did hear something about that. In fact, there was quite a flair-up afterward, wasn't there, about a CIA woman whose secret operation was exposed? I just caught bits and pieces from the news clips I saw."

"Valerie Plame," Josh said. "And, yes, she was *really* a victim in all this. But, in a way, I even feel sorry for Scooter Libby, who was forced to resign for disclosing her identity to the press. You know he was chief of staff to Cheney and national security advisor to Bush. Most everyone knows Libby is the fall guy for both of them. He's been indicted by a federal grand jury on several charges of perjury and obstruction of justice for exposing Plame as an undercover CIA operative. I doubt if the news will ever come out but there's no doubt in my mind that he did so by direct orders from his two bosses to get even with her husband for slamming the president when he misled the public in his State of the Union address."

"Speaking of 'slamming,' whatever happened to the gentleman who promised the president that finding all those weapons of mass destruction would be a 'slam dunk'?"

Josh laughed. "So you know about George Tenet's infamous two words? He's another guy I feel badly about. Like my boss, the way I see it, his loyalty to the president got him in trouble. I think what he meant by that remark was to assure the president that by declassifying enough additional information, they would easily be able to strengthen the public presentation on this subject. But that isn't how his words played out in the media. He's another one who left office about a year ago. Hey, you know, you're a whole lot more savvy than you let on, Brother."

"Not really, but an old basketball player pays attention to words like that. You thought I was kind of hip when you learned that I could dribble a mean ball in my youth. Can you imagine this ol' body shooting hoops now, much less doing a slam dunk?"

For the past few months, Josh had been hearing Larry Wilkerson speak out candidly about his anger and disappointment with the Bush administration. Josh liked the colonel and gave him a call.

"I don't know what I want to do, Larry. I've tried to hang in here but I don't think I can do it with all of you gone. I wake up depressed, I come to work depressed, and I go home more depressed."

Revelations about Abu Ghraib and the skirting of the Geneva Conventions had added to Wilkerson's anger as it had to Josh's.

"I understand, Josh. Combine the detainee abuse issue with the ineptitude of post-invasion planning for Iraq, wrap both in this blanket of secretive decision-making . . . and you get the overall reason for my speaking out," Wilkerson remarked.

"Powell was our boss and our hero, Larry. Yet he's chosen to stay fairly quiet about what happened. How did you get the courage to go public knowing that you would jeopardize your friendship with him?"

"It was my wife, Barbara, who helped me realize how important it was for me to be true to my conscious. She said to me: 'You have two choices, my man. You can think more about him or you can think more about your country. I suggest you do the latter.'"

Josh understood knowing that Emmy would say the same to him.

"Josh, you gave it your best. It's time to move on now. I've got friends over at USAID. They are always looking for good people and I could make a call for you."

Josh respected the people at the U.S. Agency for International Development. This would be a natural transition for him in that USAID was an independent organization whose administrator reported directly to Condoleezza Rice, the new secretary of state. The agency was responsible for U.S. foreign economic assistance to developing countries around the world and helped countries with democratic and economic reforms, recovering from disaster, and attempting generally to rise above poverty. It was a mission well-suited for Josh. It took only a week for the colonel to make the call and Josh to receive the offer. Without hesitation, he accepted.

Kyle had been serving in his role as president of the U.S. Institute of Peace for more than three years, and he was thriving. He was immersed in searching for solutions to the tragedy amid the continued U.S. attack on Iraq. Focused on creating peaceful solutions to global issues, he vowed to direct more of USIP's activities at this time toward Afghanistan, Palestine, and Iraq.

The previous year, at the request of Congress, the institute had successfully coordinated a bipartisan effort to evaluate the nation's role and relationship with the United Nations. Now, this month, as the institute's president, Kyle was asked to facilitate the Iraq Study Group. With more than 70 foreign policy specialists whose expertise bring decades of government, military, university, and other valuable experience to the international arena, Kyle knew that USIP analysts were uniquely poised to advise, assist, and convene efforts for this committee. He looked at the political career he walked away from and felt worthwhile that his work now so far surpassed the impact he could have on world peace.

In addition to his job, he had also agreed to serve on the board for the Peace Alliance Foundation, which currently had a bill before both houses of Congress to establish a cabinet-level Department of Peace and Nonviolence. The department would be charged with imbuing the U.S. government with a culture of peace alongside the existing Department of Defense which, of course, cultivated the primacy of war. The spirit behind the establishment of this department was to have the DOD take over only after all other options have been tried by the peace department. Kyle felt honored to be a part of this organization and believed that this historic measure would provide practical, nonviolent solutions to the problems of domestic and international conflict. Absentmindedly, he thought about how Jenny would be proud of his efforts for this cause.

Sitting back on the couch in Josh's den on Thursday evening, March 9, Kyle and his twin watched a press conference being replayed from the UK.

"I know these Brits," Kyle said excitedly. "John and Hamit are great guys. I met them at a peace conference last year. They're co-founders of a group in London called the Iraq Body Count."

John Sloboda opened the press conference with an alarming statement about the U.S presence in Iraq.

> Today's figures are an indictment of three years of occupation, which continues to make the lives of ordinary Iraqis worse, not better. . . . This conflict is proof that violence begets more violence. The initial act that sparked this cycle of violence is the illegal U.S.-led invasion of March and April 2003, which resulted in 7,312 civilian deaths and 17,298 injured in a mere forty-two days. The insurgency will remain strong so long as the U.S. military remains in Iraq and ordinary Iraqi people will have more death and destruction to look forward to.

"So if all we're doing is stirring up shit," Josh yelled at the screen, "then why don't we get the hell out?!"

> So why is the U.S. still there? And if the U.S. military can't ensure the safety of Iraqi civilians and itself poses a danger to them, what is its role in that country? How many more must die

before the architects of the 'military solution' for Iraq realize
that the only sure way to reduce violence is to stop inflicting it?

"Thank you! I couldn't have said it better myself." Josh muted the
sound and turned to Kyle. "Our whole strategy was based on a set of
false assumptions, bro . . . put forth, of course, by comb-licking
Wolfowitz and the three stooges. Did they *really* think they could waltz
in and steal the Iraqi oil, and everything would be hunky dory?"

"I think they really thought we'd be viewed as good guys coming in
to liberate them," Kyle said.

"How many do you think understood that we were going to send
in our own dictator in the person of Paul Bremer? I can't believe that
the first thing he did was throw the frickin' baby out with the Ba'ath
water. The guy removed everyone remotely affiliated with Saddam
Hussein out of any top-level ministerial or corporate position."

"Is it really true that over 120,000 top-ranking Iraqi civil servants
were fired?"

Josh nodded. "Our side didn't understand that these workers had
to be members of the Ba'ath party in order to be employed in the
government under Hussein. It wasn't in any way a gauge of their
endorsement for his actions."

"I thought those Iraqis had the most expertise about the country's
water, electricity, sewage, transportation, finances, health care—you
name it."

"They did. But with the U.S. takeover, Bechtel is in charge of
getting the electricity up and running again, and until recently some
areas were getting only about four hours of power each day. Can you
frickin' imagine how Americans would react to this?"

Kyle shook his head in disbelief.

"Electricity controls water and sewage in Iraq, so without one, they
don't have the others," Josh mused. "Some people would keep their
faucets on for days at a time just hoping for an occasional trickle. And
when they do get water, it's not safe to drink. Plus they look out their
windows and see raw sewage in the streets."

"Why isn't everything at least back up to pre-war standards, Josh?
My God, we've been there three years."

"Bechtel claims to have run out of money, and the U.S. government can only account for a fraction of the $24 billion dollars given to Iraq reconstruction. Halliburton was found to have over $1.5 billion in overcharges for its Iraq services. And they were also found to have colluded with the U.S. Defense Department to keep these charges out of public purview for more than five months."

"Gee! You don't suppose that the fact that Cheney is the former CEO of Halliburton has anything to do with their getting the contract, do you?"

"Of *course* not," Josh said in mock surprise, echoing his brother's sarcastic tone. "And Cheney's tie to Rummy doesn't have anything to do with the frickin' cover-up either."

Without disturbing the brothers' conversation, Emmy brought in glasses and a bottle of wine and set them on the coffee table.

Aware that it was unusual for Josh and Emmy to serve anything but beer, Kyle picked up the bottle out of the ice bucket and looked at the label. It was Rombauer chardonnay—*Jenny's favorite white wine,* thought Kyle. *Is Emmy trying to give me a not-so-subtle nudge?*

Kyle struggled to shift from sweet memories of Jenny back to the turmoil of the never-ending war.

"You would've thought Iraq had no running government before our invasion but—from what I've learned setting up the USIP's redevelopment work there—they ranked rather high," Kyle said, leaning up to pour glasses of Rombauer for himself and his twin. "Before 1990, Iraq had the highest percentage of college-educated citizens in all of the Middle East, and its health care reached nearly all of the urban population and more than three-quarters of the rural population."

"Iraq is a bigger mess now than before we invaded the country, and hardly anyone frickin' knows or cares," Josh said. "Everyone assumed the combat part would be over quickly and the postwar stability operation would begin almost immediately."

"It might have if Jay Garner had been allowed to stay on," Kyle added as he handed a glass to his twin. "The national infrastructure completely broke down after Paul Bremer enacted over one hundred orders, the worst of which was Order #39. Talk about creating a neocon Utopia…"

"No kidding," Josh. "That Order effectively privatized all of Iraq's state-owned enterprises; gave one hundred percent foreign ownership of Iraqi businesses to global corporations; offered no priority of local over foreign businesses; provided unrestricted, tax-free remittance of all profits; granted forty-year ownership licenses; and took the right of legal disputes out of the Iraqi courts and into international tribunals." Josh raised his glass. "Here's to corporate greed…not!"

"And Bremer gave every advantage to *U.S.* corporations, ensuring them long-term economic rewards while the Iraqi people got screwed."

Josh nodded. "And Rummy is the one who got Garner out of there and replaced him with Bremer. What really pisses me off is that no one challenged him because Rummy scares the shit out of people. There were a lot of guys who could've stood up to prevent this, but they didn't speak up because they were afraid for their jobs."

"There's just no hope with the current administration, Josh. And it's still too early to speculate who'll emerge as a viable presidential candidate in 2008, but we need to find someone who'll take us in the right direction and deal more judiciously with other countries. I don't care if it's a man or woman, democrat or independent. All I know is that we have to find someone who understands and has the courage to act on what JFK meant when he said 'mankind must put an end to war, or war will put an end to mankind.'"

"We've got just over two years to put together a foreign policy plan," Kyle noted. "If we're going to support a new kind of administration, I think we should focus our efforts primarily on foreign policy and domestic issues that relate to peaceful solutions."

"I agree, bro. We need men and women who can think outside the box of aggressive war behavior and who are willing to make some effort to understand the culture of the country before going in to *save* it. Most Americans and Iraqis would like to see us bring our troops home and replace U.S. military forces with a multi-national peacekeeping force."

"We also need to cancel all U.S. corporate reconstruction contracts in Iraq, take the reconstruction funds out of U.S. hands, and turn the work over to Iraqi companies and workers."

"And what about the economic invasion this administration has planned for the rest of the Middle East?" Josh said. "I think we need to pull out of the U.S.-Middle East free trade negotiations."

"Yeah, and provide Iraq with the means to set its own terms for foreign companies operating there."

"You boys still figuring out how to save the world?" Emmy said as she entered the den.

"With the right people in place, Emmy, the rest will take care of itself," Kyle said with hope in his voice.

"Well," she noted as she poured herself a glass of wine, "since the Bush administration brought together two threats that were much more deadly in combination than they were separately—radical Islamism and weapons of mass destruction—it's going to be a challenge to get other countries to trust us or want to work with us again. The Bush administration has really shot itself in the foot."

"Yes, and before other countries accept U.S. leadership, they'll have to be convinced that America is not a corpocracy. Referring to the the special "marriage" of big business and big government, Josh asked "how the hell is the U.S. ever going to turn that around?"

"Not with the usual arrogance shown by the Bush administration," Emmy said. She picked up the bottle of Rombauer. "By the way, boys, dinner is served."

Josh and Kyle rose and followed Emmy to the dining room.

"Yeah, well, right now, Bush is entitled to the blame, "Josh said. "And considering all the repercussions in London, I think even Poodle Boy Blair is regretting his blasted decision to jump in Bush's lap."

Hearing the word "blasted" made Kyle recall Ellen with fondness. That was the word she used when she really wanted to let go and swear. Josh, who was completely uninhibited when it came to expressing anger, could have given Ellen a lesson in self-expression, Kyle thought.

"With one more of these, Josh," Kyle said, holding up his wine glass to make a toast, "you and I could solve all the world's problems this evening." Then he added in a more reflective tone, "I have to admit, I understand the power grab thing. I think I've been just as arrogant in my personal life as I've been professionally."

"No arguments from me there, bro."

Kyle was suddenly thrust back in time to his own self-absorbed way of dealing with Jenny. Feeling his own pain had prevented him from feeling hers. *How true is this of America?* Kyle wondered remembering his visit with Marion Barker. *Are our fatalities of innocent men and women on September 11 somehow worse than those experienced by the innocent victims in Afghanistan and Iraq now?*

Kyle awakened the next morning with Jenny still pervading his thoughts. He reflected on one of the many lessons he had learned from her: that human beings can change and grow. As he stood looking at himself in the mirror after his morning shave, he realized how much he had grown emotionally over the years since he'd seen her last. He had dated other women, but thoughts of Jenny kept getting in the way. For the moment, he felt relieved to have left all of that behind and come to Washington to do something worthwhile with his life. As he drove to work, Kyle decided he felt good about the life he'd chosen.

"One thing I know from personal experience," Kyle announced to his staff later in the morning as they gathered in the conference room for their weekly meeting, "is that we need to pull together a diverse team who can help us create a well-rounded foreign policy plan for the next administration. One of the mistakes of the present government is that officials haven't been willing to listen to anyone who differed from their own way of thinking. Believe me, I can understand that behavior. I've been prone to that style of operation myself in times past. But we need to gather information from as many different sources as are available to us."

Millie, Kyle's chief of staff, was especially enthusiastic about the subject of this week's meeting. "Why don't we start by sorting out what we feel was done right and what was done wrong after 9/11?"

"That's pretty obvious," said a younger staffer. "Although it still has a lot of problems, Congress did the right thing creating a Department of Homeland Security. It also established the Patriot Act so that law enforcement had more power in siphoning out and exposing would-be terrorists."

"Personally, I don't like the Patriot Act. It invades the lives of American citizens," said another staff member. "I can see the present administration abusing this power."

"I understand the need for it," Kyle said. "Something had to be done to break down the wall between intelligence and law enforcement so that they could share information. One thing the Patriot Act does is to give agents a chance to connect the dots. But, beyond that, I see the problem you're bringing up."

"The government was pretty strongly supported in its invasion of Afghanistan and deposing the Taliban regime that had sheltered al Qaeda," another added.

Kyle still had reservation about *how* the United States had invaded Afghanistan. He reminded his staff that the primary purpose of invading this country was not, and still has not been, accomplished: capturing Osama bin Laden and displacing the Taliban. "And is the good we've done there worth the thousands of innocent lives that have been lost in the process?"

"Yeah, and look what happened with their country's new American-backed government," the young man added. "Once it took control in Kabul, Afghanistan was on the brink of surpassing Colombia as the illicit-drug-capital of the world. I read that the country was producing eighty-seven percent of the world's opium supply. Heroin became its leading export."

As the staff continued to look for the good, they agreed that the January 2005 election by the Palestinian Authority was a welcome event. And Syrian forces had departed from Lebanon although Syria continued to influence the internal situation through Lebanese allies. The elections in Saudi Arabia represented an expansion of the process even if women were still excluded. And democracy seems to be taking root in Afghanistan . . . but not in Iraq."

"No, democracy is far from a reality in Iraq," Kyle affirmed. "The way the Iraqis see it, America replaced one dictator with another. When Paul Bremer was appointed the administrator of the Coalition Provisional Authority, for fourteen months he had full authority to single-handedly enact laws for Iraq . . . laws that were self-serving for the U.S."

"Exactly," Millie agreed. "No one could run for office without his approval. He disbanded the military, taking 400,000 men out of duty and refused to pay their salaries. He even abolished benefits to war widows and disabled vets who were senior party members. I guess he wanted to remove any remnant of Hussein's government but, in the process, he threw out over a hundred thousand of Iraq's most knowledgeable and distinguished civil servants."

"You're talking about engineers, university professors, scientists, physicians, community organizers, and government administrators," added another staff member.

Millie nodded. "I think that was the beginning of the end for Iraq having any semblance of democracy. But once the so-called 'democratic voting process' began, with only the hand-selected candidates approved and the laws written by Mr. Bremer being put forth, few Iraqis could have known that the constitution they sanctioned locked in the most essential aspects of the Bush Agenda into law—things like the continuation of the U.S. military occupation, offering economic advantages to U.S. corporations, and especially America's increased access to Iraq's oil."

"And what was even more atrocious was the administration failing to anticipate the negative global reaction to its decision to go into Iraq," said the young man.

"It's almost as if we didn't care what anyone else thought and still don't. President Bush makes it sound like winning this war will somehow bring safety to America. In my opinion," Millie said heatedly, "we are much more vulnerable now. All we're succeeding in doing is to make the Muslims around the world hate us more. And the majority of these people are *not* in Iraq."

"But the worst mistake of all, in my opinion," said a young woman who hadn't yet spoken, "was not anticipating how to go about the reconstruction of Iraq. The Bush administration expected it to be a short war and, once Hussein was out of the way, an easy transition to post-Hussein Iraq."

"And that is the primary purpose of our organization," Millie affirmed. "We need to beef up our Middle Eastern program and not only work with the differing cultural groups to help them find ways to get along, but we also need to educate our own government about how to do this."

"Exactly," affirmed the younger man. "Here we are . . . in a war that has no obvious end and with uprisings from within that have no obvious solution. We have serious work to do to prepare for whatever lies ahead."

Thanking everyone for their contributions, Kyle felt more certain about the direction their organization was moving. He was gratified by the united front shown by the staff. *If we couldn't create a peaceful coalition within our own institute how would we ever create it on a larger scale?*

Dressing for work the next morning, Kyle turned on CNN. An announcer was reporting that close to 160 dead bodies had been found in Baghdad that week alone. Since the bombing of a holy Shiite shrine in late February, hundreds had been killed in sectarian violence over the past month. The host, Miles O'Brien, brought on the network's senior analyst, Jeff Greenfield, and asked him if what was happening in Iraq would be defined as a civil war.

"How do you define 'civil war'?" Greenfield asked. "When the administration says we're not in one, they may be right. But is that the relevant question? You don't have armed militia fighting each other across Iraq. You even have people from both sides saying 'we've got to pull this thing together.'"

"So what are the relevant questions as you see it?" O'Brien asked.

"It seems that the forces pulling Iraq apart are becoming stronger than the forces keeping it together. The key elements of the Iraqi security forces are working less for this government and more for the Shiite sponsors. And that work includes the killing of Sunnis. You've got people moving out of neighborhoods if they're not part of the dominant force. You've got people trying to change their names. And that's only the more obvious evidence. Civil war or not, those are the areas that are really troublesome."

Kyle cringed as the screen flashed to Rumsfeld speaking: "If you put up a scoreboard and say, gee, how's it going for the last year? They tried to stop the January election, and they failed. They tried to stop the October referendum, and they failed. They tried to stop the December election, and the terrorists failed."

"Muslims going to the voting booths have to walk right by the bomb craters that wiped out their families," Miles O'Brien said, turning back to Jeff Greenfield. "Do you think having an American-style democracy will make them forget who slaughtered their husbands, wives, and children? So, okay, there are some positive things on the scorecard but . . ."

"But the problem is," Greenfield continued, "every time you take that step forward, there is a step or two backward. And again it raises the question of whether these centrifugal forces, these ancient enmities between these forces are stronger than this notion about pulling the country together. Never mind what we accomplished. Outside of this administration, you'd be hard pressed to find anybody who thinks what we did after Saddam fell really set the stage for a coalition government to deal with all these enmities."

Kyle related well to the discussion. He and Jenny had been in this same pattern: one step forward and two steps back. And the forces pulling them apart had been stronger than the forces pulling them together. He and Jenny each had their own established beliefs that they could not negotiate through in finding a new way to pull together.

As Kyle's attention was drawn back to the television screen, Miles O'Brien suggested a quick history lesson was needed. "Great Britain took a land called Mesopotamia and artificially drew lines in the sand after World War I, thereby creating a country it named Iraq. Its population is composed of Shiites and Sunnis and Kurds and dozens of other groups that are not known for getting along with one another. What you're talking about is bringing people together in an artificial way that would have no other reason or desire to be together."

"I wouldn't argue whether you can or can't *impose* democracy here because it happened in Japan," Greenfield said. "The question is, okay, the Sunnis ran this place because the British told them 'you're in charge.' They did that for decades. Now they are going to be left out. And they are in the one place that is now left with no oil. Do you think we're going to resolve this simply with a new democratic governance?"

"All the king's horses and all the king's men may be required. Thank you, Jeff Greenfield."

"It's amazing that the war mongers didn't see this coming," Kyle said to Millie as he met her in the coffee room after he described the CNN interview to her.

"The Bush administration should have stopped at ousting Hussein," Kyle said. "But no. It had to also oust the existing class structure of Iraq. The new policies were taking power away from the Sunnis and delivering it to the long-suffering Shiites. Since the Shiites are the majority, it is certain they will come out on top in any election."

"In my attempts to understand this internal warfare," Kyle continued, "I did learn that the Sunni Muslims are, so to speak, the Roman Catholics of Islamic history. They've never been particularly keen to embrace radical ideas en masse, let alone the ruthless violence that is an integral part of bin Laden's message. Even so, did the administration think the Sunni's were going to sit back and do nothing?"

"The top administrators didn't think at all," Millie said. "That's the problem. It was all about grabbing the oil and rearranging the Middle East. They didn't have a clue about the aftermath. Still don't. Our role here at USIP is to pick up where they blew it. They've made our job a lot tougher but we have a lot more experience using diplomacy than these idiots in the Defense Department."

"We can't do it alone, Millie. We have to help create an entirely new kind of administration in Washington." *No one can make changes of this sort alone,* Kyle thought. He had Josh. He'd had Harvey. He had Anthony. He had so many people to turn to when he was giving up on his relationship with Jenny. Why didn't he seek their advice then? For sure, he would not make that mistake now.

Over the next few weeks, while Kyle continued working with his organization, Josh began to line up interviews with people who, in his opinion, had the experience and wisdom to offer intelligent and varied input on establishing a sound foreign policy. He chose knowledgeable political scholars, senators, former Washington officials, authors, and peace organization board and staff members who were open-minded to alternative ways beyond war to deal with U.S. relations throughout the world. After some thoughtful discussions, Josh and Kyle gave this group an illustrative name—PEACE—Peaceful Effort to Achieve Coalition Everywhere.

"How's that for the ultimate in idealism?" Kyle quipped to his twin. Josh's first interview was with Daniel Benjamin and Steven Simon, two men who had served on the National Security Council. Benjamin was director for counterterrorism and Simon had an earlier career in the State Department as an expert in Middle Eastern security affairs. Together they had written a book called *The Next Attack: The Failure of the War on Terror and a Strategy for Getting it Right*.

The two men met with Josh in his conference room. Josh handed out bottles of water as he sat down with the recorder playing and a yellow pad in front of him. "Okay, guys, let me begin with the obvious question: how do we get it right?"

Daniel began by explaining that a comprehensive counterterrorism strategy must focus on four goals: "First, by whatever means, stop terrorists from committing acts of violence. Second, keep the most dangerous weapons out of their hands. Third, protect those facilities in the United States that, if struck, would cause the most damage. And, fourth, halt the creation of new terrorists by dealing, to the extent possible, with those grievances that are driving radicalization."

"In each of these areas, the U.S. could do better," Steven added. "But in the last point, we could hardly do worse. The grievances of Muslims in Western Europe cannot be disassociated from their native countries. Iraqis are unhappy with the U.S. for invading their home country. They are unhappy with the European's lack of acceptance of them. They feel disconnected and disgruntled. Online capabilities put dissatisfied Muslims in touch with each other everywhere. This is why the present administration is narrow-minded if it thinks it can contain the jihad war inside of the Middle Eastern borders."

Josh was awestruck by the insight of the two men. It was clear the so-called war on terror was so much more expansive than our fighting Muslims in the Middle East.

"The administration is off-track in assuming that the number of terrorists is limited and that the violence won't reverberate significantly outside of Iraq," Daniel pointed out. "There is something to be said for taking the war overseas so we don't fight our battle here in America. But it's a mistake to think that an aggressive offense eliminates the need for a strong defense. We need to set up far more protection at home."

"Let's get into that," Josh said. "I realize that part of a good foreign policy is domestic safeguards."

Daniel deferred to Steven, who said, "The Department of Homeland Security needs clear priorities defined and put into practice: (1) the need to secure ordinary infrastructure that could be turned into weapons; (2) the need to prevent deadly weapons or the equivalent from being smuggled into the country; (3) the need to prepare for a biological attack; and (4) the need to know who is entering and leaving the U.S. and to monitor and disrupt terrorist cells that might be forming here."

"There are a number of areas of serious vulnerability where the U.S. needs to beef up its defense," Daniel added. "Unsecured and unregulated general aviation, remotely fired aircraft, kit airplanes, shoulder-fired missiles, railroad transportation, biological attack, port security, and cyber systems, just to mention the most obvious." Daniel looked to Steven to see if he had forgotten anything.

"Also," Steven said, "we need to cultivate the cooperation of American Muslims and professionalize domestic counterterrorism."

Josh was taking notes but counting on the recorder to pick up what he was missing. He found this to be invaluable information.

"What we're saying is that this is one of the major areas where the White House is flawed," David said. "We've failed to achieve the necessary balance between the offensive and the defensive elements of our counterterrorism efforts, and we've fallen short in getting our homeland security program up and running. The Bush administration's belief that striking terrorists in Iraq would remove the threat to

Americans at home led the White House to leave the complex political and organizational challenges of the home front to officials without the necessary stature and authority."

"So what I'm hearing is that leaves us, even now, extremely vulnerable," Josh concluded. From his five years in the State Department, he had experienced firsthand what these men were saying.

"At some point in time," Steven concluded, "ambitious jihadists will carry their fight back to the U.S. When that happens, we'd better be ready."

"Yes, we'd better!" Josh exclaimed. "The weight of America's future cannot rest on the shoulders of one person. I pray that a leader will emerge who is humble enough to embrace a more peace-driven foreign policy plan and surround himself—or herself—with experts who believe that there must be a better way to interrelate with the rest of the world." Josh's head was spinning from taking in so much information. It was obvious these men had given enormous thought to this topic. He thanked them for sharing their valuable time and well-thought-out strategies. At his prompting, they agreed to serve as part of the PEACE team.

Josh was energized by his first interview. "We're on the right track, bro," he said to Kyle when he stopped by the next day for morning coffee at his brother's condo. He summarized the meeting for Kyle.

Kyle was especially drawn to two points of their meeting—directly addressing grievances that are driving radicalization and fostering the support of American Muslims. It is so obvious, he thought, as he applied these principles to himself. Why didn't he delve more deeply into understanding Jenny's side of what drove them apart? And why didn't he turn to some of her friends for suggestions about how to solve their problems? Lost in his own reflections, he tuned in as he caught his brother's last words.

"Imagine if we can talk to twenty or thirty people who have insight like these guys."

Kyle agreed that the PEACE team had an opportunity to play an important political role behind the scenes. This was the single most threatening issue facing America. "You're right, Josh. We can put together a team that recognizes the power of international diplomacy and believes in striking with that weapon first. Military force may be necessary, but it doesn't always have to be our first line of attack."

Josh, who had carried in *The New York Times* from his brother's porch, opened it and scanned the national section.

Cheney's Aide Says President Approved Leak

WASHINGTON, April 6, 2006—Vice President Dick Cheney's former chief of staff testified that he was authorized by President Bush, through Mr. Cheney, in July 2003 to disclose key parts of what until then was a classified pre-war intelligence estimate on Iraq, according to a new court filing…

The testimony by the former official, I. Lewis [Scooter] Libby Jr. . . . provides an indication that Mr. Bush, who has long criticized leaks of secret information as a threat to national security, may have played a direct role in authorizing disclosure of the intelligence report on Iraq . . .

Mr. Libby is scheduled to go on trial next year on perjury and obstruction charges connected to the disclosure of Ms. Wilson's name. . . .

The previous day [July 7, 2003] the White House, for the first time, had publicly admitted that Mr. Bush's statement in the State of the Union address earlier that year, alleging that Mr. Hussein had sought uranium in Africa, should not have been in the speech. . . .

The leak was intended, the court papers suggested, as a rebuttal to an Op-Ed article in *The New York Times* on July 6, 2003, by Joseph C. Wilson IV, a former United States ambassador and the husband of Ms. Wilson [Valerie Plame]. Mr. Wilson wrote that he traveled to Africa in 2002 after Mr. Cheney raised questions about

```
possible nuclear purchases by Iraq. Mr.
Wilson wrote that he concluded it was
"highly doubtful" Iraq had sought nuclear
fuel from Niger.
```

"Holy shit!" Josh cried out. "Libby *has* been lying his ass off, covering up for Bush and Cheney! We knew Rove and Libby actually talked to the press. Everyone knew that whole Niger report was bogus, but I *never* thought it would come out that Bush himself authorized leaking the information."

"What?" Kyle took the paper from his brother and scanned the article as Josh kept ranting.

"Oh, man, the White House cherry-picked what they declassified but had they declassified the whole National Security Estimate, we would've seen that in the same document, the CIA negated the claim that somehow Saddam Hussein was trying to buy uranium in Africa. Bush just leaked the frickin' parts he wanted to mislead the country so he could go into war! Kyle, it's impeachment time."

Josh was seething. He had seen firsthand the top officials using and abusing key men in the administration. He continued to put the pieces together for his twin. "See, bro, sixty days after the president ordered the release of highly selective and misleading nuggets out of the National Intelligence Estimate, he went on television and said, 'Oh, it's bad to leak classified information.' Do you remember that?"

Recalling all of it now, Kyle furrowed his brow and took on a presidential air as he imitated Bush: "'If there's a leak out of my administration, I want to know who it is . . . I don't know of anybody in my administration who leaked classified information. If somebody did leak classified information, I'd like to know it.'"

Josh gave a bitter chuckle.

"I guess the threat of thirty years in prison didn't leave Libby with much of a choice," Kyle reasoned. "And even the White House press secretary admitted he was lied to."

"It's all over but the shouting," Josh ranted. "Bush and Cheney and Rummy may have finally, once and for all, unilaterally demolished the neoconservative Republican succession in office. Now all we have to do is put together a solid foreign policy plan and find a worthy presidential candidate to take over, and we're home free!"

"But Bush and Cheney have an inexorable ability to dodge bullets," Kyle warned. "Only time will tell whether they take the hit on this one or whether Scooter Libby becomes the fall guy."

"I can frickin' predict what will happen," Josh said irately. "Whatever Libby's sentence turns out to be, in order to repay him for his 'loyalty,' Bush will commute his sentence and eventually pardon him. You just wait and see."

"Loyalty, schmoyalty," Kyle said. "Bush will do whatever he has to do to keep himself, Cheney, and Rove from being implicated. That's the bottom line."

"Rumor has it that Rove will be stepping down soon," Josh said. "He's become a lightening rod about numerous issues."

"Good riddance," said Kyle. "The extent Bush has gone to put his own spin on the reasons for taking us into war make Nixon's paranoia look like a mole hill. How could the media and the American public make mountains out of this incident and let Bush get by with misleading us into war and then committing war crimes that have caused the deaths of hundreds of thousands of innocent people and the maiming and inhumane torture of countless more?"

Shaking his head, Josh walked over and turned on Kyle's television. CNN faded in announcing that another military cover up in Iraq had just been exposed by *TIME* magazine. Several U.S. military troops had been accused of going on murdering sprees. Having originally claimed that the deaths were the result of a roadside bombing, seven Marines and one Navy corpsman have been placed in military confinement in the brig at Camp Pendleton Marine Corps base in California, pending charges of murder, kidnapping, and conspiracy for the deaths involving women and children in Haditha. One of the witnesses to this attack was a 12-year-old girl who pretended to be dead and lived to describe the horror of seeing both her parents, her sister, and others shot at close range by U.S. soldiers.

"It's a good thing I'm not still California's attorney general," Kyle muttered. "I'm afraid I might kill those mother fuckers with my two bare hands."

Prime Minister Nouri al-Maliki then appeared onscreen saying he was outraged that the Americans were supposed to be freeing Iraqis by helping form a democracy but instead "they crush them with their vehicles and kill them just on suspicion. The U.S. military violence against Iraqi civilians has become a daily phenomenon."

"I guess the big shots in Washington aren't the only ones weaving some mighty tangled webs," Josh sorrowfully concluded as he turned off the television. "The military may be right that these are isolated incidents, but it doesn't excuse covering them up."

"Apparently the truth about the war in Iraq is not yet all out," Kyle added dejectedly. "Three and half years into the war, the military is a little late starting to teach the troops core values. But I hope part of the training is to engage their brains before they engage their weapons."

The following week, Josh shouted into Kyle's phone, "Trouble in River City, bro. Check your fax. I'm sending over a report that just came over from my old buddies in the Secretary of State's Office. Catch you later."

Kyle pulled the report out of the machine shortly afterward.

> A small group of senior Republicans are defying the president and have passed a measure out of the Armed Services Committee on how terrorists are treated—a measure the president is vowing to block. The biggest source of contention is how the U.S. will interpret or define Article 3 of the Geneva Convention, which sets international standards for how prisoners are treated. The White House wants greater leeway in how they interrogate suspects; the Senate measure gives prisoners more rights. This is setting off a stunning display of Republican division. Former Secretary of State Colin Powell fired off a letter saying that he disagrees with President Bush. He says the Bush proposal would put U.S. troops at risk and concludes: "The world is beginning to doubt the moral basis of our fight against terrorism." The president claims he merely wants to clarify a vague international treaty.

Spurred on by all the reports coming to light, the brothers were more motivated than ever to complete their mission. While Kyle was engaged in his own set of interviews, Josh made an appointment with James Bamford, who lived in Washington, not far from Josh. Kyle had known him as a visiting professor back in California at the Goldman School of Public Policy at U.C. Berkeley and recommended that Josh talk to him because of his extensive knowledge about both pre- and post-9/11 facts.

"We have to know everything about what went wrong if we are going to attempt to make things right," Kyle had said repeatedly to Josh. In preparation for the meeting, Josh got a hold of Bamford's book, *A Pretext for War,* wherein he described how the intelligence agencies had failed to share valuable information and connect the dots of the forthcoming terrorist attack. When asked by Josh, Bamford confirmed in no uncertain terms that Cheney and Rumsfeld, together with Wolfowitz and Josh's three stooges, used every means possible, including the Niger report, to concoct the weapons of mass destruction story in order to convince the American public and the world that an attack on Iraq was warranted.

Kyle's schedule opened up on the afternoon Josh was booked to meet with Francis Fukuyama. He was excited to join his brother for this interview. Mr. Fukuyama formerly worked under Deputy Secretary of State Paul Wolfowitz at the State Department and was himself a former neoconservative who lost faith in those in power and described this in his book, *America at the Crossroads.*

The brothers chose Josh's conference room for the meeting. After explaining their goals, Josh asked Mr. Fukuyama if he was comfortable with them pounding him with questions.

"Call me Francis, and that's why I'm here. I'll give it to you as straight as I know how."

"There are certainly better ways to promote political and economic development in other countries beyond preemptive war. I know you would agree," Kyle began.

"The United States needs to define an approach to foreign policy that's concerned with what goes on *inside* other countries and not just their external behavior. But our government tends to impose the

American way on these people instead of allowing institutions to emerge out of the habits and experiences of the local people.

"That's such common sense," Kyle replied. He thought about how things would have come out with Jenny if he had been more concerned with what was going on *inside* of her and not just what he perceived as her external behavior. Refocusing his thoughts, Kyle asked, "Tell us, was a regime change in the Middle East the right goal?"

"This administration has placed regime change front and center in their foreign policy," Francis replied. "The upside of that is the regime change in Afghanistan and Iraq are the best guarantees that they'll not threaten the U.S. But the downside is that establishing a new political order is a difficult business, and doubly so for those not immersed in the habits, mores, and traditions of the people for whom they're setting up a new style of government."

"Bringing about a regime change is exactly what a lot of us want to accomplish right here at home," Josh said. "But we want to learn from what's happened in Iraq. Otherwise we could end up with a civil war breaking out here at home. It wouldn't be the first time."

"When no weapons of mass destruction and no ties between Hussein and al Qaeda were found, the Bush administration could only rely on its third motive for the war, human rights and democracy," Francis said. "You're in an entirely different situation with your strategy planning."

"What do you see was their real motive for going to war in Iraq?" Josh probed. "Helen Thomas raised that question to President Bush only yesterday."

Francis was candid. "Obviously it's a composite of reasons: paving the way for Israel's triumph in the Middle East; securing our energy supplies from the world's second-largest oil supplier; who knows, maybe even Bush getting even with Hussein for nearly taking out his entire family back in 1983 . . ."

" . . . And if our government could make this work in Iraq, then the plan was to use this as a model to rearrange the entire map of the Middle East, setting each county up to our liking," Josh added.

"The motivation for this war was certainly not rooted in self-defense, let alone altruism," Kyle offered. "It's becoming clear to me that this administration had a totalitarian vision of America as ruler of the world."

"And somewhere way down on the list," Francis added, "perhaps there *really was* the legitimate desire to create a regime that would work cooperatively with the U.S. But this administration doesn't know the first thing about how to do that. So what we've ended up with is an outbreak of civil war, isolationism of the U.S. from many other countries, and increased hatred of Islamic people toward the U.S."

"I was in Bali at the time of the attacks," Kyle said. Again his thoughts slipped back to Jenny and their memorable time there. He shook them off and refocused. "I didn't get the impression at all that America is hated by the vast majority of people there."

"Muslims don't dislike the U.S. or the West as such," Francis told him, "but rather they dislike our foreign policy. They believe that the U.S. supports Israel one-sidedly against the Palestinians and supports Arab dictators like Egypt's Mubarak and the Saudi ruling family at the expense of democracy. This makes it easier for hard-core terrorists to recruit supporters."

"Our foreign policy has to account for the fact that there are groups of susceptible young Muslims rising up all over the world who don't take orders from Osama bin Laden," Kyle interjected. "They aren't directly connected to him. They're inspired by him and eager to carry out Allah's mission wherever they can." Then he added, "I learned this from an elderly Muslim man while I was in Bali. He said that taking out bin Laden wouldn't in itself stop this diffusion of hate in various pockets around the world."

Francis agreed. "The liberal democracies of Western Europe, Canada, and the United States face clear challenges in integrating Muslim immigrants into their countries," he said. "The greatest obstacle is that many Muslims, particularly those who are second—and third-generation, have been unable to achieve a clear sense of identity, resulting in a disenfranchised group of people who've failed to become assimilated into mainstream culture."

"You're saying Muslims need to be incorporated into society as fully as the Jews have been made a part of the U.S.," Josh suggested.

"Exactly," said Francis. "As long as Europeans, for example, keep these young people from joining the privileged ranks of society, Muslim immigrants will resort to desperate measures to extricate themselves from a repressive existence, with disastrous consequences for an unsuspecting majority that marches forward in the interest of one national identity."

"So many marginalized European Muslims embrace Osama bin Laden as a visionary figure because, as long as they lack a national connection, he offers them a way to identify with their larger Islamic community," Kyle said.

"So what's the answer?" Josh asked Francis.

"I suggest taking multiculturalism more seriously," he replied. "Immigrants should be able to look forward to attaining not only jobs but status within their newfound homelands, so that one day Muslims can feel as French or as Dutch or as Spanish as they are in name. Laws should be amended so that citizenship is open to immigrants at an earlier stage, as the Germans did in 2000. Traditions that are integral to the established national identity should not be exclusionary of groups whose ancestors were not a part of their creation."

"Francis, you're suggesting the good ol' melting pot that's been adopted in the United States," said Josh.

"Yes, if Europeans continue to regard their national identity as a blood and soil creation that inhibits the integration of new ethnic groups, then the prognosis for a harmonious and productive European society is quite bleak."

Josh got up and returned to the table with bottles of water for them. As he placed them on the table, he asked, "What about our *National Security Strategy?* I know that could use some reworking."

"The *National Security Strategy* ought to be officially revised to provide clear criteria for going to war," Francis offered. "An integral part of our U.S. strategy should include actions that fall within the realm of soft power. Hard power is the stick; soft power is the carrot. Hard power is the strictly militaristic approach to solving all problems. The neoconservatives calling the shots in the Bush administration only understand hard power, thereby over-emphasizing the use of force.

You know the saying: 'When your only tool is a hammer, every problem looks like a nail'?"

"Hmm," Kyle muttered, suddenly recalling his issues with Jenny. *Hard power was all I knew then,* he thought. *When she didn't accept my offer to help, I wanted to shove it down her throat.*

"The United States is a powerful nation," Josh said. "Everyone knows it. We don't have to blast the world with a reminder. After all, power is most effective when it's not so heavy-handed."

Kyle came back to the present. *Put her out your mind,* he told himself. But the analogy Francis had offered stuck with him. Kyle knew he was a commanding personality in his own right. He realized he hadn't needed to be so oppressive with Jenny.

"Out of respect for the administration," Francis said defensively, "it's more likely that officials were guilty of exaggerating rather than lying. They probably truly believed or wanted to believe that Hussein was trying to get nuclear weapons."

"JFK counseled that the great enemy of the truth is very often not the lie, deliberate, contrived, and dishonest, but the myth, persistent, persuasive, and unrealistic," Kyle quoted.

"I talked to a former National Security Council expert on Iraq, Kenneth Pollack, and he told me that what the Bush people did was dismantle the existing filtering process that for fifty years had been preventing the policymakers from getting bad information," Josh said. "They created stovepipes to get the information they wanted directly to the top leadership. Their position was that the professional bureaucracy was deliberately and maliciously keeping information from them."

"So this way, for better or for worse, they *had* the information," Kyle reasoned.

"Yes," Josh agreed, "they always had information to back up their public claims, but it was often bad information. They were forcing the intelligence community to defend its good information and good analysis so aggressively that the intelligence analysts didn't have the time or the energy to go after the bad information."

"Their deeper fault was not having the humility to engage in a more open-minded review of the evidence before launching into war," Francis added.

"So how can this be prevented in the future?" Kyle asked.

"I recommend working toward a multi-institutional world," Francis responded without hesitation. "Few trust the U.S. to be sufficiently benevolent, and so they would like to subject American power to more formal constraints. The U.N., while useful for peacekeeping and nation-building, is structurally limited with regard to both legitimacy and effectiveness, and it's doubtful that any set of reforms currently contemplated or politically feasible will solve the organization's problems."

"So to build trust, we need to create new institutions and adapt the existing ones to new circumstances," Kyle offered. Again, he thought of his time with Jenny. Instead of demanding that she fit into old traditions, he realized that perhaps he could have been willing to adapt to something all together new for both of them. But, at the time, he was too locked into the old, the only way he knew. He chuckled to himself, thinking, *Ever consider becoming a marriage counselor, Francis?*

"Bottom line," Francis offered, "is that American foreign policy must promote a world populated by a large number of overlapping and sometimes competitive international institutions, what can be labeled multi-multilateralism. In this instance, the U.N. wouldn't disappear but would become one of several organizations that fostered legitimate and effective international action. The problem with the U.N. is that it makes no practical demands on its members to be democratic or to respect the human rights of its citizens. We need a multiplicity of international organizations that can provide both power and legitimacy for different types of challenges to world order."

"I can see that this is another form of softer power," Josh stated. "The U.S. is seen by many as greedy, isolated, and self-absorbed. Using a multilateral approach might focus our efforts on building stronger institutions and governance in poor countries."

By now, it was apparent that Fukuyama was fully engaged in exploring options. "Josh, we could consider raising USAID to cabinet status," he said, pointing to the USAID plaque on the conference room wall, "or it might make sense to break out the really effective parts of the agency, such as the disaster and reconstruction teams or the Office of Transition Initiatives, and roll them into a single agency for reconstruction. Or instead of trying to reinvent USAID, it might be better for the U.S. to try to reinvent the World Bank and other multilateral financial institutions."

"So what you're saying is that the most important way that American power can be exercised is not through the exercise of military power but through the ability of the United States to shape international institutions," Kyle said.

"That's exactly right. Effective institutions must have two qualities: power and legitimacy. Power is needed to deal with threats that may employ weapons of mass destruction. Legitimacy must avoid unilateral decision-making and instead work through international institutions. Even though they're inherently slow-moving, less flexible, and crippled by cumbersome procedures and methods, it's all necessary to provide the respect that legitimacy brings. You won't accomplish this all in one or two terms of office. But this will be the prime task for the coming generation."

"What about NATO?" Kyle asked.

"NATO has fewer legitimacy problems than the U.N. All its members are genuine liberal democracies, and all share important core values and institutions. But when NATO was unwilling to support the Bush administration in Iraq, the Bush administration rejected NATO as well. It goes without saying that being willing to work within a multilateral framework does not mean accepting other's positions only on your terms."

Kyle let these last words linger as he mulled them over. "NATO supported the Afghan intervention but not the invasion of Iraq. Had the U.S. submitted itself to a test involving most of the world's developed democracies, it would not have launched the second war and, in the end, would have been better off for having observed self-restraint," Kyle said.

"There's a lot of room for creativity in designing other new multilateral security organizations," Francis said. "Trust me. Had the idea for a 'broader Middle East' democracy initiative come from the community of democracies rather than from Washington alone, it might've had a better chance of being adopted."

As the meeting wrapped up, Josh and Kyle thanked Francis for spending time with them and asked if he would join the PEACE team to help lay out their foreign policy for the next administration. For Kyle, the meeting had been a personal learning experience as well as a professional one.

"Do you think we're getting somewhere?" Josh asked his brother after the meeting had ended.

"Look what we've learned from a handful of interviews. Just think where we'll be after a few more like this guy. He's so insightful. He'd be a powerful asset to any president's cabinet."

"There's a frickin' barrel full of wisdom out there for anyone who cares to dip into it," Josh concurred as he turned out the lights and closed the door to the conference room. "If these blockheads in power would just be open to expanding their own mindsets . . ."

"Open is right," Kyle exclaimed. "I hope the administration is open to listening to the report that comes out of the Iraq Study Group. I'm enjoying my work with Jim Baker and Lee Hamilton. In fact, I'm impressed with the whole committee. It's not about politics for them but about finding rational recommendations for resolving our presence in Iraq."

"What's with these guys in the administration? Are they all so damned arrogant and unwilling to listen?"

"Well, I can personally relate to that," Kyle said quietly. "I didn't used to be very willing to listen and remain open to any other possibility than the one I knew."

"Woah." Josh looked intently at his brother. "What's up with you?"

Kyle started to say something sarcastic and then changed his mind. "Josh, it's taken me more than three years out of office to begin to see myself the way I really am . . . or was."

"Bro, I thought you were an excellent public servant. I'm not just saying that because you're my brother. I'd tell you if I thought you fucked up."

"I did okay . . . publicly."

"Aha. But behind those closed doors, out of the public eye ... You wouldn't be referring to Jenny, would you?"

Kyle looked at his brother with sad eyes. "I've come to realize that it's the worst mistake of my entire life. I don't feel proud of how I behaved back then."

"Well, it's never too late, bro. September 11 taught me that. My entire life changed by making it out of that building. Emmy and I have never gotten along better. We both appreciate that we were given extra time to make things really right in our lives. And with what you and I are doing right now, we are taking steps to make things right."

Kyle gave his brother a knowing nod but said nothing as he walked out the door toward his car.

"Hey," Josh called out to his brother. "It's election night. Why don't you come over for dinner?"

Kyle turned and smiled. "I'd love to."

Emmy set out some pre-dinner nibbles for the twins as they watched the evening news, and she went back to the kitchen.

After a few minutes, Josh exclaimed, "Oh, my God! Emmy! We won the House!"

"And only two votes away from winning the Senate," Kyle shouted with excitement.

Emmy rushed into the den. "Alleluia! Alleluia! I knew that champagne I bought wouldn't go to waste," she happily declared, and rushed to the fridge to retrieve it. As they toasted the Democratic victory, they all felt renewed hope for the country.

The next morning, each at their respective jobs, neither brother could focus on his work. When it was finally known that the Democrats were fully in control of both houses, Kyle began to believe that all of their work just might pay off. He phoned Josh.

"The American people have spoken! And they've sent a loud and unmistakable message. Man, have we got our work cut out for us! But with Harry Reid as Senate majority leader and Nancy Pelosi as speaker of the House, there's hope."

"There's only one thing that could top all of this, bro," Josh said.

"What could be better than this?"

"I just got word from some of my old buddies in the Secretary of State's Office. Rummy's been fired! He's frickin' gone. It'll be all over the news tomorrow."

Kyle was speechless. He had hoped but never really thought it possible—the House and Senate had a Democratic majority, and Rumsfeld ousted!

"My word, Josh, it looks like God isn't a Republican after all!"

By the next morning, Kyle had learned that Robert Gates was the nominee for the new secretary of defense. He recognized President Bush's tactics. He was on the offensive as he prepared to work with a democratically controlled Congress. Kyle would have taken the same political tact.

Three weeks after the election, the president was scheduled to speak at the University of Latvia, where he planned to attend a two-day NATO summit and then meet with the prime minister of Iraq, Nouri al-Maliki.

"We may not have to wait until 2008 to begin implementing our foreign policy," Kyle said to Josh as he joined him in his office to listen to the president's speech. "So much depends on what the president will do now in light of these changes. Maybe Bob Gates can convince him to give more credence to diplomacy and economic solutions."

"I doubt it, bro. All the Bush supporters seem entrenched in believing that we have to stay the course in Iraq; that to leave is to admit defeat."

"And if we stay until we win, we'll be there for decades," Kyle responded softly.

Revved up even more by the political turnaround, the brothers scheduled an interview the following week with Sister Kathleen Pruitt of Pax Christi, a Catholic peace movement that rejects war and every form of violence and domination. Its mission is to seek peaceful ways to deal with differences on all levels whether personal, social, or international.

Kyle and Josh drove over together to meet at the Pax Christi office. As they approached the intersection, Josh slammed on the brakes, barely avoiding a collision with a car running a red light. The other teenage driver gave him the finger, rolled down the window, shouted expletives, and then sped away.

"So much for world peace," Josh said as he took a deep breath before attempting to move forward in traffic. "Guess that was a young Republican."

Upon meeting Sister Kathleen, Josh was surprised. She looked nothing like a nun. She was dressed in tasteful professional clothes and wore her hair short and stylish. Once they were comfortably seated, the sister explained that Pax Christi's international program was a nonprofit, non-governmental Catholic peace movement working on a global scale to promote a variety of issues including human rights, security, disarmament, economic justice, and ecology. The U.S. branch strove to create a world that reflected the peace of Christ by witnessing to the call of Christian nonviolence. "The work begins in our personal lives and extends to broader communities, where the goal is to transform structures of society."

Curious about the inner peace the nun projected, Kyle asked her, "Exactly how do you live out the principles of Pax Christi in your personal life?"

"For me, peace and war begin in the individual human heart. The work of Pax Christi really calls all of us to prayer, action, and study to enable us to be in touch with our own gifts and limitations. We're striving to *be* people of peace. And as we live within that spirit, each of us deepens that commitment to bring peace to every corner of the world that we touch. I'm sure you would agree that there'll never be peace unless there's justice. So a good definition of peace is the sharing of resources. That's why part of the Pax Christi International mission is to help with development work in foreign countries," she said.

"It definitely sounds like your work and ours at USAID are compatible," Josh said. "But how do you ultimately decide where to offer your services?"

"The process typically begins with a study of the situation," the Sister replied. "Then we form a delegation that assesses the conditions of the country. From there, we're better able to determine what can be done both in and out of the country."

"Would that our illustrious government would be that methodical before launching into a country," Josh quipped. "So what kind of action might you take?"

"Often we make efforts to find funding or we call on governments to apply greater justice to its people," she explained. "Then we set up the appropriate delegation to address issues with the governments of those nations.

"Let me ask you, Sister," Kyle asked, "if you were in a position of authority in the Pentagon, what changes would you make in our foreign policy?"

"Well, for starters I'd get rid of Bush," she said, laughing.

"It's really a shame, but our current foreign policy is based on reckless incompetence of the highest order. Our government goes into places they have little knowledge of the culture and even less interest in studying it. Why not learn about the ethnic conflicts that exist? Why don't we come to an understanding and respect of the differences in religious beliefs? If the Iraqis elect a very conservative fundamentalist Islamic government, it *will* be democracy but the U.S. is *not* going to be happy with that."

"It's pretty evident that our current administration doesn't want democracy," Kyle said. "They only want a government that will favor American interests. Period."

"Absolutely," the sister responded. "It's a monolithic view, but the government doesn't seem willing to do its homework to get down to the fine details. What the current administration does is alienate, frustrate, and trod where we don't belong. We need government that will really address the needs of all people, one that isn't based on brute force but rather on the distribution of the wealth of Iraq. We could be offering the technological capabilities and the resources we have to confront illness and poverty there. Can you imagine what a positive image we would have in countries around the world if our foreign policy were built on honest relationships instead of trying to force others to be like ourselves?"

I too have changes to make, Kyle thought. *Building on honest relationships instead of trying to make others behave the way I want them to.*

"When Osama bin Laden sent a message suggesting a truce early this year," Sister Kathleen continued, "a government exercising the kind of foreign policy I'm describing would have seized the opportunity to listen more carefully."

"You mean instead of our standard line: 'We don't negotiate with terrorists,'" Josh stated.

"JFK was right: 'Let us never negotiate out of fear. But let us never fear to negotiate,'" Kyle quoted. "There was one noteworthy part of bin Laden's message that shouldn't have been ignored."

Kyle opened his thick file and pulled out a transcript of the January 2006 message purportedly from Osama bin Laden and read the section aloud.

> In this truce, both parties will enjoy security and stability and we will build Iraq and Afghanistan, which were destroyed by the war.
>
> There is no defect in this solution other than preventing the flow of hundreds of billions of dollars to the influential people and war merchants in America who supported Bush's election campaign with billions of dollars.
>
> As for us, we do not have anything to lose. The swimmer in the sea does not fear rain. You have occupied our land, defiled our honor, violated our dignity, shed our blood, ransacked our money, demolished our houses, rendered us homeless, and tampered with our security. We will treat you in the same way.

"We will never know what could come of a truce talk," Kyle continued, "but he's making a valid point. We have everything to lose and, from al Qaeda's perspective, they have little or nothing to lose. They want us to help rebuild their countries that we've destroyed and leave them alone. We want to be left alone as well and to trust that a truce will be respected. Would it make the U.S. look weak if our representatives at least explored ways to make this happen? There was a time I might have thought so, but not anymore."

Sister Kathleen seized the opportunity to take the conversation to another level. "There's a biblical passage in Romans that says, 'Bless those who persecute you, bless and do not curse them. Do not repay anyone evil for evil; be concerned for what is noble in the sight of all. Rather, if your enemy is hungry, feed him; if he is thirsty, give him something to drink; for by so doing you will heap burning coals upon his head.'"

"What does that last sentence mean?" Kyle asked.

"For christsake, bro," Josh piped in with frustration in his voice, "it means if we showed a little frickin' compassion for their plight, we'd take the wind out of their revengeful sails. We can kill them with kindness instead of weapons and torture. If we did this, there'd be a whole lot less motivation for the spin-off terrorist acts happening all over Europe and in other parts of the world." Kyle quickly shot Josh a glance of reprimand for his cursing, and Josh looked sheepishly at the nun. "Uh, pardon my language, Sister."

Sister Kathleen surprised them both by laughing. "No offense taken, Josh. Believe me, I've heard worse! Leaders who have the courage to be forthright are much more inspiring."

"Personally, I'm fed up with our leaders putting their own spin on the truth." Taking on the voice of a pompous leader, Kyle said, "America, the perfect country, has been wronged by the evil one." As if coming into his own awakening, Kyle continued in an unusually serious tone. "Until we as Americans look inside of ourselves and ask what part we have contributed to the hostility that other cultures feel toward us, we will never regain our standing in the world. Why does the Muslim world hate us so much? What have we done to contribute to their willingness to even die for their beliefs? Is it possible that it has something to do with America's self-absorbed need to preserve its lifestyle in consuming an exorbitant share of the world's resources to the detriment of other countries? Until we begin to live our lives with a concern for others' needs as well as our own, we will never create peace out of the conflict that exists."

Admiring his brother, Josh added, "And knowing the scarcity of truly honest leaders, Mother Theresa said it best: 'Do not wait for leaders; do it alone, person to person.'"

Sister Kathleen nodded in full agreement. "That's exactly what the members of Pax Christi are about."

Referring to the Peace Alliance, Kyle informed the sister that he was currently serving on a board that was promoting the addition of a department of peace to the government.

"I'd strongly support that concept," she said, "particularly if it included our participation in world organizations in a collaborative rather than dominating fashion. There must be a forum for people to talk with each other and work out their differences. It's unrealistic to have all like minds gathered around a table. People who feel isolated need an opportunity to voice their opinions and be heard, even if they're dissonant. In my opinion, the U.S. isn't a democracy; we're an oligarchy. Unless we sit down and talk to people who are *not* like us, how will we ever learn to work out conflicts?"

"A lot of respect has been lost for the United States throughout the world," Josh stated with sadness. "When the 9/11 attacks first happened, the whole world came to our support. But now they feel they've been lied to by the White House. Other countries simply don't trust us to use our power wisely."

"And why should they?" Sister Kathleen responded, throwing her hands in the air. "Of course other nations want nuclear weapons. If the U.S. is going to have a policy of preemptive war, if we're going to have a strike-first policy, why wouldn't other countries want that, too? What we need to ask ourselves is how we get people who disagree to come together in a constructive way to resolve issues. We can point our fingers at other nations, but we're not as pure as we'd like to think we are. We all know that, as individuals, we need to constantly work on ourselves. But the same is true with us as a society, as a nation, as a world community. How can I reflect on the sins of another if I haven't reflected on my own? What's happening in the world at this moment is a social sin of the greatest magnitude."

Kyle was lost in his own thoughts as he reflected back on his decision not to talk to Jenny after their breakup. And yet, at the time, talking seemed to have no redeeming value. Right or wrong, regretfully he could understand a government's reluctance to negotiate.

"Sister Kathleen," Josh said, ""given where we are in Iraq, what would you recommend we do now?""

"I think we need to look at the strengths and values of globalization," she replied. "But we need to replace the need for power and greed by creating a world community. I truly believe that one world government can happen someday. We can find a way with all of our differences—somewhat like the European Union—to develop a way in which individual nations can work within their own construct and, at the same time, work cooperatively with each other. Globalization is not all bad, but it cannot be driven by an attitude of greed that says: 'This is mine, and I'll take yours, too.' A peaceful globalization is one that shares its resources and that truly desires social justice for *all* of humanity, not just for our own country."

As the meeting ended and the brothers acquired one more member for PEACE, Kyle found himself nearly immobilized. So much of what this good sister said hit home with him. Sister Kathleen seemed clear about her philosophy of life, which ran consistently throughout every phase of the world she touched. How he longed for that in his own life: consistency of behavior, consistency of values, consistency in loving a woman. This nun reminded him of Jenny, both of whom had helped open his mind to new ways of thinking . . . on a global front for certain, but even more powerfully on a personal level.

Kyle and Josh watched the replay of a grainy video of Saddam Hussein's final moments. Shortly before dawn on December 30, this tyrant dictator struggled briefly after American military guards handed him over to Iraqi executioners. As masked executioners slipped a noose around his neck, in one last act of defiance, he refused a hood to cover his eyes. In keeping with the philosophy of "an eye for an eye," Saddam faced the same fate he was accused of inflicting on countless thousands during a quarter-century of ruthless power.

"This is not what we are about," Kyle said softly.

The screen transferred to a scene of President Bush speaking from his ranch in Texas. He announced that the execution marked the "end of a difficult year for the Iraqi people and for our troops" but cautioned that Saddam's death would not halt the violence in Iraq.

Thirty-three

Looking for Jenny

When Kyle checked his email while waiting to board United Flight 297 for California, an instant message popped up from Josh.

"HEY, BRO, JUST WANTED TO REMIND YOU NOT TO MISS THE STATE OF THE UNION ADDRESS WHILE YOU'RE OUT OF TOWN."

"WHY WOULD I WANT TO WATCH THAT?"

"SOME OF MY BUDS FROM THE STATE DEPARTMENT SAID THEY RECEIVED A MEMO FROM THE PRESIDENT'S SPEECH WRITER ASKING FOR 'A LINE THAT'LL GUARANTEE THE PRESIDENT A BIPARTISAN STANDING OVATION,'" Josh wrote. "I THINK I FOUND ONE THAT WOULD ABSOLUTELY KEEP BOTH SIDES APPLAUDING 'TIL THEY COULDN'T STAND UP ANYMORE."

"OKAY, LET'S HAVE IT,"

Kyle braced himself for his brother's wit.

"'I HEREBY RESIGN . . .'"

He closed his laptop, laughing until he almost choked. He didn't mind that everyone in the waiting room was eyeing him. Maybe he would watch the address after all. There was always hope.

A well-dressed, middle-aged man with dark hair and glasses approached Kyle and, as the man got closer, Kyle recognized him: Leon Panetta, a distinguished gentleman who had served as part of the Iraq Study Group.

Leon and Kyle had little opportunity to visit during their intense work the previous year. But after a brief discussion, Kyle realized that, besides their time spent together in the ISG meetings, they had met several times at functions in California. He remembered that Leon was best known for his work with civil rights and environmental issues during his nearly two decades of serving in Congress. Since leaving public office, while serving as Fort Ord's chief of operations and planning of the intelligence division, Leon was instrumental in converting the army base into part of the California State University system in Monterey. Afterward, he and his wife founded the Panetta Institute for Public Policy there.

"Are you here in Washington for more meetings regarding your infamous report?" Kyle asked him jokingly.

"Yes, I'm just on my way back home after a meeting with the guy who councils the president on national security affairs," Leon said shaking his head.

"You mean Stepehen Hadley. Man, you look like you've had the bejesus beat out of you."

"Some of the others in our group are taking Bush's disregard of our work better than I am. Even though the Iraq Study Group created seventy-nine recommendations, you may remember that we have three that are the heart and soul of our report that *weren't* included: the drawdown of U.S. troops by next year, the need to penalize the Iraqi government if certain benchmarks aren't met, and the call for diplomacy with Iran and Syria."

"Oh. I remember." Kyle thought back to the long, involved, painstaking meetings he helped facilitate for the Iraq Study Group. He remembered how well Jim Baker and Lee Hamilton chaired the meetings and how the bipartisan representation was the epitome of *negotiated* resolutions. "Those are critical issues to ignore," Kyle continued. "I remember how hard your committee worked to arrive at those proposals. I'd feel kicked in the gut if I were you."

"Mainly I'm offended by the way the administration created the impression that it gave our recommendations serious consideration but really didn't."

"The White House will come around to your recommendations eventually," Kyle reassured Leon. "They'll have to. The Iraq Study Group Report is the only bi-partisan guide that makes any sense."

The two new-found friends boarded the plane and rearranged their seats to sit together. Kyle caught Leon up on his Peace Alliance meeting in California and the PEACE group that he and Josh had formed. Leon asked to be kept in the loop.

The annual board meeting for the Peace Alliance Foundation was in Palo Alto. Kyle felt chills run through him as he set foot back in his home state for the first time in three years. With his mother having passed away, both of his sons away at college, and Josh back in Washington, he had rationalized that there was little reason to return. *Well, maybe one*, he thought.

Walking across the tarmac after his plane landed in the San Francisco airport, he felt good to be back. It was early afternoon, and he had the evening free before the meeting the next morning. He had pondered going to see Jenny while he was there, and she was just a two-hour drive away.

Should he call her? Should he just show up on her doorstep? Was she alone or with someone? Those and other questions ran through his head as he walked to the rental car counter. After getting a car, he headed out to Highway 101. Going south would take him to Palo Alto, and north led to Sacramento. Opting to take a risk, he turned right . . . taking him toward Jenny.

The drive seemed to take no time at all. Kyle made his way down the all-too-familiar tree-lined street in Land Park. He parked the car next to the curb, feeling too presumptuous to park in the driveway. After staring at her house for a few moments, he exited the car and walked up to her front door. His heart was pounding. He said a prayer, asking God to give him strength, and rang the door bell and waited. Nervously, he reached up to give it a second ring when the door opened. It was not Jenny but Chad.

"Uh…hello, Chad."

"Hi, Kyle, it's been a long time." After an awkward pause, Chad invited him in.

"So, where's your mother?" Kyle asked as he stood awkwardly inside the doorway.

"She's been away for nearly a month. I'm just here picking up her mail and stuff."

"Oh? Where is she?"

"Working with the Red Cross. She started with them over a year ago when she went down to work with the Katrina victims in Dallas."

"Is she enjoying Dallas?"

"No, she's not there anymore. She's in Iraq now."

"What?? Iraq?" *Oh, my God,* Kyle thought. "Where? Have you heard from her? Is she okay?"

"Well, it's not easy for her to communicate," Chad told him, "but I've had a couple of emails from her."

"Why? I mean, what's she doing in Iraq? For godsake, people are getting killed by the hundreds over there!"

"She's visiting detainees and providing emergency assistance to Iraqis displaced as a result of the insurgencies and attacks."

"My God, she could be killed! Why is she doing this?"

"To tell the truth, you had a lot to do with it," Chad said.

"Me??"

"She told me you got her thinking about how wrong this war is, and she said she felt called to do something worthwhile with her life. You know how she is when she sets her mind to something."

Boy, do I ever, Kyle thought.

"Is there any way I can reach her?" Kyle asked.

"Well, she doesn't have regular access to a computer."

"But she *has* written to you?" Kyle asked. He longed to read whatever he could from her.

"Mm hmm. Come on, I'll show you what I've gotten so far." Chad led Kyle into the back office and clicked on Microsoft Office Outlook. He did a search and pulled up two messages.

```
-----Original Message-----
To:      Chad
From:    Jenny
Re:      Happy Birthday
Date:    Sun 1/12/2007 3:19 PM
```

Dear Chad,
I just wanted to wish you a happy birthday and let you know I have arrived safely. I'm staying with other Red Cross volunteers in a flat just inside the central area of

Baghdad known as the green zone. Not far away are the main palaces of the former president, Saddam Hussein, which now look like abandoned opulence. I can only imagine what stories those walls could tell.

Most of the U.S. authorities live and work inside this well-guarded area walled off from the rest of Baghdad by coils of razor wire, chain-link fences, and armed checkpoints. Once inside, the streets are closed-off, and people go about their daily business.

My team spends our days going out into other parts of the city. When we leave, we are taken by armored car with an armed military escort. The green zone is one of the nicer parts of Baghdad, even though it has been frequently hit by rocket fire and suicide bombers. Once I leave this complex, the neighborhoods aren't so lovely. You can't even begin to imagine the horror here. The neighborhoods are made up of small, sandy-colored houses. There are people living in them, but they are all boarded up with blinds shut. And these are the lucky ones. The people I am working with have been completely displaced from their homes. I think I had to see this for myself to believe it. So much tragedy. So many tears.

I love you. I will write again when I can. Don't expect it to be too often. The setup here is not exactly a five-star hotel. Take care of yourself and give everyone my love. Mom

Kyle was filled with emotion as Chad pulled up the next email.

-----Original Message-----
To: Chad
From: Jenny
Re: Life in Baghdad
Date: Wed 1/25/2007 6:42 PM

Dear Chad,
How are you, sweetie? I have never been busier in my life. Remember those old World War II movies that we used to watch together? Well, I am definitely in the midst of battle. I feel safe. Really I do. I spend some of my time visiting detainees, as they like to call them, even though they look like prisoners to me. Other times we provide emergency assistance to people who have been displaced. We find

them places to sleep and get them fed. If the wound is simple like when you would skin your knee, I am even playing Florence Nightingale. But there is a pretty good medical staff here that takes care of the more serious injuries.

I've never seen a civil war up close and personal but this definitely seems to go beyond what everyone is calling "sectarian violence." The sad part is that our military have not only fueled the fire; we have given the Iraqis the ammunition with which to kill each other. There are fewer air bombings now, but the ground bombings are still going on. From what some of the wounded tell me, the news back home sugar coats what is really happening here. It's far worse than anything I've ever envisioned.

I am where I belong right now. If this ever calms down, I would love to do what I do best and help educate some of the people who are young enough that there is still a chance to influence their thinking.

I love you, sweetie. Don't do anything I wouldn't do. That should give you a pretty broad range.   Take care of yourself, and I'll write again when I can. Mom

Kyle's face was flushed. He stood in front of the computer, staring at the screen. Finally, he spoke.

"I remember your mom always saying that she felt optimistic as long as she could think of one more step to take that would solve a problem. It was only when she ran out of things to do that she'd let herself get discouraged."

"Yeah, I heard her say that a lot."

"Well, I know how she feels," Kyle said.

Kyle asked about his schooling. Chad proudly reported that he had successfully finished his degree and was now working as a student counselor at Cal State.

Kyle told Chad that he thought his boys might follow in his footsteps and also complete their college education. Then he described the reason he returned to California.

"Wow, a department of peace," Chad pondered. "I never imagined the U.S. could have such a thing. If you need any volunteers with the organization here in Sacramento, it'd be awesome to be a part of it."

Kyle said he'd keep Chad informed, and turned to leave. As Chad walked him to the car, Kyle threw a protective arm around the young man's shoulder, and asked him to keep in touch with any news of Jenny. Then they hugged each other, and Kyle got into his rental car and slowly pulled away. He felt empty inside, and terrified for Jenny's well being.

Had I decided to try to find her even a month ago, she'd still have been here, he thought. *God, my timing sucks.*

As he headed to Palo Alto, he sent up a prayer.

Please, God, please keep Jenny safe.

Thirty-four

Jenny in Iraq

The short time Jenny had been with the International Committee of the Red Cross had been the most transforming of her life. Other than living as a tourist in a safeguarded American hotel, she had never spent time in third-world countries. Living and working in the Middle East was taking her out of her sheltered environment and opening her up to a far more expansive worldview. She hadn't actually seen the carnage of the war—only the aftermath: The abandoned homes, the burned buildings and cars, the homeless wandering the streets. There was little local news of the disasters but she kept up by reading reports on the Internet.

Some aspects of the war, however, were kept out of even Internet news reports, the most disturbing of which was the large, shadow army hired by the Bush administration. These private military contractors— about one hundred thousand in number—were granted impunity from their actions. Their deaths and injuries they caused were not counted and their crimes went unpunished. Shrouded in secrecy, the contractors were shielded from any effective oversight or accountability. It wasn't until 2004 that the public even became aware of their existence when four of its employees were captured, killed and burned by a mob in the Sunni city of Fallujah a large town about forty miles west of Baghdad.

What Jenny hadn't understood until arriving in Iraq was that event was the day the war turned. The Bush administration had issued a

massive revenge attack for the murdered contractors. The military laid
siege to the city of Fallujah, killed hundreds of people, and displaced
thousands more. And more recently, one of the contractor's convoys
indiscriminately and unnecessarily killed eight Iraqi civilians. If tension
wasn't already strained enough, this gave Iraqi citizens even more
reason to hate America.

Sporadically, Jenny was able to keep in touch with Chad and a few
of her friends via email although she omitted many details in her
correspondence, sharing with them only her supposed safety being in
the green zone.

Jenny was especially struck by the diversity of women's self-images
in Iraq. Some were university professors who dressed professionally
and were respected for their knowledge and talents. Some wore
makeup. Others did not, considering it an offense to their religious
beliefs. Most dressed tastefully in skirts and blouses. About half of the
women wore head scarves with regular clothing while others, mostly
older women, were in head scarves and loose fitting black robes, in
keeping with the more traditional beliefs held by their husbands or
families. Jenny dressed inconspicuously, in jeans and tennis shoes,
usually wearing her hair in a ponytail with Chapstick and sunscreen as
her only makeup.

Her roommate, Karima, was an Iraqi woman who went to work for
the Red Cross in hopes of improving the plight of women in her
country. About ten years younger than Jenny, she spoke perfect
English and was able to explain to Jenny some of the issues that Iraqi
women faced.

"Many Iraqi women were hopeful when the elections occurred,
believing that women's rights would come to the forefront," Karima
told her. "But in reality, under Islamic law, women were better off
under the Ba'ath party regime than now. Since the new government
took over four years ago, women are less protected in the work
environment and some feel pressured to go back to wearing the veil."

"I'm surprised," Jenny responded. "Reading the news reports at
home, I got the impression you were making some headway with
women's issues."

"Freedom is so much in the mind," Karima explained, "so what it
means to women here varies from one extreme to the other. Some are

perfectly content to wear the *hijab* as a sign of modesty but they are still fighting for equal pay, maternity leave, and reduced work hours during pregnancy. Others have set their sights higher. They want to serve in an elected capacity and have equal rights to men."

"It's similar to American women," Jenny replied. "It's been less than a hundred years since we've been allowed to vote and look how far we've come since then. Over twenty years ago, a woman in the U.S. was chosen to run for the vice presidency, although she didn't win. And today a woman, Hillary Clinton, is actually a frontrunner for the presidency. It just takes time."

"Would this woman make a good president?" Karima asked.

"She could win the nomination but I think she's less likely to win the election," Jenny said.

"I bet she has strong backing from women," Karima said, imagining how passionately women would support a woman leader in Iraq.

"Surprisingly not," Jenny exclaimed. "A large percentage of women and the majority of men have declared they will vote for 'anyone but Hillary'. She has knowledge and experience but many are not happy with her support for this war and her lack of authenticity. Many see her as a chameleon adapting herself to be whatever it takes to win votes."

"So if she's chosen by her party, what is her biggest challenge?" Karima asked.

"Sixteen years of Clintons and twelve years of Bushes is seen as too much power for two families. But mostly they fear that her presidency would polarize our country. Unlike her Democrat counterparts, the Clintons have old baggage that'd be used as ammunition against her."

Struggling with her own desire to see women advance in her country, Karima asked, "Don't you want to see a woman as your president?"

"Of course, but after the devastation of our current administration, most Americans are looking for someone who can unite our country and bring about change. This does not appear to be her persona. She is extremely controversial. But, if she should become the first woman leader of the free world, Iraq will be her first call to action."

"I know many women in Iraq who would be effective in office. And they are very clear about their stance on issues—not just women's issues, but matters of human dignity, secular versus Islamic law, even sectarian and international relations."

Jenny greatly admired her new friend. "Karima, it will be because of women like you, with convictions and dedication, that women will eventually be emancipated in Iraq. Don't give up your dream."

"Despite their reserved demeanor, women are quite savvy here, Jenny. One good thing that's come out of the new government is the increased attendance of students at the university here. And the education offered is high caliber."

"Education is the only way we can ever change the cycle of poverty and violence," Jenny said. "Slum education begets slum jobs, begets slum living, begets poor people's children receiving slum education. It's a never-ending cycle unless it's broken at the educational level."

"Jenny, I have a friend who's a history professor at the University of Baghdad, and his class this morning is comparing the Vietnam War to this war. Would you like to attend? It's a small group of students, and I'm sure he wouldn't mind us sitting in."

"We've got time now before our team goes out today," Jenny said excitedly, looking at her watch. "Let's go."

A Red Cross driver took them to the university, passing through the cement wall topped with barbed wire and the heavily guarded security point of their semi-protected green zone and headed south to drop the two women in front of the liberal arts building. Stepping out of the car, Jenny thought how much the setting resembled many campuses in the states.

Like the river setting of Sacramento State at home, the grounds were nestled in the curve of the Tigris River. Students were milling about in front of the brick building with heavy ornate iron grating on the front. The attire was different: no low-cut jeans and bare midriffs. Most of the girls were wearing skirts and blouses with no veil, and the boys were dressed in shirts and casual slacks. Jenny scurried inside, following Karima up the stairs. Karima introduced Jenny to the professor, who invited both women to join the circle of about a dozen students. Class was ready to begin.

"In light of our American friend visiting today, let's begin by addressing the issue of what it's like for you to come to class in the midst of this war," the professor opened.

Karima translated this for Jenny, who bowed to the class in appreciation.

One of the students, Yassar, responded in reasonably good English. "Imagine you arrive on campus day to find out that the dean of your program has been—" Yassar then spoke a word to the professor that Jenny didn't understand.

"Assassinated," the professor told him.

"Yes, the dean has been assassinated and another student, your friend, who recently completed his course work, has been murdered before even receiving his diploma," Yassar continued.

Jenny couldn't imagine being a student in such an environment.

Another student, Mohammed, raised his hand, and the professor nodded to him. He spoke in Arabic, and Karima translated. "Every day I feel anxious. I worry for my family. I attend the university because it is my only hope for improving our lives."

Jenny wanted to reach out and hold him or, better yet, take him by the hand and walk him home from school. Meet his family. Somehow assure them that life would be better.

Moving on to the topic of the class, the professor raised the question of whether the students saw any comparison between the Iraq war and that of Vietnam.

Yassar spoke up again. "In both times, the U.S. military is quick to find a reason to go to war."

As the discussion continued and Karima quietly translated, Jenny heard bombs going off in the distance. No one seemed to react.

Responding to the look of concern on Jenny's face, Yassar said, "Of course bombs worry us, but we're used to them."

"Will you stay here after you finish your schooling?" Jenny inquired of the group.

Most everyone nodded yes. A young girl, who identified herself as Sabeen, spoke up. "These explosions have united us here as much as the sectarian violence is dividing them out there."

It suddenly dawned on Jenny that these students sitting in front of her were not merely from one sect. They were Sunnis, Shiites, and Kurds—all sitting together in one classroom exploring ideas together. That's what Sabeen meant by feeling united.

"I feel like I'm the one who got the education today," Jenny said to Karima as they were driven back along the Qadisiya Expressway to their headquarters.

When they reach the security gate, there was commotion on both sides of the cement wall. Militia, police, and ambulances were blocking their entrance. They waited patiently until they were waved through and told that a bomb had exploded in the parliament's cafeteria. So far, two people were found dead and 10 were seriously wounded.

And this is within the safety of the green zone, Jenny thought. She said a quick prayer as their driver pulled up in front of the Red Cross headquarters and she was able to confirm that her co-workers were not in harm's way.

"Thank you for taking me there today," Jenny told Karima as they walked to meet their team. "Just look what can happen when differing sects are brought together in one room to discuss their views." She thought back to a movie, *Silent Night*, which she saw several years earlier on a forlorn Christmas morning. The same message was depicted in that storyline as she had witnessed firsthand today.

While waiting for her team to gather at the Red Cross headquarters, Jenny found a rare opportunity to access a computer. She immediately sent an email to Chad telling him not to worry about her if the story was broadcast on the news, that she and the Red Cross volunteers were not in the vicinity of the blast. She asked his prayers for those injured and killed. Next, checking the general Red Cross email, she found a response from an Iraqi man with whom she had corresponded. His brother had been imprisoned for almost two years.

> Thank you for your email and your concern about my brother, Ali. There is no change and no development in the case. And it is very difficult to visit him because he is now in Camp Sather. Sunnis face many problems when they try to go there to visit their relatives. Besides, it is very difficult to get permission from American soldiers to cross

Shiite territory. Now we have lost hope of getting to see
him again.

Jenny made a mental note to seek out the man's brother on her
next visit to Camp Sather.

Walking into the common room, still waiting for the rest of her team
to arrive, Jenny let her fingers brush the spines of old reports stacked on
the bookshelf. One of the files caught Jenny's attention. It was submitted
from Amnesty International to express concern to U.S. authorities
regarding their use of a restraint chair for detainees. Someone had
photographed an individual—reportedly a juvenile detained in maximum
security at Abu Ghraib prison—strapped into a four-point restraint chair.
Military police reportedly said that he was being "punished for
disrespecting them" and would remain for two hours in the chair.

Jenny knew there was no accurate account of how many juveniles
were being detained at this time but, according to one of the reports, at
the end of September 2005 there were about 200 held by the multi-
national forces. These young people were scheduled to be transferred
to the jurisdiction of the new Iraqi government. Jenny asked one of her
co-workers and the man explained that, given their life exposure in
Iraq, a 15 or 16-year-old was just as capable of insurgency as an adult.

After weeks of fighting bureaucracy, Jenny finally won permission
to visit with a few teenage Iraqi boys being held at Abu Ghraib. The
detention center was just a few miles southwest of the green zone.
When her group arrived at the prison, they spread out to visit as many
detainees as they could. At last, after so many tries, Jenny found herself
in a conference room waiting for two boys to be escorted in.

An Iraqi guard led them into the barren room and sat them at the
beat up table. The boys' wrists and ankles were cuffed. Jenny nodded
to the guard, indicating that she would be fine if left alone with them.
Over the years of her work in radio, Jenny had developed her
interviewing skills. Her strength was getting guests to speak candidly
about personal issues. She knew that getting these boys to open up
would not be easy. Reluctantly, they told her that their names were
Hakim and Gabir. Hakim was the more outgoing of the two.

"You both seem so young. Why are you in prison?" Jenny asked.

Looking down at the floor, the boys shrugged their shoulders.

"How long have you been held captive?"

Hakim, whose English was better than Gabir's, spoke angrily, indicating that they had been held for a few months by American soldiers before being transferred to Abu Ghraib two years ago. Since being turned over to the Iraqi ministry, they had been allowed to see their families, but only on rare occasions. When Jenny asked, Gabir acknowledged that he had been in "the chair." He described, more with his hands than words, how painful and horrifying the experience was for him. He prayed he would never have to face that again.

"What do you do all day?" Jenny asked.

Again, looking down at the floor, they shrugged their shoulders. Hakim spoke up and explained that occasionally they were allowed to study, and a teacher came in to give them homework. But that didn't happen often. Other times, they were given dirty jobs to do like cleaning toilets—jobs that were beneath the guards.

"What were you doing when you were arrested?" Jenny had saved this question until she thought they might trust her enough to tell her the truth.

The boys looked at each other, and Hakim answered. "We were helping our father fight for our families. We are Sunnis and, since the attack here, everything has been taken from us. We lived a normal life before. Now, with the Shiites in charge, we are treated badly. We have nothing. No money. No food. Our mother is mistreated, too."

"You're brothers?"

They glanced at each other and nodded somberly.

"Can you help get us out of here? We've done nothing wrong," Hakim whispered.

Gabir wiped a tear off his cheek. Jenny felt convinced that, given half a chance and some extended time with these young people, she could help to educate and rehabilitate them, benefiting them far more than being strapped in a restraint chair or made to fight an unwinnable war. She could picture them sitting in the classroom with the students she had met this morning. Before she left, Jenny promised to do everything she could for them and to visit again soon.

Thirty-five

Department of Peace

Before leaving Sacramento, Kyle stopped by the governor's mansion. Kyle was invited to seat himself in the living room to wait for Governor Bradley.

"Good to see you, Kyle," Jed said when he entered the room. They exchanged a warm hug, and the governor joined Kyle on the couch. Kyle filled him in on the past three years and his work with the U.S. Institute of Peace.

"More power to you, my boy. I personally have no objection to your attempts to work things out non-violently. Obviously, if it can be done, it should be the first course pursued. I've just always had my beliefs that there are certain people, certain terrorists, and certain foreign heads of state with whom you simply cannot negotiate."

Kyle described the board meeting that he had come to Sacremento to attend. The meeting's objective was to urge Congress to establish a Department of Peace.

"That sounds mighty idealistic," Jeb told him. "Don't you think we have enough internal problems within our government as it is? It sounds like you are going to end up pitting the Department of Defense against the Department of Peace. When President Bush appealed to congressmen to support his war on Iraq, he told them that relying on diplomatic and other peaceful means alone wouldn't protect the United States against the continuing threat posed by Iraq. After all, who will carry the ultimate authority to decide when it's time for the peace department to step aside and the defense department to take over?"

"As it is now, Jed, I don't think anyone calling the shots at the Pentagon has even considered a peaceful solution, much less taken tangible steps in that direction. America spends more on its military than all other countries in the world combined. No country does this merely for protection or even for peace. The way we see it, we need another segment in our government that will look for other avenues. And now with Rumsfeld out of the way, that just may be possible."

"Let me ask you, son: if the administration knew that there was no threat of weapons of mass destruction and they knew Hussein had no ties to bin Laden, then why did they invade Iraq?"

"Why? Pure and simple: to protect our oil rights and to establish a power base in the Middle East. But I don't think they ever thought it was going to be so costly, both in terms of the hundreds of thousands of lives and the billions of dollars."

"But why wage a war to safeguard what we already have protected under oil contracts?" the governor asked. "It doesn't make sense."

"Contracts can be broken. Other countries, like China, are building eight-lane freeways where their little cobblestone roads used to be. Don't you think *they* are going to need some of that oil? Don't you think American businesses and consumers might suffer if the Middle East should decide to trade with someone else?"

"But China isn't limited; they can turn to other sources, like the Saudis," the governor countered.

"Yes, and in the likely event that the relationship we now enjoy with the Saudis comes to an end, China has positioned itself as the next likely favored partner to consume Saudi oil, Jed. The next president, whoever he or she may be, will be ensconced in making sure that America has enough energy. We can consider ourselves lucky if we don't end up in a world oil war."

"I supported Bush because I think he's a good man with some basic Christian values," Jed said. "I'd like to believe something better of him. But, I must admit, even I am becoming disillusioned."

"I don't see him as a bad man," Kyle conceded. "Weak, perhaps, and certainly not the world's brightest president. But he is responsible for surrounding himself with strong-willed men who had an agenda, men who took him along for the ride. Once that course was set, Bush was like a dog with a bone."

"He's certainly put himself on the line defending this war, which to most of us seems pretty indefensible."

"More like unconscionable," Kyle said. "Jed, I'm so angry about our government and what we're doing with our wealth and power. I have to do something to try to stop this insanity."

"What do you think it's going to take to turn things around?"

"It'll take more than just throwing out the neocons. There also has to be a change in the mindset of the American people. Our country represents less than five percent of the earth's population yet consumes one-quarter of its energy. Poor nations can't get what they need, and their citizens suffer because America's greed demands so much. We have to begin sharing our resources, cutting back on our extravagances, and thinking about other nations that are less fortunate than we are. For that matter, we have to begin doing the same here at home. How can the wealthy in America be so focused on preserving their own little empires, —so worried about their taxes being raised—that they are blind to those losing their homes, working for minimum wage, and, going without healthcare for themselves and their children. Don't they feel any responsibility to balance the scale . . . even a little bit? And when they support the continuation of the war with no end in sight, where do they think that money is coming from?"

"I will say one thing for President Bush. He deserves credit that something he has done has prevented another attack on us like 9/11. But even as a crusty old Republican, I can understand your passion and determination, Kyle. When I signed on another lifetime ago, the Grand Old Party was about lower taxes and less government. With the trillions of dollars being poured into this war, that vision got lost somewhere along the way. . . . Do you have anyone in mind who can carry out your vision in the coming election?"

Kyle shared with the governor that he and Josh had scheduled a meeting with Senator Barack Obama.

"This may surprise you," the governor said, "but I can't find anything wrong with this young man. Maybe only that he *is* a bit young and still inexperienced in running a government."

"Jed, Bush put *experienced* men around him," Kyle retorted, "and look where that got him. Obama is older than John Kennedy when he was elected president. But, more importantly, he has showed sound judgment . . . enough to speak out against waging war in Iraq months before the actual invasion and at a time when popular wisdom was rallying support behind the president. "

The governor nodded, taking in Kyle's words.

"I find his ideas about bringing change to the way politics is conducted to be refreshing," Kyle continued. "Adhering to the constitution—imagine; challenging the control special interest groups have over Washington; sifting down the needless layers of medical care so as to make it more efficient and more cost effective; giving college kids help with their tuition but asking them to give something back to their country when they graduate. He seems to be addressing the ordinary day-to-day needs of people struggling to survive. He's not afraid to take a stand on any issue. I get the feeling that what he says is really what he thinks, regardless of whether it will win him votes or not. I'm really looking forward to meeting him in person."

"Kyle, you know you're like a son to me. And I admire your passion. I always have. I'm not as sure about these things as you are, but on the other hand, you raise some mighty good points."

"I appreciate your friendship, Jed. I really did want to talk this over with you just so I could get your perspective."

"You're an intelligent and competent man, Kyle. If I'd had a son, I'd have liked him to be just like you."

"Surely he would have loftier goals than mine," Kyle said humorously. "Jed, if I were half as good in my personal life as I am in my professional life, then I might accept what you say."

"So how's your personal life, Kyle? Whatever happened to Jenny? I always liked that girl."

Kyle explained the situation and concluded by telling him that she is in Iraq.

"So I guess you're putting it on your shoulders that somehow you drove her there?"

"No, Jenny is there because of her own convictions. I just want a chance to talk with her and apologize for my part in what happened with us. It was all about my pain. I just couldn't empathize with hers. I want her to know . . ."

"Sounds like all this peace work has rubbed off on you. Let me make a call to the Red Cross office here. I may be able to get more information about where she is and how you can reach her."

Kyle thanked Jed for everything he had been to him over the years and, with thoughts weighing him down, made the two-hour drive back to Palo Alto.

The next morning, Kyle walked into a room where about two dozen people were gathered. Maneuvering his way to a table with coffee, he poured himself a cup of the roasted java from one of the metal dispensers.

A man approached him and let Kyle know how much he has been missed. "Senator Feinstein may make it here today," the man said. "She's been weighing the pros and cons of this proposal for some time. She seems really frustrated with the president's vetoes over every bill Congress passes. His entrenched position may have finally pushed her over to our side."

"Her support would certainly step up our cause. It's obvious that we need the backing of more congressional leaders like her."

Kyle was new to the board and not nearly as familiar with the campaign as he should be. With the news of Jenny being in Iraq, Kyle found it difficult at first to focus on the foundation meeting. But as the agenda was laid out and the meeting was called to order, he found himself enthralled with the speaker who was approaching the front of the room. A petite, slender woman with shoulder-length brunette hair, Marianne Williamson was introduced as the chair of the Peace Alliance and welcomed everyone and she began by explaining their campaign.

"As many of you know, the Peace Alliance will be gathering in Washington, D.C., next week to support the proposal for a U. S. Department of Peace," Williamson announced. "During the twentieth century, over a hundred million people—mostly noncombatants—

have lost their lives to war. Now we're well into the twenty-first century, and the extent and current speed of nuclear proliferation makes the achievement of non-violent alternatives to war the most urgent need of the human race."

Kyle listened attentively as she spoke. He made a mental note to alert all the members of PEACE about the rally.

"Peace is more than the absence of war; it is a positive state of being predicated on the presence of a peaceful heart," Williamson said. Then she reminded the audience that there was a long history of legislation dedicated to creating a department of peace, actually originating with Benjamin Rush, one of the signers of the Declaration of Independence. Over the years, there had been repeated attempts to introduce bills calling for such a department. Most recently, in September 2005, legislation was introduced in both the House and the Senate to create a Department of Peace and Nonviolence. But the bill hadn't yet been debated or voted on. "With the support of Congressman Dennis Kucinich, we now have hope," Williamson concluded. "He personally wrote our current bill before Congress."

Kyle felt someone slide into the seat next to him; then he felt a tap on his shoulder. He looked around to see Dianne Feinstein. "And Kucinich is preparing another calling for the impeachment of Vice President Cheney," she said to Kyle as they applauded the presentation and Williamson left the dais.

"That's long overdue," Kyle remarked. "Cheney should be tried for war crimes and violating the constitution."

Feinstein nodded in agreement. "Welcome home, stranger. It's good to see you back in your home state."

"So what's your take on this Dianne?"

"Well, Kyle, diplomacy is the order of the day. I don't know what the United States thinks it is—keeper of all the world, apparently. If we can't get along with a government, we've got to change that government . . . but to do so by preemptive war is the wrong choice. I think diplomacy needs to work to its fullest. I think we need to put some of our best diplomatic minds forward and sit down with people and solve this situation. Stop Bush from anymore saber-rattling. It seems that these days all America knows is the threat of force when, in fact, that is just *one* thing. And it should be the *last* thing. Why we have always moved it up to the very first thing, I don't know. But it's a mistake. It's a mistake for our future and it's a mistake for America's presence in the world today."

"Well, if you are going to say a few words to the group, I guess I don't have to stick around to learn how you really feel."

The senator laughed. "The real reason I'm here is to make a recommendation to this group for the person whom I think would best serve as the first Secretary of Peace. So, Mr. Former Attorney General, or whatever official name you go by these days, if nominated, would you serve?"

Kyle was caught off-guard, honored, and unsure that he was up for it—all in one breath. The room's lights were dimming, and an image appeared on the presentation screen as Marianne Williamson returned to the dais. Kyle looked up at the screen and imagined the emblem being a part of the U.S. government . . . and his office.

With the senator from California sitting by his side, Kyle watched as the plan was laid out to establish a cabinet-level department in the executive branch of the federal government. The secretary of peace would be appointed by the president and confirmed by the senate. The department would include pursuing both domestic and international peace. Kyle noted that some of the initiatives—such as conflict prevention and dispute resolution—bore similar resemblance to the program he established before leaving his AG position. Kyle listened carefully as Williamson spoke.

"In a case in which a conflict between the United States and any other government or entity is imminent or occurring, the secretary of defense and the secretary of state shall consult with the secretary of peace concerning nonviolent means of conflict resolution."

Dianne nudged Kyle. "I really like that part . . . and here comes the best part." Kyle looked up the see the slide indicating that the cost for the department would be "equal to two percent of the total amount appropriated for a fiscal year for the Department of Defense. The present Department of Defense budget is $400 billion. The proposed Department of Peace budget is $8 billion."

"That's less than what Halliburton 'misplaced' in its Iraq reconstruction budget," Kyle whispered to Dianne. "How could anybody object to that?"

The vision of the concept was so much more developed than Kyle had even dreamed. He was beside himself with excitement, eager to get the information back to Josh and incorporate it into their foreign policy plan.

Then Dianne was called to the dais. After delivering essentially the same message she shared with Kyle, Feinstein concluded, "Recognizing that the appointment of the secretary of peace is a presidential decision requiring senate approval, we anticipate that a new president will be open to a recommendation. After due consideration, it is my proposal that Kyle Anderson be the alliance's nominee."

"All in favor," Marianne said.

A thunderous "aye" echoed throughout the room.

Kyle was humbled by the confidence shown in him. For him, an appointment of this magnitude overshadowed any previous elected post for which he had ever served. If his appointment was confirmed, he vowed to serve with all the energy and passion that was within him.

Back in Washington, Kyle was intrigued with the presidential candidates emerging on the scene. Josh and Kyle had organized what they had learned from their interviews into a new foreign policy plan. One by one, the brothers were personally introducing the PEACE plan to each candidate. The depth and thoughtfulness that the twins had given to the plan could not be missed and precluded any prospective leader from treating it lightly. In turn, they had the opportunity to gain a sense of each candidate and anticipate which ones might be open-minded and ready to take the leadership of the country to a new level.

The PEACE plan seemed to fit particularly well with the platforms of Senator Obama and former Senator Edwards and, of course, Congressman Kucinich. In light of those candidates' plans, the brothers had scheduled interviews with each of them. Both Josh and Kyle agreed that with so many solid candidates in the running, the Democrats would have to shoot themselves in the foot to lose the 2008 election. But with still a year and half to go before the election, who knew what other candidate might step out from the wings? However, one thing was clear: the Republican Party would be a long time recovering from the destructiveness caused by the Bush administration.

At Marianne Williamson's suggestion, Kyle met with Dennis Kucinich early after his return from California. He found the congressman to be a man of peace and a true advocate of peace, as Sister Kathleen had stressed in their interview. He could well understand why Kucinich had introduced the bill establishing a department of peace into the House.

Next, the brothers had a rousing meeting with John Edwards and his wife, Elizabeth. Like the Kennedys, they were wealthy but committed to bringing the two Americas—the America of the haves and the America of the have-nots—into greater alliance. They had created a strong email campaign and, with John *not* in the Senate, he could afford to be more vocal about what Congress should be doing to end U.S. participation in the war in Iraq.

Both Kyle and Josh grew more excited as they anticipated their interview with Barack Obama. Both brothers held the deepest respect for him. Arriving at his office on the Hill, the senator, instead of speaking to them across his desk, joined them in a nearby seating area.

"So, where would you like to begin?" Barack asked them with a warm smile.

"I guess all things begin and end with Iraq these days," Josh said. "Let's start there."

"You know my position," said Obama. "I think it's safe to assume that those in power would think longer and harder about launching a war if they envisioned their own sons and daughters in harm's way."

Kyle thought about his own boys and nodded. He could not imagine the pain he would feel if anything were to happen to them.

"I believe a stronger sense of empathy would tilt the balance of our current politics in favor of those people who are struggling in this society," the senator added.

"Do you feel empathy for the president?" Kyle asked, not meaning for it to be a trick question.

"I am obligated to try to see the world through George Bush's eyes, no matter how much I may disagree with him. That's what empathy does—it calls us all to task, the conservative and the liberal, the powerful and the powerless, the oppressed and the oppressor. We're all shaken out of our complacency. We're all forced to look beyond our limited vision."

Kyle understood in very personal terms exactly what the senator was describing. He reflected on his lack of empathy for Jenny on the day her mother died, and on the day of Mike's burial. He regretted that he wasn't shaken out of his complacency and self-absorption then. But he could feel it now. He could feel so much more now.

Regaining his focus, Kyle raised the issue of oil. "We produce about three percent and use about twenty-five percent of the world's supply of oil. If this current war isn't about oil, the next one will be. With China and India adding millions of cars to the road and expanding their need for oil, what do you propose that we do to prevent an all-out oil war?"

"It's safe to say that without any changes to our energy policy, U.S. demand for oil will jump forty percent over the next twenty years," Barack answered. "And over the same period, worldwide demand is expected to jump at least thirty percent for the very reasons you state. I'd suggest that we need to do a complete turnabout. Instead of subsidizing the oil industry, we should end every tax break the industry currently receives and demand that one percent of the revenues from oil companies with over $1 billion in quarterly profits go toward financing alternative energy research."

"Finding a sensible solution to our oil crisis will have a direct effect on our economy," Josh said.

"Absolutely! And on our national security! A large portion of the $800 million we spend on foreign oil every day goes to some of the world's most volatile regimes—Saudi Arabia, Nigeria, Venezuela, and, indirectly at least, Iran. They get our money because we need their oil."

"Are you optimistic about the long-term prospects for our economy?" Josh asked.

"Within the coming year, this will be the issue on everyone's mind," Barack predicted. "My greatest concern is for the lower and middle-class Americans who are worried about their jobs, their mortgages, and their healthcare coverage."

"Specifically, what can you do about this as president?" Josh asked.

"Nearly two-thirds of Americans do not itemize their taxes. I'll make it just as easy for them to take advantage of deducting their mortgage interest. I'll restore fairness to the tax code and provide 150 million U.S. workers with the tax relief they deserve by offsetting the payroll tax on the first several thousand dollars of their earnings. Of course, I will eliminate the ridiculous income taxes for seniors who make less than $50,000. And if the healthcare package that we have in Congress is good enough for us, it should be available and affordable to all Americans."

"Do you think the U.S. can ever really compete in a free trade environment?" Kyle asked.

"Yes, but only if we distribute the costs and benefits of globalization more fairly across the population. If we stay on the course we're on, we'll become a nation even more stratified economically and socially than we currently are, one in which an increasingly prosperous class will be able to purchase whatever it wants in the marketplace—private schools, private health care, private security, and private jets—while a growing number of citizens are consigned to low-paying service jobs, pressed to work longer hours, and dependent on an under-funded, overburdened public sector for health care, retirement, and their children's education."

"Back to Iraq for a moment," Josh said. "Now that we're there, are we stuck there indefinitely?"

"Contrary to some of my esteemed Republican colleagues," Obama said with a grin, "I don't believe it's an option for us to maintain an indefinite occupation in Iraq so that we are sending $100 billion to Iraq every year; so that every year we are watching hundreds if not thousands of Americans die; so that we continue to see a deterioration of America's standing in the world. I don't think that serves the best interest of the United States and its citizens, and it would certainly be the wrong message to send to the Iraqi government."

"So, if you are sworn in as president in 2009 and the situation is still essentially the same in Iraq, what'll be your first steps?" Kyle asked.

"We have to be as careful getting out as we were careless getting in," Obama replied. "We would want to pull our combat troops out of Iraq in a phased, systematic way. I have a bill before Congress now that suggests we begin getting them out this year and have them all out by next year. If the Iraqi government meets certain benchmarks, we would continue to provide the country with logistical and training support. We would have the necessary forces to respond to the crises that spill over into the remainder of the region. And, most importantly, we would have to have an aggressive diplomatic initiative with all countries in the region to make sure that we are a part of a broader conversation about how we can stabilize Iraq and the region."

"That sounds like the main guidelines recommended by the Iraq Study Group," Kyle said.

The senator nodded as he smiled.

"Senator, you've also talked about our need to broaden the distribution of opportunity for all Americans," Josh said, "but how?"

"At the end of Bill Clinton's presidency," Obama explained, "we had the answer. Even after the economy was forced to absorb the shock of 9/11, we had the chance to make a downpayment on sustained economic growth that would have provided a broader opportunity for all Americans."

"But that's not the path Bush chose," Kyle noted.

The senator's secretary then appeared at the door to signal his next appointment. Turning back to the brothers, he answered, "No, instead we were told by our president that we could fight two wars, increase our military budget by seventy-four percent, protect our homeland, spend more on education, introduce a new prescription drug plan for seniors, and initiate a successive round of massive tax cuts—all at the same time."

"I guess that pretty well sums it up," Josh said.

Obama looked poignantly at the brothers. "Gentlemen, it's time for us to return our government to one that truly represents *all* Americans, but we must recognize what Martin Luther King described as 'the fierce urgency of now.' I'm running for president because I believe we find ourselves in a moment of great challenge and great promise—a moment that comes along only once in a generation. From what I've read, you've drafted an excellent foreign policy that addresses the key issues today." The men stood to shake hands and Obama thanked them for their time, agreeing to be a part of the PEACE effort.

Out in the parking lot, Josh, looking more serious than usual, turned to his brother. "This man is the best of JFK and MLK combined. Can you imagine running our country based on his values?"

"Can you imagine *living our lives* based on these kinds of values?" Kyle countered. "Barack Obama won't take PAC money. He was a constitutional lawyer and actually believes in the Constitution. He is the voice of integrity that America needs in these critical times."

"Well, we can't change American politics overnight, but we sure as hell can begin taking some kind of action ourselves," Josh vowed.

You're absolutely right, Josh, Kyle thought. *It's time to take action.*

The following week, Josh was keyed up to get things moving forward but frustrated by the proceedings going on in Congress. He complained to a colleague.

"Withdraw troops? No, increase troops. Debate the issue? No, debate whether to debate the debating of the issue! How frickin' pointless is all of that?"

"I loved Senator Harry Reid's comment today in reference to Bush," his colleague replied. "'He is *president* of the United States, not *king* of the United States.' Bush has to learn to work with somebody. He may have veto power, but he doesn't get to play emperor and completely ignore Congress *and* the American people."

Kyle was pleased when Congress was at last able to agree to a *binding* resolution that tied additional funding for Iraq to combat troops being brought home by a set time.

"Finally!" Kyle exclaimed to Millie. "What took them so long? The president may veto their resolution but at least they've agreed on one."

"There're rumblings that a number of Republicans are getting restless," Millie told him. "I hear they're planning a meeting with the president to express their fear of losing their seats in 2008. And there are rumors that more than one Republican is considering a serious run for the presidency as an Independent," Millie said.

Kyle saw all of this as positive and anticipated there would be many Independents and Republicans shifting their party loyalty.

"Well, whether or not Democrats win this round with the president, each veto by Bush and each new set of floor debates are bringing both sides of Congress closer to a united front. Things are set in motion for a new regime to take over in 2009 and introduce a new kind of politics in America. Barack Obama could do for our generation what my hero, President Kennedy, did nearly half a century ago."

Opposing arguments continued to run rampant between Congress and the White House. And the deployment of more U.S. forces in Iraq continued to draw hostile responses from around the world. Nearly thirty six hundred American soldiers had died, another thirty thousand wounded, and thousands upon thousands of civilians continued to die as abuses were being propagated from all sides. Despite the world situation, for the first time in years, Kyle Anderson felt at peace with himself and with the direction of his life.

Thirty-six

Pilgrim Soul

Jenny was being drawn more and more into her work with detainees. The next afternoon, she found a free moment to continue to explore the old reports. She desperately wanted to understand the circumstances behind the detainee system in Iraq and its handling of inmates. She read testimony made by Major General Antonio Taguba before the Senate Armed Services Committee. His report on the U.S.-run prison complex at Abu Ghraib found numerous "sadistic, blatant and wanton criminal abuses," and its release created worldwide outcry. As she scanned the report, she learned that he found our government's policies tragic and devastating to America as the beacon of democracy. Not surprising, soon after, he lost his job because of his forthrightness.

In one of the U.S. government's periodic memorandums to the U.N. Committee Against Torture, Jenny learned that Dick Cheney played an early role in revamping the torture rules permitting interrogators to go well beyond the human treatment guidelines set forth by the Geneva Conventions. She read that Rumsfeld had said he didn't consider U.S. soldiers who *see* inhumane treatment of detainees to have any obligation to intervene to stop it. She was appalled, and relieved that Rumsfeld was gone. Further down in the report, she learned that Rumsfeld admitted that, a few months after the war began, he had ordered military officials to detain a senior member of Ansar al-Islam without listing him in the prison's register.

Several members of this administration right up to the top should be tried for war crimes, Jenny thought.

In visiting with many of the detainees and their families, Jenny had learned that the practice of holding detainees in secret, with no contact with the outside world, created extreme hardship on their families as well as placing the prisoners outside the protection of the law. They had no access to lawyers, doctors, or even their families. They were unable to challenge their arrest or detention, and the lawfulness of it was not assessed by any judge.

The secrecy of their detention allowed the concealment of all further human rights violations they suffered, including torture or ill treatment, and allowed governments to evade accountability. It was obvious to Jenny that any deprivation of liberty, even when carried out in accordance with international humanitarian law, inevitably caused some degree of mental suffering to the internee and his family. But *indefinite* detention was horrific, especially for those who had been held for more than two years. What bothered Jenny was that these so called "ghost detainees" were being hidden to prevent even her and fellow Red Cross workers from visiting them. And when she learned that much of the detainee interrogation had been carried out by private contractors who were exempt from all prosecution, she became even more outraged.

When Karima entered the room, Jenny looked up from what she was reading.

"We have to do something about these injustices," she pleaded. "As part of the Red Cross, we are supposed to be able to help protect these prisoners."

Karima told her that the Red Cross had tried to intervene by submitting regular reports to the coalition forces. "We described the situation in detail and we actually got the attention of the secretary to the U.N. He was extremely concerned about the prolonged detention of so many without due process. But somehow the U.S. always manages to override the United Nations and convince it that detainees have full access to lawyers and their rights are being met under the Geneva Conventions."

"I understand now why when detained Iraqis are lucky enough to finally be released, they come out angry and wanting payback."

"Yes, if they weren't hostile toward the United States before being detained," Karima said, "it's an absolute guarantee they will be when they come out."

"I don't understand," Jenny said. "*We're* here. Why don't U.N. representatives just come over and see what's going on for themselves. Why all the protocol?"

"Believe me," Karima said passionately, "they've tried to get into Afghanistan, Iraq, and Guantánamo Bay on what they call fact-finding missions. But every time they've been denied entrance to see any detainees held by U.S. forces."

While making visitations to prisoners, Jenny befriended one of the USAID staff. Like herself, David Liberstein was idealistic and an avid believer in human rights. A New Yorker in his mid-forties, he had dark hair and a protruding chin that accentuated the determination in his face. From David, she learned that five independent experts of the U.N. Commission on Human Rights had tried for the past three years to visit prisoners arrested and detained for alleged terrorism.

"I had assumed that last year's ruling by the U.S. Supreme Court regarding Guantánamo Bay would've had a positive effect on the detainee system," Jenny said to David as they walked out of Camp Cropper, the central booking for all detainees in Iraq.

"When the Supreme Court determined that the president had overstepped his bounds in Guantánamo Bay, it seemed likely that this would spill over into the detention centers in Iraq, but it hasn't had much effect," David said, expressing his anger at the Bush administration for maintaining that the Geneva Conventions don't apply. Even so, he was relieved that the justices declared that the military tribunals are not properly constituted and cannot go forward. "Calling the detainees 'enemy combatants' rather than 'prisoners of war,'" he added irately, "is a game of semantics to avoid compliance with the Geneva Conventions."

"Here another year has passed," Jenny pointed out as she looked around at the beleaguered surroundings where they were standing, "and the question still remains what to do about the 400 detainees at Guantánamo Bay and the thousands here. Some are guilty and should be tried somewhere, but according to our records with the Red Cross, close to ninety percent of the people being held are not guilty and were picked up in random U.S. sweeps."

"Jenny, it'd take a person of deep faith to forgive America for the treatment they've received after leaving one of our detention centers."

"I just don't understand. It's as if our country has grown numb," Jenny replied, sadly recognizing that the same point had been made repeatedly by her Red Cross teammates. "For a short time, when the treatment of detainees first got exposed, there was a public outcry but, without continued media coverage, the atrocities are forgotten to those back home."

"Yes, when we see Americans or Brits taken hostage or mistreated, there is widespread outrage. But how many understand we're doing the same and worse to the Iraqi soldiers?" David said. "What ever happened to the ideals of our founding fathers, who wanted nothing more than life, liberty, and the pursuit of happiness for everyone?"

"I see that same wide-eyed look in many of the young men when they first come here. They're barely through their adolescence, and some not even," Jenny said, thinking of Hakim and Gabir. "And they're all just thrown into this war zone for believing fully in their respective causes." Her sadness was not just for the Americans as she realized that the frontline of battle was youth fighting youth, regardless of what side they were on.

Overhearing their conversation, an American soldier approached them. "Excuse me, but could we speak privately?" he asked cautiously.

They found a place out of sight and sat down on a low cement wall. The young man introduced himself as Timothy with the 123rd Main Support Battalion under the First Armored Division of the army.

"I've been deployed here since May of 2003," Timothy explained. "About six months ago, I filed for conscientious objector status, but I'm having a hard time getting it through. My assignment here is for another six months, and probably more if Washington decides to extend our stay."

"On what grounds have you filed?" David asked.

"Are you kiddin' me? You see what's goin' on here. I'm assigned here as an assistant interrogator, and I can't take it no more. If I don't use the goddamn methods—'scuse me, ma'am—I'm ordered to use, I'm reported for insubordination."

"Where are you from?" Jenny asked.

"Indiana, ma'am. I'm Catholic, and it's a bit harder to get objector status for us."

Jenny acknowledged that she, too, was Catholic and well understood the challenge. If a soldier is Hindu or Buddhist, their religious values are opposed to war in all forms. But Catholicism holds that there are circumstances where war is justified.

"A guy named Josh is trying to help me get the discharge."

"Josh." Jenny thought of Kyle's brother immediately. This sounded like something he would be involved with. "What's his last name?"

"Casteel. Joshua Casteel. He was serving in the army back in 2004 doing the same job I am here. He managed to get through the bureaucracy and get the hell out o' here. Now he's working for CPF." Timothy glanced at Jenny to see if she was familiar with the peace organization. She didn't seem to recognize it. "It's the Catholic Peace Fellowship and he serves as a kind o' go-between for guys like me."

Jenny expressed interest in knowing more about the group.

"He and two other guys from CPF went to Rome recently to promote the issue of conscientious objection to war with the Vatican. They weren't sure how they would be welcomed, but I just heard from Josh that they were received with open ears. So I'm hopin' I'll be released any day now. Anyway, thank you for listening."

As the young soldier walked away, Jenny turned to David. "Rome can't decide this issue but a letter from the Vatican would definitely have strong influence on Timothy's chain of command."

"Some accept the killing and maiming as part of what they signed on for," David said. "Others, like this young man, find it devastating."

"That's true of all sides fighting in this war, isn't it?" Jenny asked. "Sometimes I think back to the early pilgrims who were escaping religious persecution. Has America forgotten what started this great country of ours? How did we go from being the persecuted to becoming the persecutor?"

"Crusades were fought in the name of God. Wars break out to achieve peace," David said. "And the funny thing is that each side always believes it's right."

"Isn't that always the way? We all want to believe we're the ones who are right."

"You have a lot of idealism, Jenny. Of course, I guess we all do or we wouldn't be here."

"Working here makes me feel that we're all like the early pilgrims striving to establish true freedom for this country."

"I can see that pilgrim soul in you," David commented.

"I've been told that before," Jenny replied with a smile.

Waving goodbye to David as the armored car arrived to take the Red Cross workers to Camp Cropper, Jenny walked into the facility with her team, angered by the very ambiance of the place and the senseless detainment of so many innocent civilians. The vast majority of the detainees were, according to the records, no guiltier than the 3,000 victims killed in the World Trade Center.

Upon their arrival at the camp, Jenny and her fellow workers went through their usual ritual. They presented the purpose of their visit to the detention authorities; they inquired about internment conditions, population and movements of persons deprived of their liberty. The International Committee of the Red Cross was particularly interested in releases, arrests, transfers, deaths, and hospitalizations. After touring the prison, the volunteers were permitted to hold private interviews with various inmates of their choosing. At the end of each visit, the delegates held a final talk with the detaining authorities to inform them of the ICRC's findings and recommendations.

The following week, an armored car drove Jenny's team along airport road as they headed toward Camp Sather, a temporary base at Baghdad International Airport. Going through a similar ritual as before, Jenny had an opportunity to meet with Ali, the brother of the man with whom she had corresponded by email. He was an exceptionally bright and well-spoken Islamic detainee. Although only in his forties, he appeared much older. With a graying, overgrown beard, he reminded her of the elderly Hindu man she'd met in Bali. His eyes revealed his despair as he told Jenny how worried he was about his wife and whether she was able to keep the family together in his absence. His boys were teenagers, and he was concerned that they would be dragged into the sectarian warfare. He explained that he believed his brother was doing all he could, but he was allowed so little information from the outside world. He would just like to know that his loved ones were surviving without him.

Jenny felt his pain and assured him she would contact his brother and his wife for him. Perhaps, Jenny suggested, she can serve as an intermediary so they can communicate better. After learning more details about his family, Jenny inquired how he got here.

"I was a member of the Ba'ath party that was thrown out of office. I guess you understand that belonging to the party was mandatory to preserve our jobs under Saddam then. I was a community analyst. My job was to evaluate the needs of each ethnic group and determine how our government could best accommodate them. Believe me, I was way down in the pecking order but because I was a part of Hussein's government, the U.S. military must think I know something of value to them. I don't. I'm glad Saddam is gone, but I'm distraught at what has transpired since he was taken down. The overall condition of our country is worse now. I never thought that could happen."

"What do you think it will take to bring peace to the Middle East?" Jenny asked.

Ali took a deep breath as if exasperated by the question. "For starters, you need to close down your military bases and get the hell out of here. The desire for democracy has to come from us. You can't use a bomb to force it on us. The factions here have to decide for themselves whether the differences that separate them are greater than the bonds that could unite them."

"So, Ali, how would you suggest that our troops make their exit from here?"

"Obviously, the U.S. needs to maintain some kind of presence here. But as soon as is reasonable, your country needs to begin withdrawing its combat forces and replace them with peacekeeping forces. I can almost guarantee you that hatred for the U.S. is at such an all-time high in the Middle East that if America would simply take a back seat and serve in a training capacity, it would quiet down some of the insurrection."

Jenny moved her wooden chair closer to the table so that she could take notes on a yellow pad. The setting was the same bleak environment as the meeting room at Abu Ghraib, only smaller. Ali was wearing nondescript prison garb, but she noted that his eyes were beginning to exude more life as she drew him out to share his views.

"Many Americans, particularly my Republican friends, feel that a reduction of our troops will declare victory for al Qaeda. They think this so-called 'failure' in Iraq would endanger America for generations to come. So how would you respond to them?" Jenny asked.

"You see, it's going to require the coalition leaders to try to understand the al Qaeda movement. From where I sit, it doesn't appear that anyone has ever really tried to do that. Al Qaeda's overall strategy is to bleed the U.S. and its allies in a series of quagmire wars in places like Afghanistan, Iraq, and maybe Samalia. It's obvious that, since Sept 11, al Qaeda has gone on the offensive and their most successful plans have been in Iraq."

"President Bush would say that's why he declared war here—to fight al Qaeda and bring an end to terrorism."

"No, it's the other way around. Your ambitious president decided to come here first . . . for his own political reasons. *Before* 9/11, it was a well-known fact that America planned to invade this country. Bin Laden merely responded by urging his followers to go to Iraq and prepare a trap for the occupation. Where your leaders were blindsided is that al Qaeda has been successful in precipitating the Sunni-Shiite war which now grips our country. Don't you see that the continuance of the Iraqi war supports the overriding goal of the al Qaeda network?"

"You're saying that we are playing into their hands by staying and that by leaving we will thwart their plans?"

"Exactly! If the American troops go, two things will happen: they will leave the Shiites to dominate our country, which would ruthlessly repress al Qaeda and, even worse, America will leave the historic trap al Qaeda set up for them, thereby depriving them of the opportunity to destroy American forces."

Jenny was fascinated. "Americans who still support this war—and they are declining by volumes every day—believe that by keeping the war here, they are keeping it from being fought on our own turf."

"That's what I mean, ma'am. America simply hasn't taken the time to try to understand bin Laden and the al Qaeda network. They don't want to fight on your soil. Their intent is to fight long battles in Muslim countries where they have all the advantages—fighting on their home turf and fighting where they think their intelligence will be better than America's and where they will weaken the United States' will to fight back."

"But they are planning to attack us," Jenny protested as she flipped some straggling hairs behind her ear. "Last August, had their plot been successful, we would have seen the downing of ten simultaneous aircraft over the Atlantic."

"These are what they call raids—as in the bombing on the U.S., London, and Madrid—and they're useful in that they take the war to the far enemy from time to time but that is not the central point of al Qaeda's strategy. They know they can never conduct a raid that is so devastating that it will destroy the West. They want to entice the U.S. into these quagmire wars so they can defeat you on *their* own turf."

"I must say, Ali, you have a fascinating insight into the innuendoes of this war."

"You would too, my dear friend, if you were imprisoned as long as I've been with nothing more to do than to analyze this situation and pray for some solution."

Jenny felt drawn to Ali. He was wise beyond his years. Perhaps his imprisonment had made him so. She thought how Father Mike would have been in complete sync with this so-called enemy combatant. The fine man across from Jenny was anything but an enemy or a combatant. He was expressing Mike's basic philosophy of life.

"If America only understood," Ali said wearily. "What motivates Osama bin Laden and the al Qaeda network is not to turn Westerners into Muslims but rather to end a century of what they see as Western domination—the widespread plundering, pillaging, and raping of the Muslim world."

"So what do you think we should be doing?" Jenny asked.

"America should be using its military to go after Osama bin Laden and the senior leadership of his organization. The very fact that he has survived six years creates a mystique about him and his ideology. He started out as one man with a few followers. He has become an ideology and a movement. Besides the 3000 lives lost on 9/11, he is credited with the nearly 4000 U.S. soldiers' lives that have now been taken since the war began. He is the Robin Hood of the Muslim world. Back in 2002, the U.S. had him cornered. Instead your country decided to go to Mesopotamia and fight another enemy in a different dessert. The cost of that strategic mistake is one that all of us—Westerners and Middle Easterners—are paying for with our lives and our freedom. There is no greater sacrifice."

Jenny was mesmerized by the concepts of this gentle man. Not wanting to leave yet, Jenny found herself searching for ways to prolong their conversation. "Do you see bin Laden as actively involved in Afghanistan operations as he is those in Iraq?"

"Beyond any doubt, he still has influence there as well, which accounts in part for the Taliban resurgence. Despite what your bellicose Mr. Rumsfeld declared, the Taliban was never really defeated in 2001; they merely disbursed and bided their time. Of course, it helped the Taliban immensely when the coalition, especially the U.S., took its eyes off the Afghanistan ball and directed its attention to Iraq. Afghanistan was given little reconstruction assistance after the Iraq war began. Do you realize that less than one billion dollars was put into Afghanistan in 2002 and 2003, the most critical years in the battle against the Taliban?"

Jenny shook her head in disbelief.

"And, finally," Ali continued, "the Taliban benefited enormously from having a safe haven and help in Pakistan, which has proven to be a fertile recruiting ground for operations against the West and Israel."

"You're not suggesting we invade Pakistan?"

"No, of course not. If anything, America needs to help Pakistan get out of its conundrum. For example, the timing is right for a senior level official from the U.S. to help India and Pakistan resolve their fundamental differences over Kashmir. Be assured of one thing: until we break the nexus between Pakistan and jihadism, we are not going to defeat al Qaeda."

Jenny felt as if Mike was somehow speaking through Ali. He seemed to have such a clear vision for solution.

"America needs to change the story. Al Qaeda's narrative is that the U.S. and its allies are seeking to take over the Muslim world for their own reasons."

"Isn't there a lot of truth to that?" Jenny asked as she looked up from her note-taking.

"Yes, but that perspective is dominating the jihadist discussion groups. If the U.S. wants to succeed with its mission, you need to get out of the business of looking like you're pillaging and raping the Muslim world and get back into the business of working with Muslim leaders to resolve underlying issues of concern to the Islamic world."

"I see what you're saying. We have to change our approach. As long as we see ourselves as the good guys who have never done anything to incite this crisis, we will remain at war."

That was certainly true of my relationship with Kyle, Jenny thought. *As long as I saw myself bearing no blame in our downfall, we were destined to be at odds. It is so easy in hindsight to see things as they were.* Bringing herself back to the present, she continued her conversation with Ali. "Okay, Ali, for peace to be possible, we must try to understand what it is bin Laden and al Qaeda truly want, why they have such hatred for us, and begin to change our tactics. If we are to be *perceived* as good guys, we must begin to *behave* as good guys."

"You have a good grasp of the situation, ma'am. It is not by more pillaging and killing that you will succeed. You need to take Osama bin Laden out of a position of influence and help the Muslim world regain its dignity. My family and I are Sunnis but I'll tell you that Shiites in particular have no more respect for al Qaeda than America does. If given the opportunity, they'll work with the U.S. military to move al Qaeda out."

"How else could the U.S. change its approach?"

"They could begin by showing the slightest bit of care for the country from which it is extracting its resources—like giving back some of the private foreign oil interests in the Middle East to the country where they originated. The U.S. corporations that have come in here to do reconstruction work—especially Halliburton and Bechtel—have abused their privileges and wasted more money than it would have taken an Iraqi company to do the job, and they've been ridiculously slow in getting things done."

Behind a small glass window, the guard tapped loudly, signaling to Jenny that time was up. Winding down the interview, she thanked Ali for his candor. "What I've learned from you today is that, if the U.S. is to help in the peacemaking process, we must show the Muslim world that the West does have a positive agenda to pursue and has the desire to make real improvements in the lives of Muslims."

"Yes ma'am, this would dramatically change the atmosphere in which radical Islamists make the United States a villain," Ali concluded.

As she prepared to leave, Jenny once again reassured Ali that she would be in touch with his family.

Jenny could not give up the hope that peace in the Middle East was feasible. But she had lost hope that it would ever happen under her party's administration. It would take a new kind of leadership with an entirely fresh viewpoint. Somewhere in the near future, she prayed, a presidential team will emerge that has the wisdom and compassion to interface with other countries far better than the bungling job the U.S. has done here in Iraq.

David was waiting outside for Jenny as she emerged from the building. "You're going to love this," he said holding a faxed copy of a document in his hand. "The Foreign Relations Committee led by Senator Joe Biden has unanimously taken a hard line against the president's current policy on this ludicrous war. Enough Republicans have crossed the line to join the Democrats. Despite the president's blind optimism, enough members of Congress are finally convinced that the Iraqis will *never* get together and form a unity government that can be trusted by all sects of the Iraqi people. It simply can't happen."

"My God, it's about time," Jenny exclaimed. "If they'd made any effort to understand these cultures, they would've figured that out a long time ago. So what are they proposing?"

"Instead of escalating the war with no end in sight, this committee is proposing to begin bringing our combat troops home *now* and withdraw most of the rest by early next year, leaving behind a small peacekeeping force to train Iraqis, protect our embassy, and guard against growing terrorism."

Jenny nodded approvingly.

"They've come up with a detailed plan to form a decentralized federal government here," David continued, "that separates the warring factions while retaining some common concerns of guarding their borders and fairly distributing oil revenues."

"That's critical," Jenny pointed out, "especially for the Sunnis who have no oil revenues in their little triangle of the country."

"They've also arrived at the brilliant conclusion that the U.S., having lost most of its credibility in the region, can no longer be the sole voice for the world on decisions made about the Middle East. So the USAID headquarters back home has announced that it is sending over an expanded team to work with Iraq's government. Congress has finally realized that the surge needs to be one of increased *aide*, not increased *troops*."

David explained to Jenny that, as part of this effort, his team would be working in a myriad of areas, including education, health care, food, security, rebuilding infrastructure, airport and seaport management, and economic expansion. "I see myself helping with local governance and community development," he said.

Jenny was thrilled with the news. She appreciated how much USAID's work dovetailed with her involvement with the International Committee of the Red Cross.

On Thanksgiving Day, a calm prevailed over Baghdad. As Jenny came out of Camp Sather after completing her morning round of visits, David was waiting for her. He told her that the USAID team members were about to arrive at the airport, and asked her if she'd like to come with him to welcome them.

Since Camp Sather was a temporary base located at the airport, Jenny thought it would be fun to walk over with him. On the way, she wondered in passing if Josh Anderson would be in the group. Emmy had contacted Jenny to tell her of Josh's transferring from the Secretary of State's Office to a position with this organization.

As they approached the new arrivals who were taking in their first breaths of life in the panic-stricken town, Jenny spotted Josh.

"Josh, Josh Anderson! Over here! It's Jenny!"

She began waving wildly and started toward him. His face lit up and he headed her way.

"You look great," Jenny shouted as the two rushed to embrace. But Josh didn't relax his embrace when Jenny did. He continued to hold on, and Jenny suddenly recognized the familiar way in which she was being held. She gently took a step back from him, and stared up into his eyes.

It can't be, she thought. "Kyle??"

His grin confirmed it. They hugged again, and this time they held on even longer. Jenny's heart was racing. Baghdad was the last place in the world she would have expected to see Kyle. And especially after all these years. She stood back so she could really look at him. He didn't appear much older but something was different—the look in his eyes and the way he was looking at her.

"So you've come to save the Iraqis?" she asked demurely.

"No, I've come to find you." He took her hands in his.

She gazed at him, not fully grasping his words. A range of emotions flooded her being.

"Jenny, I switched places with Josh because I had to see you. I have so much I want to tell you."

She embraced him again, cautiously opening herself to accept all that he wanted to share with her.

"I finally *understand* what you were feeling back then, Jenny. It took me too long, but I've been able to put myself in your place. I don't know why I couldn't do that before. But I can now. I really can. I'm so sorry, Jenny. I'm sorry for everything I put you through. I love you. I never stopped loving you. Could you still … love me?"

As Jenny gazed into his eyes, she saw his genuineness, and she tried to imagine what events had brought him to this place standing here, now, in front of her.

"I'm different, Jenny. I've stabilized. I really have. I don't skip my meds. And I've grown; I've changed."

"Kyle, you know I believe every one can change and grow but—"

"Please, sweet pea. Hear me out. I've never been so sure of anything in my life as I am that I belong with you. When Harvey . . . after his plane crashed . . . I wished I'd gone down with him. I didn't know if I could make it on my own. But I did, Jenny. I continued to get help. I tried to forget you; I dated other women, but none of them could measure up to you. What I said a long time ago was true. No one else could ever find that secret chamber of my heart that I'd reserved for you."

Jenny didn't try to conceal her feelings. A tear trickled down her cheek. "Kyle, no one else could ever find that secret chamber of my heart, either." Then she raised up her right hand to show him that she still wore the silver band that he'd once slipped on her ring finger as a sign of their commitment.

He was elated that she had continued wearing his ring. *Why did I think we had to have a license to love?* Kyle thought. He realized now there was more than one way to exchange vows in the eyes of God.

"Jenny, I've learned so much about myself from so many people that God sent into my life. I can honestly put myself on the other side now and . . . and understand."

"Understanding is the key, Kyle . . . for *both* of us." She tilted her head back and stood on her tiptoes to kiss him. Kyle's eyes filled with tears and they embraced again, kissing passionately, tears on both their faces mingling together.

"I would almost bet that Mike is smiling down on us about right now," Kyle whispered into her ear.

"I think you'd win that bet," Jenny teased. "So are we going to stand here all day or get to work saving this country?"

Kyle took her hand, and their fingers entwined as they strolled toward the baggage claim area.

"Well, no one understands conflict better than you and I," Kyle said. "And if we can resolve ours, there may be hope for the Sunnis and the Shiites."

"Maybe," Jenny responded softly as she fixed her eyes on him. "Maybe even hope for America as well."

Afterword

Since September 11, 2001, nothing about our lives has been the same. Set during and after the most significant crisis of our time, the fictitious characters of *Peace Amidst Conflict* have been given an opportunity to carry out what could be in a more perfect world. I had a threefold objective in writing this reality fiction book: to tell a compelling story, to give an accounting of the facts of pre- and post-9/11, and to encourage change in both personal relationships and world affairs.

The message of this story is crucial to our times. "Change we can believe in" is the outcry of so many of us as we look to a new presidential administration to lead us into a world desperately searching to find peace amidst global as well as personal conflicts. Just as this book was in the final stages of publication, Caroline Kennedy, daughter of the late President John F. Kennedy, came out with a letter that touched me deeply:

> I have never had a president who inspired me the
> way people tell me that my father inspired them. . . .
> But for the first time, I believe I have found the man
> who could be that president — not just for me, but
> for a new generation of Americans.

Of course, she is referring to Senator Barack Obama. He is asking us not just to believe in *his* ability to bring about real change in Washington. . . . He is asking us to believe in *ours*. But for that to happen, change has to begin on a personal level within each of us. I am pleased that Kyle, the devotee of President Kennedy in *Peace Amidst Conflict*, could see early on the parallel between the two men and fictionally arrive at the same conclusion as the daughter of President Kennedy. The hero of this story has "the audacity to hope" that, in spite of all odds, the son of a black Kenyan father and a white American mother will be the 44th President of the United States of America.

All references to political organizations, medical facilities or procedures, psychological disorders, and religious practices mentioned in this story are authentic, and all facts have been honestly described based on the best research available to me.

Political: The recounting of the events leading up to and following 9/11—including how the terrorists slipped through our intelligence agencies and how we ended up waging a war on Iraq—is accurately presented and based on published accounts. All references to the torture and mistreatment of detainees of war are based on official reports. The presidential electoral process of 2000 is accurate as reported in the media. Certain political organizations, such as the School of Americas and the SOA Watch, do exist but are placed in a different location to comply with the story setting. The U.S. Agency for International Development and all peace organizations, such as the National Peace Foundation, the U.S. Institute of Peace, the Peace Alliance, the Catholic Peace Fellowship, and Pax Christi, are also real and successfully serving the cause of peace throughout the world.

Medical: Information regarding alternative cancer treatment programs such as Immune Augmentative Therapy, located in the Bahamas, actually exists. Certain hospital procedures intended to extend the life of those with liver disorders are also accurate, and real doctors' names are used.

Psychological: All details about emotional disorders—bipolar state, narcissism, abandonment syndrome, and bereavement—are all based on available published information.

Religious: For Catholics and former Catholics who believe that they are automatically excommunicated from the Church once they remarry, the internal forum is a legitimate alternative to bringing them back into compliance. Additionally, all information about Hindus and Muslims is based on research.

The characters in this novel are fictional, though inserted into the reality of sickness, death, and the 9/11 terrorist attacks. The reader assuredly recognizes the true characters of all Washington senior officials as well as Osama bin Laden and other known terrorists. All other characters are fictional including Josh, but his experience of getting out of the South Tower of the World Trade Center on the day of the attack is based on one person's factual account of his experience.

For me, this is a book born in the anguish of letting go of one life and looking forward to another. Some people accept life for what it is and feel no need to question. But I am one of those people destined to go on searching for a life that some might think beyond our reach. And I am not alone. There are countless others like me. We continue to look for deeper meaning in our lives and relationships. We grieve uncontrollably over the loss of those we love through death or breakup. We continue to look for visionary leaders who can lift our spirits and inspire us to believe in our dreams. We recognize that the pursuit of peace, whether between nations, communities, or couples, must never be abandoned, no matter how unattainable it may seem.

Acknowledgments

I am grateful to the following authors whose writings served as a background resource and helped shape many of the concepts and theories that went into the dialogue and actions of my characters. In some instances, I have fictitiously portrayed some of these authors as characters in the book offering their opinions about solutions to the war in Iraq. Their responses are as close to their own words as I could recreate them, and they deserve full credit for their ideas.

- *The Grief Recovery Handbook* by John James and Russell Friedman, which is written for those going through the grieving process, serves as the basis for the process used by Jenny to recover from her losses.
- *The Next Attack* by Daniel Benjamin and Steven Simon, which describes the failure of the war on terror and helps my characters develop a strategy for getting it right.
- *A Pretext for War* by James Bamford, which explains how knowledge of the terrorist attacks slipped through our intelligence agencies, and how they were manipulated for the purpose of documenting evidence that didn't exist to justify the war in Iraq.
- *America at the Crossroads* by Francis Fukuyama, a former neoconservative who lost faith in those in power and shares his observations of where they went wrong in a conversation with one of my characters.
- *State of Denial* by Bob Woodward confirms how the Bush administration avoided telling the truth about Iraq, not only to the American people but to Congress as well.
- *The 9/11 Commission Report* helps solidify my facts and findings.
- *The Iraq Study Group Report* offers recommended actions to be taken to improve the situation in Iraq.
- *DisInformation* by Richard Miniter helps formulate points to defend the present administration in some of the dialogues.
- *State of War* by James Risen explores the secret history of the

CIA and how it became involved in a political crossfire in the Bush administration.

- In *House of Bush, House of Saud*, Craig Unger presents an account of the thirty-year relationship between the Bush family and the House of Saud, explaining how, two days after the 9/11 attack, the White House approved the departure of 140 Saudis, many of them kin to Osama bin Laden.

- In his book, *Why America Slept*, Gerald Posner details the reasons for our failure to prevent 9/11 and reveals the connection of the royal Saudi family to al Qaeda, showing that family's own Prince Ahmed met with al Qaeda operative Abu Zubaydah.

- *The Audacity of Hope* by Barack Obama offers his thoughts on reclaiming the American dream and inspires readers to believe it is possible.

- *At the Center of the Storm* by George Tenet, former Director of the CIA, provides an insider's view from 1998 to 2004.

- Counterterrorism expert, Bruce Riedel, provides valuable insights through his article, "Al Qaeda Strikes Back" written in May 2007. His thoughts are expressed through the character of Ali, who is interviewed by Jenny while detained in prison in Baghdad.

- *The Italian Letter* by Peter Eisner and Knut Royce, describes in detail how the Bush administration used a fake letter to build the case for war in Iraq.

- *Fair Game: My Life as a Spy, My Betrayal by the White House* by Valerie Plame Wilson sets the record straight as to why Vice President Dick Cheney's chief of staff, Scooter Libby, was directed to retaliate against her husband, former ambassador Joseph Wilson, for his challenging the Bush administration's use of the falsified Niger Report as a justification for going to war in Iraq. Directed by the president and vice-president, Libby exposed Plame as a CIA operative, for which he was tried and convicted.

I am appreciative to the following peace organizations that helped formulate a theory of a more peaceful, non-violent approach to America's foreign policy:

- All ideas surrounding the creation of a department of peace and non-violence came from The Peace Alliance, founded by Marianne Williamson. There is currently a bill before Congress to establish a United States Department of Peace.
- I am grateful to Sister Kathleen Pruitt, who is affiliated with the Catholic peace movement Pax Christi for contributing her ideas for the formation of a peaceful foreign policy.
- The U.S. Institute of Peace's mission is to search for peaceful solutions to global issues. The activities of this institute inspired me to make the character of Kyle Anderson serve as its director allowing him to fictionally carry out USIP's goals of preventing, managing, and resolving threats to international peace.
- I am appreciative to Esther Pank, the director of The National Peace Foundation, for previewing excerpts of this book and helping me accurately describe various peace organizations mentioned in this story.

I acknowledge these insightful individuals and organizations for their well-thought out concepts, which I have woven into the mindset and thoughts of my characters. It is my hope that by reinforcing these ideas in this book, together we will bring our shared dreams of world peace into closer proximity.